THE DRAGONS OF THE RHINE

THE DRAGONS OF THE RHINE

DIANA L. PAXSON

An AvoNova Book

William Morrow and Company, Inc.

AVON BOOKS
A division of
The Hearst Corporation
1350 Avenue of the Americas
New York, New York 10019

Copyright © 1995 by Diana L. Paxson
Published by arrangement with the author
Library of Congress Catalog Card Number: 94-31982
ISBN: 0-688-13986-8

Library of Congress Cataloging in Publication Data:

Paxson, Diana L.
    The dragons of the Rhine / Diana L. Paxson.
        p. cm.—(Wodan's children ; bk. 2)
''An AvoNova book.''
1. Siegfried (Legendary character)—Fiction. 2. Mythology, Germanic—Fiction. I. Title. II. Series: Paxson, Diana L. Wodan's children ; bk. 2.
PS3566.A897D7   1995   94-31982
813'.54—dc20   CIP

First Morrow/AvoNova Printing: January 1995

To
Laurel Olson
who knows where the valkyries ride . . .

Foreword & Acknowledgments

"Perlectus longaevi stringit inampla diei." (l. 20)

"**R**ead through, it makes the lengthy day a little shorter." Thus says the poet of the ninth century Latin poem "Waldharius," which recounts an obscure adventure of Gunther and Hagen. The sentiment is as appropriate now as it was when the story of Sigfrid was new. Despite the heroic meanings with which the legend has often been invested, most particularly by Wagner, the first requirement for any successful retelling is that it keep the reader entertained long enough to appreciate its significance.

It is in this spirit that I present Book II of *Wodan's Children*, which tells what happened when Sigfrid and Brunahild encountered the Burgundians—the people of the Gundwurm—the dragons of the Rhine.

I would like to acknowledge the contribution to the writing of this book made by my long-suffering friends and family, who have put up with various fits of despondency, excitement, or abstraction in order to help me see this project through. Most of the people who got me through Book I are still in there pitching—my thanks to all of them once more!

One person who never got to read the book should be

vii

mentioned—Dr. Elizabeth Pope, longtime professor of English at Mills College, who died in August of 1992. Dr. Pope, author of _The Perilous Gard_, and an authority on mythology, was both a mentor and role model. I will miss her insight and encouragement.

Contents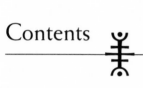

Characters & Places

CHARACTERS

(Note: most names and other Old Germanic words used in this book are early forms, in many cases simplified out of pity for the reader. Where only Roman names for tribes, etc., are known, they have been used.)

CAPITALS = major characters
( ) = a personnage who died before the beginning of the story
* = historical character
[ ] = form of name in later sources

Gods and Spirits:
Aesir—function gods
alfar—male ancestral spirits
Baldur, or Fol [Phol] (the Beautiful, son of Wodan and Fricca)
Donar [Thor] (the thunderer, god of storms and strength)
disir, idisi—female ancestral spirits
Erda (Earth Mother)
Fricca [Frigg] (the weaver of fate, wife of Wodan)
Fro [Freyr] (god of luck and fertility, brother/lover of Froja)
The Frowe, Froja [Freyja] (dish of the Vanir, goddess of love
and fertility)

Hella (queen of the Underworld)
Huginn, Thought (one of Wodan's ravens)
Idunna (keeper of the apples of youth)
landvaettir—nature spirits
Loki (the trickster, a *jotun* allied with the gods)
Muninn, Memory (one of Wodan's ravens)
Nanna (wife of Baldur)
norns—the fates
Tiw [Tyr] (god of war and justice)
Walburga (another name for the earth goddess, worshipped
    on May Eve)
Wanes [Vanir]—earth and agricultural gods
WODAN [Odin] (lord of the Aesir, worldwalker, god of
    wordcraft and warcraft and magic, also called High One,
    Old Man, War Father, Victory Father, the One-Eyed, Grim
    (Hidden One) etc., sometimes appears in human form)

Demigods or Legendary Figures:
Andvari, an earth elemental who in pike shape guarded the
    Niblung treasure
sons of Haki, legendary heroes, mentioned in the *Völsungasaga*
Starkad, legendary hero who killed King Vikar, from Saxo, etc.
(*Walada [Veleda], legendary seeress of the Bructeri in the
    first century)
(*Wallia, king of the Vandals)
(*Airmanareik [Ermanaric], third-century king of the Goths,
    defeated by the invading Huns)
(*Alaric, king of the Visigoths)
(*Hermundurus [Arminius], first-century leader of Cherusci
    and Hermunduri against the Romans)

Romans:
(*Jovin, attempted to usurp Empire of the West, 412)
(*Julian, Emperor of the East, 361–363, tried to restore pa-
    ganism)
*Honorius, Emperor of the West, 395–423
*Castinus, the Patrician in the time of Honorius

*Joannes, Primicerius Notariorum, attempted to usurp the Empire of the West, 423
*Valentinian III, Emperor of the West, 425–
*Galla Placidia, sister of Honorius and mother of and regent for Valentinian
*Bonifatius, general in North Africa, favorite of the empress
*Felix, Magister etc., Patrician, Galla Placidia's compromise choice for supreme commander
*FLAVIUS AETIUS, Magister Militae of Gallia
*Carpileon, his son, a hostage with the Huns
*Litorius, his second-in-command
Father Priscus, Orthodox Roman Catholic priest
Father Severian, Arian priest

Burgunds:
the Burgundians, an East Germanic tribe living in the area between the Neckar, the Main, and the Rhine and from Mainz to south of Worms.
(*Gipicho [Gjuki], father of Gundohar)
GRIMAHILD, Gundohar's mother
Ordulf, her servant
*GUNDOHAR [Gunther], king of the Burgunds
*GODOMAR [Guthorm] (Godo), his oldest brother
*GISLAHAR [Giselher], his youngest son
GUDRUN [Gutrune, Kriemhild], his sister
HAGANO [Hagen], his half brother
Ostrofrid, lawspeaker (*sinista*)
Chieftains:
    Heribard, a counselor
    Ordwini Dragobald's son [Ortwin of Metz]
    Sindald [Sindold]
    Unald [Hunold]
    Laidrad
    Deorberht, son of Folco
Ecward, a young warrior interested in Gudrun
Members of Gundohar's house-guard:
    Betavrid, Gerwit and Randalf, Eleuthir, Helmnot, Trogus, Gamalo, Apius

Gundrada, a cousin of Gundohar, married to a Visigothic prince

Gundiok, her newborn son

Ursula and Adalfrida, maidens attending Gudrun

Marcia, an attendant of Brunahild

Gunna, Ordleib, noble maidens in the queen's household

Other Germanic Figures:

SIGFRID Fafnarsbane, son of Sigmund the Wolsung

Alb, a Frankish king and Sigfrid's stepfather

Fafnar

*Hengest, an Anglian warleader, formerly in service of Alb's brother

King Hiloperic, father of King Alb

(Hiordisa, Sigfrid's mother)

Huld, a wisewoman of the Walkyriun (Walada = her magical name)

*Theoderid, king of the Visigoths of Tolosa

Ra

Waldhari, son of Albharius, nephew of Theoderid, hostage of Attila

Hildigund, daughter of Hairarik, a Frankish king, betrothed to Waldhari

Huns and Associates:

(Balimber, son of Uldin, Hun chieftain who defeated Airman-areik)

Ruga, king of the eastern Huns

Oktar, king of the western Huns

Mundzuk, his brother

Bladarda, son of Mundzuk, prince of the Acatiri Huns

ATTILA, son of Mundzuk, warleader of his clan

Ellak, his son

Tuldik, Attila's messenger

Kursik, one of Attila's counselors

Bertriud, Bladarda's older daughter

Heimar, a Marcomanni, husband of Bertriud and foster father of Brunahild

BRUNAHILD (called Sigdrifa among the Walkyriun), Bladarda's younger daughter
Asliud, her daughter by Sigfrid

PLACES

Waters:
Albis—Elbe
Danu, Danuvius—the Danube
Moenus—the Main
Mosella—Moselle
Nicer—the Neckar
Rhenus—the Rhine

Mountains and Forests:
Broken Mountain—the Brocken, Harz Mountains
Charcoal Burners' Forest—Odenwald
Holy Hill—Heidelberg
the Taunus—Hochtaunus, above Frankfurt
Forest of Vosegus—the Vosges
Wurm Fell—the Drachenfels, above Königswinter on the Rhine

Towns:
Arelas—Arles
Argentoratum—Strasburg
Augusta Treverorum, Treveri—Trier
Bonna—Bonn
Colonia Agrippina—Köln/Cologne
Constantinople, Mundberg—Istanbul
Divodurum—Metz
Halle—Schwäbisch Hall
Mogontiacum—Mainz
Roma—Rome
Ulpia Traiana—Xanten
Walhall—Hall of the Slain, Wodan's hold in Asgard

Geographical Divisions:

Aquitanica—southern France, Aquitaine

Asgard—home of the gods

Belgica Prima—eastern France

Belgica Secunda—approximately the Low Countries

Borbetomagus—Worms

Gallia—northern half of France

Germania Prima—lands just west of the Rhine, Koblenz to Basel

Germania Secunda—lands just west of the Rhine, North Sea to Koblenz

Iberia—Spain

Midgard, Middle Earth—the world of men

Muspelheim—the world of elemental fire

Nibelheim—the world of ice and mist

Noricum—lands south of Danube, Austria

Pannonia—plain west of Danube, Hungary

Family Tree

(*Italics* indicate a character invented to fill a gap in the legend)

THE NIFLUNGAR

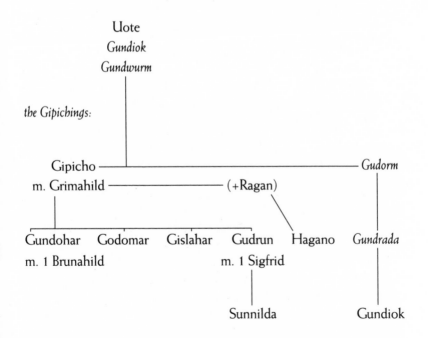

Uote
Gundiok
Gundwurm

the Gipichings:

Gipicho ———————————————————— *Gudorm*
m. Grimahild ——————————— (+Ragan)

Gundohar   Godomar   Gislahar   Gudrun   Hagano   *Gundrada*
m. 1 Brunahild   m. 1 Sigfrid

                                          Sunnilda   Gundiok

"All is clear to me now!
Hark to your ravens!
Hear them rustling?
With tidings long awaited,
Let me send both of them . . ."

Richard Wagner: *Götterdämmerung III*

THE DRAGONS OF THE RHINE

Prologue Muninn's Tale

$\mathbf{D}$o you see that raven that flies over the trees, a moving spill of ink upon the grey sky? He is thought on the wing, each fold and flex of black feathers forms the rune of a new reality. High Huginn flies, for his work here is done; the thin wailing of Brunahild's babe echoes from Heimar's hall. Huginn follows the setting sun westward as the thought of our master turns to Sigfrid, who is fighting in Frankland. But I will sit awhile on the rooftree, for I am Muninn, and I remember. . . .

I watched from the ridgepole of King Hiloperic's hall when the north wind swirled across the grey sea and Sigfrid's first cry split the air. I heard Hiordisa proclaim him the child of Sigmund the Wolsung, heir to his father's treasure, and his magic, and his enemies. I heard Hiloperic agree to foster him, though that lasted only until the sons of Hunding learned that a Wolsung walked the world.

In the hall below, Brunahild is still refusing to name the father of her child. She will swear only that he is a hero, and her sister Bertriud and Heimar, her sister's husband, have sworn to raise it as they did Brunahild herself not so long ago. Bertriud is past bearing now, and she has no child. She hopes that this little lass, bright as a sunbeam, will learn to love her as Brunahild, black-haired like the

1

prince of the Huns who is their father, never could do.

I watched when Brunahild and the Burgund princess Gudrun looked into the sacred well, and Brunahild was sent to study with the Walkyriun, and I saw how Sigfrid was sent away with the earth-smith Ragan to save him from the sons of Hunding. I saw how the wisewoman Huld taught Brunahild her magic, and how Sigfrid learned forge-craft with Ragan and watched the wolves. But Brunahild studied ravens, and when she lay unconscious in the snow it was Huginn and I who guided her through the Otherworld to Wodan, and heard him claim her as his child.

Sigfrid's mother gave him Sigmund's wolfskin and the boy grew shapestrong; the berserker's blood awakened in him when the Hundings attacked Hiloperic's hall. It was then that Ragan demanded the fee for his fostering, and Sigfrid promised to kill Fafnar if Ragan could make him a sword.

In the Taunus, Brunahild was learning swordplay and battle-magic. When the Walkyriun sent her to the Huns she learned to use it, but Attila told her to go back to the west. He is here now, in Heimar's hall. He has not pressed his niece to name her lover, but he watches her, and even I, peering down through the smokehole, cannot read what lies behind his dark eyes.

"You are Bladarda's daughter," Bertriud is saying, "and the child proves your fertility. We will find you a noble husband."

"I need no husband," Brunahild replies. "I am a Walkyrja."

It is true. I feasted on the scraps of the feast when the Walkyriun celebrated Brunahild's initiation, and she named herself Sigdrifa, Bringer of Victory. And I feasted on the slain after the battle in which she betrayed them by serving Wodan's will instead of theirs, the battle in which she spared the life of the Burgund king.

"They have cast you out," Heimar's voice comes now.

"I am Wodan's Walkyrja," she whispers then. "I will ride with the hero who rescued me."

It was Sigfrid Sigmundson who released her from the rock where the Walkyriun had imprisoned her; Sigfrid, the new and reluctant master of Andvari's hoard. My brother and I saw him kill the battle-wurm, the berserker, and we heard how

Ragan goaded him until he found his own death on Sigfrid's sword. It is we who lured the boy southward to find Brunahild.

Throughout that winter they lived together in the mountains, wolf and raven hunting together. That much happiness their own natures and the Norns allowed them. It was not until the beginning of summer that they parted, he to get arms worthy of a hero from his Frankish kinfolk, and she to wait for him among the Huns.

"Sigdrifa—" he called her when he swore to come for her in a year and a day—the Walkyrja title that was the only name she had given him. He did not know she was Bladarda's daughter. And it was not until Brunahild had reached her sister's hearth that she knew she was carrying Sigfrid's child.

The babe, swaddled warmly, has ceased her crying now. Heimar sprinkles her with water from the sacred spring and takes her under his protection. "Asliud," he calls her, and blesses her in the names of the gods. A tiny finger tightens on his own, and his heart is lost.

"Take care of her, foster father," says Brunahild, watching, "for only Wodan knows where my path will lie."

"It leads to a king's hall—" Attila speaks from the shadows. He comes forward, peering from the crumpled features of the infant to the white face of the mother. "You have run free long enough. It is time for our clan to fulfill its destiny, and you must do your duty to your kin." He gestures toward the child. "Surely you cannot pretend to dislike the thought of a man."

"One man—" Brunahild begins, but Bertriud shakes her head.

"Where is he, then? How can you believe that he will come for you?"

"He will come!" She touches the golden neck ring she wears.

"And if he does not?" says Attila then.

"I told you—" Wincing a little, she pulls herself up to face him. "I am still Walkyrja, and Wodan's child. And this I swear by the wise god's spear and the war-god's sword, that I will seek death rather than allow a man who cannot defeat me in battle to call me his bride."

A wind from beyond Middle Earth ruffles my feathers. Brunahild's words ring out through all the worlds, and I understand now why I have stayed. This is what I was waiting to hear.

The wind blows cold, calling me home. It is time to seek the Hall of the Slain and the high seat where Wodan watches his warriors, and I must whisper this word into the High One's ear. I spread my wings and let the wind lift me, a flutter of black fading into the darkening air.

Or perhaps there is no raven, and I am only a shadow within your mind, cast by the god.

Chapter One
Currents of Spring

Valley of the Rhenus
Ostara's Moon, A.D. 420

The river lay still under moonlight, its power sheathed by a dimpling of silver serpent scales that coiled around the cliff, then straightened between wooded shores. From a distance the serpent did not appear to move, but close, the air trembled with the sound of its inexorable flow. The creature who bent to lap water from the river's edge twitched as he sensed that leashed energy, memories of his battle with another serpent competing with the messages his heightened senses were sending him now.

Across the river, cliffs rose sheer above the narrow strand, their upper slopes thickly covered with trees. *The Taunus . . .* With the name came a rush of longing that rocked him backward. He shut his eyes, but the images only grew sharper— a girl's body glowing pale in the firelight, ravens circling, blood on white snow.

Whimpering, he turned away and took a deep breath of the cool air, sensing apple blossom from some distant orchard, damp earth, a whiff of fish from farther up the shore. Gradually, the impressions faded and he grew calm once more, listening to the chuckling of the waters. Then, from the cliffs came another sound that brought him upright, every hair quivering. After a moment, he settled onto his haunches, golden eyes turning silver as the moon they reflected. His head tipped back and he returned the howl.

For a moment it seemed that even the river paused in its relentless flow, waiting for an answer. For the space of time it might have taken for an owl to fly across the river he listened, and then howled once more. The call rose and fell into silence, and all other sounds became its echoes, a distillation of longing that hung in the soft spring air until the breeze from the river carried it away.

He crouched down again with a sigh. If others of his kind roamed across the river, they were not answering. He was still alone. But at least there was clean water, and coming down to the river he had caught the scent of deer. The ache in his breast faded. With luck, he would feast well before dawn. He shook himself, got to his feet, and trotted back across the stony shore toward the trees.

The first light was beginning to restore color to the world when Sigfrid stepped into the clearing where he had camped the night before, though the mist that had risen from the river with the dawning made a mystery of the trees. The grey horse stamped a little at the wolf smell, but in the past months he had grown accustomed to the scent of the brindled pelt slung across Sigfrid's shoulders, and while his master went on two legs he had nothing to fear.

Sigfrid sighed, rubbing his eyes. He supposed he would have done better to spend the night in sleeping, but soon he would be coming into the settled lands. A winter penned in his stepfather's hall with the war-band had prisoned his soul and deadened his senses, and the night had called to him. Running free in the moonlight relaxed him as he could never be rested by any sleep within men's walls, and the deer he had chased down had fed not only his body, but his soul.

No human had seen him, and so he had not broken his self-imposed law. The world knew him as Sigfrid Sigmundson, or perhaps these days, as Sigfrid Fafnarsbane. That was bad enough. But to be called Sigfrid the Shapestrong would have been worse still.

For a few hours he had been free, lacking nothing but a companion with whom to share his joy. But it had been a mistake to call out to the local wolf pack. He was not a wolf, even though he was not entirely a man, and the only creature who could truly understand him was the slim dark girl who spoke with the ravens as their kin. His loins tightened at the thought of her. Soon, he and Sigdrifa would be together again.

He pulled off the wolfskin that had once been his father's and began to roll it, his skin pebbling at the touch of the cold air. Despite the chill, he eyed his piled gear without enthusiasm. The loose wheat-colored trousers and the front-lapped tunic dyed the hue of Gaulish wine lay folded carefully atop a rectangular cloak of tightly woven grey wool, the byrnie of riveted leather with its insets of mail, and the wolf-crested spangenhelm adorned with plates of figured gold. There was gold on his shield-boss, golden tags on the straps that gartered his trousers, gold on his belt and brooch and his horse's trappings as well.

King Alb had spared nothing to fit his stepson out as a Frankish princeling, adding his own gifts to the wealth Sigfrid had won in last summer's campaigning and a few choice pieces from Sigmund's hoard. At this moment, with the memory of a night of freedom still singing in his blood, Sigfrid felt strongly tempted to tip the whole lot into the river and continue southward with nothing but the wolfskin and his sword. But he had vowed to Sigdrifa to return to her armed as a hero, and for men to accept him in that role, he would have to display the trappings he had won.

His lips curved beneath the soft Frankish moustache he had begun to grow. For Sigdrifa's sake he could endure worse hardships than smothering his body in these rich garments. The outpost of Bonna lay far behind him. Just past the cliffs the river bent eastward through open land. If he struck straight across country, sometime tomorrow he should reach Borbetomagus, where the Niflungar ruled. He would need to make a good impression there.

Still, he could put off dressing until he had taken the grey stallion down to water. Grani, despite his noble breeding, did not care whether his master wore fancy clothes. Sigfrid unknotted the tether, and then, moving with a predator's unconscious grace, led the horse down to the water's edge.

Gudrun tossed on her narrow bed, fighting her way out of an uneasy slumber. But there was no light in the chamber, and the thick walls of the old Roman building deadened sound. She sighed, trying to persuade herself back to sleep once more. She had never rested well in this stone palace that had once housed a legionary commander. Sometimes it helped if she could imagine herself somewhere else. She lay still, listening to her own breathing, and found herself sliding into a state that was neither sleep nor waking.

Memory seized on an image of trees and grass; she let the vision grow clearer, until she could hear the whisper of wind in the leaves and watch the dappling of moonlight on the forest floor. For a time it was enough simply to wander, but gradually she began to realize that she was lonely. Surely that was nothing new. Why should it matter now? Perhaps it was the beauty of this place that required sharing. Each new leaf seemed edged in silver, and the white trumpets of the larkspur glowed.

She stared around her, willing a companion to appear. The wind grew stronger; something moved in the undergrowth and suddenly what she had thought was a shadow took shape and she saw a grey wolf watching her with amber eyes. For a moment she felt a flicker of fear. But the wolf stood with one paw lifted as if it were about to flee, and she realized that, for all its strength, it was afraid of her.

"Come then," she whispered. "I'm alone too. Walk with me."

Her breath caught as the beast stirred and she saw its size. It stood nearly to her hip, its bulk increased by the thick pelt. Her fingers closed in the brindled fur, and she felt the muscles beneath ease. There was strength in that great frame, but she could sense no hostility. Indeed, the animal seemed as glad as she was to be companioned. Suddenly the forest was no longer a place of fear. She took a deep breath, thrilling to the sweet pungence of crushed thyme, as if the beast had lent her its sharp senses. Then the wolf started forward, and Gudrun, walking with it, found herself relaxing as well.

When her maid came to wake her a short time later, she was curled in the bedclothes like a little child, and she was smiling.

"So, you have consented to join us at last—" said Queen Grimahild, frowning as Gudrun hurried down the path toward the river. The other women were gathered already in the meadow, shivering in the chill wind that had picked up with the approach of dawn. "You must have slept well."

"I was dreaming. I was wandering in the woods and a wild wolf came to me and walked by my side," Gudrun answered, a little defiantly. Her maid had bundled her into her clothes and ornaments and hurried her through the river mists that veiled the old stone and new timber of the town, but her mind was still full of moonlight.

The queen's heavy lids lifted from eyes curiously colorless, as if they had looked too long into the Otherworld. Gudrun bit her lip. What had possessed her to say that? Now her mother would be after her again to learn her magics. Even Gudrun could not deny this had been a dream of power, not when her mother's seamed face was less real to her, even now, than the wolf's amber gaze.

"Did the wolf speak to you?" Queen Grimahild began, then her head came up as softly the women began to sing. "You will tell me after. Take your place quickly. In another moment the sun will be over the hill!"

For some years now Gudrun had been taller than her mother, but she felt like a child again as the queen gripped her elbow and dragged her toward the harrow of heaped stones that served as altar, and hastened her steps in an attempt to preserve some dignity. The singing grew louder, a flow of liquid syllables whose meaning, if there had ever been one, had been worn away by the years.

The growing light was diffused by the mists into a glimmer of sourceless radiance in which tree and stone had less substance than her dreams. Just so the mists had risen when the fires of Muspel touched the primal ice. The feast of Ostara marked summer's beginning, but to Gudrun, it felt like the beginning of the world.

And then an eye of light blinked suddenly above the ragged line of the hills across the river and the mists seemed to catch fire. For a breath Gudrun stood in the heart of the flames and was not consumed. Hills, fields, and river were suddenly revealed as the newborn sun lifted fully above the ridges.

What need to invoke the goddess? thought Gudrun, transfixed by that revelation. She was already here.

"Now—" the queen's voice hissed in her ear. Blinking, Gudrun saw the tinder laid ready on the flat stone beside the altar. She threw back the heavy folds of her blue mantle and fumbled with the flint and striker, painfully aware that all eyes were on her, and as the first spark leaped, her sigh of relief nearly extinguished the flame.

"Hail, Ostara!" cried the women around her. Gudrun stepped back as others thrust sticks into the infant fire and carried it to the wood piled in the pit beneath the cauldron. The queen's voice rang out suddenly as the shouting became a song.

> *"Hail, Ostara, eastward arising,*
> *Laughing goddess, Lady of Light—*
> *To dawn, dominion over darkness*
> *Thy glory has granted, gone is the night!"*

Now that her part was done, Gudrun was uncomfortably aware of dew-damped skirts clinging to her ankles. But the Presence she had sensed at the moment of the sun's rising grew stronger as women brought up their offerings, pouring milk, crumbled barley cakes, and flasks of mead over the heaped stones.

> *"Winter's wrath by winds of warmth*
> *The maiden's might has melted here;*
> *Everywhere green plants are growing,*
> *Flowers flourish, she-beasts bear;"*

Ursula, who was sister to one of the warriors, stepped forward, holding a large hare by its bound feet and ears. Gudrun suppressed a shiver, for the hare was sacred, offered and eaten only at this festival. The creature was still struggling, but when she laid it across the stones of the harrow it stilled. As the queen drew the short knife that hung from her belt, the hare stared up at her, and Gudrun wondered what message was passing between them.

At the end of each cycle there was always a moment of uncertainty, when one wondered if life would go on. In the sacrifice the balance between death and birth was reestablished; folk offered up the old life in exchange for the new. She wondered if the beast accepted its role in these ceremonies. It was always a good omen when the sacrifice went consenting.

> *"Let Thy light's illumination*
> *Banish sorrow, blessings bring,*
> *Grant success, and a good season*
> *To those who seek thee here this spring!"*

The sound of the singing faded to silence; as the queen severed the head the animal's blood burst bright across the stones. Gudrun blinked. For a moment the air seemed to shimmer above the harrow, and there was a shape in it—a woman, a hare, a blaze of radiance that was more than either.

Shining One, she said silently, *receive the offering, and let your light bless the world.*

In a few minutes the creature was limp and emptied. It seemed to Gudrun that the vortex of energy above it did not so much diminish as dissipate into the surrounding air. Did she feel a tingling as it passed? If so, it was only for an instant, but suddenly she was as alert as if she had never been awake before. The long grasses by the edge of the Rhenus whispered as the power passed, and for a moment the gentle murmur of the waters seemed to grow louder in reply.

Swiftly, the women were gutting the hare and stripping off the hide. They disjointed the carcass and dropped it into the cauldron, where the water was already steaming. Barley went into the cauldron as well, and spring greens and herbs.

With the completion of the sacrifice came a general release of tension. Servants spread hides and cushions upon the wet grass, and women began to sit down, chattering. One of the older women started singing something about sprouting shoots and opening flowers that made the girls blush and the married women laugh. The sun was well up now, beginning to burn off the mist from the river. Damp logs steamed where the sun touched them, white smoke interweaving with the blue smoke from the fire.

Gudrun began to distribute the boiled eggs that she and the other younger women had spent most of the day before decorating to the wives and daughters of the Burgund chieftains, murmuring the old rhyme.

> *"On Ostara's feast this wish I bring,*
> *That love and joy your life should ring;*
> *An egg I give to you today,*
> *That love and faith will not betray!"*

Goose eggs and duck eggs and the smaller eggs of hens had been painted in red with symbols ancient beyond the memory of the tribes. There were sun-crosses and spirals separated by meanders, and strange woman-shapes with round heads and striped triangles to represent a gown. Father Severian shook his head at such doings, and Father Priscus had frowned, but they were willing to wink at the women's superstitions while they continued their efforts to win the men to their new god.

"I have been thinking," said a quiet voice behind her, "about your dream."

Gudrun turned, still holding her empty basket, and met her mother's considering gaze. "I put no apple beneath my pillow to conjure my true love's image; I chanted no spells. It was only a fancy of the night, no more."

The queen sat down upon a fallen tree trunk brought down

by the winter's floods and gestured to Gudrun to sit by her side.

"All that is dreamed at the Spring Turning has power. There is a moment, when day and night are equal, when you can see past Midgard's bounds. Such visions are all the more significant when uncalled. Why do you still refuse to believe in your own magic?"

Gudrun stared at the tangle of branches, where new leaves fluttered, though half the tree's roots were in the air. *Because I do not want to be like you,* she thought rebelliously, *valuing everything and everyone only for their usefulness to your ambitions and the Burgund cause.*

"The wolf came to me and we wandered in the forest, that is all!" she said aloud.

"Not quite all—" Grimahild's eyes narrowed as she surveyed her child. "For when you spoke to me before, your eyes were wide with wonder. What did you feel for this creature as it walked by your side?"

Gudrun's awareness went inward, remembering, and her eyes filled with tears.

"Love . . ." she whispered. "I felt safe with him, and loved. . . ."

"The wolf is won by maiden's charms," said the queen into the silence. Gudrun cast her a swift glance, for her voice had thinned suddenly to the sibilance of incantation. "The warg wins refuge in her arms. Ostara's dawning bless the day a mighty warrior comes this way!"

Is that a prayer or a spell? Gudrun started to reply, but what came from her lips was a question.

"Who? Who is the wolf that will come to me?"

Grimahild's heavy lids lifted. Gudrun read curiosity and calculation in her smile. "I think it is the son of Sigmund the Wolf-king who rides this way. I have heard that he is shapestrong, and a hero. He is your wolf, my daughter. I will have to consider how we may fittingly welcome him."

She fell silent as one of the women came to them with bowls of stewed hare. Gudrun had not thought herself hungry, but the morsel in her wooden bowl made her mouth water and she ate eagerly. *My dream and her delusion . . .* she thought as she remembered her mother's words. *How can I trust them?*

Her mother had as good as promised her the hero for her husband, and yet she knew well that the marriages of princes had little to do with maidens' dreams. The queen had never yet done anything that did not serve her own dream of glory for the Niflungar. If she wanted Gudrun to marry Sigfrid, she had other reasons than her daughter's happiness. Suddenly Gudrun felt afraid.

The hare's severed head still sat atop the stones, and she could not help remembering the look in those eyes before death had dulled them. There had been fear, at first, and then acceptance. Perhaps the men were used to this. More often than not they themselves killed the meat they ate in the hall, and risked their own lives to get it.

Some always have to pay the price so that others can live, she thought as she swallowed. Some speculated that Baldur had been offered at the end of the age of the gods, so that Wodan might continue to rule through the age of men; even the god whose festival the Christians would celebrate on the morrow had died in the spring. *If Sigfrid is to be mine, who will have to pay?*

For a moment the world seemed to still around her, and she saw each leaf and blade of grass limned with a terrible clarity. Then someone handed her a cup of wine and as she took it, blinking, the world flowed into motion again. The grass and the trees seemed no different, but Gudrun knew that she herself was no longer the same.

Between Mogontiacum and Borbetomagus, the Rhenus flowed between the marshy margins that bounded the water meadows and plowed fields, its dimpled grey-green surface concealing the powerful current below. From the porch of the feasting hall that the Burgunds had made from the old basilica, the king could see a ferry angling across the river, laden with warriors, as well as the cookfires of those who had arrived already and camped in the fields outside the town.

"So many . . ." he whispered. "Will they all fit into the hall?"

Hagano, beside him, gave a grunt of laughter. "It gives us a good excuse to reduce the size of the escorts they bring with them, brother. And maybe that will mean less blood flowing with the wine."

Gundohar grimaced. Quarrels were always a danger when men drank deeply with weapons to hand. When warriors in their cups got to brooding, an unlucky word could reawaken old feuds to venomous life.

"Aren't you looking forward to it?" asked Hagano. "Don't you want to eat until you bloat and drink till you puke with the rest of them?"

"You can afford to laugh," said Gundohar, cracking his long fingers nervously. "You won't be the one they are watching, whispering you're not the king your father was."

"That is certainly true—" said Hagano dryly, and Gundohar realized suddenly that he had been tactless, for Hagano, though it was never spoken of openly, was not King Gipicho's child. It should not matter, for as far as the folk were concerned, he was as royal as Godo or little Gislahar. But his brother's blunt features never showed what he was thinking. It was hard to tell if he cared.

"—At least for the older men," Hagano went on. "But the younger warriors will think only that you are the hero of the Longstone field."

Gundohar sighed. He recalled mainly the terror of that day, but the beauty of the Walkyrja who had spared him burned in his memory like a dark flame. And after that there had been a short space filled with blood and shouting when perhaps he had been a hero.

"Oh, I have learned my lessons," the young king said bitterly, "both kingcraft and bardcraft. Our folk would rather follow a hero, but what they need is a *hendinos*, a king of kings. Either way, reputation is worth an army. But how do I build one? I don't even know what I did in that battle, much less whether I can do it again! Counsel me, Hagano—you have our mother's wisdom. How can I be the king the Burgunds need?"

Hagano, who had been watching the struggles of the latest

batch of newcomers to disembark their horses from the ferry, turned to him, the sunlight glowing in his dark eyes.

"The first thing you must do is to order the thrall who serves you to water your wine." He waited out Gundohar's laughter. "And then you must lead the talk around to alliances."

"Do you mean marriage?" The king grimaced.

"Perhaps. Old Ostrofrid was wise to counsel you against entanglements when you were young. Godo and Gudrun can bring us useful connections, but you are the the most valuable prize. Your marriage must buy us the support of a major power."

"I am sure that the chieftains will have plenty of suggestions," said Gundohar quickly. There was only one woman he had ever wanted to wed, and she was as unattainable as one of the Walkyriun in Wodan's hall. "But such arrangements take time. What can we do now?"

"Gain the allegiance of heroes—younger sons and masterless men who will be loyal to you alone. You have some good men in your house-guard already—warriors like Gamalo and Randalf and old Eleuthir. But you need somebody more notable to inspire them. That Anglian, Hengest, comes to mind, but I believe he's hired out to Hnaef Half-Dane in Juteland. There are others, like the sons of Haki, and Starkad, who killed King Vikar, or Sigfrid Sigmundson, who slew Fafnar up on Wurm Fell."

"I don't think we can afford the kind of fame Starkad would bring us, brother, and Sigfrid has made a name for himself this past year fighting for the Franks. I doubt his stepfather would let him go." Gundohar frowned. "Forming my own company of heroes is a good idea, though. I'll ask the bards who the people are making songs about these days. Perhaps if I can get one hero, others will come too." He would have twelve, he thought, that was the traditional number.

"You will lead them, Hagano," he grinned, and was rewarded when for once his brother's eyes widened in surprise. "You're a good fighter, and a cunning one, and the men respect you."

Hagano stared at him. "Respect! Well, perhaps they do. But they do not love me," he added bitterly. "You will have to look elsewhere for a warleader if you expect the heroes to flock to your standard."

Gundohar felt the color rush to his face and reached out to his brother, but what could he say? From the river's edge came the sound of singing—the women were returning from their ritual. He saw their mother trudging up the path, swathed in a dark mantle, and the gleam of sunlight on Gudrun's golden hair. Soon enough the men would be gathering for the feasting. With a sigh, he let his hand fall away. Each man followed his wyrd as well as he could. That would have to do.

"To all those gathered in this hall I give good welcome." Queen Grimahild stood like an image, her dark cloak replaced by a Byzantine mantle of heavy dull green silk drawn over one shoulder and under the other arm, edged with pearls and gold. Lappets of pearl and peridot swung from the flat gold round of her diadem. Its cabochon stones glowed balefully as the torchflames flared in the draft when they closed the great door. "Victory to those who bring honor to the Burgund name!"

She looked like an empress, thought Gudrun, standing behind her. But long strands of amber weighted the queen mother's neck instead of pearls, and the inscription graven on that crown was in runes. The chieftains stood to receive her greeting, nearly two hundred voices rolled and echoed from chipped plaster which still bore paintings of the old Roman gods as they replied. Once this had been a temple of Jupiter. Now, with its tile roof replaced with thatching, it served as a feasting hall for a barbarian king.

"The mother of the Gibichings drinks to you, heroes—" Grimahild lifted the silver-mounted aurochs horn. She sipped at the mead, then poured for her son and the men who sat at the raised end of the hall. When she had finished, she stepped down from the dais and began to make her way along the northern aisle, pouring a little for each man.

Gudrun tightened her grip on the mate to the horn her mother bore and started down the other side of the hall. Her own attire was scarcely less elaborate than Grimahild's. The ivory damask dalmatic was figured with wheat sheaves, belted with golden plaques chip-carved in the Frankish style and weighted with goldwork at the neck and hem. But beneath the jeweled band, her hair flowed freely nearly to her knees in a mantle of living gold.

There might be more honor in being served by the queen, but it seemed to Gudrun that those for whom she poured smiled more appreciatively, and gradually she began to relax. It was some comfort to think that whatever husband they eventually gave her to might find her fair.

The boards were already scattered with pieces of the hard loaves which had been baked to eke out the king's supply of wooden trenchers and platters of unglazed Gaullish ware. The boiled pork and beef had already been consumed, and now they were starting in on the venison. Platters of spring greens and bowls with the last of the winter's cabbages and apples boiled up together were placed at intervals along the boards.

It seemed to Gudrun that her brother could take pride in his people. Since the death of Gipicho a new generation had come to power. Despite a leavening of greybeards like the lawspeaker Ostrofrid, most of the heads along the benches were brown, or red where the Gaullish blood was strong, or fair. *We are not so numerous a people as the Goths,* she thought then, *but we are growing. We can become a great nation if we root ourselves into this land.*

Ordwini, the son of Dragobald, gave her a cheerful smile as he held out his horn. He was only a winter or two older than Gundohar, but he had filled out in the two years since becoming the chieftain of his clan. Solid and stalwart, he seemed as unmoved by the babble of the hall that swirled around him as a rock in a stream. It was a pity, thought Gudrun as she went on to the next man, that Ordwini was married.

As she moved along the tables she was aware that young Ecgward Fairhair was watching her as if the drink she bore had been pressed from the apples of Idunna's garden and would bring him immortality. It was the hair, she thought critically, that made him look so like an unfledged chick, though he was the same age as she. There was one who would be glad to marry her, but he was only here because his clan's lands were too far away for his father to come. Though he was a promising warrior, the family was poor, and an alliance with him would win the Niflungar no advantage. Still, his adoration was flattering, and she smiled especially sweetly as she poured the last of the wine from her horn into his.

A slave appeared with more mead and she continued along the table, serving Helmnot and Tanastus and the others in her brother's house-guard. Soon she had served her half of the hall.

"Royal Woman, we drink to you, and to your children, and to Gundohar, son of Gipicho, hendinos of the Burgund clans!" Ostrofrid the lawspeaker held out his horn, and along the rows of benches arms lifted like branches in a wind.

"Hail to Gundohar! Hail to the Niflungar! Honor and Victory!"

For a moment Gundohar's face colored as crimson as his robe. Godomar was grinning, but Hagano, as usual, appeared unmoved. On the rounded wall behind them a faded painting of Jupiter, the hendinos of Olympus, could still be seen, but the throne of the old Roman god was shadowed by the high seat of the Germanic king. That gave Gudrun a certain satisfaction, but as she looked at her brother, clad in a silk tunic from Constantinople and holding a drinking horn blown from Roman glass, she wondered who was replacing whom?

She and her mother took their places next to Gundohar's high seat, as slaves with great jugs of the pale local wine began to move among the tables to refill the horns.

"We drink to our fathers who came down from the northern sea and up the Danu, who held back the Huns and defeated the Alamanni, conquerors of lands the Romans could not hold!" Old Heribard raised his horn.

"To Gipicho!" "To Gundiok!" "To Gundwurm!"

The clamor grew as the chieftains shouted out the names of their ancestors. This would go on for some time, as each lord toasted the heroes from whom he was descended. Even so recently as Gudrun's childhood, later rounds would have honored Donar and Wodan and the goddesses, but although more than one of the men made the hammer-sign to bless his horn, the conditional Christianity required by the Romans forbade such dedications at a public festival. Still, as the leaders of the great clans all traced their lineage back to some god, she could not see that very much had changed. Certainly they consumed just as much wine and ale.

"My lord, I wish you victory indeed," said Ostrofrid, at the other end of the table. "But for the moment we can do no more by force of arms. Tomorrow, when we meet in council, we must consider how to strengthen our alliances."

"I will not jeopardize our treaties with Rome—" Gundohar began.

"No need to—" Heribard broke in. "Our greatest danger now is the Huns, who are beginning to test our eastern borders. Until now, they've been busy digesting the Goths and taking Roman gold to fight her enemies. The Empire can hardly object if we make an alliance with *them*." The other older men laughed, but Gudrun's middle brother, Godomar, stirred impatiently beside her.

"I would," he whispered. "I'd like to fight them. I'll wager that man to man, we would win!" A glare from their mother silenced him, and Gudrun looked at Gundohar's counselors once more.

"But what can we offer?" asked the king. "The Romans buy them off with gold."

"A marriage—" said Ostrofrid. "Is there a woman available among their royal kin?"

"The king of the West-Huns has a granddaughter of the right age," answered Heribard. "She had a Tervingi mother. Hild, that's her name."

"Brunahild . . ." Gundohar's voice cracked. "Bladarda's daughter. But she is vowed to the Walkyriun."

"Not anymore—" Heribard grinned craftily. "They cast her out—for saving you! She's with her kin now among the Marcomanni."

"Indeed!" Ostrofrid exclaimed. "Then that is a proposal worth considering . . ." He glanced over at Gundohar, who was gaping with the same stunned-ox stare with which Gudrun had once seen him gaze at Brunahild.

He is still in love with her! she thought then. *He'll not try to evade this alliance.* She remembered then how she had once longed to have Brunahild as her sister, and how impossible it had been to imagine the older girl's wild energy harnessed to the duties of a queen.

Oh my brother, don't try to tame Brunahild! But she was not one of Gundohar's counselors, and she said it silently. It occurred to her then that she was just as foolish, dreaming of a man she would probably never even see.

Borbetomagus dozed in the golden light of morning like a dog in a patch of sun. Hagano gazed out over the town, leaning against a pillar of the porch of the feasting hall. Behind it the old governor's palace stretched in a maze of wings and courtyards, where those who had drunk most deeply the night before were just now beginning to stir. If he looked to his right, he could see down to the river. Straight ahead lay the Forum and the houses of the city fathers of Borbetomagus. From the little church on the knoll to his left he could hear the sonorous chanting of the priests as they celebrated the Easter mass.

The priests said that on this day the White Christ had risen from the dead, which even Baldur had not been able to do, but Wodan had hung on the Worldtree for nine nights, not three, Hagano thought then, and never died at all. All religions proclaimed the greatness of their own gods, but growing up in the shadow of his mother's magic he had learned how much was superstition, and how much illusion. Better to trust, he thought, in his own wit and will and the strength of his right arm.

The town lay at peace, but despite his stillness, he was restless. Even though the sky was clear, it was too quiet, like the pause before a storm. His lips twisted as he realized that his disquiet came from within. Wood scraped on stone behind him and he turned.

"You are not at the service, Mother? Father Priscus will scold."

Queen Grimahild came forward, leaning on her stick, and sank down on a bench set against the rail. "My joints are bad this morning, I told Gudrun to tell him so, and if the good fathers do not believe that, they will not dare to give me the lie."

For the first time since he had awakened, Hagano felt genuine amusement. "Well, the shave-heads have three of your children to gabble at this morning. Let that content them. I do not care what they think of me."

"My son, what is wrong?" She had turned her face to catch the sun, and the ruin of her beauty was clear, but her eyes were closed. From all others he could cloak his thoughts, but Grimahild did not even need to see to know his mind!

For a moment, then, he hated her. Gripping the rail, he gazed unseeing over the town. "I want to go away," he said then. "I would seek my fortune in the north."

"Would you spend your strength for some stranger when your kindred need you?"

"My half kin!" Hagano exclaimed. "And what do they need me for? Gundohar has counselors to advise him and Godo to be his strong right arm."

"He will need you because you can do both," she said softly, "because you understand the things he cannot afford to know."

Hagano snorted. "Do you mean me to stand always in his shadow? I will not do it! I am enough a Burgund to want to earn my own fame!"

"Do you want them to make a statue of you by the riverside, as if you were an emperor?" She gave a short laugh. "I have read the runes for you, and looked into the well. Your name will live, Hagano, I promise you, but only if you remain faithful to the Niflungar."

He looked down at her bent head, wondering if he could believe her, or if she were using him as she used them all. Even his conception, he thought sometimes, had been part of a plan. The doors of the church swung open and people began to move blinking into the sunshine, chattering. His unease grew suddenly stronger.

"I will give you a little time to prove those words—" he said, watching the crowd. "Until they have made this marriage for Gundohar and he is settled in his power."

"Going or staying, you will serve the Niflungar," Grimahild said softly. "The fate that will bind you is riding through our gates even now . . ." Her voice had sunk to the monotone of trance, and he bent to look into her closed face.

"What is it, Mother? What do you see?"

For a moment she swung her head back and forth, muttering. Then she shuddered and opened her eyes. "Have they come from the church yet? What is happening?"

Hagano stood once more and looked up the hill. He could see Gudrun, all white and gold in the sunlight, and the blaze of Gundohar's crimson gown. But they were looking toward the Forum, where a man came riding on a storm-grey stallion with a grey cloak thrown back from his mail. Everywhere about him gold was gleaming, from the wolf-crest on his helm to the ties of his shoes, so that he seemed to move in a bright haze.

"A warrior," he whispered, "with the hero-light around him." There was a beauty in that glittering figure that made him feel suddenly ill.

"Ah—" she breathed. "Help me get up, Hagano, I would see."

The men had gone into the church unarmed, but Ordwini stepped between the king and the stranger, who surveyed them in silence, his eyes glittering from within the helm.

"Who comes armed on this day of peace? Stranger, if you mean us well, I give you the blessing of this holy day. Who are you, and what is your business here?"

"Victory to the Burgunds and to their king," the horseman replied politely. He fumbled with the chin strap and pulled off his spangenhelm, running his fingers through a tangle of sun-streaked brown hair. He looked strong, but younger than one would have supposed to have earned such riches. Then, with a supple economy of motion that made Hagano blink, he slid to the ground.

"I am called Sigfrid Sigmundson, and I bear a message from the lords of the Franks for King Gundohar."

Sigfrid stood still, but his eyes never ceased their assessment of all around him. Hagano flinched as that amber glance flicked toward the villa and then away.

The queen sighed. "He is come, then, and it is true. He has wolf's eyes. . . ."

Chapter Two   Hunting

Burgund Lands near Borbetomagus
Ostara's Moon, A.D. 420

"It is long since you have walked this path, Burgund Queen—"

The voice was soft, as if the words had been spoken by
the wind in the rowan trees. But here, on the path through
the forest, there should have been no one at all. Hagano
stopped short behind his mother, staring at the shape that
had appeared among the tree trunks, swathed in a cloak
and leaning on a staff, and his hand went to the hilt of his
sword.

"Who are you?" he asked sharply. He had escorted his
mother resentfully, for his brothers were feasting with Sigfrid
around the fire at the edge of the woodlands, boasting of the
deeds they would do in the hunt the next day, but perhaps
there was a reason for him to be here after all.

"Would you challenge me? Your mother knows who I am."
The man moved forward, peering at them from beneath the
brim of a broad hat that left half of his face in shadow, and
Hagano heard a sharp hiss of caught breath from the queen.
"Indeed, you are far from your royal hall—"

"No farther than you, Hidden One—" Grimahild replied,
her voice tight with some emotion Hagano could not identify.

Hagano twitched, wondering why she had used that name.
But the voice had been real, and though the dappled moonlight obscured as much of the stranger as it revealed, Hagano

25

could see that his hat was tattered, and the cloak could have belonged to any masterless man who wandered the roads. But it was hard to focus, for the leaves behind him glimmered with silver light.

"And why does the she-dragon brave the night?"

The queen took another step forward. "To call the spirits, to stir the cauldron. As you know—so why do you question me?"

Hagano's heartbeat, which had almost steadied, skipped once more. Who was this, to whom his mother boasted of skills which were hidden even from her children? Of them all, only he had been to the house in the forest where the queen brewed her potions and sang her spells.

"Indeed—" The stranger stroked his beard as if to hide a smile. "You are a mistress of magic. . . ."

Grimahild snorted. "I have gathered a few crumbs of lore. But they fell from your table. Have you come to teach me more?"

From beneath the broad hat came laughter, and Hagano shivered.

"Ah, but you must win *my* wisdom. Will you read a riddle for me?"

Queen Grimahild's fingers tightened on her staff.

"A wolf killed a wurm; a bird guided him. What is his name?"

"His name is Sigfrid," said the queen. "I have answered your question, and so, Father of Wisdom, I may ask one of you. Will the magic I mean to work this night succeed?"

"As a spear from a skilled hand strikes the target it sees. Would you know more?" For a moment he paused. "A raven lay on a rock surrounded by fire but was not burned. Who is she?"

"She is Brunahild," came the answer. "Tell me, Wise One, if Gundohar weds her, will the Burgunds become a mighty people? Will my sons sire kings?"

"And I—" Hagano pushed forward. "Will my name live?" He trembled as the lightless gaze beneath the broad hat shifted to meet his own.

"That is three questions. I will answer . . . the last one. You will be remembered so long as the Rhenus flows beside the city of the Wurm."

Queen Grimahild glared at her son. "But you have not told me what *I* need to know!" She turned to the wanderer once more.

"Then you must answer again—" For a moment he was still. "Fafnar guarded golden treasure. Who is the heir of the rod and the ring?"

Grimahild stared at him. "What do you mean—" she asked angrily. "You ask not for wisdom, but prophecy!"

The stranger shrugged and started to turn away. "That is what you have asked of me."

"Wait—" she cried. "When will you come to me again?"

"What use would that be?" he asked gently. "You do not know what you need to know."

"What about me?" Hagano found his voice once more. The wanderer considered him, and seemed to sigh, though perhaps it was only the rising wind in the trees.

"Are you also one of my children? Then you must learn to see as I see. . . ."

The wind stirred the branches, confusing vision with a shimmer of light and shadow. When they stilled once more, the wanderer was gone.

Hagano rocked back on his heels, staring around him.

"Who was he?" He turned to the queen, who stood with head bowed, clinging to her staff. "He was real—I could hear his breathing—but you spoke as if he were the High One himself. Woman, answer me!"

Grimahild turned to him, her face contorting. "Foolish child, have you learned nothing, sitting by my fire? How should the gods walk among us but in the bodies of men!"

"Wodan?" Hagano whispered. "Is he my father then?"

The queen shook her head with a harsh laugh. "Do not be so eager to claim that ancestry—he is not kindly to his children. Be glad that your father was heir to an older wisdom even than the god's."

Hagano blinked. Once, when he was small and the world

still seemed a bright place to him, another child had taunted him with bastardy and he had run weeping to his mother. Her reply still resonated in his memory. *"When you were born, King Gipicho held you in his arms and gave you your name. What more certain acknowledgment could there be?"* But he had known then that what his tormentor said was true. Until this moment, he had not spoken of it to her again.

"Come. Night is passing—" Grimahild said, "and we have work to do."

The morning resounded with the music of the horns, echoing from tree trunks, throbbing in the clear spring air. Gundohar stopped with one hand on his spear, for a moment no more than a sounding board for that melody.

"Come on, brother—the deer won't wait while you stand gaping!"

Godo's shout brought him blinking back to awareness of laughing men and bounding dogs, and his blood leaped in answer. The Burgunds were ready for the hunting trail! He lifted the spear away from the oak tree and turned, blinking, into the sunlight. His men cheered him and Gundohar grinned. A morning like this balanced all those times when he was uncertain or afraid. His men were splendid, glowing in dyed leather and wool with their golden arm rings glittering in the sun, and he was young, and their king.

"Then let us tell them we're coming!" he cried.

Laughing, he gazed around the circle, as man after man lifted his horn. Only Hagano, looking as if he had not slept at all, was silent, but that was nothing new. Gundohar's glance passed to the man beside his brother, in his undyed hunting leathers seeming almost a part of the woods behind him, until you met his eyes.

The northern warrior looked as a wolf might look, observing the antics of dogs, and all the shouting men seemed suddenly like so many puppies beside him. But at his hip hung a great silver-mounted horn.

"Blow your horn, Sigfrid," the king called out to him. *Bay with the rest of my hounds; do not break the harmony!* Heart pound-

ing, he held the other man's golden gaze in a long stare, until
at last Sigfrid lowered his eyes and smiled.

He unhooked the horn, and Gundohar blinked, realizing
its size. Only a wild aurochs of the woods could have borne
it—perhaps one day he could get Sigfrid to tell him the tale.
Then Sigfrid lifted the horn to his lips.

At first, the king heard nothing. Then he realized that the
note of Sigfrid's horn began so far below those of the others
that at first he had not recognized it. But as without apparent
effort the northern warrior continued to blow, the sound
grew, that single, deep note gathering strength until Gundohar felt it in the earth beneath his feet, he felt it in his bones.
In all the world, nothing existed but the sound of Sigfrid's
horn.

And then eternity ended and they were standing once more
in a forest glade. But for a moment, as the last echoes died
away, the shifting sunlight clothed Sigfrid in a haze of gold.

Who are you? Dazed, the king stared at him. *What are you,
that you can shake the soul in my breast this way?*

He felt a hand on his arm and knew that Hagano was leading him after the others. When he shook his head his sight
cleared, but his pulse was still pounding.

"We must have that man for the war-band. He has to be
ours!"

"He will be, brother," murmured Hagano. "He will."

Hagano rubbed his eyes and wished that he had been able
to snatch more than an hour or two of sleep. But it had been
well past midnight before the queen had finished her work.
He patted the pouch at his side where the small stoppered
bottle of Roman glass lay hid. It was nearly noontide, and the
dogs and the beaters had driven two deer within range of their
spears. Surely they would be stopping soon. From ahead he
heard the sound of running water and quickened his pace.

"Is no one else hungry?" he called as he caught up to the
others, who had paused in a clearing beneath a stand of linden
trees. "Beyond those lindens is a spring of good water. Let us
sit down in their shade and eat something. Sensible creatures

like deer rest in the middle of the day. We'll have more sport later when they come out to feed!"

Gundohar turned with a grateful look, and the others began to throw down their javelins and game bags with the smaller fare they had found on their way. Hagano gestured to the servants who had followed them to bring up the baskets of bread and cheese and ale and start a fire.

Someone spread a cloak for the king, who eased down with a sigh. Hagano leaned against a tree, feeling the ache of unaccustomed exercise in his bones. He would sit down after his task was done. If he allowed himself to relax now, it might be hard to rise again. Sigfrid was squatting on his heels, plucking two grouse with quick, efficient motions. He had brought them down on the wing, Hagano remembered sourly, with cast stones. In a few moments they had been spitted on green wood and were roasting above the fire.

"Is it true the envoys you sent to the Huns have returned?" Ordwini asked.

The king grew crimson, and Godomar guffawed.

"Oh, they've returned, all right—" His brother laughed again, and Hagano sighed. "But Gundohar is going to have to fight for the girl."

"Are they so unwilling?" Ordwini looked from one to the other, confused.

"Oh, the Huns are eager enough for an alliance. The problem is with the bride. This Brunahild thinks herself a warrior, and won't marry until she meets a man who can lay her on her back in the ring! I'd get her on her back quick enough if she were mine to master—" Godo leered. "You'd best get back in practice, brother mine!"

Hagano stirred, wondering if he would have to intervene.

"Godo—" said the king, and there was something in his voice that made his young brother flush and fall silent.

"I will do what I must to win her. The alliance is too important to us to let her go—"

To you. . . . thought Hagano with a twinge of pity. But he remembered the Wanderer's riddle. He must ask his mother why Brunahild had been surrounded by fire. There was a mystery here, and Gundohar might be getting more than he expected if he married this girl.

"Do the Huns train all their women to war?" asked Sigfrid, his gaze sharpening.

"I believe that they teach them to ride and to shoot the bow," said one of the older men, "but it is not usual for them to learn the sword. Why do you ask?"

Sigfrid looked suddenly much younger as he smiled. "I knew another Hun maid who was a warrior," he said softly. "I hope to see her soon."

Not if my mother has her way, thought Hagano grimly. He called to one of the servants and instructed him to bring out the ale and the drinking horns.

"Here—this will ease your thirst!" He moved across the clearing, the paired, silver-mounted horns in his hands. "To your health, brother—" Carefully he gave the horn in his right hand to the king. "And to yours, honored guest—" He offered the other to Sigfrid. The horns were identical, and the same brown ale filled them both. But the one he had given Sigfrid had received in addition the contents of the glass bottle his mother had given him the night before.

"To the king!" he cried, and shouting, the men lifted their horns. Sigfrid grimaced as he drank, but he knew enough of custom to drink his draft down.

"Too strong for you, stranger?" asked Godomar.

"This southern ale is bitter," answered Sigfrid. "But I'll run it off when we get on the move once more."

Hagano stifled a snort of laughter, remembering what his mother had said. Running was what he would be doing, but not after deer.

"Well, this bird smells done, and it will take the taste away. My lord, will you share my kill in return for your hospitality?" He lifted the grouse from the fire and laid it down on a mat of clean leaves, disjointed a leg and thigh and offered them to Gundohar.

"Hagano gives me drink and you give me meat!" exclaimed the king. "You should be my brother as well!"

Gundohar grasped Sigfrid's shoulder. His face was glowing,

triumphant, and for a moment Sigfrid's eyes, unguarded, betrayed a longing that Hagano understood only too well. Then, as if he had caught fire from the king's enthusiasm, he smiled. For a moment the two men seemed to share a single identity.

Though they had come from the same womb, Hagano knew that he could never be so at ease with his brothers as this stranger was now. He watched as Gundohar laughed, and felt his gut twist as if he had swallowed the potion instead of Sigfrid.

Wolves hunted silently until it was time to close in on the prey, but he was hunting with dogs now, thought Sigfrid as he trotted after the Burgund king, in more ways than one. Ahead of them the hounds were baying hysterically, but the men who followed them were nearly as loud. One would think any deer with ears would be miles away by now, but perhaps they were confused as well.

The noise of the hounds rose in pitch as they struck a new scent, and he quickened his pace.

"They've found something—" he called as he came up with Gundohar. "Come on—"

The other man grinned breathlessly. His face was pink with exertion and he was sweating, but he pushed his long limbs gamely onward despite his obvious fatigue. Gundohar had treated him like a brother, thought Sigfrid, restraining his own easy stride to keep pace with the king. It was almost like running with the pack again, despite the noise. Indeed, even among the Franks he had never felt so at ease. It was a pity, really, that he must move on, but perhaps when he had found Sigdrifa they could come back again.

For a moment, then, he could almost forget where he was, and who he hunted with today. The world narrowed to this whirl of varied green, the rich scents of last year's decaying leaves and the delicate perfumes of spring. His body took over, memories built into muscle and bone by a boyhood of ranging the forest guiding him as he raced through the trees, feet striking the earth lightly, body twisting lithely to avoid branches through which other men blundered, swearing. But in the excitement of the moment he could forget them, and imagine that the yelping of the hounds was the calling of his wolves.

His belly griped suddenly and he missed a step, frowning. This had happened from time to time before, when he ate bad meat, but he could not think of anything he had eaten that the others had not had as well. He swallowed nausea and forced himself to continue. He was not going to impress the Burgunds by puking behind every tree.

The deer was a brown blur ahead of them. The shouts of the men who were driving in from the other side echoed their own. Inexorably the circle tightened around the hunted creature so that its dash became a maddened whirl, and at last a frantic plunging that stopped only when the men halted a spear length away. Sigfrid could smell the sharp musk of its fear. It was a young stag, fat enough for the table, but inexperienced, and perhaps all the more dangerous because it would be unpredictable. He hung back a little, wondering if Gundohar would claim this kill. It was a fine beast, and in prime condition, plunging from side to side in mingled fury and terror as the dogs closed in.

The noise level had dropped, but its tone had deepened. Sigfrid recognized the sound of a hunger that transcended any need of the body—a hunger to kill. As if in response, his belly cramped again. He grimaced, but his body had become like those of the others, weapons aimed at a single goal. He had no time now to consider its pains.

Men stepped back to let Gundohar through, and for a moment Sigfrid saw not men but wolves, deferring to the pack-leader at the moment of the kill. Gundohar was the king-wolf here. The Burgund king lifted his spear, eyes burning with a desperate intensity. Sigfrid watched him intently—such moments were a good test of a wolf, or of a man. He could see tension in the set of the bony shoulders, the jump of a muscle in his cheek, and the tremor along the king's thigh. *He wants it too much*, thought Sigfrid. An experienced predator saved its energy.

Sigfrid had learned to judge a creature's spirit from the way it moved during those years in which the only society he had to study was that of the wolves. This king was awkward in motion, like a cub that had not quite achieved coordination between its body and soul. And yet his men followed him. Did leadership depend less on physical qualities among men? Sigfrid bit his lip as the uneasiness in his own gut returned. He was never ill, but perhaps there had been a bad bit in last night's stew.

He forced his attention back to Gundohar. At least there was no doubting the king's courage. He stalked forward, grip tightening until the knuckles showed white against the shaft of his spear. The deer's head came up, eyes white-rimmed and nostrils flaring.

Yes—thought Sigfrid, and felt a telltale flutter beneath his ribs that had nothing to do with the roiling of his belly, *he knows you; he has agreed to his death. Finish it now, Gundohar!*

The king took a deep breath, and for a moment the look in his eyes mirrored that of the deer. Then the muscles clenched beneath the tight-drawn cloth of his tunic, and he cast his spear.

Even as it blurred through the air, Sigfrid could see that the blow would not strike true. As the spearpoint tore its way along the buck's side the spell was broken. The beast reared, its forehooves, sharp as any spear, striking out before the king even realized his danger. In the same moment instinct unleashed Sigfrid in a spring that knocked Gundohar aside and brought his own spear driving up between the flailing forelegs and into the lungs. He wrenched himself away, jerking it free as the deer staggered, blood spraying across the leaves.

Gundohar was trying to rise. He went down again as Sigfrid rolled into him. Sigfrid crouched where he had fallen, sheltering the king's body with his own. He could feel the shudder of the other man's breathing against him as slowly, one muscle at a time it seemed, the deer collapsed and lay still.

For a moment there was silence. Then the men began to cheer. Gundohar stirred convulsively beneath him, and Sigfrid pulled away. The blood of the deer had soaked his leathers. Its reek filled his nostrils. His belly cramped as if the spear had gone not into the deer's gut, but his own.

"You saved me—" came Gundohar's voice in his ear. "Stay with me, Sigfrid. I need you here—" The others were saying things too, words of amazement or admiration; suddenly he was too sick to hear.

He lurched to his feet, looking past the grinning faces for some green shadow in which he might go to ground. Ignoring all the hands that reached out to him, he crashed into the bushes, and for the first time in his life vomited after a kill.

"It is only a gut cramp; I need no help, truly, just to be left alone—" Sigfrid felt his whole body heating with shame, or perhaps it was the illness. His head was ringing and he could not be sure. By the time they got back across the river it was nearly sunset, and it had taken all his will to stay in the saddle that long.

A hard hand closed on his shoulder, and his reactions, dulled by internal preoccupations, were a second too slow to keep Hagano from drawing him into the room. He glimpsed white walls, a low bed beside a brazier where coals were glowing, and the dark figure of the Burgund queen.

"Be easy, it is you who confer the favor," came Gundohar's voice behind him. "My mother is renowned for her skill with herbs, and will be glad of the chance to use her craft. We'll have you fit again for the feasting, never fear."

The door clicked shut and he was left alone with her. Swathed in her shawl and veils she seemed shaped from shadows. *My own mother was the sunlight*, he thought then, shivering. He felt trapped. Instinct told him that his trouble was only a systemic upset that would pass with time, but now that he was here, he risked insulting his hosts if he did not let the woman dose him. He supposed that her nostrums, whatever they might be, could make him feel no worse than he did already.

"I am sorry that you are not well. Lie down. It will be better soon."

Her voice was a surprise to him, low and honeyed. *Women's magic*, he thought, twitching. Just so Sigdrifa had spoken when she worked her protective spells. That ritual had linked them in a bond that led finally to love, but he supposed he need fear no such outcome from this crone's magic. With a sigh he stripped off his tunic and sat down.

"Drink this—" The woman held out a beaker.

The stuff tasted foul going down, and worse coming up, but she was at his side immediately with a basin.

"It is well, well," she whispered. "First we must purge you of the poison. This that I give you now will be better, I promise."

Head swimming, Sigfrid drank, and though there was an odd acrid taste that puckered his mouth, she had added honey to this potion, and it lay heavy in his emptied belly. Soon a slow warmth spread outward, weighting his limbs.

"What . . ." Sigfrid tried to speak. *What have you given me?* But his tongue did not seem to want to obey. She touched his shoulder and he collapsed backward onto the bed.

"Do not fight me, wolf-child. This is part of the magic. Lie still, and soon all will be well." She lifted his legs onto the bed and straightened his arms, humming softly.

That part of Sigfrid's mind which could still reason doubted that, but he found it hard to care. It was very warm in the room. Vague images filtered through his awareness . . . the nest of furs where he and Sigdrifa had lain curled together after making love . . . lying in the meadow near the forge on a summer's afternoon . . . warm arms around him and a soft breast. . . . Blindly he turned his head and tasted sweetness.

"Warm . . . yes, you are warm and secure . . . sink into the warmth . . . sink deeper, still deeper, rest, be at peace . . . be still. . . ." He heard, and did not know if the words came from outside or were his own.

"When did you ever feel such ease before? When did you know love? You can speak now, to answer me. . . ."

That was not hard—there had been little enough love in Sigfrid's life, and the tale made no long telling. He thought of his mother with an ache that had never left him; and then it seemed to him that he was talking about her, or perhaps he was only remembering.

"She did not want me to go, but even though I was only

eight winters old I understood that I must leave Hiloperic's hold or my father's enemies would kill me. I went with Ragan to live in the forest voluntarily. But it felt as if my mother were sending me away. I saw her only two more times, once when we went back for the king's funeral ale, and once when she was dying. I only wanted to comfort her, but I was nearly her death when the Hundings came after me and tried to burn us in our hall. In the fighting the berserk fit came on me and I became a wolf. I saved her, for a little while, but after that I could not stay. Even my little sisters were afraid of me!"

"It does not matter..." came the words, and they sounded sweet to him now, *"I will be your mother. I will care for you...."*

A gentle hand was stroking his brow. He lay against a soft breast and some last tension left him. When the sweet voice asked him about his childhood, once more the words began to flow.

"I would have loved Ragan if he had let me, but he did not know how. I got more affection from the wolves. In the end death was the only repayment I could make him—he forced me to it, he wanted it! But he made me a kin-slayer, and I will never lose that pain. He left me alone...."

"Be clanless no longer," came the reply. *"Let the land of the Burgunds be your home, and Gundohar and Godo and Gislahar will be your brothers...."*

Sigfrid remembered how he had leaped in to save Gundohar from the horns. The other man had embraced him, and he had found himself hugging him back, for that moment at home and accepted as he had never been before. Was that how it felt to have a brother, to be part of a family? He heard a thin moaning, like an animal in agony, and after a moment realized that the throat it came from was his own.

Memory filled his vision with wolves, hackles bristling as a stranger approached the den, but this time it seemed to him that the queen wolf barked in welcome, and then suddenly all of them were nosing at the newcomer, whining eagerly, tails wagging in an ecstasy of welcome. Sigfrid stiffened, shaken by emotions almost beyond bearing; then something touched his forehead, and a soothing murmur thrust him back down into the passive stillness of dream.

For a time he drifted, neither knowing nor caring what passed, but presently he became aware that the sweet voice was calling to him once more. Reluctantly he moved toward awareness.

"Tell me of women, Sigfrid—whom have you loved? Who has touched you like this . . . and this?"

A sweet fire spread beneath his skin, and he gasped as his phallus stiffened. He reached out blindly. Where was Sigdrifa? Suddenly his whole body had become one ache of need. Trembling, he whispered her name.

"Who is Sigdrifa?"

"A dark fire," he breathed, "a raven in the snow . . . the Walkyrja who guards my soul. . . ." His skin twitched at a change in pressure, as if someone were stroking the air around him.

"Ah—" came the voice, *"that is what I sensed before—she has warded him."*

"With runes and herbs she spelled me against all evil," he whispered. "Her spirit shields me wherever I may go. For nearly a year we have been parted, but still she is with me. Sigdrifa, soon I will see you! Soon I will take you in my arms!" His body strained, but there was nothing there.

"I will not touch the protections, but the bond must be broken—"

Sigfrid heard without understanding; the words seemed to come from very far away. Once more he heard the humming, a babble of meaningless syllables that nonetheless sent a chill through his bones. Then came a sudden, sharp severing—he cried out, feeling the loss like a physical pain. But he could still feel all his limbs. What had gone? It was as if one of his senses were suddenly missing; lacking it, he could not even guess what it had been. The humming grew louder, distracting him.

"Be easy, child . . . be still . . ." came the soft murmur. *"It was only a dream. . . ."*

"Sigdrifa—" he murmured the name, but the humming absorbed it. "We lived together, hunted together, made love—"

"It was a dream, such as comes to lonely men in the wilderness. . . . She was never real."

Once more he felt the touch that set his senses aflame, but now his desire had no outlet. He thrashed and whimpered, tormented by his need.

"Turn from the dark woman of your nightmares to the bright maiden of the day—" sang the voice in his ear. *"A wondrous woman awaits you, a golden girl, tall and deep-breasted. She is fair as the Frowe herself, a bride of royal kin."*

"A bird once led me to a fair woman . . ." Sigfrid whispered, "but she is gone . . . what happened to her?"

"Forget the bride of the forest, the life of the outlier, severed from kind and kin. Now you are in the world of men, Sigfrid, and you must win a wife to make a home for you and bear you children. . . . Forget the past. Forget all that went before. Soon you will see the golden maid, Gudrun. You will desire her, and seek to win her love."

He groaned as passion stiffened him once more; through closed eyelids he sensed the light growing brighter, a sweet, spicy scent teased his nostrils, he burned in a blaze of gold.

Then the light faded. He felt the warm weight of a blanket, a gentle hand stroking his hair.

"Sleep now . . ." the sweet voice was murmuring, *"sleep without dreams. When you awaken, all that is past will be as if it happened to another, dim, without meaning. No vows bind you. Your future is with the Burgunds now, your family is the Niflungar, and you will love Gudrun. . . ."*

For a moment longer he struggled, then the darkness rose up around him. With a sigh he let it take him and knew no more.

"This was an ill thing you did this day," said Hagano, looking down at the sleeping man. At first he had felt satisfaction to see this hero powerless before his mother's magic, but he was a warrior as well, and there was no honor in such a victory.

The queen straightened her shoulders and looked at him. "It served the Niflungar—"

"And that justifies everything?" he asked curiously. He could see from her face that it had been no easy task. The work had carved deeper grooves from nose to mouth and in her brow, but triumph burned in her eyes like a dying flame.

"You told Gundohar that the war-band would not follow you," she said quietly. "But *he* is already renowned. Men will flock to the Gundwurm when it is known that Sigfrid Fafnarsbane is here."

"And what will bind him?"

"Your sister's bright eyes . . ." said the queen, and smiled. "Go now, and tell her to attend me here. When he awakens she will be the first thing he sees, and if he does not desire her above all things, from that moment on I will forswear magic!"

"Drink health to Sigfrid! Were it not for him, you might have been mourning me instead of rejoicing in the deer!"

Gundohar swung up his drinking horn, and ale splashed onto the straw on the floor as the others echoed him. Sigfrid, blinking at the sudden blaze of torchlight, thought the king's cheeks looked unusually rosy. The hour was late, and clearly the hunters had been consoling themselves with the ale vat while the stag was cooking—*and while I slept off the old woman's magic!* He was still weak, but he was emptied of all the poison—in fact he felt so light that he squeezed the hard muscle of his arm to make sure the old witch had not turned him into a spirit while he was asleep.

Or perhaps what was making him so buoyant was joy. Gudrun was coming toward him with a full ale-horn, and as he met her eyes he felt a tingling throughout his flesh, like a shower of gold. Her serene loveliness had overwhelmed him when he awakened to find her looking down at him, but he thought now that she was even more beautiful in motion, her golden hair rippling like a field of ripe barley in the sun.

"I drink to Gundohar and the Dragons of the Rhenus!" He took the horn from her hands, and trembled as his fingers brushed hers. "Wassail!"

The king sat at the table on the dais with his brothers beside him, Godomar leaning forward with a beaker of ale in his hands, stout as a young oak tree; Gislahar, a lad about nine winters old, holding a flagon to refill it, and Hagano, standing as usual a little behind the others. Their hair, every shade from wheatstraw to amber, was burnished to the same rich gold by the torchlight. Sigfrid looked from them to their sister and recognized the common stamp of blood and bone. And in that moment he wished to be one of them more than he could remember ever wanting anything. Then Gundohar grinned.

"Come, Sigfrid, and sit beside us—there is room here between Godo and me!"

The wolf within him tensed, still not trusting, but Sigfrid suppressed it. Why should they not welcome him? The Burgunds thought that the wolf on the crest of his helm was only a totem such as any man might honor. Carefully, lest his weakness betray him, he went forward.

"I am glad to see you on your feet. It was a shock to have you looking so pale." Gundohar moved on the bench so that he could sit down. They were bringing in the deer at last, and the scent of cooked meat filled the hall.

"It was a surprise to me, too," said Sigfrid ruefully. "I can hardly remember the last time I was ill."

"You have been here only a few days, but already I have learned to value you. I shall be sorry indeed when you ride on. I would like it well if you could see your way to joining us in this summer's campaigning." The king spoke diffidently, as if he were asking the favor, not a great lord honoring a landless wanderer.

A pair of slaves came down the center of the hall, staggering beneath a slab of wood on which smoking joints of venison lay. They brought it to the high table and Gislahar supervised the transfer of choice pieces to figured plates of red Roman ware. Sigfrid's belly clenched with hunger as the scent reached him, but in his heart was a sharper hunger still.

Sigfrid knew that as men counted such things he was rich. But what was that worth, really? Wealth was useful to bolster a chieftain's position, but you could not eat gold, nor would it shelter you. Fighters could be bought, but hired swords would not defend you with a kinsman's loyalty. Sigfrid knew well enough that all he truly had to offer was his strength. He thought of the plans he had made with Sigdrifa and reflected that the life of a wandering sword, hard enough for a man, was no kind of existence for a woman.

"Must you go?" asked Godomar. "What can you find to do in the east that would be more worthy of your skills?"

"I have . . . an obligation . . ." Sigfrid said, trying to remember why it had seemed so important to him.

Sigdrifa was a fine woman, and by now, safe among her kinfolk, she must be wondering why she had ever agreed to ride with him. He had to go to her, of course, but to release her, not to take her away. Then he would be free to return to Borbetomagus, and—he could not finish the thought, but his gaze followed Gudrun as she moved through the hall. She was like a young doe pacing through a meadow, grave and self-contained.

Gundohar saw where he was looking and laughed.

"I have a quest of my own this summer," he said in a low voice. "And would be glad of your company. The Huns have agreed to a treaty at last and they would seal it with a marriage tie."

"So there is to be a wedding?" Sigfrid was still watching Gudrun. He had never dared to imagine himself settled with a wife in the usual way, but he was thinking about it now.

"First I must win the bride," said Gundohar. "She is a warrior-maiden, and has sworn to wed with no man who cannot defeat her. Sigfrid, men sing of my deeds on the Longstone field, but that day I was desperate. I have not the warrior craft to overcome an opponent without trying to slay. If your path lies east, will you at least ride with us and teach me as we go?"

"This does not sound like a match made by royal counselors—" said Sigfrid, his gaze still following Gudrun. She had been gazing down at him when he awakened, and though night had long fallen, for him it was suddenly morning. She had a quality of repose that was like his mother's, but there was a promise in her smile that made his blood sing.

If fighting were all that was needed, he would have known how to win her. Perhaps when he had discharged his debt to Sigdrifa he could return and woo her—but what did he have to offer? It always came down to that. He was a landless, kinless man.

"And perhaps he could come back with us afterward," said Godo like an echo. Sigfrid stared.

"I need you, Sigfrid Fafnarsbane," said Gundohar. "Not just to help me win the Hunnish princess. I need your fame to bring heroes to my war-band, to guard my back in battle, to add to the glory of the Burgund name. But what can we offer you? You are wealthy already, and renowned."

"Wealthy?" said Sigfrid, and his yellow wolf-eyes met the grey gaze of the king. "You are rich in kindred and followers, with brothers around you. . . ."

"Become our brother, then," said a soft voice behind them. "Marry Gudrun. . . ."

Sigfrid looked round, met Hagano's considering gaze, then turned back to the king, whose eyes were blazing with sudden hope. His own heart had begun to pound so painfully he wondered if he would pass out again.

"Will the Council agree to it?" asked Godo. "It will take time to talk them around."

"He brings us wealth and glory, and we do not lose our sister," said Hagano. "That is a good enough basis for alliance. If he proves his value by helping the king to win Bladarda's daughter, they will agree."

"Sigfrid, will you do it?" Gundohar clasped his arm.

"Will *she* agree to it?" he whispered, and Gundohar laughed.

"Gudrun is the daughter of a king, and knows she must marry to serve her family. But I have seen how she looks at *you,* and I do not think you will find her an unwilling bride!"

"The marriage must wait until we speak with the Council," Hagano's deep voice echoed, "but you need not wait to make him your brother. Swear your oaths now." He lifted down one of the spears that was hanging on the wall, and a murmur of speculation ran through the hall.

Sigfrid saw the twining of silver inlaid into the black blade and felt his skin chill. Ragan had forged that spearhead long ago, when the Burgund king first went to war. He himself had plied the bellows, watching in fascination as the shape emerged from the steel.

By Ragan this spear was forged, Ragan my kinsman, loved and hated, who doomed me to walk alone . . . But this pack is willing to welcome me—there is a pattern here indeed!

"I will swear—" he said hoarsely.

"There is a garden just outside," said Hagano, "where Mother Earth can witness." He started toward the door and the others followed him, snatching torches from the walls.

The garden was only a circle of shrubs around an empty plinth, where once there had been a shrine to some Roman god. But the turf was thick, and it was easy enough for one of the swordsmen to carve a strip and lift it, unbroken, with the two ends still joined to the ground.

Gundohar's men grew silent as the king and the stranger knelt to either side of the opening and the blade swung down between them. In the torchlight its silver traceries ran with fire.

"Take your oaths," said Hagano, "and let them be as binding as if you swore on Wodan's spear."

Gundohar laid his hand upon the king-spear, closed his eyes for a moment, then smiled.

> *"Sigfrid Sigmundson, strongest of heroes,*
> *become now my brother! Thus do I bind me:*
> *by love and loyalty be our lives linked;*
> *my hall be your home, here shall you prosper;*
> *if you are wronged I will avenge you;*
> *faith kept between us, fortune will follow.*
> *This oath I offer, and need no other,*
> *by blood of brothers shall we be bound—"*

Crimson welled up in a thin line as he drew the fleshy pad of his hand suddenly across the sharp edge of the blade and let the blood drip into the dark opening beneath the strip of grass.

The place had gone very still. Sigfrid looked across the spear and saw a blur of faces staring down him. Beyond them, Gudrun stood at the door to the hall, the flagon of mead still in her hands, like a figure carved in ivory and gold. In all that company, only she was real. He gashed his own hand with the spear and held it up so that all could see.

"Thus do I swear also, to live with you as a brother in love and loyalty. Your cause shall be mine, your enemies my own. May my heart's blood flow as my hand bleeds now if ever I break faith with you." He thrust his hand under the turf and felt his blood dripping into Earth's womb.

Then he straightened and held out his hand, and the young king clasped it. He felt the wet warmth and did not know if it were Gundohar's blood or his own. Godo grinned and scratched his own hand and gripped Sigfrid's, then kissed him on both cheeks.

"So swear I also!" he cried. But Gundohar took Sigfrid's face between his two hands and kissed him on the lips, and in that moment, his eyes were very much like Gudrun's, and Sigfrid loved him.

"By kiss of kinsman we call you to witness, Gipicho's sons give this oath gladly!" the king cried. "This night we have become brothers—in Erda's dark womb our blood is mingled." He sat back, and the men let the strip of turf drop back into place.

Even little Gislahar hugged Sigfrid then. They were all embracing, grinning like wolves returning to the pack after they have scattered for hunting. All except Hagano, who was holding the spear.

Sigfrid looked up and saw Hagano watching him, and it seemed to him that Gundohar's brother looked at him with Ragan's eyes.

Chapter Three

Leaf King & Spring Queen

Borbetomagus
Milk Moon, A.D. 420

The feast of Pentecost was coming, when the Holy Spirit descended in wind and fire. But for the people, it was the season when the fire of life kindled in the blood, and flowers sent forth their incense on every breeze. The Christian priests might call it Pentecost; but for those of the old Celtic blood it was Beltane; for the Romans settled in the Rhinelands, the joyful festival of Floralia; and for the Burgunds, Pholstag, when they remembered the joining of Baldur and Nanna by celebrating the marriage of the Leaf King and the Spring Queen. A fine time, said Gundohar, for a royal wedding.

Sigfrid agreed with mixed emotions. When he looked at Gudrun, his body thought for him. He wanted her as he had wanted no woman before. But though her brothers assured him that the girl was willing, he had not been able to get close enough to her to tell if she also felt desire. Only, when he could get her to meet his eyes, he thought he saw interest there.

Sigfrid had hoped that before he married he would be able to settle things with Sigdrifa. It seemed obvious to him now that the future he had planned with her would be no good for either of them. If she needed wealth to make a good marriage among the Huns, he was quite willing to dower her from Andvari's hoard. But as Gundohar pointed out, there was not time enough to go to the land of the Huns and return before the Burgunds started their own journey there. It made far more sense to marry Gudrun now and seek out Sigdrifa after he had helped Gundohar win Bladarda's daughter.

Unless, of course, he wanted to put it off until after the king's wedding. But when Sigfrid looked at Gudrun, working in her garden with the spring sunlight gilding her hair, he knew he could not do without her so long. And so the weeks of waiting went on till the Spring Festival. But if there was not time enough to journey to the Huns, it was only the work of a few days for Sigfrid to go back up the Rhenus to Wurm Fell to recover Fafnar's treasure, and hide it anew in a cleft above the spring of the linden trees where the hunters had rested, just across the river from the city of the Niflungar.

The night before the festival there had been a high wind, chasing clouds across the sky, whistling in the thatching and bringing down a few more of the remaining Roman tiles.

"The demons are riding to revel with the witches," said the priests, crossing themselves.

"Wodan is leading his Walkyriun to keep the feast with old Walburga and the wisewomen on the mountaintops," whispered the old women when the priests had gone.

And if some folk were absent from their beds that night, no one ventured to comment. But everyone, whether they followed the old faith or the new, took care to ward their stock pens and their houses, for whatever human folk rode to the mountains, it was certain that all the wild powers were abroad this eve.

Gudrun slept badly that night. She told herself it was the wind. A German house, rooted in the earth, would groan and sway in a tempest and be little the worse in the morning, while the old Roman building stood rigid and shook to the blast. But in the morning, looking out at a world swept clean and shining with promise, she could no longer delude herself. She was afraid.

Her brothers had assured her that Sigfrid was as hot for her—as Hagano put it—as the horse for the mare, and it was true that when his gaze followed her she felt an odd tingling, not unpleasant, that she did not understand. Even her mother wanted this marriage. Perhaps that was what disturbed her, for when had her mother and Hagano ever had her good at heart? And Sigfrid had no claim on their loyalty, only the enthusiasm of Gundohar, who seemed ready to worship his new brother as one who possessed by nature all the qualities that he had been struggling to acquire. Why should they give their sister, one of their chief assets, to a stranger, even if he was the most famous hero to come along in years?

But she had not refused him. How could she, seeing the wolf of her dream look out of his eyes?

From the streets beyond the villa she could hear singing. The young men of the town had been out before the dawn to gather birch branches, which they twined into wreaths and decked with flowers to hang above the doorways of their girls. From farther off came the deep heartbeat of a drum.

Then she heard laughter. The door swung open and the maidens who attended her burst into the room, babbling.

"Oh, mistress! Someone has put up a wreath over the gateway to the women's wing of the palace!"

"It is Sigfrid! He loves her! He claims her as his bride!"

Gudrun thought it more likely that the idea had come from Gundohar, for how should Sigfrid know their ways? But it was the kind of thing her brother, who sighed over old tales and loved to join in the village festivals, would do. She wondered if Brunahild would appreciate him.

"Lady, you must hasten." Little Ursula was already lifting her new gown from the chest while Adalfrida tugged at her nightrobe. "The men are getting ready to march down to the field for the races and you must be there."

Among the Romans, even the most staid of matrons blossomed out in colors for the Floralia. It was warm enough for Gudrun to wear her leaf green linen wrap in the old way, without an undergown, pinned at the shoulders with golden fibulae to leave her arms bare, and girdled with a belt of gilded leather. Grimahild's women had embroidered the gown till it blazed with flowers, and her mantle, of light wool left the natural creamy color, was bordered with flying birds. By the time they had hung necklaces about her neck and golden earrings in her ears, Gudrun felt as bedecked as the birch tree that had been set up in the square.

But no one could feel anything other than rejoicing on that morning once they had stepped out of doors. Soon the cobbled streets of the old Roman town were left behind them, and they moved along the moist earth of the road. Sunlight showered through the new leaves in a dappling of liquid gold, and the snowy petals of the hawthorn, shaken down by the night's wind, strewed the path as if the tree spirits were dancing just before them, scattering flowers. Gudrun found her steps growing swifter; her maidens had to hurry to keep pace with her as she danced along.

Then they came out into full sunlight, and saw the meadow blazing before them. For most of the year the water meadows between the town and the river were common grazing land, but since Borbetomagus had not been important enough to justify building an arena, they served also as a playing field for festivals. A platform had been built for the princes at one end with benches and a thatching of greenery.

As Gudrun settled into her place a cow horn blew from the other side of the field. The men were coming, with drums and banners, crowned with leaves in honor of the day. She saw her brothers, their fair heads gleaming. The magistrates of Borbetomagus marched with the Burgunds in their best tunics and mantles, the Romans resplendent in snowy togas. Behind them were the men who would compete in the games; blond heads and brown, Gaullish redheads and dark-haired sons of legionaries from every corner of the Empire who had taken up land on the frontier, all crowned alike with spring green.

With drum and horn and twittering flutes they marched around the field. Gudrun felt her pulse race as the procession turned back toward the platform. There was her brother, grinning like a boy, and behind him, Sigfrid. Gudrun stared, wondering why she had not seen him before. Perhaps Godo's stockier figure had hidden him, but now she could look at no one else.

The other men marched to the deep pulse of the drum as if they shared one heartbeat. But Sigfrid, even in the midst of the crowd, moved with his own feral grace. He was not so much out of step as moving to a music that flowed through the others but was uniquely his own.

They call him brother, but he will never be like them, she told herself, and smiled.

The procession came to the platform. The drums boomed demandingly, then stilled. Gundohar clambered up the ladder and took his place beside her, still standing, grinning out over the crowd.

"Men of the Burgunds!" he cried. "Men of Borbetomagus! All you who work this land—compete with one another, put forth your strength and skill; for your power is the power of the earth, and as you strive so shall the crops grow!"

The men began to cheer, and their families, and almost every living soul in Bortebomagus, joined in. Gundohar laughed in pleasure and then sat down at last, and one of his men handed him a horn of beer.

The boys' races were beginning; at the horncall, a dozen small figures pelted down the track that circled the field. Their elders, stripped down to breeches, were warming up in the center, casting an occasional glance toward the crowd.

"They know we are watching them," whispered Ursula to Gudrun. "See, they display themselves like fighting cocks."

"And we are the hens?" asked Gudrun. She was not sure she liked the comparison.

But there must be some reason why male animals pranced and preened. She supposed that humans were not so different from the other beasts, who fought for food, status, and the right to mate. The relationship between the games humans played and these realities were usually less obvious, that was all. What were these men fighting for? For a moment she saw the confusion of the field and the town beyond it and the land itself as part of a larger pattern, in which the meaning of it all came clear. Then the boys' race ended and everyone began cheering, and the thought was gone.

"Father Priscus says that women should not look at men lest

the sight inspire lust," said Adalfrida, watching the next group of runners, youths just coming into manhood with the long-legged awkward stride of young horses and an androgynous grace that would have made a Greek sculptor sigh. "But if we did not desire them, why would we let them lie with us? And if they did not, how could the next generation be born?"

Gudrun stared straight ahead, but in her cheeks she could feel the betraying color rising. She had been to enough weddings to understand what was happening. The teasing had been going on since the announcement that she was to marry Sigfrid. Tonight would be the worst, she told herself, and then—but she could not think that far. Perhaps after tonight she would know the answer to Adalfrida's question.

"Look, they are lining up for the men's race now—" said Gundohar. "I see Godo has joined them." He shook his head. Godomar's strength as a fighter was not in his speed, but in his blows. "Perhaps I should have joined them to defend the family honor." Long and lean, running was almost the only exercise at which the king did excel.

"But you have Sigfrid to race for you now—" said Ursula brightly.

As if he had sensed that they were all watching, the sun-streaked brown head turned, and Sigfrid grinned up at them. The other men were hunkering down, digging in for a fast start. Sigfrid stood a little crouched, but at ease, as if he had no idea the race was about to begin.

"That is true," said Gundohar thoughtfully, leaning forward to see.

And then the horn blew, and the taut figures exploded into motion. Sigfrid loped along with the same loose grace with which he had been standing, holding even with the others. Gudrun had a sense that he was still not taking this seriously, and reflecting on a few of the things he had said about his early life, she thought that was probably true. What could this dash over good ground on a spring day mean to someone who had run with the wolves?

He stayed with the pack all the way around the far curve. It was only when they began to labor down the homestretch and the people that lined it were cheering themselves hoarse with excitement that he seemed to rouse. There was a change in him then, though Gudrun could not have found words to describe it, a focusing of power.

Now his strides were longer, smoother, directed toward his goal. No increase in effort was apparent, and yet he was pulling away from the others despite their struggles, and he made it look so easy, as if they were running through water. Men caught their breath and forgot to shout as he flowed past them. There was a moment of silence as he passed between the endposts and pulled up, barely breathing hard. Then they realized what they had witnessed and began to cheer.

The others came pelting after and collapsed to the grass. An impromptu honor guard formed around Sigfrid and led him toward the platform to receive his crown.

"Patience at the beginning and plenty of power coming home. If he makes love the way he runs," said Adalfrida, grinning wickedly, "you will be a happy bride."

Gudrun watched him approach and felt herself coloring once more. The slabbed muscles of chest and the ripple of muscle over his abdomen were lightly sheened with sweat that highlighted every curve. The fine hairs that downed his belly and grew like a cape across his shoulders glistened in the spring sun. She found herself wondering how his skin would feel beneath her hands. Then he was looking up at her. Fixing her gaze on the top of his head lest he read her thoughts in her eyes, she settled the wreath of oak leaves there.

Other competitions followed—casting a javelin, throwing a boulder, jumping over hurdles and across a stretch of sand combed in waves to represent a stream. Godomar came close to Sigfrid's distance in the boulder toss, but could not quite match him. Gamalo of Gundohar's house-guard did almost as well with a javelin, and several of the country folk were almost as good at jumping as he. But none of them could surpass him, none could boast that particular blend of coordination and power.

Gudrun, giving him one crown after another, saw his face grow flushed, not with effort, but with excitement. He took in the adulation that the crowd was awarding him with a kind of astonished delight that made her heart ache. Had he not known that he would win? Was it possible that he had never been in such a competition before?

Gundohar leaned forward, eyes shining as he watched the play.

"Do you wish you were down there?" she asked. There was not much about being king of the Burgunds that her brother really seemed to enjoy, but he was clearly having a good time today. He snorted and shook his head, but she could hear the bitterness beneath his laughter.

"How can you ask? When my life is at stake I can summon up the skill to defend it, but I should look a fool down there, little sister, as you know well! But I can appreciate the prowess of other men."

"Like Sigfrid . . ." she said softly.

"Look at him!" the king exclaimed. "He leaps like a stag!"

For the hurdle race the men had stripped down to their clouts. Gudrun bit her lip, seeing Sigfrid's long limbs extended, body in perfect balance as he soared over one obstacle, powerful muscles rippling as he landed, contracting smoothly to launch him toward the next. It was true. He was winning because he moved like a wild thing that passes silently through the thickets where a man would fight his way. She saw then that he was beautiful, and her eyes stung as they did sometimes at the transient beauty of a sunset or a flower.

"Perhaps *you* should marry him—" she said acidly, fighting for control.

Gundohar sat back and stared at her. "Don't you want this marriage? I thought you were willing. I am giving you to the greatest hero of our time!"

"I know," Gudrun sighed. *He is a legend, a creature of the old magic, but I am only a human woman. What good can come of such a mating, wonderful as it may be?* And then she sighed again, because even now, that magic was making her heart beat faster, and she knew she would forget all her wisdom when she lay in his arms.

They watched in silence as Sigfrid won the race and the runners started back across the field.

"I don't want him, sister, though I have heard there are men whose desire runs that way in the Romani lands," Gundohar said then. "I want to *be* him . . ."

And so you are giving your sister to become one flesh with him. Was it not enough that you shared your own blood? She knew the thought for truth, but she did not speak. Growing up in her mother's shadow, Gudrun had learned to keep her own counsel.

The sun was sinking toward the western hills before the games concluded. Every contest that Sigfrid had entered, he had won. Gudrun fingered the wreath of gilded leaves, watching them escort him toward her yet again.

"Sigfrid Sigmundson, well have you played and fairly won. I am happy to crown you as victor of these games!" She knelt on the edge of the platform to set the wreath on his brown hair, curling even more vigorously with moisture now. He looked up at her, and this time she could not evade his gaze.

"Fair is the crown," he said in a low voice, "but fairer still the hand that gives it."

"You shall have my sister's hand as well, and no later than this evening!" said Gundohar, behind her. "You see, sister, I am giving you to a king after all."

"A king—" The men around him took up the cry. "Let us make him king of the wood. To the forest with him—away, away!"

Something dangerous flashed in Sigfrid's eyes as they laid hands upon him; then he realized that they were grinning, and allowed them to carry him away.

"And Gudrun shall be our Spring Queen," cried the herb-woman who sometimes sold her wares to Grimahild. "Bring her, maidens, that she may be crowned!"

Gudrun had time for just one accusing look at Gundohar before Ursula and Adalfrida, laughing, hustled her down from the platform and the women bore her away as well.

Sigfrid sighed with relief as the forest closed around him. He still had his escort, of course, jabbering like magpies, and a few convulsive rustlings in the undergrowth told him where various small animals had gone to ground But he knew that in one step, or perhaps two, he could disappear into the greenery so completely they would need dogs to trail him. And he could have outrun the dogs.

Knowing his freedom, he felt the hairs that had lifted along his spine lie down again, and allowed himself to enjoy the game. He knew what play was—the otters made slides into their pools and fawns raced across the meadow; wolf cubs attacked one another, and sometimes their elders, with furious growlings. But he had always been an observer. Until today, he had not really known how humans played.

"This is far enough," said Godo, grinning. "Do you have the axe and the thongs?"

One of the countrymen was already cutting branches and tying them into a rough skirt. Sigfrid stood patiently as they bound it around him; more thongs made a harness to suspend another row of branches beneath his arms; they wove more into a cape that covered his arms and shoulders and bound shorter lengths to a crude hat of birch bark so that some covered his face while others thrust outward, fluttering leaves like the antlers of a stag in velvet. They even managed to incorporate his gilded wreath into the contraption, and someone added a string of bells that tinkled merrily with every move.

"The King of the Wood has come to us!" they cried. "All hail to the King! Now comes the Green Man, and the world is in bloom!"

By the time they were done he could hardly see, but he soon discovered that they had left him an opening to drink through. Someone had brought thin Roman wine in a goatskin bag, which they passed around as they started back down the path. When that was emptied, he found he could manage a mead-horn as well. Then they had left the patch of woodland and were stopping at the first holding. Folk came out with more food and drink, and Sigfrid began to understand.

They rolled him into the first pond they came to, but this time Godo warned him, and gave him to understand that once he was ducked he had the right to splatter everything he could reach with his birch wand.

"It is to bring rain, and make the crops grow," said the old farmer who seemed, as much as anyone, to be in charge.

Sigfrid nodded. Now he was remembering a rite he had seen in his childhood, though in the north they covered the Green Man with reeds, not boughs. Among the Franks they called him Yng, and in Juteland, Frodi. He understood better than they could know. Here, they had been Christian too long to give a name to the god of the growing things, but no folk whose lives depended on the soil could deny him. He grinned, and whipped at all and sundry with a will.

As the sun sank lower, the procession wound among the outlying houses. There was one more dunking, this time in the shallows of the Rhenus. Then they brought him, dripping from every leaf and giddy with laughter, for he had not eaten since early morning and by this time he had consumed a fair amount of wine and mead and ale, up into the town.

In the center of the Forum they had set up a Spring Tree, a tall birch pole crowned with streamers and flowers. Cow horns blared insistently and the drums beat out a summons that pulsed in his blood. And then, from some hidden alley, new figures came lumbering out to join the procession. By their movements he knew them for men, but like him their forms were completely hidden, encased in shirts and breeches tufted with colored wool that looked like fur.

"The wild men! Here come the wild men!" The children were the first to take up the cry.

As they cavorted around him Sigfrid blinked, trying to bring them into focus. Ragan had told him about wild men, the real ones, survivors of a people even older than his own, who lived in the most secret places of the hills. Sigfrid had found a track once, manlike, but longer than any human foot, with strongly gripping toes, and once he thought he had seen a man-shaped shadow disappearing into the trees.

These wild men were furred with colored wool, one saffron, one red-brown, another blue, but their movements were a blurred reflection of the shambling gait of the creature he had seen. They pushed past him into the square, and danced around the Spring Tree, whirling with odd, mewing cries.

Then they fell into formation around the Leaf King like a guard of honor. On the steps of the palace Gundohar was waiting. For a moment Sigfrid felt dizzy, as if his head were weighted by something heavier than his headdress. Scarcely knowing what he did, he plunged his wand into the fountain and ran forward.

"The King of the Wood brings abundance to the King of Men!" he cried in a voice he did not recognize, splattering Gundohar vigorously. "Long life to thé king, peace and good seasons! To all here, abundance—" He whirled around the circle, sprinkling the crowd, and the wild men followed him, howling.

He finished the circuit and stumbled to a halt, staggering as the strange enegy left him. It was then that he realized that it had not been himself speaking, but the god. His attendents held him upright, shaking with reaction and dripping onto the cobblestones, but as he caught his breath, he realized that they were no longer looking at him.

He heard flutes twittering, and the sweet jangling of bells. A new kind of shivering took him then as a flock of small girls came skipping into view, scattering flower petals. Above the flutesong came the sweetness of women's voices.

> *Tempus adest floridum, surgunt namque flores,*
> *Vernales in omnibus imitantur mores,*
> *Hoc quod frigus laeserat, reparant calores,*
> *Cernimus hoc fieri per multos labores . . .*

"The time of flowers is here, the blooms burst forth, and what cold attacked the warmth restores," murmured one of the men, translating.

More women followed the maidens, laughing, crowned with flowers. They moved to one side or the other as they entered the Forum, and a murmur swept the crowd. In their midst a woman came walking, half-covered by a long, gauzy veil that hung down in front and was carried by her attendents behind her and to either side. It was held to her head by a great crown of flowers. The drums had fallen silent but Sigfrid did not notice. His heart was the drum.

> *Sunt prata plena floribus iucunda aspectu,*
> *Ubi iuvat cernere herbas cum delectu,*
> *Gramina et plantae quae hyeme quiescunt,*
> *Vernali in tempore virent et accrescunt.*

And surely it was true that the herbs and flowers that decked the Spring Queen had flourished. The procession circled the Tree, blessing the people. Beneath the veil Sigfrid caught the gleam of golden hair. His breath caught, for surely it was more than the crown that made her seem taller; there was a glamor about her that made him keep looking away. But always his gaze returned.

> *Terra ornatur floribus et multo decore,*
> *Nos honestis moribus et vero amore,*
> *Gaudeamus igitur tempore iucundo.*
> *Laudemusque Dominam pectores ex fundo . . .*

Earth is bedecked with flowers and many things of beauty . . . The whole great crowd fell silent, understanding, with a wisdom the Christian priests could not deny because it was not put into words, Who it was that walked among them now.

They came at last, as Sigfrid had known they must, to the place where he was waiting.

"Behold, oh King, we have brought the Lady to you—how will you welcome her?"

Her face was a pale blur beneath the veil. Golden ornaments glittered as her breast rose and fell. He felt himself growing hard, but that had been happening for weeks now every time he looked at Gudrun. He felt a flicker of panic, but some knowledge deeper than his own gave him the answer.

"As the seed to the earth, as the tree to the sun, as the wood to the fire," he said hoarsely. "So may it be!"

* * *

Gudrun blinked as the Green Man claimed her. That part of her mind that was still her own supposed it must be Sigfrid, but through the veiling he looked larger, as if the spirit of the forest had indeed taken this shape to walk among men. Men pushed him toward her; she felt the shock of contact as human hands reached out through the greenery and clasped her own. There was no question of kissing, clad as they were, but it was not needful. The power that passed between them as they were escorted to their seats on the steps was rolling in waves up and down her spine.

They were seated, and someone brought them more mead. The people danced around the Spring Tree; a group of boys sang a song. The long sweet dusk of spring hung veils of gold and flame over the sky and purple shadows gathered between the houses and spread across the square. From somewhere nearby, wonderful smells of roasting meat were drifting through the air.

And then, as the first stars began to prick through the darkening sky, the hand that had been her link to the world was pulled away. Her women helped her to rise and led her to the palace. It was only when they had lifted the flower crown from her head and taken the veil away that she remembered with any certainty who she was and why she was here. They clad her anew in her white dalmatic brocaded with wheat sheaves, bedecked her with necklaces and earrings of amber and pearl, brushed out her hair in waves of gold, and set a hawthorn wreath upon her brow.

When they escorted her back outside, darkness had fallen completely, but torches flared around the forum, and before the Spring Tree burned a great fire. A long table had been set up on the broad porch in front of the palace, and boards on trestles filled the square. Gundohar stood on the steps, draped in his crimson mantle and wearing his crown. Godo and Hagano and little Gislahar stood beside him and their mother was seated nearby. Gudrun paused, appreciating the drama. The scene was set, awaiting only the players. Why did she feel so numb, when she should have been filled with joy?

There was a stir at the far side of the square and she felt her pulse leap. They were bringing Sigfrid to her, clad now in dark green breeches and a knee-length lapped tunic in the Frankish style of moss green silk heavily ornamented with gold. His champion's wreath was on his hair. She supposed Gundohar had planned that as well. Despite their change in costume, they were still the Leaf King and Spring Queen.

Gudrun suppressed a smile. Father Priscus, the Orthodox Roman priest, and Father Severin, the Arian, who had begun to bristle like two dogs eyeing the same bone over which of them would get to perform the wedding, had united in their expostulations when they heard that Gundohar intended to give his sister in marriage with a feast and contract in the ancient way. After all, Sigfrid had not been christened, and Gudrun suspected that her brother did not want to bind her in a way that would involve Roman law.

In the old days, of course, there would have been prayers and offerings to the gods who give prosperity and offspring; it was rather clever of Gundohar, really, to have attached the wedding feast to a festival which honored those same powers. She understood enough of her mother's teachings to know that through her, Gundohar was linking his line to the land in a way that his own position as a Christian prince would never have allowed.

Bells chimed softly as they were led forward to face each other on the step below the king.

"Burgunds, Romans, people of Borbetomagus—" he cried. "Men of many bloods, you are gathered here as one kindred to witness my sister's marriage to this man. With her hand, I give to him a brother's share in the holdings of the Niflungar; henceforth he shall rank as a prince of our people. In return, he has agreed to endow her with a legendary treasure. Is this a fair contract? Will you witness this marriage with a good will?"

"It is!" said Godomar with real enthusiasm. Others, well primed with ale since morning, were shouting approbation, and the king smiled. Then he took Sigfrid's hand.

"Sigfrid, son of Sigmund of the Wolsungs, will you take

this woman to be your wife, to provide for her and protect her?"

Gudrun, staring at the pavement, felt her heartbeat shake her body as she waited for his reply. When it came, it was no longer the hoarse voice of the Leaf King, but low and clear.

Then Gundohar grasped her hand. "Gudrun my sister, will you accept this man as your husband, to honor and serve him?"

Her response seemed to come without her volition. "I will."

"Be joined then as man and wife, and at bed and board may you be a joy to one another." Gundohar put her hand into Sigfrid's, and the tingle of sensation leaped once more from his flesh to hers. "I call all men here to witness that I have given my sister Gudrun to Sigfrid Sigmundson to be his wife in all honor. I invite you now to share this feast, that the bond may be witnessed. And tonight Sigfrid and Gudrun shall preside over this table as our king and queen."

The master smith of the town came forward to bless the bride with his hammer as they were seated. *Yes,* she thought as she felt the weight of it in her lap, *I do want Sigfrid's children. I accept the blessing the hammer brings!*

All around them, folk were feasting. Gudrun scarcely knew what she was eating. Sigfrid had not even kissed her yet, and she had scarcely dared to look at him, but she was aware of every movement he made. As the evening progressed the jesting grew broader; even the mimes who entertained them had a bawdy theme. If she had been in any doubt about the expected outcome of the proceedings, they would have dispelled it. But she listened without blushing, too preoccupied with her own sensations to care.

Gundohar's counselors lifted their horns to wish the new couple happy. She could hear her women giggling behind her. Soon, now. It would be over soon.

Then she heard the first words of the wedding song. With broad jests and with music they were escorted to the chamber that had been prepared for them. Gundohar kissed her. Her mother handed her a golden goblet and she drank without tasting it. Sigfrid was doing the same. Then, with a few last words of advice which she did not understand and she doubted he needed, they were left alone.

Sigfrid listened to the fading footsteps of their well-wishers as once he had listened to beasts in the wild. The last thing he could distinguish was Gundohar's high peal of laughter. Then there was no sound but the rustle of their breathing. The scents of flowers and the herbs with which the chamber had been decked lay heavy on the air. Listening, he knew the woman's breath was too controlled; she stood too still. *What have I done?* he thought in panic. *She is afraid of me!*

"Gudrun, did your brother force you to marry me?" he said at last, glad this Roman building gave them the privacy for conversation. It would have been impossible in a curtained box bed with the rest of her family reveling just outside.

She continued to look at the floor. "He explained his need. I know that I am the bait to keep you here—"

Sigfrid laughed with soft self-mockery, but some of the fear went away as he began to understand. *I was a fool,* he thought then, *to let another man do my courting.*

"Do you think so?" he said aloud. "Gudrun, listen—I was frantic for some justification that would allow me to approach you. I could hardly believe your brother's offer to let me marry you, but he cannot give you to me even with a feast and the vows. Only you can make that choice, Gudrun. If you cannot like me, I will not trouble you, but do a brother's duty to Gundohar so long as he has need."

"*Like* you?" she said in a strangled voice. "Your deeds are bread in the mouths of bards up and down the Rhenus. Why would you want *me?*"

A strand of golden hair lay across her shoulder. He lifted it, and through it, felt her trembling.

"Look at me, Gudrun," he whispered. "Please, *look* at me! Am I so terrible? When you look at me, what do you see?"

She lifted her eyes, limpid as water; it seemed to him he could see into the depths of her soul.

"I see a hero, I see a wolf, I see a god. . . ."

He stiffened—how could she know? "And when you see the wolf," he breathed, "are you afraid?"

"Not of the wolf," she answered, "but I do fear the hero and the god."

He laughed softly, dizzy with relief at her words. "Well, I have never desired to be either!" He pulled off his golden wreath and tossed it across the room, and then, very gently, lifted the crown of flowers from her brow.

"I look at you and see a goddess, I see a royal woman . . . and I see . . . a garden, protected and secure." He looked at her and frowned, wondering if he could match her truth with his own. How could she understand the tangled path that had brought him here?

"I am only Gudrun," she whispered, "but if you will come into my garden, I will try to welcome you there. . . ."

He set his hands on her shoulders and kissed her, hardly having to bend, for her height nearly matched his own. Her lips were soft; he could taste the sweetness of the potion her mother had given them there. He kissed her, holding himself under rigid control, until he felt the trembling go away. Then he let her go.

He saw in her eyes the little flicker of disappointment and thought she was far too quick to hide it—was she so used to rejection? Had no one ever truly loved her until now? He was beginning to realize that this proud princess whom they had condescended to give him was as vulnerable as any creature of the wild.

"Can I help you take that thing off?" he asked plaintively. "I cannot appreciate you properly so long as you are swaddled in that gown."

By the time they had gotten free of all their fine clothes they both were laughing. Gudrun fell silent when he drew her down to lie beside him, but by then he was kissing her again, tasting the sweetness of her flesh with a hunger that grew the more it fed.

"Not a garden, an orchard . . ." he murmured indistinctly as he found her breast. He felt her shiver at his touch, and knew that this time it was not fear, for her hands were fluttering along his sides, growing firmer as he continued, learning his body as he was learning hers.

Sigdrifa had begun his education in the craft of love, but that memory was now only a vague impression of darkness and fire. He had as much reason to be grateful to the girls he had met since then, who had taught him that each woman must be courted differently. He could tell from the change in Gudrun's scent when she grew ready for him. The skin of her thighs was like the petals of a flower; she gasped as he touched the sacred place between.

"Open to me ..." he whispered. "Lady, please, let me in. . . ." He could feel her quivering as he stretched himself upon her, but the gate was open, and in the last moments of coherent thought as he entered, Sigfrid knew that the place he had found there was home.

Chapter
Four   Journeys

Borbetomagus, Marcomanni Lands
Milk Moon, A.D. 420

Brunahild ran through the forest, forcing laboring lungs to suck air and aching limbs to take the next step, leap the next obstacle. Her black hair, grown past her shoulders in the two winters since the Walkyriun had cropped it, flared out behind her; a body still slender as a maiden's slipped between the trunks of the trees. The woodlands around Heimar's steading were thick with new growth, limber as switches and feathered with green. The blood sang in her veins as she fought her way through it, parrying each whipping branch with the wands in her hands.

The forest battle was an old training exercise of the Walkyriun. Repeating it brought back painful memories. The faces of those who had cast her out rose up before her as she slashed at the branches and she shouted their names—Hlutgard, their leader, Thrudrun, who had taught her runes, Galemburgis, the Alamanni girl who had been her greatest enemy. Only old Huld the seeress had not betrayed her. Childbirth had weakened her body, but the Walkyriun had tried to destroy her soul. She still hated them. Still, each day it grew a little easier to rise, to fight, to run.

Her labor had been hard, for her hips were narrow, not built for easy bearing. Brunahild had been slow to heal, confined to her bed for a moon thereafter, until the messengers came from the Burgund lands with the offer of marriage from their king. The next day she had left her box bed, though Bertriud fussed around her like a nervous hen, and made her first, faltering foray into the fields. She must be fit to ride when Sigfrid came for her—she had known that from the beginning. Now she had a more pressing reason to recover her health. She had to defeat this suitor so that she would be free to leave when Sigfrid finally arrived.

If he ever came. Through all these moons she had sensed the life in him and known he fared well, though she could not say where or how. But suddenly, two nights ago, the link had broken, and that, more than any other, was the agony that drove her through the forest now. She had called on Wodan, but there was no answer, only an emptiness, as if the part of herself that had shielded Sigfrid was her link to the god as well. And so she ran, striving to discipline her mind to the motion, to cast aside all fears, all other thoughts, so that there was only the harmony of muscles in motion, and for a moment, peace. . . .

Brunahild burst through the trees at the edge of the wood and faltered; strange horses were drawn up before the gate, folk were clustering round. Her heart lurched—was it Sigfrid? But no warrior would ride such a placid nag. The people parted and she saw a familiar dark blue cloak. For a moment she stiffened—how *dare* one of the Walkyriun come to Heimar's home? Then something in the woman's movement stirred memory, and she recognized Huld.

Need spurred tired limbs into new motion. She ran across the pasture, the wands forgotten in her hands. She could see the old woman's features, worn with years and the pains of the road. Her hair was completely silver now.

"Huld!" she shouted, and heads turned to watch as she neared the log wall that surrounded Heimar's home. "Huld, you are here!"

Brunahild shifted Asliud awkwardly from one shoulder to the other, patting the child's back as she walked up and down beside the long hearthfire that burned in Heimar's hall. To Huld, watching, her face showed a kind of grim patience, unexpected in a new mother with her first child.

"She is a lovely baby," Huld said softly. And that was true. At the moment the child seemed fretful, but for a babe three moons old she was remarkably finished looking, with delicate features and wisps of pale hair shining in the firelight. She looked gravely over her mother's shoulder, as if already aware that whatever others might think of her, she would have to work for Brunahild's regard.

"She is well enough, and if she is not, her nurse has the worst of it. Where is that girl?" She looked around her as the baby began to whimper again.

"Let me take her—" said Heimar, rising from his high seat at the end of the hearth. Its pillars were carved and painted, the back hung with woven cloth from Byzantium. He held out his arms, and Asliud blinked at him and smiled. "There, my little one, there you are—" He settled her against his broad chest and she reached for his beard, gurgling delight-edly. It was a strange sight, for Heimar was as massive as an oak tree, with silver in his brown hair. "Gently, child—" He disengaged her tiny fingers. "What, do you think this is a toy for you to play with?" The baby laughed and reached for him again.

"He is very good with her," said Huld. Heimar's gaze had softened as he looked down at the child, and the baby was relaxing in his firm grasp. Her next grab for his beard was halfhearted. Already her eyelids were drooping, and in an-other moment she was asleep.

Brunahild shrugged. "He should have been her mother. Even when her nurse can do nothing with her, she always quiets for him." She moved restlessly to the hearth, poked a branch into the flames, and came back again. Leaping flame picked out the designs of the hangings, the luster of the furs cushioning the long benches, the glitter of weapons hanging on the wall.

"I wish I could sleep so easily," said Huld. "When I close my eyes I grow dizzy as if I were still jolting along the road."

"You have had a weary journey—I am sorry." Brunahild moved to trim a bronze lamp suspended by a bracket from one of the house pillars and came back again. "If I had known where you were, I would have sent for you before the child was born."

"After the fire the Walkyriun were scattered—" said Huld. The nursemaid came to take Asliud away, and Heimar eased the sleeping infant reluctantly into her arms. *Brunahild is right,* she thought then. *Whatever happens, he will take care of the little one.*

"Wodan's fire . . ." Brunahild said with a strange smile. "He protected me."

"I guested over the winter with the Hermunduri, but for a turning of the seasons I could get no news of you. I thought you were dead, child. Not until last autumn did word come that you had returned to your kinfolk, and I am too old to travel in the snows."

"How I have missed you!" Brunahild exclaimed, kneeling beside the wisewoman as she had so often when they lived with the Walkyriun. But Brunahild was a girl no longer, thought Huld, seeing the softness that once had gentled those angular features pared away by pain. In another moment she was up again, pouring ale into a beaker and offering it to her guest.

Brunahild was a woman now, matured by suffering, and not a happy one. But how could Huld find out what was wrong if she would not be still?

"Brunahild, will you sit? I am tired enough from the road without whirling about to keep you in view!"

Brunahild paused, biting her lip. "I think that if I tried to sit still I would scream. Huld, I cannot sense Sigfrid, and that has not happened since we parted. He cannot be dead—I would have felt it—there was simply a moment, a few nights ago, when he was no longer *there!*"

"That is true. You transferred your own fetch to him in that warding," said Huld. "If Sigfrid had died, it would have returned to you. You were foolish to try that kind of magic, when the bonds between your own soul and body were scarcely secure."

Brunahild shrugged. "I had to. I had to prove I could do it, for him, and for me. It hardly mattered if I gave him more than I intended—in every way, we were one. You must help me to find out what has happened before the Burgunds come! I have cast the runes, but I can find no meaning in them. The Walkyriun tried to destroy my magic, and in Sigfrid I regained it—but now it is gone!"

"Do you think he has betrayed you?" Huld asked carefully.

"How could he? We were a single person. No—something has happened to him, and I must learn what it is. Go out for me, Huld. Journey on the spirit road. Find him, and wherever in the nine worlds he may be wandering, there I will go!"

Sigfrid rode out with the Burgunds on a morning of such radiance that he wondered how his body could contain the joy that filled his soul. He and Gudrun had had only a few days of marriage, but she said she loved him, and he knew she spoke truly, for he could scent her desire. He remembered how he had left her, safe in the walled garden, surrounded by young growing things. It seemed to him that she *was* the garden, the hidden center, the sanctuary. She was the source and focus of everything he had envied other men.

Even among the Franks he had never been truly at home. His stepfather held him in affection, and all of the warriors had respected his skills, but the tilled lands around Ulpia Traiana were not the same wild marshes where he had grown up, and there was no one there who loved him now that his mother was gone. But now he rode with warriors who hailed him as a brother, with the promise of a royal woman to be his bride.

It was a three week journey to the land of the Huns, but the weather held fair as they passed eastward across the river to the Holy Hill, and along the Nicer south through the old Burgund lands, then cut through the mountains to reach the Danu and follow it eastward toward the country of the Huns. Most of these lands had once been held by the Romani, and the orchards they had planted there filled the country with the scent of apple bloom.

Gudrun is like a young apple tree, thought Sigfrid, breathing deeply of that heady perfume, *clad all in white and shining in the sun.* For a moment then, memory supplied the image of a woman who had been like a fire in the darkness, but though the image made his flesh burn, there was pain behind it—her pain and his. He and Sigdrifa had been each other's healing, but now he was Gudrun's husband, and it would be better for both of them to forget the past.

Grani, feeling the rein loosen, started to trot, shaking his head and snorting as Sigfrid reined him in.

"He wants to run," said Godomar, who was riding beside him. "He looks as if he could go to the land of the Huns and back again without sweating. I did not know the Franks bred such beasts on their sandy shores."

Sigfrid laughed. "There are not many, even in my stepfather's herds. Grani's dam was a big Gaulish mare of the Tolosan breed, but as for his sire, who can say? The mare ran loose for a time in the marshes, and was already in foal by the time they recaptured her. When the colt grew up swift as a flying swan and so wild no man could touch him, some swore that Sleipnir himself had gotten him on the mare."

"And were you the one to break him?" Gundohar, scenting a story, turned in his saddle.

"I helped Alb to drive off some Heruli raiders, and after the fight, he told me to take my pick of his herds," Sigfrid answered him. "It put me in some confusion how to choose, for I was never brought up to have much to do with horses. But on my way I met an old man with a long beard who told me to test their strength by driving the herd out into a strong-flowing stream."

This was not the place to say how his skin had prickled when he saw the way the battered hat hid the old man's left eye. When they separated to drive the herd and he heard the howl of a wolf, he had been sure it was the god. But in his own throat he had felt an answering howl building, and as wolves together they had driven the young horses, whinnying with terror, into the river. Some of them stayed plunging in the shallows. A few, the weaker, were swept off their feet. The rest forgot their panic soon and came ashore. One only, a storm-grey colt with a pale mane, had snorted defiance and forged his way steadily upstream.

"I sped through the woods alongside and came up with Grani just as he was climbing out of the water. He was off-balance and tired from swimming against the current, or I would never have gotten a rope on him. Even so, he fought, and plunged back into the water, but I went with him. I got upon his back and though he churned the water like a mer-ewip, I stayed with him until he knew I was his master."

"He was tame then?" asked Godo.

"For me—" Sigfrid laughed. "But as you can see, he wears only a headstall. The last man who tried to bridle him with a steel bit lost a hand. Grani serves me because he has chosen to yield."

Gundohar's grey gaze lifted from the horse to Sigfrid in a long look. *He is thinking that I am the same,* he realized suddenly, and knew that it was true. But Gundohar was the king-wolf here. It was necessary to serve him in order to become part of the tribe.

"May you ride Brunahild as hard," Godo told his brother, "and may she yield to you as readily!" Godo burst out laughing. Gundohar flushed darkly.

"Be still! You soil our honor, speaking of the future queen of the Burgunds in such a way!"

Godo shook his head. "I was only teasing! You will hear worse when you lead her to the bridal chamber, brother mine! If indeed you do—" he went on. "They say she is a vixen in battle, though that time she visited us she did not look it. Still, she was trained to fight by the Walkyriun, so she must be dangerous. Why take the risk, Gundohar? Surely the Huns have other princesses. What do you want with such a skinny, dark little thing?"

Sigfrid, whose attention had drifted to follow a flight of wild ducks off the river, stiffened.

"Are all of the Hun women dark-haired?" he asked carefully.

"Are you thinking that any other Hun girl he might go for would look the same?" Godo frowned. "Perhaps, but their khans have been taking wives from among the tribes since

Airmanareik's time. From all accounts, they're pretty much of a mixture by now. Anyway, Brunahild is not *ugly*, just not much of an armful to my mind."

"Then it is just as well that you will not be marrying her!" said Gundohar shortly, and the men who were within earshot laughed.

That evening Sigfrid and the king worked out with sword and shield as they had almost every night since they had crossed the Rhenus. Over the past year he had come to realize that forge-trained muscles and forest-trained reflexes had given him an advantage over most men when it came to fighting. Gundohar had been well trained according to the usual practices of the Burgunds, but as they continued, Sigfrid's respect grew for old Helmbari, who had been his own teacher.

"No, no, keep your shield up!" he cried, driving Gundohar back with regular blows of his oaken stave. "You do not want to kill the girl, but she may not feel the same about you! You are light of build, but if she is a small woman, you will still have the advantage of weight. You must use it! She will undoubtedly be quicker"—the stave shot out, and the king yipped as it caught him on the upper arm—"as I am. She could hurt you if you do not maintain your guard!"

"Hold!" Gundohar stepped back, eased his shield to the ground, and leaned on it, panting.

Sigfrid hesitated a moment, then did the same. "Your woman will not hold her hand to give you breathing room."

"She held her hand from me once," said Gundohar quietly. "She could have speared me on the field of battle, for I was unarmed and exhausted. If she had even pointed the spear at me I would have been a dead man, for I would have had no heart to withstand my foes. She said it was because the god did not want me—but I suppose I find it hard to believe that she would feel nothing, seeing me again. What woman, where once she has spared, could turn to slay?"

Sigfrid stilled; he had heard something about this before, but could not think where. Perhaps men had spoken of it in Borbetomagus, when they discussed the marriage. But why, then, did the story fill him with such unease?

"She does not care for me now," said the king. "How could she? But I will teach her to love me."

Sigfrid sighed. *Will you play the harp for her?* Not thus, he knew from his own experience, were Walkyrja women won.

"But first I must conquer her—I am learning from you, Sigfrid, but can I gain enough skill, in time? She must not defeat me! This alliance will save my people in our eastern lands. As a king and as a brother I beg you—if I am not good enough to win Brunahild, will you take my place in the battle? We are much of a height, and if you bear my gear and weapons no one will know. Promise me, Sigfrid—" Gundohar straightened, and Sigfrid flinched from the naked need in his eyes.

He wants this Brunahild as much as I want Gudrun, he thought. And then, *is this what I agreed to when we mingled our blood so short a time ago?*

He sighed. "Very well. I swear to help you if it proves to be the only way. But perhaps it will not come to that. You have rested enough. Attack me now, and see if you can get a blow past my guard!"

That night, Sigfrid lay wakeful, listening to the soft snorts and creakings men make in their sleep, and farther off, the sound of the nightwind in the tree tops and the call of a hunting owl. The late-rising moon was a little past the full, glimmering through streamers of cloud. The wind made him restless. If he had been alone, he would have unrolled the wolfskin and gone for a run, but there were guards posted who would surely see. Once only, when he was serving with the Franks, he had given in to the temptation to put on the hide and race through the night. A mere glimpse had been enough to set tongues wagging, and he had had to fight two more battles for them before men looked at him without that lingering doubt in their eyes.

Lying still in the darkness, he found himself mulling over all he knew of this journey and its goal. The princess whom Gundohar was wooing was little and dark, but so were many women of the Huns; she had been trained as a Walkyrja, and spared him in battle. . . .

But my Walkyrja was named Sigdrifa, he told himself, *and she was not a princess—surely she would have told me if that had been so! Perhaps it is common for the Huns to send their girls to the wisewomen. Perhaps this Brunahild can tell me where Sigdrifa is now.*

And then, between one thought and the next, sleep took him. In his dreams he had put on the wolfskin and was hunting across the skies. As he ran, he realized that he was pursuing a winged figure that flew just out of reach. He increased his pace, knowing he must overtake her, but she kept changing, now dark, now bright. Abruptly he realized that there were two birds, a raven and a swan. And in that moment they separated, the raven winging eastward while the swan flew west, the way they had come.

For a moment he hesitated, but the raven was a part of the night while the swan glowed in the moonlight, and she was singing. He howled in response, and raced after her.

Brunahild led the way along the path, her torch casting flickering shadows upon the trees. She had to force herself to slow so that the old woman could keep up with her—her feet knew this path even without a light. Once it had been well-worn, for it led to the ancient sacred grove. But most of the tribe who had worshipped here were gone now, or had become Christians, and Heimar's household made their offerings in the fields or at the family hearthfire. Brunahild had claimed it for her own, and it was here that she had ordered the thralls to build the raised seat of lashed poles from which the seeress could journey between the worlds.

When they reached it, Huld sank down upon a log to catch her breath, while Brunahild got a fire going in the pit beside the altar of heaped stones. By its glow she arranged the elkhide over the rough wood of the high seat and laid out the offerings. The waning moon was already high, but racing clouds alternately obscured and revealed it; there was no depending on that fitful light.

"The offerings are prepared, the high seat is ready," she said at last. "I call upon thee, *hailiuruna*, to go forth. Seek even to the world of the dead if you must, so that you learn those things that I must know!"

Huld snorted. "It is long since I have heard that name."

Brunahild laughed. "They say that the Huns are the off-spring of *haliurunae* who were driven out from among the Goths and mated with the demons of the steppes. What better word for me to use for one who knows the holy mysteries? Please, Huld, in the name of all the gods, you must help me now."

The old woman straightened with a sigh. "I have told you of my doubts. It is not enough for the gods to speak—you must be willing to listen."

"There is no more time," exclaimed Brunahild. "The Burgund king and his comitatus are coming, and tomorrow we must leave for the Danu to meet with them. I must know now!"

"By the vows that I have sworn I may not deny you," Huld said at last. She put on her headdress of wildcat skins. "Let us begin."

Brunahild cast the sacred herbs onto the fire, and as the smoke billowed up, fanned it first over Huld and then herself with a spray of leaves. She uncovered the pot in which she had brought the sacred food and offered it to the seeress—hearts of beef and lamb and goose from the farmstead, and hare and deer that Brunahild herself had hunted, all stewed together. Huld ate a little, and the rest was poured out over the altar.

"Now you are linked to this land—" said Brunahild softly. "May the spirits that share this food protect you." Her own heart was beginning to beat faster. She could feel a change in the night already, as if something were waiting to see what they would do.

She made her hands a step that Huld could use to ascend the high seat. Timbers creaked as the old woman climbed into it, but it seemed steady enough once she had settled down. Brunahild helped the seeress to wrap her cloak around her, then covered her with a second elkhide, for the night was already chill.

"Hearth and garth and all the human world we have left behind us. To Out-gard we come to begin our journey. With

these holy runes I ward you—" Brunahild drew first the rune
of riding and then the elk rune in the air in front of the
seeress. "All hail to your coming, all hail to your going, all
hail to you hence and hither! I sing a sacred song to send you
on your way—"

She moved around the chair, humming softly. It had been
a long time since she had done this, but she had not forgotten.
Once, she herself had sat in such a chair, letting the singing
carry her away. She could feel her own senses altering as she
sang, and fought to retain control.

> *"Seeress, thy way through the worlds thou must win,*
> *farther and faster and deeper within,*
> *fare onward, ever onward, ever on. . . ."*

The song emerged from her humming, rising and falling as
she moved around and around the chair. The boughs had
ceased to creak as Huld grew ever more still. The wise woman
yawned as the trance began to take her, and Brunahild heard
her breathing grow harsh and slower. It was almost time to
call her, before she sank too deeply into trance to respond.

"Sigdrifa I hight, and far have I wandered, seeking the seeress whom now I summon. Walada, Walada, can you hear me,
in depths of darkness where you're dreaming? Grandmother,
hearken; holy one, hear me, tell me what you see!"

There was an indistinct muttering from the chair, and Brunahild stepped closer, continuing to call Huld's spirit name,
talking her back to a level where she could speak as well as
see.

"I see mists . . . I see darkness. . . ." came the answer, slowly,
as if the words were indeed drawn from some place beyond
the world. "From Middle Earth to the roots of the Tree my
wildcat has carried me, through dark forests, across the river
of swords and the river of blood; I have seen the glow of
Muspel's fires and the shimmer of the Rainbow Bridge. Passage
have I won from the etin-maid who guards the way, and the
roaring river that girdles the world I have crossed. For me
Hella's ironbound gates swing open; the spirits throng about

me. A dark pool glimmers, I see the life of all the worlds reflected. What would you ask of me?"

"Where is Sigfrid? Where does the wolf run? When will he come to me? Speak now, seeress, till all is said. Answer the asker till all she knows!"

Huld grunted and muttered a little, shifting position in the chair. Then she turned as if to look at Brunahild, but her eyes were closed. It was not this world she was seeing.

"The wolf runs through the sky-fields . . . his spirit ranges the stars. He is hunting . . . he pursues a shape as white as the moon. A swan—it is a swan he is hunting. He is well and happy. His spirit is near, but he has left his body far behind. . . . This now you know. Would you know more?"

Brunahild frowned, considering. It was something to know that Sigfrid was alive, but clearly he was sleeping, and she would learn nothing more with this kind of questioning. But there was another way, and she had suspected all along that she must pursue it.

"If you can see no farther, then we must ask of one who will know more!" Brunahild said softly. "I call now on my father. I call on Wodan, the High One. Seek him, Seeress, even if you must journey to the garth of the gods. Summon him to speak to you, since he will not come to me."

There was a silence, and Huld slumped against the framework of branches. She twitched, muttering, then suddenly she laughed. "There is no need to seek Asgard. Is he not also Lord of the Slain? Child, child, he is already here. . . ." The chair creaked as she moved.

"My cat rubs against me, pushing me toward Hella's hall. From within I can hear the laughter of folk at their feasting. Torchlight streams through the open door. It is Baldur for whom that board has been spread, for whom the golden shields are hung upon the wall. The door is open as if to welcome all comers, but there is one who does not go in.

"I can see him now, standing in the shadows, listening to the rejoicing that he cannot share. Through all lands has he wandered, but this one hall he can never enter. I feel his sorrow—" Her breath caught. "I think he comes here when he can bear the pain of separation no longer, for Baldur, alone of all his children, is dead to him. This son, the brightest and most beloved, may not dwell in Valhall with the heroes. He will not return to Middle Earth until the end of the age, when Wodan himself is gone."

"I am sorry for his sorrow," said Brunahild, "but what about mine? Speak to him. Perhaps he will be glad for a distraction. Ask him when Sigfrid will come to me. Ask when we will ride out as hero and shield-maid to serve his purposes in the world."

"He turns, he looks at me . . ." said Huld slowly. "And I am glad of my wardings. This was not a good time to disturb him. And now he sighs. He has heard your question. He knows your grief, but he asks, are you so sure that you know his purposes?"

"He promised me—" Brunahild began, but Huld's shivering had increased. For a moment she thought that the old woman would fall out of the chair. But before she could touch her, the huddled figure straightened, and Brunahild's breath caught, for suddenly she was not sure who was sitting there. Swathed in those dark draperies, it was ageless, sexless—but surely now the shoulders were broader. The hood fell over the face at an angle; she saw the gleam of one bright eye.

"Brunahild . . ." The harsh whisper set her back hairs prickling. "Brunahild—my Walkyrja. . . ." It was certainly a man's voice this time, deep, its harshness laced with honey and a little mockery, though she could not tell whether it were directed at her, or at himself.

"My father," she cried, "where have you been? I have called to you and found only a void. You said you would always be in my heart, but I have searched it—what else have I had to occupy me these past moons? I have searched, and found only my own fears."

"Fear is a good barrier. You were too full of your own complaints to listen to me."

"I am listening now. Tell me, will Gundohar overcome me in battle?"

"The Burgund king will not defeat you," the answer came.

"And when will Sigfrid come for me?"

"Very soon . . ." There was a sigh. "You will ride home with your husband, and you will do my will, Brunahild, as you have promised, but remember that things are not always as they seem."

"What do you mean? I am a Walkyrja—your Walkyrja. Is it not your will that Sigfrid win battles for you, and that I choose those whom you want for your war band?"

"Do you think that is all I need?" the god said then. "In each age, Ragnarok threatens, but its battlefield changes. Perhaps the forces that I will need to fight in the future will be different. I must know, my daughter; I must experience what happens in the world of men. Old tribes give way to new nations; old ways of thinking are transformed. Those who do not understand such changes will be swept away by them. I need you, and Sigfrid, to go into the world and learn these things for me."

"But what do you want us to work for?"

"The world changes, and so do I; why do you think I have so many names? Erda has been since the beginning, but even she is always changing. As for me, I become a new thing each day. But I would be nothing if I ceased to learn. You too must learn not to cling to what is done."

"This makes no sense," cried Brunahild. "Speak clearly. I have been faithful to you, father, will you not keep faith with me?"

"My daughter, I will do everything I have promised," the god said then, but his voice had grown grim. "You and Sigfrid shall be together, and you will rule the fates of nations. In the end, if you have the courage to know yourself truly, you shall also know ecstasy, but do not ask for content—it is Erda who gives that, to those who live in harmony with her seasons. Willingly or not, you will serve me, for your oath binds you. But the burden of understanding lies upon you."

"If Sigfrid and I are together, I will be satisfied," Brunahild said then.

Wodan laughed, a sound that made her flesh creep. "Remember that when he comes for you."

"What do you mean?" Brunahild grasped the side of the chair.

"Mean . . ." mumbled the figure that sat there. "I am . . . meaning. . . . This mount grows weary," he said more clearly. "Bring her back quickly, if you value her—"

There was a long sigh, and then Huld's body began to twitch violently. Brunahild flung her arms around it, felt the tension release suddenly. Huld slumped and she held her, hearing the fluttering heartbeat steady and slow.

"Walada, Walada, can you hear me, from depths of darkness where you're dreaming?" Her voice deepened to incantation.

> "By stock and stone, by blood and bone,
> by time and tide, by waters wide,
> by breath and breeze, by fire that frees,
> come now to my summoning!"

Huld muttered indistinctly, and Brunahild talked her out through the gates of Hella's kingdom and back to the World-tree. Then she began to sing the song that summoned the wandering spirit home. The old seeress had been trained to respond to it for more years than Brunahild had lived, and she could feel the changes in the flesh she held as Huld moved back into Middle Earth and the clearing in the forest, and the chair.

"Ouf—" That was Huld's voice, and Brunahild let her go with a sigh of relief. "I feel as if I had made the journey from the Hermunduri all over again! I remember that you made me go looking for the god, but not what happened after." She fixed the girl with a bright gaze. "Did you get your answers, or have I wearied my old bones for nothing? Did he speak to you?"

"He spoke—" Brunahild stared at her. Now that Huld was safe, memory came flooding back. "He told me he would keep his promises. But Huld—I am afraid . . . I am afraid!"

* * *

The moon had waned and the bright spring weather was giving way to a fine rain when the Burgunds rode into Attila's encampment on the Danu. A few thatched houses in the Gothic style stood on a rise by the river, but the round tents the Huns called *gers* filled the meadow behind them, painted with strange figures and hung about with tassels of colored wool. Tethered horses whinnied in greeting and a cloud of riders swirled up the road to meet them.

Grani trumpeted his own challenge, and as Sigfrid wrestled him down he had a confused impression of flashing hooves and gleaming weapons, of men who moved with their mounts as if they were one being. He adjusted the spangenhelm that hid his face and pulled his cloak closer. He and Grani understood each other well, but he felt like a sack of grain in the saddle as he watched the Hun horsemen ride.

"Their princes are waiting for us up there—" Hagano pointed to an open space between the houses. A piece of stout cloth had been stretched between them to keep off the rain. "The man in front is Attila—the one with the piercing eyes and reddish-dark beard. His brother, the khan Bladarda, is the heavier man who is standing beside him. On the other side— yes, that will be Heimar. I saw him at a meeting of the tribes long ago."

Sigfrid's gaze sharpened. Sigdrifa had told him to seek her in Heimar's hall. "Is he one of their great chieftains?" he asked. To the waiting Huns, the Burgunds would be a mass of armor and horses. Sigdrifa had never seen Grani; she would not be able to distinguish him among them, if by some chance she were there.

"He is a *reiks* of the Marcomanni, married to Bladarda's older daughter. They fostered Brunahild."

Sigfrid felt his gut clench and wondered if he were going to be sick again. His vision had always been excellent, and now he could see another figure standing beside Heimar, smaller, dark-haired, glittering with Hunnish gold. She moved, and his entire body tingled as if he had been plunged into an icy spring. With a sense beyond sight or hearing he *knew* her; he recognized her with an emotion beyond joy or pain. *Sigdrifa* . . . his heart cried out her name.

"And there is the princess herself beside him," said Hagano. "That is Brunahild."

Chapter
Five
⚲ Judgment of the Sword

The Danu flowed strongly eastward between marshy banks, pale as straw with mud brought down from the mountains, swollen with spring rain. Brunahild walked beside the river, feeling through the soles of her feet the faintest vibration from its powerful movement, listening to the soft hiss of water flowing over stones. She knew how many lands and peoples the Danu would pass before it finally reached the sea. Her people had come from that direction; she had heard the tales. But for most of her life she had looked westward. From the west came both her hope and her greatest fear.

"Danu, Danu," she whispered, bending to cup the water, "wash away all uncertainty! Wash away my weakness! Give me your strength, great river, and your unswerving purpose!" She wet the top of her head, touched her breast, let the water flow through her hands.

Behind her she could hear the sounds of men and horses. The Burgunds. They were meeting with the khans even now to work out the details of the treaty. A stick came floating down and she plucked it from the water.

To swear away my freedom! Brunahild thought bitterly, stabbing it into the soft soil. Her father was with them. He had not come to see her after her child was born, but he was here now, ready to take his share of the Burgund gold.

At least, she thought then, *they understand that I will not be bartered like some swaybacked milk cow.* Her father had smiled when they met at last, and Brunahild realized that he had not the least idea that he owed her anything other than his presence here. She remembered him as a huge, loud man like a summer storm. But now he seemed small, and his black beard was streaked with grey.

Gold may buy an alliance, but they will have to find some other princess to seal it—if Gundohar is in a condition to be of use to any woman when I am done with him! She whacked at the reeds, but they only gave way with a hiss and bent back again.

Gundohar's shield will shatter when I strike it, she thought viciously. She straightened, tossed the wood back into the river, and turned up the path to the encampment. Behind her, the stick continued on its eastward way.

"But the marriage, you understand, is a marriage by capture—" Attila said silkily, stroking his auburn beard. "Two fights out of three, your king must win the girl with the sword."

That beard was very bright for a man of his age; Hagano wondered if the khan dyed it with henna. Perhaps not—Attila was younger than his brother, and raw energy seemed to crackle from his body with every move. An interesting man.

"And if he fails, or if the girl is killed in the fight, will you still hold to the alliance?" asked old Heribard. Hagano felt Gundohar twitch beside him, but etiquette required him to remain still.

"We will keep the borders. We would ask for a hostage from you in any case," said Bladarda. "A man of your family. The king of the Salic Franks has sent us already his daughter Hildigund, and from the Tervingi of Tolosa, Waldhari, Albharius' son."

There was an abrupt silence as Gundohar stared at his brothers, but Hagano felt hope leap within him, seeing a way to fulfill his promise to serve the Niflungar and get free of them at the same time.

"You can spare yourself the pain of choosing," he said to the king. "I will stand hostage for the Burgund kin."

"But you cannot—" Gundohar began.

"Why not?" Hagano whispered back. "You have other brothers, and other warriors. But we need to know more about the Huns, whether they are our allies or our enemies. This is the best way for me to help you now—and I will enjoy learning—" he added as he saw Gundohar getting ready to object again.

"So, you give us one of your brothers, Burgund king, and I give you another daughter of mine if you fare ill with Brunahild!" Bladarda laughed, broken teeth gleaming within the black beard.

"I only want—" Gundohar began, but Hagano jabbed him in the ribs.

"What we *want* is peace," he whispered, and knew as he spoke that he lied. They needed peace, but every man in the comitatus was wondering how he would fare against the Hun warriors they had seen here. It seemed a pity that the only fighting was to be between his brother, who had shaped better than anyone could have expected but was still hardly the Burgunds' greatest warrior, and a girl.

How would I do against them? he wondered then, watching from beneath his eyelids in the way his mother had taught him. The Huns were not, as a race, big men, though the Goths among them were tall and strong as any Burgund warrior. What marked them, he thought, was a quality of balance, as if they could strike instantly in any direction. It would take more than strength to defeat them, he thought then.

The eyes of the warriors who stood guard over the conference were constantly in motion, but they always returned to Attila. *Interesting,* thought Hagano. *Even those who follow Bladarda are Attila's men.* His own gaze returned to the khan. *There is more kingcraft in this man's suggestions than there was in all Gipicho's blusterings. What will he be when he comes to his full power?*

"So," said Heribard, "we have an alliance. An agreement between equal parties." He nodded, and the Hun princes smiled in their beards.

But Gundohar is not Attila's equal, thought Hagano, watching them. *Tomorrow we will see if he is Brunahild's. . . .*

* * *

At least today I will cut a better figure than I did last time I saw Brunahild on a battlefield, thought Gundohar as he came out of the round, felt-covered *ger* the Huns had set up for him to get ready in.

His royal spangenhelm, inset with golden plates modeled with the deeds of gods and heroes, had been polished until it gleamed in the sun. He wore a full shirt of riveted rings sewn to a backing of good leather and a cloak as scarlet as a Roman officer's with a garnet-set brooch of Frankish gold. His shield was of stout linden wood covered with bullhide, newly painted with the Gundwurm in crimson and gold. No one else would ever walk with Sigfrid's feral grace, but in the past weeks, Gundohar had studied him, seeking to know him as he knew no other, as if the blood they had mingled had indeed made them one. He moved now with a pride that was new to him, and hoped that in the carriage of his head and the balance of his shoulders there was at least an echo of the other man.

They had set up the hazel wands as if for a trial by combat on a little holm in the midst of the river. Four posts with carved heads and ropes stretched around them marked the enclosure. Gundohar stepped on to the flat boat that awaited him and tried not to hold on to the seat as the boatman poled him across the narrow expanse of water. He could feel the steady regard of his brothers and his arms-men on the bank behind him. Sigfrid was there somewhere as well, hidden in the crowd. He did not entirely understand why Sigfrid had insisted that his presence be kept secret—he had been acting strangely ever since they arrived—but he had come to the *ger* to help Gundohar arm, and he had promised to watch the battle.

The boat grounded, and the king got ashore with as much grace as he could muster. The judges already stood at their corners, Heribard and Ordwini for the Burgunds, and for the Huns, a bearded Goth and one bowlegged ancient who looked as if he had ridden with the horde since they first saw the Danu. Gundohar took his place at the western opening of the enclosure, and turned to watch the shore.

There was a stirring among the Hun tents; he saw a horse-tail standard tossing above the crowd and felt his gut knot. The khans were coming, then, and Brunahild with them. Now the people parted and he could see them. Bladarda was laughing. Gundohar gritted his teeth. He knew that the Huns, and even some of his own men, found the situation funny. But there was no amusement in it for him, or for Brunahild.

Now he could see her, a shadow in blackened mail. There were raven feathers on her helm, though she no longer wore the dark blue cloak of the Walkyriun. She carried her sword and shield with a kind of deadly grace that chilled him even as he found it beautiful. For a moment Gundohar recognized that the counselors who had advised him against this marriage were right, and that to cast her in the role of a Burgund queen was to catch a wild mare of the fells and harness it to a plow. But if he did not win her, his kingship would become a cage to him as well.

I will tame her! he promised himself. *Even she could not have expected to spend her whole life as a warrior-maid. Now she will settle down a little sooner, that is all!*

Brunahild remained standing as the boat brought her over, balancing easily, and sprang lightly onto the grass. She came up the path as eagerly as a maiden hastening to her bridal bed, thought Gundohar bitterly. But even in her wrath she was beautiful.

"Warriors, you are met on the field of judgment. Are you both still determined to do this battle?" asked the Goth.

"I am!" Brunahild replied swiftly, and Gundohar echoed her.

"Are you willing to try your dispute by force of arms alone, making no use of spell or charm or device of magic to gain the victory?"

Once more they agreed.

"Then come into the sacred ground, and may the gods judge between you."

Brunahild stepped eagerly into the enclosure; Gundohar, more slowly, with his best approximation of Sigfrid's swinging grace. They stopped, facing each other.

"The last time we met on a battlefield you were the victor, and I lost everything I held dear because of your victory." Brunahild's voice rang hard and clear. "If you are thinking I spared you from some misguided partiality, Gundohar, you are mistaken. I should have speared you then, but the god did not want you. This time I will not be so merciful!"

Gundohar swallowed. He heard her words, but her very presence spoke to him in a more powerful language.

"Raven of battle, railing rider, black thou art, ablaze with beauty," he answered, falling, as always when stressed, into poetry. "With sword and scorn dost seek to slay me; but a worse wound I won when first I saw thee."

He saw the pure curve of her lips twist beneath the blackened steel of her helm.

"Do you think death a worthy payment for one glance from my bright eyes? I will not kill you, King. My people need this alliance. But before we are done you may wish I had, for I will shame you, Gundohar!"

Gundohar nodded, settling into the swordsman's crouch that Sigfrid had taught him. All his life he had been hedged about by rules and responsibilities: by his mother's ambitions, his father's expectations of his heir. His only escape had been his harp, and his dreams. Now they called him king, but the old men of his Council were as demanding as ever his father had been. Brunahild was a vision made reality; marrying her the closest he would ever come to fulfilling at once both his duty and his dreams. This fight might well be folly, but to stake all on such a chance fed his soul.

He came alert with a start as Brunahild blurred toward him, got up his shield just in time to take her stroke, and felt the blow jar all the way up his arm. Gods! He had thought Sigfrid fast, but the girl moved like the flickering shadow cast by a leaping flame. Training brought his sword around in answer, but he was slow—too slow. By the time his blow fell Brunahild was gone.

At least Sigfrid had taught him to defend himself. Gundohar moved his shield back in place to meet her next attack. It felt as if she had hit exactly the same spot as before. But as he swung up the shield he sensed the slightest wavering, realized abruptly that she had struck there on purpose, and would continue to do so until the shield was destroyed.

Gundohar knew that he must attack her. But in battle, a fury of exhilaration took him. He could do deeds beyond his skill then, when everything except the need of the moment fell away. But he had no craft for such a cold combat as this. Any man could fight for his life; it was harder to overwhelm than to kill. Gundohar did not fear what she might do to him as much as he feared harming her. How could he fight to win?

He shifted his stance, turning as Brunahild danced around him, waiting for an opening. There—he swung for her shoulder, remembering to turn the blade so that it would not hit edge-on, but again she was gone. Her return blow blurred in, sheared off a chunk from the side of his shield, and grazed his thigh.

Shock surged through him; he struck, his blade passing her shield and scraping her mail. Aghast, he stumbled backward, his shield sagging as he saw her sway. Had he killed her?

In that instant Brunahild recovered, and before he could get the shield back up her blade swept in, slicing through iron rings and soft leather and into the top of his arm.

"Hold!" cried Ordwini. "The king bleeds!"

Gundohar looked down as the wound began to sting and saw blood welling from the rent in his mail. Then came the first deep throb; he blinked, dizzied by the shock of it with no battle fury to wall the pain away.

"Will you continue?" asked the Goth.

Gundohar started to say yes, but Ordwini and Heribard were already insisting that his wound be tended before they went on.

Sun flashed on steel as Brunahild swung up her sword. "Take him and tend him, Burgund lords. The first bout goes to me!"

Dizzy with shock, Gundohar had no strength to stop them from pulling him away. As Ordwini helped him out of the enclosure, Brunahild began to laugh. Gundohar could hear her laughter pealing across the river as they carried him over the water and back to the *ger*.

The noise of the crowd told Sigfrid that Gundohar was coming. At the first shout of "hold" he had withdrawn from his vantage point on the river bank and hidden himself in the *ger*. It occurred to him now that any other hiding place might have been wiser, for he had a sudden certainty that he knew what the Burgund king would say when he got inside.

He eased back against the crisscross lashings of the tent's framework as Godo thrust the doorflap aside and Hagano helped Gundohar in.

"It is nothing, only a scratch—" the king was protesting. They had his helm off already. Hagano grunted and turned his brother so that he could unbuckle the straps that held the byrny closed at the back. But Brunahild had struck a good blow, and drops of blood were already spattering the floor.

"I'll send for a healer," said Godo, but Gundohar clutched at his sleeve.

"No—it is not bad—or if it is, they must not know!" He looked wildly around him. "Sigfrid, are you here?"

"Rip off the sleeve—" said Sigfrid, the basin and swabs already in his hands. He wet one of the cloths and gently began to pat the blood away. In a moment he could see that Gundohar had been right. The wound, a long, clean cut across the muscle of the upper arm, had looked worse than it was. He finished cleansing it and clapped a dry pad across the wound. "Hold it there," he told Godo. In a few moments he had torn the ruined sleeve into strips and was winding them around the bandage.

"If you sit still, that will stop bleeding sooner!" he said to Gundohar.

"If I sit still, I will lose Brunahild."

"You're going to lose her anyway, brother." Godo shook his head. "You only need to be a little bit better to kill another man, but you have to be ten times as good a fighter to defeat him without injury. You did well—I was impressed. But those

Walkyriun bitches who trained her knew their trade. You're just not good enough to take Brunahild."

That had always been the danger, thought Sigfrid. Gundohar had said so himself, when they rested after sparring. And then he would turn once more to talking about how much he loved her.

Oh Sigdrifa, Sigfrid thought sadly, *I lived with you all one winter, but I never loved you half so dearly as this man who has only seen you three times!*

Gundohar lifted his head with a sigh. "Leave us—" He gestured to his brothers and the servants who had crowded in. "All of you, leave me and Sigfrid alone . . ."

They hesitated, but there must have been something in the king's face that Sigfrid, behind him, could not see, for suddenly they were all pushing through the door, confused or wondering, except for Hagano, who wore his usual knowing grin.

"Am I wrong? Is it wrong of me to want her so?" whispered Gundohar when they were gone.

I can hardly reproach him, thought Sigfrid. *I loved her myself.* And indeed, when he saw her striding across the field like a dark and shining raven who had assumed woman-form, there had been a moment when he could have loved her again. Then Gundohar looked at him, and Sigfrid winced at the naked pain he saw in the other man's eyes.

"Is the wound—"

The king shook his head angrily. "Sigfrid, brother by oath and blood, you made me a promise a little while ago! You have seen—you have heard! I cannot win her alone!"

Sigfrid found himself backing away, shaking his head. That had been before he knew that Brunahild and Sigdrifa were the same.

"You must help me," said Gundohar, not understanding. "If I go out there again, I may kill her, or she might kill me! If not for my sake, then for the sake of our people that must be prevented, and only you can do it. Sigfrid, my brother, will you go out and fight for me now?"

"There must be some other way," said Sigfrid desperately. "This dishonors both you and her."

"If there were, don't you suppose that by now I would have found it?" said Gundohar bitterly. "If I, a king, can bear the shame, what right have you to be so tender? You *swore* to me, brother, that you would support me in all things. Will you betray me the first time I am in need?"

Gundohar might not be a great swordsman, but he had the tongue of a bard. Sigfrid struggled for words. He had sworn an oath to Sigdrifa, too. He felt as if he had become two persons, and they were arguing.

I am still bound to her! How can I win her for another man? I should have demanded to see her, and explained. But he had been afraid to face her, he knew now, afraid of what she would say.

You had no right to bind her—that inner antagonist replied. *What could you offer her? She may think she would prefer a life of wandering to the splendor of being the Burgunds' queen, but how can she decide, who has known only the harsh life of the woods and the Walkyriun? You must take the responsibility, and set both her and yourself free!*

He realized that he was standing on the other side of the *ger*, quivering. Once he had seen a trapped wolf gnaw off its own leg in its desperation to be free. Now he understood the animal's frenzy, but the snare that held Sigfrid was the promise he himself had made.

He had sworn an oath to Sigdrifa a year ago, but he had learned, these past months, how lightly such oaths are held by men. A month ago he had sworn, by all that fighting men hold sacred, to keep faith with Gundohar. The Burgund king had given him an openhearted affection—a trust—that no man had ever offered him before.

I have no choice, he thought then. *I walked into this cage of my own will, and now I am trapped here for good and all.*

"Sigfrid, I beg you—" Gundohar reached out to him. "My honor is in your hands!"

Sigfrid drew his dagger, a lovely thing of ivory and gold that the king himself had given him. Gundohar's eyes widened, and Sigfrid thought that in that moment the other man might have welcomed death to ease his pain. He laughed then, pushed up his own sleeve, and drew the sharp blade across the muscle, just where Brunahild's sword had scored Gundohar.

"Take off your clothes," he said harshly. "We must make the change complete to the last detail if we are to deceive them. I will do my best for you."

Gundohar's amazement changed to a delighted grin that widened as he scrambled out of his tunic and breeches. He was a clumsy servant, but too soon for Sigfrid's liking he found himself arrayed in the king's arms and clothing, his face hidden by the spangenhelm, a bloodstained bandage showing through the rent in his mail.

"Hagano—" the king called. His brother slipped through the doorway, saw the two of them standing there, and stifled a laugh.

"Tell Godo off as escort for me and stay here with the king," said Sigfrid. "No one must know about the substitution. Can I trust you?"

"Always—"

There was an odd intonation in Hagano's reply, but Sigfrid had no time to ponder it. Outside, they were calling for the king. He took a deep breath, and pushed out into the sunlight and the crowd.

It did not occur to him, then or later, to tell Gundohar the one thing that would have impelled the other man to release him. Some part of him knew that if the king had understood his relationship with Brunahild, it would have been the end of their brotherhood, and that was something he needed even more than he wanted Gudrun.

Brunahild knew me as well as a woman can know a man, thought Sigfrid as he approached the enclosure, trying to imitate Gundohar's awkward gait, *better than I knew myself. I seem to have fooled all these others, but will she be deceived?* In a moment they would know. To carry this off he must become a shape-changer indeed, wearing Gundohar's clothes like the hide he put on to run with the wolves.

Off to the east, grey clouds were building. Sigfrid sent a mental prayer to the Thunderer to come quickly. They might call off this combat if it rained. Brunahild was waiting; he took his place opposite her, letting his wounded arm hang limply at his side.

"You are ready for the second fight?" the Gothic judge sounded dubious. "Your wound has been tended?"

"I am ready—" said Sigfrid in the accent of the Burgunds. Brunahild looked up sharply, but the spangenhelm covered all his face above the chin, and in the days when they roamed the forest Sigfrid had been bearded. She had never seen his face bare. He looked like Gundohar; and in his experience, people saw what they expected to see.

"You may have a new shield if you desire one," said the judge.

Sigfrid shrugged the wounded shoulder and mimed a wince as he shook his head. *I am Gundohar . . .* he told himself. *Idealistic, anxious, clumsy, noble—and a king!* He could feel his heart thumping with panic. If she tried to identify him by other senses, perhaps she would think it was fear.

"I cannot carry it," he replied.

"Then I will give up my own," said Brunahild. "I would not have it said that I did not fight fairly." There was a murmur of approval from the watching warriors as she cast her shield away.

Sigfrid nodded. Brunahild's action might be honorable, but it was also wise. A larger opponent might overwhelm her shield by sheer weight and momentum, and a shield's bulk would make it harder to use her chief advantage, her agility. Now she was free to dance circles around him. Fighting just well enough to overcome her without giving himself away would be an interesting problem. Sigfrid felt a quiver of anticipation for the first time since Gundohar had made his appeal.

Then Brunahild leaped in, and he found himself giving ground as awkwardly as he could have wished. He twisted, heard iron clang as he got his blade up and winced at the sound. He had forgotten this was not Gram he was wielding.

Gundohar's sword was a fine piece of smithcraft, but it was not star steel. It could shatter and betray him.

She was better than he had expected, and he began to have more sympathy for Gundohar's difficulties. He retreated around the enclosure, concentrating on distracting her with clumsy footwork, since the swordsmanship that defended him was beyond his conscious control. Again and again Brunahild attacked him, and each time, at the last moment or by chance, it must have seemed to her, his sword was between them when her blow fell.

At last Sigfrid began to hear the rasp of her breathing and knew that she was tiring. He stumbled, halting as if he had come to the end of his resources as well. He could feel her gathering herself for a final onslaught. A chill wind ruffled the dry grass of the enclosure. In the distance he heard the mutter of thunder. He left his guard low, as if too tired to lift his blade, waiting as Brunahild's sword lifted, judging the momentum as she started her swing.

A lightning stroke of bright metal flared toward him, and in the same moment Sigfrid leaped forward beneath the swing. The impact of his body against her shield side added to the momentum of her own blow to spin her around, a foot thrust out seemingly at random hooked her ankle and brought her down. As she struck the earth her sword went flying, and in that moment, as she lay gasping, Sigfrid's swordpoint sought her throat and hovered there.

For a moment no one moved. Then there came a sigh, as if a multitude had suddenly remembered to breathe.

Old Heribard cleared his throat. "The second bout goes to Gundohar!"

Brunahild sucked in air and the world, which had disappeared for a moment when she hit the ground, took shape around her once more. A flicker of brightness resolved itself into a swordblade, her gaze followed it as it swung away. Someone was talking. She sat up. Men's faces changed as they saw her movement and they looked away. That was when she realized that she had lost.

"Each party has been victorious once in combat," said the Burgund judge. "There must be third fight to decide the issue. Do you wish time to rest, or will you continue immediately?"

Gundohar stood a few paces away with his back to her, leaning on his sword as if that last effort had exhausted him. Brunahild scrambled to her feet, eyeing him suspiciously. Surely he must be as tired as she was, this upset a fluke born of desperation when he saw her closing in. That had to be the explanation, but there was something about the whole fight, about the warrior who had bested her, that seemed strange.

She took a deep breath, drawing strength from the earth, and widened her awareness, seeking to encompass the spirit of the silent figure who was her foe.

For a moment, it was as if he were a rock and she a flowing stream. Her awareness surrounded without knowing him. She closed her eyes, concentrating, and caught a dim impression of sorrow, and of shame.

Well, she thought, opening her eyes again. *At least he is not exulting in his victory.*

One of the Burgund judges spoke to him, and he shook his head. Old Kursik came to her with a cup of water, pity gleaming in his dark eyes.

"Will you fight now, khatun? If you need, I can ask for time."

Brunahild sighed. She felt the strain of the first two fights in every muscle, but waiting would make it no better. The sky was darkening, and she could feel the damp breath of oncoming rain. Her opponent was as tired, and he was wounded; she could see new blood staining the bandage on his arm. Better to finish it now. She took a little water and rolled it around in her mouth to moisten it.

"I will continue," she said, giving the cup back to the old man.

He gestured, and the Goth brought her sword. Brunahild took it and settled into a defensive crouch. She would not let overconfidence betray her again. A flicker of distant lightning struck sudden glints from blades and mail. She waited for the thunder.

Wodan, War Father, I am sworn to do no magic, but I beg you, lay your terror upon my foe! Give me the victory that I may do your will!

The thunder spoke, as if it had been a signal, and the staff of the judge swung down.

"Come," cried Brunahild. "You who are so eager for battle, receive the Walkyrja's embrace. Now your luck leaves you; I am your wyrd, warrior. Kill me if you can, for by my soul I swear this, that you will lie dead before ever you lie in my arms!"

Her opponent faced her and lifted his sword, but he did not reply.There had been venom in her voice, and several of those watching made the sign against evil, but as she finished Brunahild found that a kind of peace had come to her, and she knew that this time she would fight to kill.

Brunahild leaped forward, slashing at her opponent's side. But he was already moving away from her blow; she let momentum carry her past, turning as his sword swept toward her. The blades kissed, the antagonists whirled apart, withdrawal becoming the prelude to a new attack. Swords clashed in perfect alignment, as if they had planned it.

As Brunahild spun away she had an instant to wonder how Gundohar's swordsmanship had suddenly become so improved. Perhaps desperation had unleashed new reserves of skill in him, as it had given strength to her. Then the moment was past; he was blurring toward her. She responded without need for thought, the blades met, strained, then slipped apart.

She let the movement carry her sword around and up in a long sweep, and he was turning, meeting it; their shoulders brushed as he whirled past. Brunahild was dimly aware that she had never fought so well, never had an opponent who could inspire in her such battlecraft; each encounter swifter, more skilled than the one before. She had never felt so alive!

She fought, forgetting who she was, and where, and why. She and her foe were two halves of one being, locked in a dreadful ecstasy. Lightning flickered from the meeting of their swords.

She saw the joining of his neck and shoulder for a moment unguarded and began her swing. *Now! Now I will end it!* Her spirit surged through her blade. Brunahild felt his return stroke coming and knew she was unguarded, but it did not matter. Thunder rent the heavens above them and the flare of the lightning blotted out vision.

In the next moment something hit her on the side of the head and she knew no more.

Sigfrid fell to his knees beside Brunahild's body and crouched, blinking, as the reverberations of the thunder rolled away. He reached out to touch her throat, but it was a moment before he could still his shaking enough to tell if what he felt was the flutter of her pulse or his own. He sat back on his heels, breathing hard. He had almost killed her!

Brunahild had drawn him into the sword-dance, as seductive as the rhythms of love. If a year of constant practice had not given him enough control to turn the blade so that only the flat of it struck her, he would have killed her as he had killed Ragan, who had offered his neck to the sword in just that way.

Cold wind swirled around them and he flinched from the first spatterings of rain. The judges came hurrying toward them and he struggled to his feet to meet them.

"Is she dead?" asked Ordwini.

Tiredly he shook his head. The old Hun was already examining her. Gently he pulled off her helmet. Sigfrid looked down at the pale face with the black hair spilling around it—longer than he remembered—and felt ill.

Sigdrifa . . . Since coming here he had only seen her from a distance, and he thought now that if they had fought bare-faced, he would not have been able to strike a blow.

"She is unconscious only," said the old man. "She will recover soon." He looked up at Sigfrid. "The third fight, and the woman, go to you!"

There was a roaring as of the wind, but it was the people, some scurrying for cover, some exclaiming at the outcome. He saw Hagano hurrying up the bank toward them.

"You have won her! Congratulations, brother! The Burgunds have a new queen!" He clapped Sigfrid on the back, grinning sardonically. "Better not leave her lying in the mud!" He drew close, whispering. "Now you have to carry her off. Take her to that cave upriver we found on the way here. I've sent a man there with food and firewood, and a sleeping potion in case she should wake too soon. Keep her safe there tonight, and in the morning we'll send an escort to bring you home."

"Tell Gundohar to come before dawn with my clothes," Sigfrid whispered back. "I'll come out to him." He lifted Brunahild, surprised, as always, that so much passionate intensity could be contained in this slight form that weighed so lightly in his arms.

On the other side of the river Gundohar's horse was waiting. He mounted, and Hagano handed Brunahild, who was still unconscious, up to him. Then, to the cheers and jeers of the tribesmen and the roaring of the wind, Sigfrid carried her away.

By the time they reached the cave it was raining hard. Brunahild, thank the gods, was still unconscious. Sigfrid built the fire near the mouth of the cave, where the smoke could escape, and where it would warm them while casting as little light as possible on the other end, where the blankets had been laid.

Someone had had the forethought to pack a gown for Brunahild. As gently as he had tended her when first he found her, bound to the rock and surrounded by fire, Sigfrid stripped off her wet clothes and her armor. She was more rounded now than the skinny waif he remembered, her breasts fuller, but she still had bones like a bird. As he pulled off her undertunic he felt metal and saw that she was wearing the neck ring he had given her.

Was that what was maintaining the link between them? He had given it to her, but the bond it had sealed was broken, and if Gundohar should ever ask what it was, her answer would give everything away. Carefully he eased the ring around, twisted its ends open, and pulled it away. The gold lay heavy in his hand, warm from her body. Her neck looked defenseless without it. He thought a moment, then pulled off the king's torque that Gundohar had been wearing, more ornate in style, but much the same in size, and put it on Brunahild.

"That must be your morning gift now, princess—" he muttered. Then he twisted the gold that once had lain beneath Andvari's waterfall around his own neck once more. "We would not be in this tangle now if you had told the truth about yourself to me."

The wound on his upper arm had reopened, but there was no time to worry about that now. Working swiftly, he got her into the dry gown and wrapped her up warmly. He was just finishing when she began to stir.

"Sigfrid. . . ." she whispered, and his heart stopped. "The Walkyriun are watching me! They gather like crows, laughing . . . laughing! Sisters, I never harmed you—you have cast me out, cannot you leave me in peace now?"

Her head rolled against the pillow, but her eyes were still closed, and he let out his breath in a long sigh. She was dreaming herself back on the mountain where he had found her, then. Perhaps the touch of his hands had stirred old memories. He suppressed a twinge of pity. Just now her old nightmares would be kinder than the new ones. He touched her forehead and found it warm; perhaps the sleeping potion Hagano had sent would also work on fever. He set the flask to her lips, murmuring her name, and she turned, lips opening trustingly.

"Sigfrid," she whispered, "my head hurts, and oh, I have had such dreams!"

"Sleep," he answered. "You have been hurt, and you need time to heal."

She sighed and tried to lift her head, but already the drug was taking her. After a few moments her movements subsided and her breathing deepened. Sigfrid readjusted the covers and sighed. *Sleep . . .* he thought grimly, *for your waking will be worse than your dreams.*

He ate some of the food and went outside to relieve himself. Night had fallen, and the storm seemed to be growing in fury. Donar's lightning flashed on the horizon, and rain lashed the treetops as the warring hosts of heaven rushed by. Sigfrid lifted his hands to the heavens.

"Holy gods, why have you done this? Why have you wound our lives in such a tangle that there is no honorable escape either for Brunahild or for me?" Thunder boomed in the distance, but there was no reply.

When he went back in, Brunahild was still asleep, but tossing fretfully. The fire had died down enough so that he judged it safe to remove his helm, though he left the leather coif on lest she know him by the texture of his hair. To him the air seemed warm, but the girl was shivering. She seemed to calm when he touched her, so he stretched himself out beside her, holding her carefully.

Lying so, he could not help remembering how many times he had held her this way before, safe in their refuge while the winter storms howled outside. It was only when his hand moved instinctively to its familiar resting place cradling her breast that he realized that he would need more than his armor to remind him of who and where they were now.

He jerked his hand away, swearing, sat up, and reached for Gundohar's sword.

"Let you lie between us to guard what honor remains to me," he growled, laying it on the blanket. Then he eased down again.

Toward midnight, she began to toss and mutter. Her forehead was hotter, but after a head blow he dared not give her any more of the potion. If she thought she saw him now, it could be blamed on her delirium. He gave her water and bathed her face, holding her gently. She stilled, but she was still murmuring. He bent close to hear.

"Bertriud, you are wrong. Of course he will come for me. He is the noblest of warriors, and I am his Walkyrja. Can a man cast off his soul?"

Ah, Brunahild, thought Sigfrid, *these words are crueler to me than any blow you struck on the battlefield.* But he had no choice but to listen. As the hours of darkness crawled by she continued to ramble, not always clearly, but enough for him to know how

proudly she had waited and how desperately she had longed
for him. She had been ill, he thought, for at times she railed
against pain. Then she would return in memory to their days
in the Taunus, until he wanted to weep with her for the in-
nocence he had lost.

But there is no magic that will bring that time back now, he thought
dismally. *We can only make the best of the world we have wandered
into. And in this world, you will be far better off as Gundohar's queen
than you would be as an outlaw with me.*

Finally, in the grey hour before dawn, the violence of the
storm outside began to ease and Brunahild grew quiet at last.
When Sigfrid felt her forehead cool, and heard the deep and
regular breaths of normal sleep, he kissed her on the brow
one last time and pulled himself away, tucking the blankets
back around her to preserve the warmth of his body.

He stopped to make up the fire, for it would not matter if
she could see by it now. Then he went out into the dim
wasteland between darkness and dawn to wait for Gundohar.

Brunahild woke with a foul taste in her mouth and a throbbing in her head as if the dwarf-smiths had been using it for
an anvil. Every muscle in her body was complaining. She felt
weak as a new lamb, but she was dry and warm. She had
dreamed that she was back in the forest with Sigfrid; was she
still recovering from childbirth instead? That couldn't be—the
air had a dank chill to it, and she could hear none of the small
sounds of Heimar's hall. She turned and felt metal beside her,
opened her eyes, and realized that what lay beside her in the
bed was a sword.

She sat up, her heart pounding in sudden panic. Pain
slashed through her head and it took a moment for vision to
return. She was in a small cave, low and narrow, but dry. A
fire was burning cheerfully by the entrance. Beside it she could
see a folded crimson cloak, and a spangenhelm whose features
she knew only too well.

"Gundohar!" she whispered. But surely that was impossible.
He couldn't have defeated her—she fought to get past her
nightmares to the day that had spawned them. She remem-

bered wounding the Burgund king; she remembered driving him around the field; she remembered the moment when she and her opponent had become one being, locked in a deadly union more intimate than love.

That was the helmet he had worn, and this, beside her, was the sword that had struck her down. They had been here all night alone.

"Wodan . . . Father . . . why am I here? What has happened to me?" Dizzied, for a moment she closed her eyes. When she opened them again, nothing had changed. "Father, you promised that Sigfrid would come for me! Deceiver they call you, did you lie?"

From outside the cave she heard the snort of a horse and another answering. Beyond the fire the entrance was a dim oval of light. They were coming! She whimpered, enraged at her own weakness, racked by despair. But at least he had left her a weapon.

"Wodan! I curse you, grim and terrible god! My shame and sorrow come from your will! My curse on Gundohar, and Sigfrid who has abandoned me! May they suffer as I suffer, and as for you, I defy you! I will go to Hella's hall and you may find another fool to work your will in the world!"

She struggled free of the bedclothes and grasped the hilt of the sword. Gods, it was heavy, and half as high as she was. She braced the hilt in a fold of the blankets and lifted the blade, pushing herself up onto her knees. But the sword was still too long. She gripped the blade and tried to get to her feet, cutting her hands.

The entrance darkened. "Brunahild, Brunahild!" She tried to set the point beneath her heart as someone rushed toward her.

"My beloved, don't try to stand!" he cried, and then a mailed arm went around her and he snatched the sword away.

She tried to free herself, but there was no strength left in her. She glimpsed spiky fair hair, a beak of a nose between anguished grey eyes. Gundohar! She groaned, and the spinning of her head communicated itself to her belly.

"Be still, my queen, be easy. I will take care of you!" he

murmured, holding her awkwardly against him. Brunahild shook her head as nausea rose in her. Other people were crowding in after him, but she was too ill to care.

The next few minutes were a confusion. They had brought a wagon for her to ride in with a top of oiled wool. She felt the kiss of a light rain as they carried her to it, then she was covered once more.

Of the journey that followed, only one thing was clear to her. They were moving westward. She had lost everything.

Chapter
Six　 An Exchange of Vows

Borbetomagus
Litha Moon, A.D. 420

Gudrun reached out to touch an opening leaf, breathing deeply of the perfume the moist earth gave forth as it was warmed by the spring sun. It was too early yet to tell if this were one of the herbs she had planted there, but her mother had taught her that even weeds could be useful as a tonic in the spring. One thing she did like about the old Roman palace was the garden; it made up a little for losing the woods around the Holy Hill where she had roamed as a child.

"Erda, Erda, Holy Mother Earth," she murmured, holding her hands above the soil in blessing, "bring forth and be fruitful; bear these healing herbs for the good of men—" Such a prayer even Father Priscus could hardly disapprove. Every farmer did the same, adding a Christian invocation, and sometimes the priests went out with them to bless the fields. But as she spoke, her hands moved in the rune-signs her mother had taught her: *Uruz*, to give strength to the earth, *Ingwaz* and *Fehu*, to bring up the seeds hidden in the ground, and *Jera*, that they might mature in health and harmony.

When the king's household moved into the city she had found the garden overgrown with weeds, its surviving plantings sadly neglected, but she had coaxed the salvia and the lavender back to life, and trimmed down the rosemary, which was trying to take over the garden. She had taken advantage of every journey away from Borbetomagus to look for wild herbs that she could try transplanting, or later in the season, to collect seeds and sow them here.

Working in the garden, she found comfort in the regular unfolding of leaf and flower. The birds had grown used to her, and fluttered about as she loosened the earth, searching for bugs in the soil. In the six weeks since Sigfrid had ridden off to help Gundohar with his courting she had come here often.

Perhaps, she thought as she watched a finch carry off a tuft of wool to thatch its nest, she was lonely, though it seemed ridiculous to miss someone after being married to him for only three days. During the day, she could close her eyes and think of Sigfrid, and smile, but the nights were harder, when she lay alone in the great bed and touched herself where *he* had touched her, quivering with an echo of the sensations he had awakened there.

He had been gone so long! A moon had passed, and the next was swelling in the sky. Was it usual for a bride to feel as if a part of herself had gone with a new husband when he rode away? Her women laughed at her confusion, and told her how lucky she was to have such a fine, strong lad in her bed. Having expected to be married off to some old man to seal an alliance, she could not help but agree. She had never dared hope for love.

But was it love indeed that she had found? Gudrun pulled up several blades of grass that had sprouted among the violets and tossed them onto the path. Lust, she had discovered for certain, and that was a good enough beginning, if it kept her man with her long enough to give her some children. Sigfrid had demonstrated that he took delight in her body; she felt a flash of heat as she remembered it. But did he love her?

It seemed unlikely. They had hardly spoken enough for him to know her. And yet, as she found herself missing his presence even more than the pleasure he had given her, she began to fear that she had fallen into the trap that princesses were warned to beware. A royal woman might marry for policy or power; she might lie with a man for pleasure; but she was a fool if she allowed herself to love.

"Well, I am a fool, then!" she whispered as she moved on to see how the yarrow was doing. "For I am very much afraid that love is what I feel! What do you think, sister?" Smiling, she looked up at the nuthatch that bobbed on the rose tree. But the black, beady gaze of the nuthatch was fixed on something behind her. She was not alone.

Flushed with embarrassment, Gudrun turned. Sigfrid stood behind her with his wolfskin slung over his shoulder, poised like a wild thing that any careless motion might frighten away. She started to her feet, and the sudden movement drove the blood from her head; each pulsebeat showed him alternately as a black shape against brightness, a bright image on shadow. She swayed, and felt hard hands grip her arms.

He's back! He came back to me! Gradually her vision cleared. She met his eyes, the wolf's eyes of her dreams, and it was he who looked away.

"Forgive me," he said in a low voice, "I did not mean to startle you."

"My fault," she stammered. "I got up too quickly." Why was he silent? The current she felt whenever they touched was flowing between them again, so why didn't he kiss her?

"Is my brother with you? Did all go well?"

Sigfrid looked at her, forcing a smile. "Gundohar is well, but the princess was injured slightly in the combats. He sent me on ahead so that your people here can prepare a welcome. An assembly of the chieftains has been called for Midsummer, and by then they should be here."

"And no one is dead?" she asked. He shook his head, and now he was smiling, but still she knew that something was wrong. *Tell me!* she begged him silently. *Let me share your grief if I cannot share your joy!*

"Well, that will give us a little over a week to get ready," she managed an answering smile. "Did Wodan make you a loan of Sleipnir to bring you here so fast?"

"I have a good steed, but though a horse can run faster, there is none that will run as long as a man. My own legs bore me here, as a man by day, with the power of the wolf by night." He gave her a quick look, and then, as if reassured by her lack of reaction, went on, "I could do no more good there with the others. I wanted to come . . . home." He said the word as if not quite sure of its meaning. "To you." He twisted open the torque around his neck. As he lifted it off she saw that runes had been graven into the heavy gold.

"I have brought this for you."

"From the land of the Huns?" she asked.

He frowned. "It comes from Andvari's hoard. It is . . . a holy thing, Gudrun, not for the Christian priests to see. You must keep it secret, for when we are alone."

She nodded, wide-eyed, and turned her head so that he could fit the ring around her neck. For a moment, the weight of it seemed to press her down into the earth. Then she felt not so much a pressure, as a new awareness of all the living world around her, as if she were taking root in the path. The warmth of the gold spread through her with a gentle fire.

"Sigfrid," she dared to reach up to him at last, "my own dear lord. . . ."

She felt some of the tension going out of him and drew his head down, thinking he would kiss her then. But his hands slid along her arms; groaning, he sank down on his knees before her, face pressed against her belly, his strong arms embracing her thighs.

Gudrun gasped as if a sudden flame had blazed between them, and her fingers clutched suddenly at his curling hair. Sigfrid turned his head back and forth against her, and the strength went out of her. She bent, cradling his shoulders as her knees gave way, and slid down, her skirts riding upward, until she was kneeling. Then he kissed her at last, feeding on her mouth like a starving man, but by now her desire was as great as his. In another moment she was on her back on the path.

"You are the House of Life," he whispered. "Shelter me—"

"Yes," she answered him, understanding only his need. She felt her thighs parting to receive him, strained against him, wanting to open even more. Then the bright flood swept her away.

Afterward, as she became aware of the cool earth beneath her and the weight of the man who lay in her arms, it seemed to her that from somewhere nearby she could hear a contented rumbling, and wondered if the Frowe's cats were purring, or whether it was only the pulsing of the blood in her ears. . . .

"I can see the river! We'll be in Borbetomagus by sundown!" The shout came from somewhere up ahead, clear and triumphant.

Gundohar's horse reared, jabbed by an incautious heel. He clutched at the mane for balance as he reined it down. His days with the Huns had given him a healthy awe for their horsemanship. It was not to be expected that any Burgund could match such skill, but he did not want Brunahild to think him an utter fool.

But the curtains of her wagon had not even stirred. He held the horse back, waiting until the lumbering oxen came alongside. Now he too could see the grey gleam through the screen of alders along the riverbank, but low clouds hid the farther hills. A spatter of moisture flicked his cheek and he sighed. He had hoped the sun would be shining on this day.

"Brunahild," he called softly. "Brunahild, did you hear? We are almost home!"

"*Your* home. . . ." a flat voice from within corrected, but a pale hand pulled back the curtain. "But I will be glad enough to see the last of this wagon. I have been joggled and jolted till I can count every bone!"

"I'm sorry," said Gundohar helplessly. "If you feel strong enough to ride, I will bring up a horse for you. I will lead it myself if you will be more comfortable—" There was a snort, of amusement or contempt, from within the wagon.

"Prisoners do not ride horses," said Brunahild, "or had you forgotten that I am your captive?"

Gundohar sighed. They had covered this ground too many times before. "My people will not see you that way," he said quietly. "To them, you are a bringer of peace, a pledge from the Huns that their kin on the eastern side of the river will be able to live in safety. You will find the Burgunds very different from your own folk, Brunahild—I had not realized just how different until I dwelt awhile with your kin. But they are good, honest people, not so much warriors that they have forgotten how to love their families, and not so peaceable they cannot defend them if there is need. You are famed already, my queen, and they will be eager to honor you."

As I do already, Gundohar thought unhappily, *though you have given even less than that to me.*

At first he had assumed it was the head blow that made Brunahild so reclusive. But almost a moon had passed since the fight. She was a young and healthy woman; by now she should have healed. He found it hard to recognize in this bitter woman the glowing girl who had visited them at the Holy Hill four years before, or even the somber beauty whom he had faced on the battlefield.

Was I wrong to insist on marrying her? his thoughts moved round the well-worn track once more. When he heard that she had left the Walkyriun, it seemed the will of the gods that she should be his queen . . . He had been so sure that her insistence on combat was only to salve her pride.

With the thought, Gundohar found himself peering through the gap in the curtains once more. He could just see the curve of her cheek, more wan now than he remembered, and the dark tangle of her hair. And even now, even a glimpse set his heart to pounding with an astonished joy.

I love her, may the Frowe help me! he thought as the curtain was again drawn closed. *I love her, and whether she cares for me or not, now she is bound to me, and we will both have to do the best we can. . . .*

Perhaps, he told himself then, it would be better when they reached Borbetomagus at last and Gudrun and his mother could take care of her.

The rain continued for several days. To Brunahild, moving from the confinement of her wagon to the red stone walls of the palace, it seemed that she had exchanged one prison for another. But at least the new one stayed still.

Gundohar had summoned his chieftains and the men of the comitatus to a Midsummer Assembly to approve the treaty and witness the wedding. To the Huns, a marriage by capture might be binding, but it appeared there were additional formalities to be observed in the marriage of a Christian king. Sometimes, looking out at the weeping sky, she considered running away. But she did not have the strength for it, and in any case, where could she run to, now that Sigfrid had abandoned her? And so she moped like a moulting raven in a dovecote, surrounded by the chattering women who fussed over her jewelry and gowns.

The old queen had made her a rather formal welcome, which Brunahild received with the same cool courtesy. She suspected that Grimahild would have been suspicious of any woman who came to take the place that had been her own, especially one who had been trained by the Walkyriun. It might have mattered, if she had cared either about being queen of the Burgunds or about Gundohar, but how the people of this place perceived her was still a matter of supreme indifference. Brunahild thought of the stories she had heard about the old queen with a certain amusement, knowing that Grimahild would respect her own training too much to try any tricks on her.

The only thing about her arrival in Borbetomagus that engaged her interest at all was seeing Gudrun again. Her old friend had a glow about her like a spring sunrise and seemed to bring light into any room she entered, despite the lowering skies. She gathered that Gudrun was married now to one of her brother's chieftains, and clearly enjoying it, but at least the girl had the tact not to babble about her happiness.

The day before the wedding, Brunahild was escorted to the chapel to receive Christian baptism. Gundohar had proposed the idea to her with some trepidation. They would still be married without it, but only in the old way. To marry in a fashion that was recognized by the Romans as well as their own people would go far to stabilize the alliance, but to be joined in such a rite she must become a Christian. He had seemed surprised when she made no objection. But why should she, who had been abandoned by her gods?

Nonetheless, when they escorted her to the chapel the morning before her wedding, she could not help feeling some curiosity.

"Don't be afraid," whispered Gudrun, misunderstanding her hesitation. "The Christos is kinder than the priests who serve him."

Kindness! thought Brunahild bitterly. *I need a god of judgment now!* Still, the other woman had meant well, and it was good to go into this ordeal with a friend at her side.

The chapel was built of weathered red stone that looked as if it had been salvaged from some older building. Inside it was cool and dim, with crude paintings on the whitewashed walls that flared and faded intermittently as the lamps flickered in the draft.

That was familiar enough, but instead of the harsh pungence of the herbs her people used for purification, the air was heavy with a lingering sweetness, a spicy scent that made her think of sunshine in lands beyond the great mountains that touched the sky. But strangest of all was the figure hanging on the great cross over the altar, like Wodan on the Tree. She had been taught that the point about Wodan's sacrifice was the fact that he had come down from the Worldtree. Despite the many hours of earnest instruction by Gundohar's priests, it was not clear to her why the Christians should choose to concentrate on their god's suffering.

Still, she could sense that there was power here, an echo of some strong emotion composed equally of passion and fear. Clearly, in this place at least some of the worshippers of the Christos had touched their god. But she did not think that Father Priscus, stolid and frowning, was one of them.

The priest was waiting already at the altar, swathed in garments of silk brocade embroidered in gold. They said that their god preached poverty, but clearly the rule did not apply to his ministers. Brunahild thought no worse of them for that—a priest whose god had not the power to even clothe him decently would have made small impression on the tribes.

Gundohar drew her forward. She suffered his touch, wanting only to get through this as quickly as possible, and moved down the aisle. In an alcove to one side of the altar stood a bowl of white marble supported by a pedestal. There were salutations, to which Gundohar replied in the Roman tongue. He assisted her to kneel next to Gudrun and took his place on the other side of the church while the priests gabbled their Latin and moved through the ritual. Several of the Burgund chieftains and their ladies were already kneeling, men on one side of the church, women on the other, but by no means all of them. Queen Grimahild was not there.

Presently the priests moved into the alcove, chanting and swinging the censer. Brunahild found herself growing a little giddy as the clouds of sweet-scented smoke swirled about the room.

"Benedic, Domine Deus noster, hanc creaturam aquae, et descendat super eam virtus tua. . . ." the babble continued. It was only when the man's voice rose in command that she roused once more. *"Exorcizo te, creatura aquae: exorcizo te, omnis exercitus diaboli, omnis potestas adversaria, omnis umbra daemonum . . ."*

"What is he doing?" she whispered to Gudrun as the priest cast salt into the bowl.

"He must drive all the devils out of the water," came the answer. Brunahild raised one eyebrow. Surely they could have saved themselves a great deal of trouble simply by filling the font from a sacred spring. "We must rise—" Gudrun said then. "They are ready for you now."

One of the acolytes came forward to escort them to the font, face frozen in self-conscious pride. Gudrun assisted her to put back her veil. Father Priscus asked a question and Brunahild heard her own name in Gudrun's answer. He turned to her, frowning.

"Brunahilda, Bladardis filiae, abrenuncias diabolei, pompis saeculi, et voluptatibus ejus?" he asked, and then, so that there should be no mistake, added in the Burgund tongue, "Dost thou forsake the Devil and all devil worship and all the devils that ever were, Donar and Wodan and the Frowe, all those unholy

ones, and also the pomp of the world and its delights?"

She stared back at him, fighting panic, for hearing the
words in her own language had made them suddenly real.
What was she doing here? To renounce the delights of the
world was nothing, when she walked already in a grey mist
of disillusion, but to renounce the gods who were the soul of
that world would be like renouncing air or sunlight; how
could she do it and still live?

Easily, her own despair answered her. *For have they not already
renounced you?* Oh, it was true, and her heart was breaking. She
blinked back angry tears.

Father Priscus waited. They were all waiting. Boring into
her back she could feel Gundohar's stare. *What does it matter
what I say?* she told herself then. *I have already cursed Wodan,
who was the father of my soul. He was first to break the bond!* She
drew breath in a gasp.

"*Abrenuncio.*" Her response was harsh as a raven's call.

"*Credis Patrem et Filium et Spiritum Sanctum ejusdem esse potestatis?*"
the priest continued, watching her narrowly.

Brunahild did not entirely understand the words, but she
recalled enough of her indoctrination to gather that he was
beginning the series of questions that summarized their be-
liefs, and remembered the answer.

"*Credo—*" she said in a dry voice as each question ended,
but it was not true. Her heart was dead and she believed in
nothing at all. Perhaps it was not quite honorable to let this
Christos think she belonged to him, but Wodan had not
struck her dead when she abjured him, and she knew *his*
power. Why should she fear the god of slaves?

"*Baptizo te?*" the priest asked at last, and Brunahild bowed
her head, more from exhaustion than reverence. There was
another question and Gudrun answered, "Sophia."

Sophia . . . Wisdom . . . Gudrun had suggested the name, and
Brunahild had laughed, for all her wisdom had been knocked
out of her by Gundohar's sword.

"Sophia." Father Priscus turned to Brunahild, scooped up
water from the font, and poured it over her head. It was only
a handful, but she felt as if she had stepped under a waterfall

whose roar drowned out the remainder of his words. Or perhaps what she heard was the roaring of the wind.

A cross was drawn on her forehead. There were more words, but they did not need a response. Brunahild kept on her feet, but she could not have answered; it was all she could do not to cry out in a grief that was all the sharper because she did not know what it was she had lost.

The next morning she was married according to the Christian fashion to Gundohar the king.

Gundohar emerged from the chapel with Brunahild on his arm and paused, blinking in the sudden blaze of light. At that moment it seemed to him only right and fitting that the sun should bless the day on which he had achieved his dream. The sunlight shone on the golden bands and patches of embroidery that ornamented his white dalmatic and edged his crimson cloak, as no doubt it was blazing from his crown, as it shone on the warriors of his comitatus, drawn up in two ranks before him.

They were tall, strong men, the flower of the Burgunds, but browner skins and darker heads showed among them where the sons of Roman legionaries braced the line. The war-bands of kings had always been a sanctuary for wandering warriors. Gundohar had gone a step farther, recruiting with intention among the colonii who had been settled here before the Romans gave the province into barbarian hands. It seemed to him that the blood of men who had conquered half the world could not but run the stronger, mixed with that of the native women who belonged to this soil in a way the Burgunds had yet to do.

They drew their swords, and sunlight flared blindingly from bared steel. "Health and long life to Gundohar and Brunahild!" came the shout as the blades swept upward. "All hail to the Burgund King and Queen!"

Brunahild had drawn her veil around her face; beneath the gleam of the gold band that held it he glimpsed the shadow of her hair, and felt a quiver deep in his gut, thinking of the night that would complete this radiant day. Her dalmatic glowed bloodred in the sunlight. It was of brocade from Constantinople, woven with eagles, hemmed and collared and belted with bands of gold and jewels.

"Come, my wife," he said softly. "Our people are waiting."

"Our people . . ." she repeated, falling into step beside him. "Well, I suppose I must now learn to be a queen."

"Hail to the King! Hail to the Queen!" they cried. "Wassail, wassail, wassail!"

Gundohar had never before faced his people without a moment of panic. But now, on the one occasion when every man was a king, for the first time he accepted their adulation completely, for today Brunahild had taken him as her husband and he had his victory.

Cheering rolled over them in deafening waves of sound as they approached the hall. It sounded as if the whole town was following the warriors who had closed in behind them, and half the countryside as well. Women peered past the shoulders of the warriors. Fathers had set their children on their shoulders to see. Maidens pelted them with flowers. An old soldier who had lost an eye in the wars watched them from under a broad hat, leaning on his staff. Borbetomagus might be at the limits of the Empire, but the Empire in all its polyphonic variety was here.

The smell of roasting meat drifted tantalizingly from the meadow. Although only the king's counselors and his most notable warriors would find seats in the hall, everyone would join in the feasting. The king had spared no expense to help his people remember the day he had made Brunahild his queen.

They mounted the steps to the broad porch. "Wait," he said to Brunahild. "I must speak to them." He held up his hand, grinning, until at last the crowd was still.

"Burgunds! Brothers of my tribe and blood! Children of the Eagles, and you, whose fathers were bred from this soil." He reached out as if he could embrace them all. "In my marriage I celebrate a union of peoples, and I root myself in this land. As we live here and learn how to till this soil, as we nourish our own children on its produce and feed it with our bones, so shall we all become one people, a new people who belong to this earth.

"A man calls his kindred to witness his marriage, and I claim you all as my kin today. Rejoice in the feast that has been prepared for you, and today may you all be as happy as I!"

He let his hand fall, grinning as the cheering redoubled in volume. In the old days, kings had lain with priestesses who carried the power of the Goddess, that the earth might be renewed. Brunahild was even more alien to this place than he, and yet he had always seen her as a goddess, whatever the priests might say. When they lay down together, through her he would gladly serve the land. He waved farewell to the people, and side by side, he and Brunahild entered the hall.

Gudrun, he thought proudly, had done a splendid job of preparing it. Swags of flowers and greenery twined the columns and hung from the rafters; there were flowers scattered along the tables, and she had found linen enough to cover them all. The scents here were even more compelling, and he remembered that he had been too tense to eat before the wedding. No wonder he felt light-headed now.

"Ah—there's Ordwini," he said to Brunahild. "A good man, and a dependable counselor, for all that he's so young. He came with me to court you. Beside him is Deorberht, son of Folco, a bit quarrelsome, but a powerful man."

"Introduce them to me later," Brunahild interrupted him. "These golden chains with which you have weighted me are heavy, and I must sit down soon or I will fall!"

Abruptly Gundohar remembered how ill she had been. "Forgive me—" he stammered. "Of course we will move on." Waving at the others, he hurried her the rest of the way to the dais. A whispered command sent one of the slaves for water. He assisted her to sit down and fold back her veil.

"You are right," he went on when she was settled. "There's no need for you to meet the entire pack today, though you'll learn to know all of them, perhaps better than you wish to, in time. All you need to do now is smile."

"A toast to our king and to his bride!" Godomar cried, and a hundred throats echoed him. Horns were raised with an eagerness compounded equally of thirst and loyalty.

"Good—now we can drink too," said Gundohar. "But we must praise Gudrun for arranging all this so well." He saw her sitting next to Godomar with Sigfrid beside her and beckoned. "And you must meet her husband, who has been away hunting since before we arrived. It is he who killed most of the deer our people are feasting on now."

Brunahild looked up from the piece of bread she was breaking with a tired smile.

"Sigfrid is the newest of my brothers and the best friend I have in the world—" he went on. Sigfrid was approaching warily; the king had not had a chance to tell him that Brunahild had given no sign that she suspected their deception.

"All honor to the Lady Brunahild, may she be happy as your queen—" Sigfrid said softly. Gudrun gave him a radiant smile.

"Gudrun's . . . husband. . . ." Brunahild said in a stifled voice. "Sigfrid . . ."

Gundohar looked at her sharply and realized that what little color Brunahild had was draining from her skin. She stared at Sigfrid as he had seen a warrior stare once at the man behind the spear that was piercing him, and Gundohar felt an awful uncertainty twist in his own gut.

"Have you . . . been married long?" said Brunahild. Gundohar pressed a goblet full of unwatered wine into her hand and she drank it down.

Gudrun blushed. "Only since the Spring Festival. Is there anything I can get you, Brunahild? Are you unwell?"

A faint shudder ran through Brunahild's body. For a moment the king thought she was going to faint or scream, then he saw her control clamp down. "Unwell? I was hit on the head, you know," she said conversationally. "And at times I am still a little confused. Sigfrid is married to Gudrun and Brunahild is wed to Gundohar. Why should that seem strange?" Her breath caught. "Well, let me be. I am sure that I will understand in time." She cast another look at Sigfrid, and Gundohar saw his face grow almost as pale as hers, but he did not reply.

"Sit down, sister," the king said hastily as people around

them began to stare, and Sigfrid took her hand and pulled her away.

They were bringing in the meat now, with platters of bread and bowls of honied sweetmeats from Rome. The roar of conversation rose as the people began to feed. Brunahild sat frowning, but said no more, and Gundohar began to hope they could get through this without a scene

But though she drank whenever a toast was offered, Brunahild ate nothing at all.

> *"Behold the wedding torches blazing,*
> *The feast is finished, maidens scatter flowers;*
> *The bride at whom the folk are gazing,*
> *Outshines them as the sun outshines the fires. . . .*
> *Luck to the groom, luck to the bride—*
> *Long life and love with you abide!"*

Brunahild strode down the passageway, a gaggle of high-born Burgund women hurrying after her. Mixed voices echoed hollow behind them, a little slurred, for the wedding guests had drunk deeply before they decided it was time to put the bridal couple to bed.

"You go too quickly," one of the women whispered, panting, "wait for me!"

"See how high her color rises!" answered another. "It is a good sign when the bride hastens to her bedchamber so eagerly."

My face is flushed with rage, not lust! thought Brunahild, glaring. *Cannot they see?* At least the lassitude that had enthralled her since Gundohar had won their combat had lifted—if Gundohar had indeed won! *Sigfrid . . . here . . . and married to Gudrun. . . .* What could it mean? Ever since she had seen him, her head had been spinning.

"A good sign for Gundohar!" They all laughed.

She felt her color flare even higher and wished that when they put her into the silken bedgown and fur-lined mantle they had not taken away her veil. Did they think she could not hear?

> *"The bed is made, the cup is waiting,*
> *And now the eager groom the warriors bring*
> *Like a stallion to his mating,*
> *Beholding his domain he is a king!*
> *Luck to the groom, luck to the bride—*
> *Long life and love with you abide!"*

Brunahild forced herself to slow. It had not occurred to her that her haste could be construed as eagerness; she had only wanted to get out of that hall. Gudrun walked silently beside her. From time to time Brunahild could feel her troubled glance but she refused to meet her eyes.

She had thought Gudrun at least was her friend. She had trusted her.

The palace was built villa-style around a central courtyard. Its main buildings formed a square, though other wings and courts had been built onto it. From across the court she could hear men's laughter. She realized that she was hurrying again. She was eager, but not for Gundohar's embrace. When she got him alone he would have to answer her!

> *"The gods of life their gifts are giving,*
> *Wise Fricca weaves your lives in harmony,*
> *Donar will defend the living,*
> *And Fro and Froja give fertility.*
> *Luck to the groom, luck to the bride—*
> *Long life and love with you abide!"*

Why are they calling on the old gods to bless me? Don't they know I have abjured them? She fought the impulse to cry out that there would be no blessing on this union, that their king had married a woman who was cursed by the gods.

She slowed, seeing the door before her, and at that moment Gundohar himself came around the corner, supported by Godomar and Ordwini. He halted as he saw her, blinking owlishly, and his men began to cheer. With conscious dignity the king let go of his friends and pulled his mantle straight again. His face had grown radiant at the sight of her—*like a*

puppy hoping for a bone! she thought bitterly. Had he forgotten
Sigfrid? Had the drink he had downed washed all memory
away? *He must know that he is more likely to get blows than caresses
from me!*

"Brunahild," Gudrun said softly behind her. "Something is
troubling you, I know it—is there anything—"

Brunahild turned on her. "There is nothing right in all the
world, but until I know if you are as much a victim as I or
my enemy, I would accept the help of any woman in Middle
Earth before I would take it from you!"

Gudrun recoiled, paling, and the other women surged past
her.

"All hail to the bride! All hail to the groom!" shouted their
attendants. "There's the bed, let them go into it together!"

"Strip them!" "To bed with them!" Those cries came mostly
from the men, with other advice, more explicit and obscene.

Brunahild took a swift step forward. "My lord, I am not a
mare to be mounted before witnesses to be sure of the blood-
line. We will go alone into that chamber or I will not go at
all!" Some of the men started to laugh, but her glare quelled
them. The color rose and fell in Gundohar's face and he took
her hand.

"My wife has spoken truly," he said. "You may wish us well
from the other side of those doors!"

But it was Brunahild who led him into the room. She heard
the great doors creak closed behind them and let go of his
hand. Outside, they were singing still.

> *"The doors are shut and you are bedded,*
> *We leave you now with blessings and with song,*
> *May bliss be yours while you are wedded,*
> *And may your lives be prosperous and long—*
> *Luck to the groom, luck to the bride—*
> *Long life and love with you abide!"*

"Love and luck?" said Brunahild as the music dissolved into
laughter. "I do not think so—"

"Are you weary?" he asked. He poured wine from a flagon

into a golden goblet and offered it to her. "Here is a posset my mother made for us. . . ."

Her nostrils flared, recognizing the scent of the herbs mixed into the wine. "Drink it yourself," she said bitterly, "if you have not already had as much as you may carry, and much good may it do you! I need none of your mother's witcheries to heat my blood!"

He looked up at her, hope lighting in his eyes, and she laughed.

"Wrath burns hotter than passion, Gundohar. And unless your bard's tongue can frame a better tale for me than any I have heard so far, that is all you will get from me!"

"Brunahild, you are my wife—" he swallowed.

She stared at him, hugging her arms as if she were cold. "Your wife . . ." she repeated. "To win in battle, and to the victor went the prize. But were you the victor, Gundohar?"

"What do you mean?" He set down the goblet and pulled at the neck of his nightrobe until his upper arm was bared. "There is the mark where your sword bit me. What more proof do you need?"

"If I had proof, do you think I would be standing here? I know only that somehow I have been betrayed. Of all the world's warriors, only Sigfrid Fafnarsbane had the power to overcome me. When you woke me in that cave I thought I must have been mistaken. But now I see Sigfrid, here, lying with your sister and serving you. I have no proof, but I know that somewhere there has been treachery. I would be shrieking to the rooftops if I knew how it had been done." She threw off the constricting folds of her mantle and began to stride about the room.

"But why should seeing Sigfrid enrage you?" stammered Gundohar.

"Because I know him!" she whirled.

Gundohar recoiled. "Everyone in the valley of the Rhenus knows him," he began. Then, as he looked at her, his eyes widened. "Holy Frowe," he whispered, "you are so beautiful! Now you are the Walkyrja once more!"

"Walkyrja enough to kill you, Burgund king, if I were certain that you had caused my shame . . ." she hissed. "I spared your life, I never harmed you. Why did you do it, Gundohar?"

"I have made you queen of a great people, Brunahild." He pulled himself together. "Is that so ill a thing? All that I have is yours now, all my wealth, my power."

"And Sigfrid's wealth?" she answered. "Is that yours as well, or does it belong to Gudrun?"

"Why should you grudge my sister her happiness? I gave her to a man she could love, and hoped to have the same joy in you." He spoke with a fragile dignity. If she had not been enraged by her own pain, Brunahild could have pitied him. "I have loved you since first I set eyes upon you four years ago."

"Gundohar, Gundohar . . ." She shook her head with a sigh. "You are a fool!"

"To love you?" He pulled his mantle back over his shoulders, trying to resume his dignity. With his thin neck and his rumpled fair hair, he looked like some storm-battered bird.

"For that, certainly, but even more for having told me so. Now I know my power."

"I would be a fool to think that I could hide it from you—" The king shrugged and looked away. "But there is more at stake here than our feelings. Our marriage seals a treaty. Even if the Christian vows you swore this morning mean nothing to you, you must hold by the promises you made before your people and their gods. You agreed to be a true and faithful wife to me—"

"I agreed to wed the man who could overcome me in battle," Brunahild said slowly. "Are you he?"

"I fought you—" he responded. "I was waiting when you came to your senses in that cave. . . ."

She grinned mirthlessly, and then, very deliberately, pulled off her silken gown. She saw his cheeks flame as he glimpsed her body. She stood for a moment, letting him look at her, knowing that motherhood, which had filled out her breasts and hips without thickening her waist, had at last given her a figure that a man might view with desire.

"Brunahild . . ." he whispered, "please. . . ."

"If you defeated me once," she said sweetly, "surely you can do so again. Fight me, Gundohar. If you can wrestle me down upon that bed, then you will have earned the right to take me there."

He had the sense to throw off his mantle, but as Gundohar moved toward her, Brunahild thought he would have done better to remove his robe as well; perhaps the contact of flesh to flesh might even have awakened some flicker of desire. Unencumbered, she could take full advantage of her natural agility. His face gave away the moment when he mustered the resolve to reach for her; as he moved she ducked and whirled, grabbed his arm and pulled. He reeled, recovered, grabbed for her again.

Brunahild laughed. They had trained all the girls in wrestling, when she studied among the Walkyriun. She wondered suddenly if the art of grappling with larger and stronger opponents was taught to the sons of kings.

But he was trying. Grunting, he lunged at her, a callused hand closed on her wrist; she jerked free and leaped away. Her heart was pounding and her head spun. When she challenged him, she had forgotten all those weeks spent lying still. Quick she might be, but she was out of condition as well. She would have to finish this soon.

"Come, Gundohar, come to my arms!" she cried. Like a lover he turned to her, arms opening wide. And in that moment she grasped one wrist, and with a foot hooked under his heel brought him down.

The floor was of stone; for an instant he lay breathless. It was time enough for her to snatch up the cord that had tied her gown and loop it around his wrists. In another moment she had fastened the cord to the foot of the bedstead. As he began to come around she wound her gown around his feet and made them fast with the sleeves.

Then she sat back, gasping with laughter, or perhaps it was tears.

"So, my little king!" she crowed breathlessly, "how do you like your marriage bed?"

He stared at her. "You can't mean to leave me here?"

She got to her feet and wrapped her discarded mantle

around her naked body, for suddenly she was cold. "Wait and see . . ."

And wait he did, through the long hours of that wedding night, while the lamps burned low and the distant challenge of the changing watches echoed from beyond the garden. Brunahild sat huddled on a bench by the window, thinking many thoughts as she watched the wheeling stars. But all she could see in them was the brightness of Sigfrid's eyes.

A wind was rustling in the treetops. Once she would have listened for the voice of the god, but now it was only noise. Moonlight set cloaked shadows flickering beneath the trees; for a moment she thought someone in a broad hat was looking up at her window. But Gundohar's men patrolled the palace, and the gate was guarded. There was no way anyone could be there.

Presently she dozed with her head on her arms. In her dreams someone was calling her. She tried to answer, but she could only say Sigfrid's name.

A little before dawn, she roused and took up the little knife that had been set on the tray of food.

"What is it?" Gundohar saw the blade gleam, and sighed. "Do you mean to kill me? That at least would be kind."

"Do you think I have not considered it? And to kill myself after? But that would be too easy. I will have answers before I die."

She laughed mirthlessly and freed him.

"Get up, Gundohar. As you pointed out to me, I have sworn vows," she said quietly, "and I have no mind to break the treaty that means so much to your people and to my own. But from now on we should understand each other. Our marriage is for the daylight only. I will make no accusations, and while the sun shines, I will play the part of your wife and queen as well as I can. But the price of my silence is this—I sleep alone."

Chapter Seven

A Conflict of Dragons

Provincia Belgica Prima
Harvest Moon, A.D. 423

"Airmanareik, noblest of Amalings,
Great king of Goths, who got much glory,
Fought many folk and fed his people,
Lost land and life—"

Gundohar plucked another chord on his harp, seeking the right words to finish the line. In the time of Airmanareik the Goths had been a united people, ruling from the Scythian to the northern seas, with many other tribes under their sway. And yet in a few short years the invading Huns had scattered them. In those days, the Burgunds had still lived in the east themselves. The stories had migrated with them, and his foster mother had brought him up on tales of Airmanareik's tragic end.

"Lost land and life to Hunnish horse-lords. . . ." he nodded, and began to work out the next line.

The room was full of sunlight, though the king hardly noticed, wrapped in the making of his lay. They called it his workroom, as large as the royal bedchamber that adjoined it, but in truth it was his sanctuary. Shelves set against the dull red painted walls overflowed with scrolls of Latin verses; weapons leaned against the door frames. Few were aware that

126

the bed beside it was where the king had spent his nights ever since his marriage to Brunahild three years before.

"Fierce to his foes and to the faithless—" Gundohar sang. But how could he convey the danger of that fury, that had led the king to order the wife of a retainer who had betrayed him trampled to death by horses? Even in a people who lived for revenge the deed had inspired horror. Divided, the Goths were no match for the invading hordes, and Airmanareik had sacrificed himself to his gods in a final and fruitless attempt to save his people. Gundohar's ambitions for the Burgunds were more modest, but there was something in him that resonated both to the greatness and the grief of the Gothic king.

He had been working on these verses for several weeks now. It was not often he could retreat here, but it was a solace to know that his harp awaited him, a mistress that could never be untrue. *"Betrayed by trampled traitors' kin. . . ."* he plucked another chord.

A rapping on the door knocked the next words out of his memory. He swore, jerked from legend back to history, as Ordwini thrust open the door.

"My lord—the Emperor Honorius is dead of dropsy, and there is civil war in Rome!"

Other men were jostling in behind him. The king set his harp aside and got to his feet as what appeared to be half his Council pushed in.

"Silence!" A bard's training had some uses—at least he could quiet a room. "Who brought the message?" The throng shifted to permit Father Priscus, followed by an exhausted young man with the shaven pate of a cleric, to come into the room.

"This is Brother Paulus," the priest began, rather like a hen whose chick has performed some prodigy. Gundohar ignored him.

"Is the message written? Give it to me." He held out his hand. This was one of those moments when his support for the churchmen proved its worth. These days, information travelled faster, and more reliably, through the Church than it did through the Legions. He looked up at Brother Paulus. "Did you come from Rome yourself with this news?"

"No, my lord, only from Rhaetia. I was told that the Patrician, Castinus, has declared for Joannes, the Primicerius Notariorum. There is fighting in the City already, lord, and no one knows what the outcome will be."

"Is Galla Placidia still in Constantinople?" asked Ordwini. "Her little son is the Emperor's nephew. He should be next heir, I believe, and that lady is not one to see her offspring passed by!"

"They are, and the Emperor of the East has recognized the claim of little Valentinian to Rome, and is supporting her," the cleric replied.

"It will take them some time to muster the forces she'll need to win Rome," Deorberht said thoughtfully.

"What about the provinces," Gundohar asked then. "Have they declared for the House of Theodosius, or for this glorified clerk, Joannes?"

There was a short and interested silence.

"Perhaps Belgica Prima needs some help in deciding which way to jump," said Godomar, beginning to grin.

"Maybe the new emperor will need assistance in collecting the taxes." Now Ordwini was grinning too.

"And if they resist?" asked one of the others.

"It has been a *long* time since my blade saw battle. I would not have it rust away," Ordwini replied.

Father Priscus was staring from one to another with dawning comprehension. "My sons, my sons, what are you thinking of? You are here to keep the peace, not make war!"

Gundohar raised one eyebrow. Why was the priest so surprised? He had ministered to the Burgunds for nigh on twenty years. Surely he should know them by now. "Good father, we must do our duty as feoderati; we must defend the emperor."

Despite his love for the old legends, Gundohar would have been happy enough to let his own sword hang on the wall. But in three years it had come to him that one did not win a Walkyrja with harpsong. Brunahild had seen him fight only twice, when he faced her in the ring, and on that dreadful day when they battled the Alamanni on the Longstone field. Perhaps she would warm to him if he led a victorious army.

It was a chance at least. It was the only thing he had not yet tried.

"Which emperor are we defending, by the way," asked Godomar.

"Oh—the little Theodosian, I think—Honorius' sister-son." Rome might be more inclined to leave its frontiers to their own devices if the emperor were a child.

"Hurrah!" cried Godomar. "The Gundwurm goes to war!"

Brunahild sat in the sunny courtyard off the south wing of the palace, her spindle in her hand. Her attendants were still amazed that a warrior-woman could spin so well, but she had proved herself able to spin more swiftly and evenly than any of them.

On sunny days she would sit with the others, listening with half an ear to their chatter and intervening when necessary with a word or a frown. Brunahild was a raven no longer, but she still wore dark colors. Now she was a black dove, perhaps, among the white and grey. Anyone who had observed a dovecote knew that they could be vicious to their own kind.

It had not taken her long to realize that the women's half of the royal household was not so different from the House of Maidens among the Walkyriun. The girls were prone to the same petty jealousies and bickering. Besides the slaves and women with special skills, the queens were served by girls of good family sent to the royal household to bolster their kindreds' positions by forming friendships and alliances. They would marry to serve their families, but what father would refuse an up-and-coming young warrior who had become enamored of his daughter while they both were serving in the high king's hall? Those who had given their favors too freely went to old Grimahild for potions, and the lovelorn wept on Gudrun's shoulder. The girls knew better than to lay their troubles before Gundohar's sharp-tongued queen.

But as the women spun, they gossiped, and as they talked, Brunahild sifted their words. She told Gundohar what she learned each evening, when he came to bid her an unhappy good-night before retiring to his room.

She had quickly disabused the king of any idea that her concern grew out of fondness. One day he would suffer as she suffered, but not until she had found out exactly how he had tricked her. And when he did, it would be her doing, not some sordid palace intrigue, that brought him down.

She looked up as one of the maidservants appeared in the doorway.

"War—" Her first cry silenced the chatter. "The men are going to war!" The maidservant gulped as more than a dozen pairs of eyes turned her way.

"Foolish child, what have you heard?" Brunahild rose, the spindle like a weapon in her hand.

"A messenger came to the king. I heard them talking when I brought wine. The emperor is dead and the men are going to fight in Gaul!"

"No!" cried little Gunna, newly betrothed to one of Gundohar's men. She was echoed by a chorus of lamentation.

"Cease your wailing—your men won't thank you for it!" snapped Brunahild. "They'll ride off quite cheerfully to fight, and never give a thought to you, worrying at home."

"But he may be killed—" whimpered Gunna.

"Would you rather serve a live coward or remember that you were loved by a hero?" asked the queen. *As I do,* the familiar thought began, but that was not quite true. This decision to go to war could only have come from Gundohar. The outcry had subsided to a buzz of excitement. Brunahild turned, and saw Gudrun standing like a heart-shot doe, her spindle dangling from her hand. A quick step brought her to the other woman's side.

"Sit down," she hissed. "You set a bad example for these silly girls. And you, at least, have no cause for fear. This once I will prophesy—whoever else lives or dies, Sigfrid will come home to you unharmed."

One of the women, overhearing, made the horn-sign against evil, and the queen suppressed a smile. The only spell here was the one she had worked on Sigfrid so long ago, to keep him from every harm. If she had not known that, would she, too, have worried? She still felt the ache of loss when she saw him, even in the distance, or when she heard him calling to one of the other men.

Only the size of the royal household made it possible to bear her pain. Sigfrid spent his time with the men in the feasting hall or with Gudrun in their quarters. They were not thrown constantly together as they would have been in the old days, when everyone lived and ate and slept in the same long hall. But Brunahild still knew when Sigfrid was taking Gudrun in his arms.

One of Gundohar's retainers appeared in the doorway, and the women began to flutter once more. "My lady, the king would speak with you—" He stepped aside, and she saw Gundohar, his hair, as usual, all on end. Her women watched, avid as birds, as he came to her.

"My dark lady," he said softly, "sitting there like one of the Norns. Will you wind a fortunate wyrd for me?"

"Is that what you came here to say to me?"

Gundohar sighed. Then he straightened, very much aware of his audience.

"Brunahild, Queen of the Burgunds, the emperor of the Romans is dead and there is civil war. As feoderates, we must support the rightful heir. We ride, therefore, to the cities of Belgica Prima, to remind them where lies their loyalty."

To remind them where lies their treasure, more likely, thought Brunahild, but she understood him.

"My blessing upon your arms and your cause," she said formally. "May you return victorious."

"I must not leave my kingdom without a ruler," Gundohar went on. "I ask you therefore, lady, if you will watch over my people? Ostrofrid the lawspeaker and Heribard of the Council will advise you, but in you I will vest the power."

Brunahild looked up at him, touched, in spite of herself, by his trust in her. It proved, she supposed, that she had lived up to her part of the pact between them.

"My husband," she said more gently, "I will guard them for you gladly, and you will find the land no less prosperous than you left it when you return."

At her tone his color heightened, but he knew better than

to presume. He took a deep breath and stepped back, compelling attention with his gaze.

"My lords, and all you women of noble kin. I call you to witness that I have vested the authority of the *hendinos* in Brunahild, Lady of the Burgunds, until I shall return. . . ."

Grani lifted his head, nostrils flaring, and pulled at the bridle. The army of the Burgunds was plodding along the road by the river, but Sigfrid could smell the same clean scents of forest and meadow that had excited the horse. The army had marched northward through the gorge of the Rhenus until they came to its confluence with the Mosella. For three days now they had been winding westward through the hills toward the rich lands of the province of Belgica.

He grinned suddenly, loosened the rein, and the horse leaped forward. Sigfrid's long legs tightened around Grani's barrel as powerful muscles bunched and released. Trees blurred and Sigfrid slitted his eyes as the horse gained speed.

"Hai, Wind-racer," he whispered into the whipping mane, "run, run on, and leave all my troubles behind!"

When the horse slackened speed, the army was far behind. Sigfrid straightened, reining the animal in, and though Grani tossed his head, he slowed to a walk. Sigfrid looked around him, drinking in the solitude with all his senses. Green light filtered through the beeches. He could hear the gentle murmur of the Mosella nearby. Something rustled in the undergrowth, probably a bird. *Ah, little sister,* he thought, *do you have a word for me?* It had been a very long time since he had tried to understand the speech of the birds.

Sigfrid took a deep breath. He had not known he was escaping from his troubles until he had broken free. But why should he feel so happy? He had left behind him a wife so dear that even thinking of her brought a sweet tension to his loins, and a life spent in hunting and training the young men of the royal household in the use of arms.

It was, by any standards, an ideal existence, marred only by the need, which had become habitual, to avoid Brunahild.

But it was only now, when he could fill his lungs with the

clean wind, that he understood that what he had been missing was freedom. He tipped his head back and gazed up through the branches at the boundless clarity of the sky. Wolves, even with a secure den and good hunting, would leave their home range to wander far afield. Sigfrid was beginning to understand why. He needed new sights and smells and sounds as a deer needs salt; and perhaps he needed to risk his life in order to feel fully alive once more.

He heard another horse coming and turned, the lance coming up unbidden to point down the path. Sigfrid swung it back to rest as the rider appeared and he recognized young Gislahar.

"There you are!" The boy looked around him curiously. "Well, it looks peaceful enough. We wondered if the horse had run away with you, or if you had sensed some danger—"

Sigfrid laughed. The king's youngest brother had been one of his most faithful pupils, and was shaping well.

"Only an open road and horse that wanted to run!"

"I never realized that an army marched so slowly," said Gislahar thoughtfully. He had the same wispy fair hair and high-bridged nose as the rest of his family, but at twelve, he had yet to grow into his bones. "The line of helmets is like a great serpent crawling along the riverside."

"Thus the Gundwurm goes to battle—" Sigfrid smiled. "This is only a raiding party, less than a thousand. The entire army would come to three times that number."

"Well, I am glad we do not have to wait for *them* to pass!" said the boy. "How long, do you think, before there's fighting?"

"Are you so eager, lad, to see blood spilled?"

Gislahar blushed and looked away. "I am eager to know if I have the courage to face a foe . . ." he said slowly.

"Never doubt it," Sigfrid answered him. "Only a fool goes into a fight without wondering if this time he will fall. Fear gives a man the edge he needs to stay alive!" He remembered how anxious he had been when he faced Heming on the road to Fafnar's lair.

Gislahar's face cleared. They could hear the sounds of the approaching army now, and the boy turned his horse to see.

But I must be a fool now, thought Sigfrid, watching him. *It has been a long time since the prospect of battle stirred any fear in me at all. I wonder why?*

Sunlight glinted on metal and Gislahar kicked his horse into a canter and started toward them. Grani pricked his ears, and Sigfrid lifted the rein to let him follow. As they brushed past the bushes something flapped heavily upward, and Sigfrid saw that it had not been one of the lesser kindred after all, but a raven, that cawed once in greeting, and flew westward, as if to show him the way.

After a week's further travel, during which parties of warriors descended on several hapless villas and levied taxes the barbarian way, the Burgunds came to the Imperial city of Augusta Treverorum, or Treveri, as it had become in the common tongue.

The city was a rich prize, although it had been many years since any emperor had actually stayed in the Imperial residence there. Of more importance to its inhabitants were the healing baths and the arena, the shops and the slave-staffed woolen mills. What interested the Burgunds, however, were the Imperial mint and the depot, where the taxes, whether collected in coin or in kind, were held until they could be transferred to Rome.

The Romans were not unaware of their danger. Gundohar's hopes for a swift descent upon the city and an easy victory had been dashed when the *dux* of the Moguntiacensis district mustered the closest regiment of *milites* to oppose them. A thousand men now waited between the Burgunds and Treveri, whose riches grew greater in anticipation with every hour.

The Burgunds camped among the harvested vineyards, feeding their campfires with the stalks of trampled vines. They could see the fires of the Romans on the plain below, almost as numerous and far more regular; a neat line of lights delineating the human barrier that had planted itself between the barbarians and the town.

The king made his way from fire to fire, trying not to wonder how many of these men would still be hale and laughing this time tomorrow. At Godo's campfire, men were shouting out a bawdy song and refilling their drinking horns from amphorae of looted wine. At Ordwini's, they were boasting of the deeds that they would do. Dour Laidrad had brought his priest, who was holding mass for the men. Some of the warriors sat silent, thinking of those they had left behind, but most of them seemed to be in high good humor, eager for the fray.

Gundohar found it all profoundly depressing. It made it worse to know that this time it was his own doing that they were here. At moments such as this he missed Hagano's company. Any warrior of his comitatus would have been honored to accompany him, but with his men he must preserve the illusion of a courageous leader. To whom did he dare to reveal his hopes, and more important, his doubts, his fears? Then he remembered that he did have another brother, and sent his man Helmnot for Sigfrid.

He waited, sitting on a ruined wall, while first one and then another returned to tell him that Sigfrid was nowhere to be found. At the next campfire some of the men were discussing what gods should be invoked for war.

"The priests say that Jehovah is a god of battles," said Eleuthir, young and earnest. "He is the god we must pray to now. Constantinus the emperor rode to war beneath the sign of the Cross."

"That's not the way I heard it," Gamalo replied. "Christos is a peace-god who tells you to turn the other cheek when someone hurts you. What use is that to a warrior? Better call on the old gods when you're fighting, and let the women pray to the Crucified One." Of Gundohar's guard, he was the most experienced.

"But even then you have choices," said Trogus the half-Goth, laughing. "Will you make your offerings to Donar, or to Wodan, or Tiw?"

"Why not all three?" said someone, and the others laughed. "*They* aren't jealous of each other's worshippers!"

"Donar's a good defender against trolls and other unholy wights," said Gamalo. "But Tiw gives victory."

"Tiw One-hand gives *justice*," corrected his friend. "Wodan awards victory."

"When it pleases him—and who knows what will please that one?"

Who knows, indeed? thought Gundohar.

No man had ever been able to say that Wodan served anyone's purposes but his own. While a man's goals coincided with those of the god, he might prosper, but he should not delude himself that the god was helping him out of love. In the old days, Gundohar had heard, men counted the lordship of the gods as belonging to Tiw, but there was a great war, and the followers of Wodan sacrificed the priests of Tiw in their own holy groves.

Now, Wodan is a god for warriors and for the bards who sing of their deeds, and a god of kings . . . I am two out of three of those things, but I have never dared to pray to him . . . Perhaps I should learn—God knows, I need some god to help me now! But what is the god's purpose for the Burgunds? Is what I am doing here Wodan's will?

"My lord?"

Gundohar whirled. Sigfrid stood beside him, as if he had materialized from the shadows. The king gripped the other man's shoulder, studying that high-boned face, all planes and shadow in the firelight.

"Brother—" he said hoarsely. "Will you not call me brother, even now? Tomorrow morning we may mingle our lifeblood down there!"

"Come," the wolf-eyes met his. "Walk with me, and let us see what counsel the night may bring."

Gundohar allowed himself to be led away. He was shivering, though the night was not really cold. The moon was a little past the full, just now beginning to clear the tops of the trees. Its light gave a wavering, uncertain appearance to men and carts and dimmed the campfires. In the distance, the walls of Treveri glimmered like a mirage.

"What have I done?" he whispered, gazing down at them. "What are we doing here? This is like a bad dream—"

"The city is real enough," said Sigfrid quietly. "I have been down there."

"You passed through the Roman lines?" Gundohar stared at him and Sigfrid grinned.

"Like a shadow. They never knew I was there. The soldiers all speak Gaulish, and I do not know much of that tongue, but I think they are settled on lands hereabouts—they spoke of getting back to their farms. The officers talked Latin, and wondered if you could be bought off without a battle. They have declared for Joannes, and fear they may need their forces to fight for him."

"We can be bought, but not until we have fought them," said Gundohar bitterly. "It is an ancient game, and the Romans know the rules as well as we. If we win, it will drive up the price they must pay to make us go home again. But that is not why my men are singing around their campfires. They want to fight, can't you hear them? They would seek battle now even if there were no chance of booty at all!"

"What are you afraid of?" Sigfrid asked curiously. "The worst you can do is die."

Gundohar sighed, understanding now why he had wanted the other man's company. Sigfrid shared his most shameful secret. No one else would have dared to ask him that question, and he needed an answer, not for the other man's sake, but for his own.

"Death does not frighten me, or at least I do not think so, though there are nights when I lie awake, seeing in my mind all the ways that it could come. What frightens me more is failure. I am afraid that I will make a fool of myself down there, and men will laugh at me. A king cannot afford to be the butt of laughter, Sigfrid—" He bit his lip. *As I would be if folk knew how things stand between me and Brunahild. . . .*

"You know too many old stories, and you worry too much about what the bards will make of your deeds. You will fight well enough when their swords seek your life," answered Sigfrid. "You did before, as I have heard."

"That's true—" Gundohar felt some of the tension leave

him. "I have been thinking like a bard. It is time to think like a king."

"Look, and you shall see an omen that will make you hope again—" the other man said then. Metal scraped softly as he unsheathed his sword. In the moonlight Gram blazed silver, where any other weapon would have shown only a dull gleam. Gundohar had always suspected that the story of its making would make a bard's tale, but Sigfrid would say only that it had been reforged from the pieces of his father's broken blade.

"This is star steel, made from metal that fell from heaven, wrought and welded by the wise god's spells. Look now—" He lifted the weapon, and breathed out along the blade. Then he angled it to catch the light of the moon.

Gundohar stared, for Sigfrid's breath had beaded along the center of the sword, and suddenly he could see the wavy shape of a serpent glimmering there.

"This is the moonsnake," Sigfrid said softly. "How can the Burgunds lose when there is a gundwurm concealed within my sword that will fight for you?"

Gundohar looked from the blade to the features of the man who held it, half-lit by the moon like the face of a god on some old coin. He had wanted a hero, and here he was, this man of magic. But his eyes were shadowed, unreadable. Would the king ever fathom all of Sigfrid's mysteries?

"Guard my back, brother, in tomorrow's battle," he said hoarsely. There was no god he dared rely on, but he trusted this creature of silver and shadow that stood by his side. "With you behind me, I will not fail."

The morning mist had burned off early, lifted by the gentle breeze that was fluttering the folds of the Gundwurm banner. Overhead, the sky was a clear, pale autumn blue. In the sunlight, the moisture that still clung to the grass shone like silver; light sparked from helms and glinted from spear points and mail, glittered on the gold of the coiled serpent worked upon the crimson cloth of the Burgund standard. It was a good morning for fighting, thought Sigfrid, taking a deep breath of the crisp air.

Roman clarions had blared at the dawning, summoning the *milites* to battle array. They stood now, divided into three blocks in neat lines behind their brightly painted shields. The first rank seemed to be regular foot soldiers, with cuirasses of molded rawhide over dull red tunics and breeches. Behind them he could see some unarmored infantry and archers in light-colored tunics with regimental patches sewn on the skirts and at the shoulders, and breeches of fawn or brown.

"Last night I saw horses in their encampment," he said to Gundohar. "Watch out for that patch of woods—I think that's where they've hidden their cavalry."

The king nodded, the golden boar on the crest of his span-genhelm glinting balefully. "I've put Ordwini with our horsemen on the slope, ready to hit them from the side. Where do you think we should aim the point of the wedge?"

Sigfrid shrugged. The Romani warriors had a depressing uniformity. "Between the center block and the one on the right, I suppose—men tend to veer toward their shield side in battle anyhow, and we'll hit more of them as we go in that way."

"Look!" Gundohar's voice shook as he pointed. A little procession was making its way to the knoll behind the Roman line—white-cloaked officers in glittering armor, and behind them, a standard-bearer carrying something that coiled and straightened in the sun. "They have a Gundwurm too!"

"They call it Draco," said one of the others. "It has a cloth body attached to the silver head to catch the wind. It is pretty, but ours has tasted more blood over the years!"

"It will be a battle of dragons, then," the king's voice steadied. "It appears that they are ready for us. What clearer invitation do we need?" If the Burgunds could break the Roman line with the first charge, the rest would be easy.

The men began to cheer. From behind them came the hollow boom as swordhilts beat against the backs of shields. Sigfrid's nostrils flared as he picked up the rank musk of excitement and sharper scent of fear.

"Ho, Romani! Are you lonely?" cried Godomar, who had been given the honor of pointing the wedge. "Get ready to receive us—we will make you women, you have only to turn around!"

"*Spear-shafts beat a Burgund shield-song*," sang the king. Sigfrid grinned, knowing that Gundohar would be all right now that he had started chanting poetry.

> "*Heroes, hear! To battle hasten!*
> *Gaulish gore-crows soon will gather,*
> *Feed on flesh of Burgunds' foemen!*"

Gundohar lifted his spear and the horns began their bellowing. A quiver ran through the massed warriors; Sigfrid had seen just such a ripple stir the pelts of a waiting wolf pack before they closed in on a stag. Without need for an order, the Burgunds started down the hill.

Sigfrid moved with the others, shoulder to shoulder. The scent of battle lust was all around him, mixed with the pungence of crushed grass. He blinked, feeling his lips draw back over his teeth as individual awareness began to leave him, and fought to keep control. They went faster, battle-horns blaring. Shouted insults became an incoherent howling. Consciousness narrowed to the balance of spear and shield, the men to either side. They were running now.

The pale blobs beneath the Roman helms became faces. Godomar wrenched a throwing axe from his belt, and, roaring, flung it. The Burgund wedge rippled as others did the same. The men behind the Romans' first line stirred, and the air darkened as a swarm of lead-weighted darts arced upward. Burgunds screamed and fell as the *martiobarbuli* pierced them, but the momentum of the wedge was too great to be stopped now.

They were almost on them. Spears were braced and shields shifted into position. Screaming, the Burgunds smashed against the Roman shields.

Sigfrid jerked his spear from a Roman's gut and straightened as the man reeled backward. The impetus of the charge had carried them several spear lengths past the original Roman line, whose center was broken, but the blocks of men to either side were still holding, beginning to swing around to take the Burgund wedge in the rear. For the moment, the only enemies around him were writhing on the grass. He sucked in breath and looked for Gundohar.

A few paces away a knot of men struggled; he saw the gilded boar-crest gleam from the midst of them, the flare as a Roman behind it swung up his sword. Sigfrid started to run, but the blade was already descending; he balanced a moment, swung and released his spear, and started running again. The spear flew before him—doom's messenger—entered the Roman's body just above the armhole of his leather cuirass and drilled through.

The momentum of the legionary's sword continued, but the impact of the spear knocked him sideways, and the blade sliced outward to take one of his fellows in the neck as the man went down. Then Sigfrid's sword was following his spear, the star steel slicing through leather and meat and bone. Red blood sprayed as he pulled it out, scythed down the next man, knocked another aside with his shield, and reached Gundohar's side.

"It's me, brother," said Sigfrid quickly. "Keep your shield up and I'll guard your back." The king's eyes were unfocused, but at the words some sense came back into them. He nodded and Sigfrid took up position behind him.

The battle seethed around them. A shield thrust toward him; for a moment he saw it clearly, light blue with a red rim and dark green center and some kind of animal painted above. Then it shifted to let the sword through, but Sigfrid was faster; Gram swept the blade aside and cut through the Roman's arm.

He heard metal clash and knew that Gundohar was at work behind him. Two more of their men struggled toward them; now they were a tight square. Sigfrid grinned, leaping out to strike and back to guard again. More warriors joined them; the melee was curdling into knots of struggling fighters. The nearest Romans pulled back, he saw them beginning to reestablish formation.

"Charge! Don't let them form a line—" he yelled.

A dozen throats took up the cry. They started toward the knot of Romans as if they were a single being, and this time Sigfrid could not separate himself from the others. Only with the wolves had he felt this unity. As they struck the enemy, all sense of self departed, and the sound that ripped from his throat was a true wolf's howl.

Sigfrid returned to self-awareness slowly, as if from the depths of a dark pool. Once more he was alone, but this time there were many more dead around him, and it was late afternoon. He stank of blood, but though his muscles ached, none of it seemed to be his own. His shield had been hacked to fragments. With an effort of will, he forced his fingers to let go of the grip and tossed it away.

He could see the hilltop from which they had begun their charge, but now a band of woodland lay between. From somewhere beyond them he heard cries, but the calling of the crows who waited in the treetops was louder. Farther down the slope he saw more trees, and he could hear the gurgling of a stream.

Somehow the battle had carried him away from the others. He looked around him more carefully, a chill pebbling his skin as he realized that the bodies all belonged to the enemy. Painfully he knelt, lifted the corner of a cloak whose owner stared sightlessly at the dimming sky, and used it to wipe the blood from his sword.

Once, long ago, he had sworn that if he killed in battle it would be as a man. But he thought that he must have broken that vow today. The only other time he fared so far from ordinary human awareness was when he spent himself between Gudrun's thighs. But he was more than human when he lost himself in her arms. The beast in him had been the victor today. Anguish rose within him at the realization; the moan that swelled in his throat emerged as a howl, and from the darkness between the trees, the wolves answered him.

"Welcome, my brothers," he cried, "I have spread the board for you—feast well!" Suddenly the blood-smell sickened him. He got to his feet and sheathed the sword. As he rose, a raven lifted from one of the trees and soared toward the woods below. The sound of water drifted up the slope like a promise of peace. He licked dry lips, and stumbled toward it.

As he pushed through the screen of alders, he realized that this must be the sacred spring that fed the medicinal baths that were Treveri's pride. Farther down the hill the columns and tiled roof of the baths themselves gleamed in the last of the light. But the well house was shadowed and untended, for it was a pagan shrine.

The spring itself was contained by granite coping stones with a channel through which the water flowed downhill. A stone alcove had been built into the rock behind it; he shuffled toward it through the fallen leaves, caught the gleam of marble, and stopped, amazed to see that the Christians had left the goddess in her shrine.

The image was in a style he had seen only in fragments in Borbetomagus, as lifelike as if the Lady had just that moment been turned to stone. She stood with head a little tipped and hand outstretched to caress the hound that leaped at her side; smooth limbs gleamed beneath sculptured draperies that seemed to flutter in the wind. The other hand held a bow, and on her brow he saw the crescent moon.

Sigfrid gazed up at the goddess, his turmoil quelled by her serenity, abashed before her eternal, enigmatic smile.

"You are the Lady of the Wild Things," he whispered. "Huntress and protector—I am as wild as any beast of the forest! Can you find some mercy for me?" Looking at her, he realized then that the Lady herself was an answer, as the Goddess was always, giver of life and death and healing according to men's need.

"I am your hound, Lady," he whispered, "and I have hunted for you today. Let your sacred waters wash the stain of war away. . . ."

He followed the channel a little way to where the water fell into a stone-lined pool, and there he knelt, took off his helm, and scooped up some of the water in his hands. It had an odd, mineral tang, and it was very cold, but he thought that he had never tasted anything so clean. Quickly he stripped off the rest of his gear and stepped into the basin, tensing at the shock of it, remembering when he had been a boy, bathing in forest pools. He knelt in the water and rubbed at his skin, letting the chill waters carry away the blood that covered him. And presently his flesh began to tingle, and he knew that the offering had been accepted.

A wind had come up with the approach of darkness, whispering in the trees, and he had the odd fancy that there was a voice in it, engaging in a dialogue with the murmur of the spring. He stood still in the cold water, listening.

"I am the spirit the newborn breathes in; I wander the world, and bear the last breath of the fallen away," sang the wind.

"I am the blood of birth and death; forever flowing, forever renewed," the water replied.

Sigfrid felt his own spirit lift within him; there was a wisdom beyond words in what he heard. . . .

He did not know if much time or little had gone by when he came to himself again, dizzied and blinking, and realized that from beyond the alders, men were calling his name.

"Sigfrid, thank God," cried Godomar. "We feared, when we could not find you even among the slain!"

Gundohar, following more slowly, felt his breath catch as he looked from the white perfection of the goddess in her shrine to the pale body of the man who stood in the pool. He had seen the other man stripped before, but never at this vantage, poised in the pool like some wild thing. *This is what the Greeks strive for in their statues,* he thought, *but so rarely attain. This is the body of a god.*

One of the warriors came up with a torch, and as its rosy light flickered across the pool, suddenly Sigfrid's flesh was that of a living man once more. Gundohar felt something that had been tensed with dread within him begin to relax. His memories of the battle were a mingling of horror and a dreadful joy. He badly needed someone to talk to as he had spoken with Sigfrid the night before.

"Brr—the water's freezing!" said Godomar. "Come out of there, man, before you turn to ice." Sigfrid nodded and stepped out of the water. He still looked dazed.

"Are you all right?" asked the king. "Have you any wounds?"

Sigfrid shook his head, and Gundohar frowned. Not a man among them but had a bloody rag tied about him somewhere, but he could see—they could all see—that Sigfrid's body bore no mark at all. He felt the touch of something uncanny, then he saw that the other man was shivering, and thrust the thought away.

"Take my cloak—I can see that your clothes are ruined." He unslung his crimson mantle and wrapped it around Sigfrid's shoulders, glad to see the humanity coming back into the other man's eyes.

"Did we win?" he asked hoarsely.

"Win!" Godo slapped his thigh and laughed. "That's one *millenarius* that will never number a thousand again! The good fathers of Treveri have sent supplies out to us already. Tomorrow we'll collect the rest of the taxes—" All the men laughed.

They were still laughing as they made their way back across the battlefield. The scavengers were already busy among the bodies. As they neared, a wolf lifted his head and howled.

"Wodan's hounds are feasting too," said one of the warriors.

But Gundohar was watching Sigfrid, who had turned his head to listen, and for a moment it was not a man but a wolf that he saw standing there. And once more he felt a chill that did not come from cold. He had seen Sigfrid as a beast and as a god, but what he needed was for him to be a man.

Chapter Eight ☿ A Dry Season

Borbetomagus the Donarberg
Litha Moon A.D. 425

The winter after the Burgunds' bloody harvesting at Augusta Treverorum was cold but dry, and the one that followed no better. The next year the spring storms dropped only enough rain to bring up the barley. As the summer sun grew stronger, the hay ripened early, and the young corn began to wither in the fields. Folk grew fearful and whispers ran like the wind through the dry fields. God the Father was angry, said some, because so many of the folk still held to the ancient ways. Others protested that it was the old gods who were wrathful because they no longer received their accustomed offerings. And there were those who asked how they could expect the fields to be fruitful when their king, married five years now, had not yet begotten a child.

Sigfrid stood at the window of the chamber he shared with Gudrun, listening to the night wind. Now and then he would hear the scuffling as the wind harried a dry leaf across the courtyard. *Dry leaves . . .* he thought, *dry bones.* Even on the banks of the Rhenus, father of waters, dead waterweed dried on the stones.

Were the gods angry because of what they had done at Treveri? That could not be so, for the drought extended far beyond the Burgund lands, and the Romans had fought bloodier battles with each other than they had with the barbarians

146

as the forces of Joannes the Usurper contended with those of the child-emperor, Valentinian. Rumor had it that Joannes had even sent Flavius Aetius to raise forces among the Huns. Indeed, this past year, the ransom of Treveri had saved the Burgunds, for they had used it to buy grain.

But bread would not save the cattle, wandering the high pastures in search of grass. Even in these settled lands, the herds were the life of the tribe. He wondered how the beasts of the forest were faring. It had been a long time since he had taken the wolfhide from its chest in the corner of the room to range the woodlands, not since before the fight at Treveri, when he had been a wolf without the skin.

But tonight, when sleep was too wary a prey for even his hunting, the darkness called to him. He moved, soft-footed as a shadow, across the room. Yet silent as he was, Gudrun stirred in the great bed, calling his name. He turned, looking down at her. The curves of her body shaped the thin sheet, but he hardly needed sight to sense the roundness of her arms, the long sweet line of hip and thigh, or the proud weight of her breasts. In five years he had come to know her flesh as well as he did his own.

"What are you doing?" she asked. "Are you looking for the wolfskin?"

Sigfrid stiffened. He had not realized she knew it was there, but he supposed she was too good a housewife not to turn out all her chests and coffers from time to time. He stood irresolute, wondering what to do.

"It's all right," Gudrun said quietly, "if you need to go—"

The tension went out of him in a long sigh. He sat down on the end of the bed and took her hand. "I don't want to . . . ever since Treveri I've been fighting it. . . ."

"Can you tell me? Even I have heard stories—" She squeezed his fingers. "They say you turned into a wolf in the midst of the battle that day."

"Perhaps I did," he said bitterly. "I don't remember. This was what my mother feared." Her waiting silence drew forth memories he had almost forgotten.

"It is true that by birth I am shapestrong. The wolfhide belonged to my father. When my mother gave it to me, she made me promise that I would not use it to become a berserker. But the skin is not necessary if the need is strong. When the Hundings tried to burn us in our hall we broke out fighting and the change came on me. If I had not fought as a wolf that night, my mother would have died."

"So it was a good thing—" said Gudrun, curling closer in the darkness.

Sigfrid shrugged. "She died anyway, a year later. I was not there. After that, you see, I could not stay at the holding. They were afraid of me."

"I dreamed of you as a wolf before I ever saw you as a man," she said when the silence had gone on too long. "I am not afraid."

He sank down beside her, burying his face in his arms. "But what about the others? Will there come a day when men refuse to meet my eyes and women snatch their children from my path?"

"Oh, my dear, my dear—" Gudrun raised herself on one elbow and kissed his shoulder. There was another silence, then she spoke again. "Does Brunahild know about this? Is that why there is such hostility between you and the queen?"

Sigfrid stilled, torn between panic and a bitter amusement. Try as they might to conceal it, he supposed the strain between himself and Brunahild must be obvious. What could he say to reassure Gudrun without revealing what he had sworn no one would ever know?

"I doubt that would disturb her. Perhaps she suspects I helped Gundohar to win her as his bride," he said at last.

"You think Brunahild hates you because you taught my brother swordplay?" Gudrun shook her head. "I never did understand her, but that seems strange. Nor does it explain why she should have turned against me when she found out I was married to you . . ."

Sigfrid rubbed his eyes, wondering what it was about this night that should bring forth things that had been hidden for so long.

"Was it because she wanted to be free?"

"You are my wife and she is Gundohar's. And I love you," Sigfrid said more sharply than he had intended, and Gudrun sighed. After a few moments, very gently, she began to stroke his hair.

He could scent that if he made love to her now she would welcome him, but for once the knowledge stirred no desire. Brunahild had welcomed him too, and she had been his before she was Gundohar's. But did he love her? They had been very young then, and all they had needed was passion. But he had found peace with Gudrun.

And yet, as he lay beside her in the close darkness, Sigfrid wondered suddenly if peace was enough.

Brunahild was in the linen sheds supervising the flax-combing. Her sharp glance flicked from one worker to another. She saw flax stems clinging together in a bunch that one man was bringing in and descended on him, shaking her head.

"Look there; those stalks are not yet well-enough rotted!" She twitched the offending pieces from his hands. "See, they do not pull free when I break them!" She bent the woody part in two places near the middle and tugged. "This batch was not properly spread for the watering. I suppose I must speak to Durilo yet again. Not your fault—" she told the man, "but you must be more careful. Take these stalks outside and spread them out with the others. At least in this weather we will not have to dry them over a fire!"

The day was a warm one, and inside the shed it was stifling. For this work she wore only a wrap of linen pinned at the shoulders in the old style. Originally it had been dark brown, but time had faded it to the same color as the dust she trod.

The air throbbed as flails thumped the finished flax stalks. Dust rose from the mats with each blow, and bits of chaff flew everywhere. From time to time women would separate the long fibers from the mass and take them off to a second building to be combed into silky strands. Much of the linen used by the royal household was provided by the tribesfolk in payment of taxes, but a certain amount had to be produced locally, and the young women the queen was supposed to be training needed to learn how to supervise all the household crafts.

She saw Gunna's fair head through the doorway and called to her.

"My lady," said the girl, "the old queen is sitting in the arbor, waiting for you."

"Indeed," said Brunahild, "and I have been standing inside here, waiting for *you!* Take my place, child, and watch well. The day is hot and they will grow careless if your attention wanders."

The girl flushed and stared around her. Brunahild smiled sardonically and stepped out into the open air, pulling off her kerchief and using it to wipe her brow. A slight breeze provided a little relief, but the sun shone implacably from a sky like polished brass.

At least in the arbor, where some forgotten Roman had trained eglantine to form an archway, there was shade. The old queen sat hunched over her staff, draped, even in this weather, in her inevitable shawls. As Brunahild entered she frowned.

"You look like a slave in that gown. Have you no better gear?"

"Nothing that would be better for flax-combing," said Brunahild evenly.

"I'll say this for you," Grimahild went on, "you are good at this part of your job." Brunahild sighed, beginning to suspect what this was leading to. "But my son has other servants who could do the same. He needs a queen who will bear him sons!"

He could always divorce me, she thought hopefully, but she knew that if ever she managed to kill Gundohar's passion for her, he would not send his mother to tell her so.

"Surely that is up to the gods to decide!" Brunahild said aloud.

"The gods give us the means to help ourselves," the old queen said sharply. "If you will take the potion I shall give you, you will conceive!"

"I doubt it—" Brunahild could not contain a bitter smile. It would take the angel Gabriel himself to get her with child so long as she slept alone.

"Then what I have heard is true." Grimahild glared at her as if she had read her thought. "You do not lie with Gundohar!"

"I have done my duty—" Brunahild began, but the old woman struck the ground with her staff.

"That you have not, or you would be bearing! I am not asking you to love him, but to do what must be done for the health of the land!"

"And what is your own daughter doing wrong?" Brunahild spat back at her. "Do you think I have not heard how you managed her marriage, Leaf King to Spring Queen? Has she sampled your brews, old woman? If so, there is little worth in them, for from all accounts, it is not lack of trying that has kept her from conceiving Sigfrid's child!"

But I did—and bore his babe! Brunahild finished the thought triumphantly. From time to time a messenger from Heimar would come to tell her that Asliud was doing well. Huld, who was too old now for travelling, was teaching the child.

"Do you understand nothing?" Grimahild said hoarsely. "Look around you—" She plucked a leaf and rubbed it, and it crumbled in her hands. "The land is dying. Without rain, the people will die as well. If you cannot like Gundohar, open your thighs to the first beggar you meet on the road. If the queen gives nothing, how can the waters flow?"

"Old woman," Brunahild said sternly, "I have nothing to give." *Except for death. . . .* the thought came to her. But for that, the time had not yet come.

For a long moment Grimahild stared at her. Then she sat back, seeming to shrink within her robes. "Men call me an evil woman," she whispered, "because I cast spells and pray to the old gods. But all my deeds were done for the good of my family. What justifies yours?"

"Ask the gods who sent this drought to you, and this fate to me," answered Brunahild angrily.

"The kindreds have been summoned," said Grimahild softly. "They will gather on the eve of Donar's day at the top of his mountain to make offerings to the god. You and Sigfrid must be there."

Gudrun set down the sprig of mint whose leaves she was stripping and stared at her mother. "A sacrifice to Donar? What will the priests say?"

"They will say we are heathens, and it will be true." The old queen smiled grimly. "But what they say will not matter if the rite brings rain."

And if it does not, Gudrun reflected, *we will have more to fear than Christian fulminations.* She looked down at the herbs in her hand. It was early to be harvesting them, but though the leaves were still small, if she did not dry them now, they would wither on the vine.

"But why me?" she asked then. "Surely it is for Gundohar—"

"There would be too much talk if he were there, and it might be dangerous . . ."

Gudrun's eyes widened as she began to understand. In the old days, when there were too many poor harvests and the lesser gifts had not been sufficient, folk had been known to sacrifice their kings. Were the people already muttering about Gundohar? It occurred to her then that she herself might be in danger if the people decided to settle for a substitute from the royal house. No doubt her mother knew it as well.

But as she met Grimahild's implacable gaze, Gudrun understood that the older woman would have gladly stood in her son's place, if she had been vigorous enough to be an acceptable offering. For the greater good, she would sacrifice herself or those she loved, as merciless as the god she served.

In the past, Gudrun would not have understood that. But she knew now that she would give her life for Sigfrid if there was need, and as she looked around her at the dying garden, she thought that such a price might not be too great to save the land, as well.

Abruptly she remembered the neck ring that Sigfrid had given her. She knew enough of the runes to realize that those inscribed in its gold belonged to the gods of the fields and waters—they were runes of fertility. She would wear the neck ring to the ritual.

"If the old gods need an offering in order to help us, then I will be their priestess," she said softly, meeting Grimahild's gaze at last. And in the old woman's face she saw a flicker of something that had never before been there when her mother looked at her, pride.

Even before they reached the hill, they could hear the drumming, a deep pulse-beat that seemed to throb from the heart of the rolling countryside. Ahead, Donar's mountain jutted out from the hills that edged the valley of the Rhenus to the south and west of Borbetomagus, a dark hump against the sky. On the plain, pale swirls of dust drifted above the fields, marking the progress of the people and the animals they were bringing to the ritual. Each clan had been asked to provide a black he-goat or a black bull for the god. Gudrun licked dry lips and a little prickle of excitement pebbled her skin. Already the energy was rising. Though heat still blazed from a cloudless sky, she felt suddenly certain that the ritual would succeed.

Sigfrid matched his pace to hers, though it was clear he could have been up the mountain in half the time. Gudrun wiped perspiration from her forehead and sighed. When she was a girl scampering up and down the Holy Hill, this climb would not have fazed her. But for too long she had done no more walking than the circuit of her garden, or a leisurely stroll down to the riverside. She made a private vow to be more active hereafter, and stretched her legs to match Sigfrid's long stride.

She glanced at his strong profile, wondering once more at this man to whom fate and her brother had given her. His gaze was, as usual, watchful, giving nothing away. And yet she had learned to read him well enough to tell that he was interested and perhaps a little amused.

"Thank you for coming with me today," she said softly.

He looked at her in surprise. "Did you think I would leave

you to do this alone? Besides, I'm enjoying myself. It reminds me of our festivals in the north when I was very young."

Gudrun thought of the solemn, bright-eyed boy he must have been and her eyes misted suddenly with longing to bear his child.

Perhaps there was a curse upon the Niflungar, she thought then. Though Gundohar did not complain, she could tell that things were not well between him and Brunahild. But why had no fruit come of the ecstatic nights she had spent in Sigfrid's arms?

The climbers ahead of them slowed and she paused, leaning against a young oak tree. The air was close and still, even halfway up the mountain, the land below veiled in heat haze through which she could barely make out the metallic gleam of the river. The tumbled stones of the old ringfort at the base of the mountain looked like scattered bones. The heat was oppressive, and yet Gudrun found herself feeling curiously weightless. Dutifully, she sipped from her waterskin; it would be embarrassing to faint from too much sun.

"Come—" said Sigfrid. "It is not far now."

She saw sky through the trees ahead of them. A few minutes more brought them to the summit, where a single, ancient oak tree clung to the rocky crown and shaded the spring. The dry grass around it was already being ground to chaff by the crowd. Cattle lowed unhappily, tied among the lower trees. Where the ground was flattest, space had been cleared to lay a great bonfire, and each clan had prepared its own fire on the slopes below. Gudrun saw her mother, who had been here since the night before to supervise the preparation, sitting with several other old women beneath the oak, clad in white and veiled.

The sun sank through a blazing sky, as if the drought-parched world had caught on fire. Gudrun saw that it was not the official representatives of the people who had come, but brothers or sons—those who stood behind them. It seemed appropriate that they should come here to celebrate the rites that could only take place in the shadows now. Though the air was still heavy with heat, once more Gudrun felt a prickle of chill. When she spoke to her mother, she found herself whispering.

"When it begins, what must I do?"

Something Grimahild saw in her face must have pleased her, for she smiled. "You will know. The drums will tell you. The wind will tell you."

"But there is no wind—"

"There will be," said the old queen. "Be patient, and it will come."

People had begun to gather around the waiting bonfire. As the sun touched the far hills, old Ostrofrid, the lawspeaker, got to his feet and bowed toward the oak tree. Then he turned to the people.

"Children of the Burgunds, why have you come here?"

"We have come to pray for rain. We have come to honor the god. . . ." came the murmured reply.

"And why to this mountaintop?" Ostrofrid asked.

"Because it belongs to the Lord of Lightning. Because this place is holy ground."

Ostrofrid nodded and turned to face the oak tree, lifting his arms. "Donar, Donar, Thunder-father, behold our offerings. Here are black oxen with cloven hooves and curving horns. Here are bearded he-goats for you, good and strong. Listen now, and hear what we would ask of you—unto plowers and sowers give a fruitful season and sweet rain. Holy Thunder, guard our seedfield, that it bear good straw below, good ears above, and good grain within!"

"Thunder, holy Thunder! Give us rain!" the people cried.

From the rocks above the spring, men flung wedge-shaped stones into the shallow water. The air resounded as the smiths of Borbetomagus began to pound on the rocks. Where their hammers fell, sparks leaped in the gloom.

"Wind come! Thunder roar! Lightning flare as steel strikes stone!"

Men brought up the first of the bulls, leaning into the head-ropes as the clamor increased and the beasts, growing nervous, began to toss their horns. The chieftain stepped in swiftly and the butterfly bladed bronze axe rose and fell. The bull bellowed, but his death was already upon him. The severed head fell as bright blood spurted; they caught it in a bucket and poured it over the roots of the oak tree.

Shouting triumphantly, some of the kindred suspended the head from one of the branches of the tree while the others hauled off the carcass to be butchered and roasted. Upon the hillside the first of the bonfires challenged the last light of the sun.

"Hail, Donar, Lord of the Mountaintop!" they cried.

Already the next animal was being offered. The sweet stink of blood hung in the air. Gudrun blinked. Was dusk falling so swiftly? Yet it was not darkness, but as it seemed to her, a luminous mist that made it hard to focus as the bulls and the he-goats gave up their lives. The boughs of the oak tree groaned beneath grisly trophies as the eight clans of the Burgund nation made their offerings. She swayed where she stood, dizzied and exhilarated, feeling as if the top and back of her head were being squeezed by a mighty hand. She moved her head to relieve it and found herself twitching.

Then it was the great bull, the pride of the Niflungar herd, that they were bringing, and Sigfrid to whom they gave the axe, standing in place of the king. The bronze blade sent red lightnings around the circle. The bull, smelling the blood, bellowed and reared with such strength that one of the men on the ropes was lifted from the ground.

A sharp horn swept round, and Sigfrid stepped into the motion, man and beast pivoting, the axeblade the swiftest, angling around and upward so that its swing continued the bull's motion as it passed through the neck. The severed head arced upward toward the tree as the body fell.

"Donar! Donar! The god accepts the sacrifice!"

Swiftly they stripped the carcass of its hide and gutted it. Then ropes were looped around the feet and it was hauled up to swing from the crossbeam set into the forked logs that flanked the fire. Someone plunged a brand into the stacked logs. Gudrun stared as the fire licked the flesh of the slaughtered bull. But the flames were flaring at an angle, not straight up as they had been before. She turned towards the afterglow and felt a breath of cooler air stir the hair on her brow. In the distant west a breeze was rising. Her mother had been right. There was a wind!

The drums had settled into a steady booming now. Folk were beating out the rhythm, striking their thighs, shaking clappers and bells. Gudrun found herself swaying back and forth, laughing as if she had had too much mead. From the space beneath her breastbone a whirling radiance spread in curls of flame to her limbs. Someone started dancing widdershins around the fire, cavorting like a mad thing. Soon others joined him.

The wild gyrations became a circle. A woman grabbed Gudrun's hand and pulled her into it. She stumbled, not used to dancing in that direction, for no one worked against the sun's motion except to do evil magic—or to raise a storm. Her feet did not want to obey her will, but folk caught her as she swayed and thrust her back into the dance.

Ahead of her a man stumbled out of the circle and stripped off his tunic before beginning to dance once more. Soon others were doing the same. Tunics and breeches and gowns were cast away. A shriek burst from Gudrun's belly. She yelled again, flinging out her arms to release the force that surged through her; suddenly she could not bear the touch of clothing. She tugged at the knot of her girdle, tore loose the pins that held her wrap at the shoulders, and kicked it all aside. A ripple of pure well-being pulsed through her body as she freed herself from the clothing's constriction. Now only the neck ring remained—even the pins that held her hair had scattered as she whirled.

By shedding her clothing she seemed to have gained a new sense that linked her to the other dancers and to the earth they trod. The circle became a serpentine coil that wound among the fires. She danced with the others, but thought grew disconnected. Her body tingled with an excitement that flared from her breast to her groin as the grip of whatever force was moving her grew more sure. If she tried to stand still, she found herself twitching uncontrollably. The only release was in the dance.

She had found it hard to climb the mountain, but now she stamped and whirled with the endless energy of a child. She knew what she was doing, and yet she did not feel as if it were Gudrun that was doing it—she was someone else, Someone who exulted in the toss of silky hair and the play of muscle as if She had long been denied it. The dance brought her round to her mother and the old woman, seeing the neck ring, brought up her hands in the salute with which she greeted Gundohar when he was throned.

"Shining One, Who art Thou?" she whispered, gazing into Gudrun's eyes. But it was not Gudrun who answered her.

"I am the Frowe . . . I am the glory of the green earth and the radiance of the starry skies!" she heard herself saying. "I am the Lady of Life and Love." And then Gudrun knew no more.

Sigfrid heard the shouting and turned to see folk gathering around Gudrun, who stood turning her hands back and forth as if she had never seen them before. The old women surrounded her like murmuring doves, drawing her toward the edge of the trees. He slid through the crowd, seeking to see.

"What is it?" he asked Ostrofrid. "What are they doing to her?"

The old man grinned. "She will dig henbane with her right hand's smallest finger, and they will tie it to her right foot's smallest toe. It is an old woman's magic to bring rain."

Sigfrid lifted his head, sniffing the wind. Their witchery might well succeed, for he could scent a change in the air. The savor of roasting meat rose on the smoke of the bonfires. Surely the Lord of Lightning must smell it. Through the soles of his feet Sigfrid could feel the regular tremor in the earth as the dancers circled to the beat of the drum; even the flames leaped in time to that rhythm. It pulsed through the air, resounding from hill to hill. Surely the Lord of Thunder must hear!

The knot of white-clad women at the edge of the trees unraveled and Gudrun appeared in the midst of them, laughing. She moved in a nimbus of radiance, so that even in the shadows she seemed to glow.

"The gods have heard us," said Ostofrid softly. "The Shining Ones come down and walk with men."

Abruptly, Sigfrid understood. His Gudrun was lovely, but she always walked as if ashamed of her height, her shoulders curved to diminish the lovely line of her breasts beneath her gown. This woman strode with chin high and shoulders back, her firm breasts riding high and proud, their rosy nipples pointing bewitchingly.

Gudrun had a gentle beauty that soothed the soul, but the woman she had become commanded the space around her. Her laughter rang across the hillside. "Gytha! Gytha!" the women cried. *Goddess, priestess . . .* the words were the same.

"The Lady blesses us!" cried Grimahild. "Welcome her, oh ye people! Crown her with flowers!"

Sere as the season had been, still they had found a few blossoms. Soon a wreath of white-and-yellow asters crowned her golden hair. Sweet herbs were twined into a girdle that rested on the swell of her hips, its end swung tantalizingly above the joining of her thighs. Sigfrid felt desire grow within him as he gazed at her, and looking around him, knew that every man there felt the same.

"Froja, fairest, see how we honor you—" cried the women. "Will you give us your blessing, will you call the god to grant us rain?"

She frowned a little, looking around her, and then, slowly, she lifted her arms, and the babble stilled.

"Blood you have poured out upon the ground, but not your own—" she said, and the voice was deeper than Gudrun's, with a lazy purr beneath the words. "Lives you have given, but not yours—"

"Lady, does the god wish men for his sacrifice?" asked Ostrofrid, and Sigfrid knew that if she asked it, one of those who were dancing here would die. They knew it as well. Every man who had come here knew that the lot could fall on him if that was what the gods required.

But the Frowe shook her head so that the flowers trembled,

and laughed. "Is death the only thing that you can think to offer? Give life, children of the Burgunds, give us your strength and power. Dance, sing. Lie down together and make life; pour out your seed and the god will pour out rain. Look at me—*look* at me—" Slowly she began to walk among them, hips swaying, cupping her breasts in her hands.

"Do you desire me? Does the power of life fill you now?"

All around the circle that power was stiffening the men she passed. Women licked their lips, their nipples hardening visibly. As the goddess drew nearer, Sigfrid caught her scent, a heady mingling of female musk and flowers that engorged his already considerable erection to the point of pain.

"Ah—" she laughed. "I see that you do . . . Dance then, and let the power that rises through you be your offering!"

She opened her arms as if to embrace them all and began to whirl in place. The drummers, catching fire from her movement, thundered out a new rhythm that compelled motion. Even the old women were dancing now, tearing off their robes, empty breasts flapping as they bobbed and swayed. But just as the goddess shone through Gudrun's flesh, one could see in the old women the radiance of the maidens they had once been. They were all beautiful now, men and women alike, shining with power.

The goddess moved among the people, reaching out to touch a cheek or clasp a hand, brushing against them, clasping first one, then another, in a swift embrace. Someone snatched up a knife and gashed his arms, another took the blade and scored a red line along his thighs. The knife went from one man to another. They flung out their arms and red drops sprinkled the dry ground.

"Life! Life!" they cried. "Let the thirsty earth drink blood like rain!"

Men and women were beginning to reach for one another, but the goddess had acquired an escort of warriors, erect and ready, following her as wolves follow the pack-queen when her season comes. Sigfrid snarled. A hard hand closed on his arm and he saw the old queen.

"There is no need to fight." She looked at his face and

cackled. "You are the king here. You have the right. But you must claim her now or she will spread her legs for them all!"

Wind gusted suddenly and the flames flared high. Dazzled, Sigfrid understood what had happened to Gudrun, for with the queen's words, the same power that had touched him at his wedding feast tingled through him and he began to lose awareness of the man he had been, and become the king. He tipped back his head, and let the power flow out of him in a long, exultant howl.

Drums thundered, echoing. The dancers paused to stare as Sigfrid stalked past the fire to stand before the Lady and her followers.

"She is mine!" He stared around him and saw the other men flinch from his gaze.

"She is meant for him—" Grimahild echoed his cry. "He is the Wolf-King, the Leaf King, the Year King. The blood in his veins has mingled with that of the lord of this land. Does any here deny that Sigfrid is royal, and most fit to mate with the Sacred Queen?"

"You stand for the king—" First one man, then another, bowed to Sigfrid and backed away. "You are most fit to make the offering."

There was a part of Sigfrid that knew he ought to be disturbed by those words. But in that moment, he yearned only to sink down upon the woman before him and pour out his life in her embrace.

"My Lady," he said more softly. "I stand ready to serve you. . . ." She focused fully upon him, and he felt as if he had stepped into a flame.

"My Lord," she answered him, "I welcome you. . . ." Golden strands whirled brightness around her as the wind whipped back her hair. Sigfrid's skin prickled at the tension in the air. The drumbeat shifted; they swayed together. People were swirling around them. Water splashed with a shock across his back—men were running through the crowd with buckets, dipping oak branches into the water and shaking them at the people.

"It rains, it rains!" they cried. "The god gives rain!" Light blinked in the west, and after a moment there came a long mutter of sound that was not the drums. And then she came into his arms.

Their bodies molded together with the ease of long knowledge, and yet every inch of him thrilled with sensations that were new. His mouth moved on hers as a thirsty man drinks from a spring. All around them, people came together, man and woman or man and man or pairs of maidens; a man was fondled by two women, a woman kissed one lover while embraced by another from behind.

A damp wind whirled around them; they strained together; wet skin clung to skin. She balanced on one leg, wrapping the other around him. Sigfrid gripped her buttocks, lifting her, and slid sweetly home.

In that moment, sound, like two great hands clapping around them, knocked them to the ground. A spear of light struck the tree and flared from offering to offering. Dazzled and deafened, the only sense left to him was touch; as he thrust himself into the sweet flesh beneath him, sensation magnified until even that awareness was overwhelmed by an ecstasy that built past pleasure or pain. He knew only the need to give.

Now they were the heart of the storm. Sigfrid cried out, his body arching, releasing all his pent power into the body of the goddess as overhead, the god released the rain.

Chapter
Nine The Ring

Shrine of the Mariae
Harvest Moon, A.D. 425

For most of the week following the rite on Donar's mountain the storm fronts continued to roll in. After the first violence they came gently, covering the parched land with grey veils of moisture, filling sunken ponds and swelling shrunken streams. It was too late to help the hayfields, but the high meadows put forth a belated growth which the cattle devoured eagerly, and as the withering wheat and barley sucked up the water, their drooping stalks grew stiff and strong, and seed heads began to fill out with hard grain.

It was not only the grain that was growing. By the time the second moon after the ritual was swelling in the sky, Gudrun knew that she was with child.

Swiftly as the waters that now were splashing down the hillsides, word of the rite had spread among the people. The priests glowered and ascribed the storm to the mercy of their god, but who cared for their frowns when they could see the green deepening on the hillsides with every day that passed? When Gudrun walked in the town, women would come out to touch her; once, when she got back to her chambers, she found that someone had cut a strip from the hem of her gown.

In early pregnancy, some discomforts were to be expected. But when Gudrun grew pale and sickly the women of the palace began to murmur about omens. Some gesture, said Grimahild, was required to reassure the people. Gudrun must go to bathe at the holy wells below the old ringfort. There was a shrine of the Mothers where she could pray for the delivery of a healthy child.

On a swift horse, the journey to the springs would have taken no more than a few hours. But for the queens, held to the pace of the gentlest of ponies, it took all day to cross the plain. Throughout the day, the little procession wound through fields where men were getting in the harvest. Where they passed, men ceased their labor, and brought bouquets of wheat ears bound up with blue cornflowers and starry daisies to deck the wagons and hang from the saddlebows. By the time the dark hills were close enough to make out trees, Gudrun rode garlanded like the goddess when she makes her circuit through the fields.

Although it had rained throughout the summer with gratifying regularity, the weather was warm and muggy, and perspiration soaked her gown. The healing waters that bubbled from those hillsides would refresh the body as well as the spirit. Gudrun longed for them. Riding through the fields she had felt like the queen they hailed her, but in a moment the exaltation left her and she found herself weeping for the beauty of the season, so soon to fade. It was no good to tell herself that these shifts in mood were only part of her pregnancy and would pass. While they lasted, they were real.

It seemed to Gudrun that this time away from the demands of their men and the duties of the royal hall would be good for all of them. Her mother, who in these past months had grown visibly older, might regain some strength, and as for Brunahild, who had not even the excuse of pregnancy for her tempers, one could hope that the waters might bring some healing to her troubled soul.

Darkness was falling when they reached the house that her mother had built below the old Gaulish ringfort, and Gudrun was too exhausted to pay much attention to her surroundings. Thus it was dawn before she was able to look around her.

The morning mist that wrapped the hillsides was beginning to stir now, trailing away in glimmering swaths and spirals as the rising sun woke the wind. Dewdrops glittered on the grass; lifting mist unveiled now a glimpse of green meadow, now the graceful arc of a branch against the brightening sky.

Grimahild's hall was built into the hollow of the hill below the piled stones of the ancient fort. Young oaks and hazels screened the fold in the hills below, but Gudrun could hear a musical trickling where the overflow from the springs came down. Then a stronger gust swirled mist against her face and away, and suddenly everything before her showed clear. Tile and thatching gleamed through the multihued greenery on the slope that faced the ringfort, and Gudrun knew they must belong to the shrine.

Holy . . . she thought, lifting her hands in salutation, *it is all holy—the hills, and the shrine, and me!*

"A fair sight, is it not?"

It was her mother, looking, even after a single night in the cool air of the hills, more at peace. Unaccountably, Gudrun found her eyes filling with tears.

"I understand now why you love this place," she managed to say.

"It's high time you saw it so," said the queen, and Gudrun felt her throat tighten. Could not the old bitch leave her be, even now?

"Oh, you need not look at me so suspiciously," the queen went on. "Even a trained wisewoman has little time for her craft when she is bearing. You need not fear that I will seek to make you learn it while your children are small, but the gift is in your blood. Deny it as you will, you will come to it in time. But for now, it is the mysteries of the Mothers you must learn." She looked at her daughter and smiled.

Then other women came out behind them, chattering. Gudrun crossed her arms over her breasts, aware of their new weight as she sensed the other changes her body was going through. Why had she and her mother been so long at odds? She had even mistrusted the queen's motives in marrying her to Sigfrid, and that match had brought her more happiness than most women dream of, and now the joy of the coming child.

She touched the warm weight of the gold neck ring that he had given her. She had been wearing it ever since the ritual, at first because it was her link to the power of the goddess, and then for strength and protection while she was carrying the babe. As Gudrun allowed her women to drape her mantle around her, she found herself steadying to an anticipation that warmed her as they started for the shrine.

As they moved down the path, one of the girls began singing an old cradle song that Gudrun had never understood before.

> *"Ride, ride, ride a stick-horse,*
> *A fortress guards the holy source,*
> *A golden house where waters pour,*
> *Three holy maids look out the door.*
> *The one spins out the shining silk,*
> *The other cards wool white as milk,*
> *The third one cuts, as I've heard tell—*
> *Gods keep my baby safe and well."*

The temple, a square, tiled building with a portico in the old Gaulish style, was barely big enough to hold the images and a few benches. The place had always been sacred to the *idisi* whom the Romans called the *matronae*—the Mothers who gave women children and watched over their safety. The Christians had installed an altar to the three Marias in the old shrine, but that made little difference to either the ritual or the prayers—the Mother of Jesus blessed everyone, and welcomed the fruit and flowers which in the old days had been the proper offerings to the ancestral mothers of the clans.

It was apples and autumn asters they were bringing now, and a richly worked cloth from Constantinople. Gudrun watched Brunahild glide forward to lay her gift on the altar. Her words and gestures were perfectly correct, the smoothly planed features calm as always, her almond eyes as unreadable as the green depths of a forest pool. Gudrun's own eyes filled with sudden sorrow over the distance that lay between them.

For a little while, when Brunahild first came to Borbetomagus, she had thought they would resume their old friendship. What had happened between Gundohar and his queen to make it all go wrong?

Then it was her own turn. The carving built into the back wall of the shrine was a bas-relief of three female figures. Closer, she could make out among the folds of carven stone a cornucopia at the feet of one, flowers in the lap of her companion on the other side, and in the arms of the central goddess, a child. A painted image of the Virgin Mary had been set on the low table before it, but to Gudrun, the flat, hieratic features had none of the mystery of the carvings, whose expressions seemed to change with each flicker of the lamp.

"Holy Mothers, hold your hands over me and my child and bless the life within me. Which image of you is the true one? Shall I call you Maria or Fricca? What names did they call on when they set your image here?"

She stared upward, and it seemed to her that one of the carven faces was smiling, and one was twisted in sorrow, and the third looked calmly into some place that lay beyond the world. When she stared at the third face, the one in the middle, Gudrun felt the neck ring grow warm. Self-awareness faded until she, too, floated in serenity. And in that place beyond human boundaries, it seemed to her there were words.

"I am the Holy Mother, nourisher of nations. By many names the folk have called Me. My faces are as many as the babes I bear. In Roma, they hail Me as Virgin and Mother of Sorrows and as Maria, Mother of God, but you should call Me Mother of All. Listen for My voice in the murmur of the waters, look for My image in the shining face of the world. You have come to seek Me in this shrine, and because of that, you are listening. But in truth, I am everywhere. Go forth in joy, therefore, knowing that you will see Me whenever you open your eyes, and whenever you still your spirit, you may hear.

Will you serve the cause of Life? Will you serve Me?"

"I do . . . I will . . ." Gudrun responded, vision dazzled by a multiplicity of images which were still, somehow, all the same. *"Tell me—what wyrd does my future hold?"*

"Fear not, My daughter, for you will bear a healthy babe. But you will know also My face of sorrow. Beware of your passions lest you cause the very ills you fear. Great currents are moving. You must flow without fighting them, or they will carry you away."

The face of the Goddess became many, and those many a series of images that flowed into a moving tapestry of people and places, some familiar, some unknown. She saw blood and fire, and the surging waters of the Rhenus, whirling ever more swiftly around her, until her mind could no longer control them and she fell back with a cry.

When she could see again, the other women were supporting her and they were outside.

"I'm all right," she answered, taking a deep breath and shaking her head. "A moment of dizziness, that was all. I will do now."

"The waters will restore her," said Queen Grimahild. "Let us go down to the pools."

As they moved out under the trees Gudrun turned to Brunahild. "Do you remember how we sneaked off to see the sacred well at Halle when we were little girls?"

The other woman's distant gaze softened and her lips twisted wryly. "I remember that they almost killed us for it. I trust the folk who keep this well will be more welcoming—"

Gudrun nodded. Long ago, her vision had told her that help would come from the waters, but fire was her enemy. She put her hand to the neck ring hidden beneath the folds of her mantle for reassurance.

What can harm me? She pulled her mantle closer to hide her shivering. *I am the sacred queen!*

Brunahild had also been thinking about the saltwell of Halle. She could still remember the experience quite clearly— the steep slopes with the village clinging to them, the dank, briny smell of the water in the saltwell, and the Eye that had looked back at her from its depths—but as if it had happened to someone else. The girl she had been was gone. Perhaps she had died when Gundohar's sword struck her down. Or perhaps it was when Sigfrid had looked at her as if she were a stranger.

Folk had been coming to bathe in the sacred waters for a long time. The Gauls had built the shrine there, and the Romans had added a coping of stonework around the edge of the largest pool. More birch trees grew around it; the reflection of their pale trunks glimmered like the smooth bodies of maidens in the dark surface of the pool.

Brunahild unwrapped her light mantle and laid it aside and tugged at the fastening of her belt. If only she could lay aside the armor with which she had encased her spirit as easily as she did her clothes!

The other women—even Marcia, her own maid—were clustering around Gudrun, chattering as they helped her to disrobe. She supposed that given Gudrun's condition it was inevitable. Bertriud's women had fussed in the same way when she herself was bearing. And they must know, as well, that Brunahild was indifferent to their ministrations. Her lips twisted bitterly. *Why should they love me? I have never shown them more than bare civility!*

And yet she *was* the queen. She let her wrap slide to the ground and unpinned the brooch at the neck of her tunic, stretched to pull it over her head along with the shift beneath it, and took a deep breath. She felt with unaccustomed sensitivity the touch of cool air on her bare skin. When she was with the Walkyriun she had often stripped down with the other girls in the hot summertime. Why did she feel so naked here?

Perhaps it was because she had taken off more than her clothes. The peace of the shrine had been seductive. She realized that she was actually letting go of some of that invisible armor—at this moment she could even forgive Gudrun for bearing Sigfrid's child.

She laughed a little then and moved toward the water, her thigh brushing that of Gudrun, who was raising her arms so that the women could remove her shift, and then stepped down into the pool. For a moment the cool water was a shock, then she dove under, surfaced in a patch of sunshine, and rose into the light with the water streaming off her skin.

For a moment sight was dazzled, but she could still hear.

"Clumsy bitch—" one of the women said in what she thought was a whisper. "She nearly knocked my lady down!"

"She cares for nothing, that one—" said another. From the voice she thought it was little Ursula, who served Gudrun. "Who does she think she is, pushing in here?"

Brunahild turned. "I am the queen," she said distinctly, "and I go first, here and everywhere." She squinted toward the blaze of gold that must be Gudrun. "Sister, your women grow insolent. Discipline them, or I will do so for you."

"Brunahild, she meant no harm—" Gudrun began.

"What I said was true," the girl burst out behind her. "You are the Sacred Queen, you should take precedence here!"

"Sacred Queen?" Bitter amusement rose in Brunahild's throat. "The priests would frown to hear you say so. Surely we are all good Christian women here, come to worship at a Christian shrine!"

"What do the priests know of begetting and bearing? They have no power here, and you know it well," said Gudrun, her voice sharpening. "Nor will I punish my maid for saying what the whole tribe knows is true. The precedence is yours in Borbetomagus, but I am the one who went to the mountain to make the offering for the people. If you were the true queen, you would be carrying this child!" She thrust her women aside and splashed down into the pool.

I have borne Sigfrid's child already, Brunahild shook with fury, *and what honor did it bring me?*

"You are married to a servant, to my husband's sworn man," she said scornfully, squinting into the sunlight as she tried to see, "no matter how you disported yourselves in the hills. We do not give royal honors to every bondmaid who tumbles her lout behind a haystack or under a tree!"

"Sigfrid is the son of a king!" Gudrun's voice shook with outrage. "He and Gundohar have mingled their blood. He is as noble a man as walks the world, a prince of the Niflungar and master of Fafnar's hoard!"

She stepped into the light and Brunahild blinked, for Gudrun seemed fashioned of living gold. Her hair shone in the sunlight as if dwarves had crafted each strand for a goddess, brightness blazed back from her wet skin. And around her neck—around Gudrun's neck coiled a circlet of metal that seemed to glow with a radiance of its own, a pure and vivid gold whose surface was scored with runes of light.

Brunahild did not need to see them to read them. In the long days when she waited for Sigfrid to return to her she had memorized every stroke, every scratch. The ring—*her* ring! Fafnar had hoarded it, Sigfrid had won it, and he had given it to her for a morning gift after their first night of love.

But when she had wakened in the cave after her battle with Gundohar, it had been Gundohar's ring that weighted her neck, and her own was gone! She stared, and felt the fragile structure of her life giving way. She had felt this pain when the Walkyriun burned all that had made her one of them, but this time it was water that was dissolving her life away.

"Where did you get that ring!" She pointed, her voice grown so terrible that even the fluttering leaves seemed to still.

Gudrun stared, her hand going to the necklet protectively. "It is a holy thing," she began. "It came from Fafnar's hoard."

"I know where it came from." Anguished laughter tore Brunahild's throat. "Better than you do—but how did it come to you?"

"Sigfrid gave it to me. . . ." Now her other hand moved to shield her womb as if Brunahild's gaze might blast the infant cradled there.

"How did he get it?" she hissed. Seeing it on Gudrun's neck, she relived the agony of the day when it had been wrested from her own. "Did he steal it or was it Gundohar's payment for his treachery? Either way, it is my ring—mine! Give it to me!"

Speculation swept the waiting women like a wind as Brunahild thrashed forward. Her hands closed on warm flesh; but though she was strong, Gudrun was taller.

"Brunahild, let me go!" she cried. "Have you gone mad?"

"Mad? Not I—it's the world that's mad, and all vows a lie!" She grabbed for Gudrun's neck and her nails raked down the other woman's breast. Water fountained around them as they grappled, then frantic hands were wrenching Brunahild away.

She struggled, but after a few moments her wrath gave way to a grief beyond words. She hugged her arms, shuddering.

Gudrun had gone to her knees in the shallow water and was rocking back and forth, weeping. Drops of blood like liquid garnets oozed sluggishly from the scratches on her white skin.

"Queen you may be, but you will not go unpunished!" Ursula glared at her. "Grimahild shall hear of this, and so shall the king!"

"The king!" Brunahild found her voice again. "Indeed he will, and so will all the world, until I unravel this treachery. Oh yes—I shall have a great deal to say to Gundohar!" She shook off the hands that held her and began to wade toward the opposite side of the pool. When she had climbed out she looked back at the knot of women around Gudrun.

"Tend her well. It may be that she has been a victim too. Until I know the truth she has nothing more to fear from me."

One of the women made a sign against the evil eye and Brunahild began to laugh once more, a terrible sound like the caw of a raven on a battlefield. She strode around the pool and snatched up her clothing, and then, without troubling to put the garments on, she swept up the path, leaving them staring after her.

"They're saying in the marketplace that Aetius finally reached Roma with the Huns he hired to support Joannes—" said Godomar lazily, pegging his spearman into a new spot on the *tabula* board and reaching for his drinking horn.

Gundohar continued to stare at the board where his ivory kingpiece stood surrounded by foes. There was an air of subdued expectation in the hall that made his skin prickle. Everyone knew that something had happened to the women at the shrine. Brunahild had arrived before the others, white with suppressed anger, and immediately demanded a hearing. And now his mother was back with Gudrun, and she had called for judgment as well.

"But Joannes is dead!" said Ordwini, leaning forward. "Galla Placidia's back in Roma, sitting on the high seat with her little emperor on her lap like Jesu and the Queen of Heaven. She's never been a forgiving woman. Which gate did they post the head of Aetius on when she got through with him?"

Gundohar looked up and met Sigfrid's troubled gaze. Brunahild was not a forgiving woman either, and yet for five years she had seemed to accept her situation. What devilry was she planning now, and why?

"None of them! That man has the tongue of Loki and the luck of the gods. They say that when he saw how things stood he marched in at the head of his army and confronted the empress. Whether he love-talked her or threatened her I don't know, but she has made him *Magister Equitem intra Gallias!*"

"Master of Gallia?" Sigfrid whistled.

"With twelve regiments of regular cavalry, ten legions, fifteen regiments of auxiliaries, and the gods know how many special forces. Gallia has the biggest field army in the Empire!" said Ordwini with a sour satisfaction. "Well led, it is the most effective as well."

"Well lads, I can see that we'll have to choose another direction for next summer's campaigning . . ." observed Sigfrid.

"Why? Just because he talked the empress round?" asked Godomar. "Any man can control a woman—it's the Huns that bother me!"

There was an uncomfortable silence and Godomar began to flush as he remembered why that was not the best thing to have said just now. Gundohar felt the color flooding into his own face as well.

Is keeping women in order indeed so easy? the king wondered, *or would the females I have to deal with challenge any man?*

He looked down at the gaming board, where his kingpiece was beleagured by his brother's red-stained spears. Godomar was a surprisingly good *tabula* player, perhaps because he did not allow himself to be distracted by worrying about the implications of his moves. He had certainly maneuvered the king into a tight place, and this time Sigfrid could not help him. Gundohar stared sightlessly at the board and shivered, for he could see no way out of the trap that held him, no way at all.

"King of the Burgunds." Grimahild's servant stood in the doorway. "The queen your mother desires to be heard."

Gundohar swallowed. It must be serious then, or his mother would have come to him in private as she used to, before his marriage made him in her sight a man and a king.

"Let the queen come in—" he said harshly, turning on his bench to face the door. At least he would not have to finish the game.

The old man stood aside and Grimahild entered, swathed in a dark shawl. She made her way forward, her stick tapping out an ominous rhythm on the wooden floor. He looked at the charms tied to its head and the marks carved down the shaft and realized it was the staff she used in her magic.

"Gundohar, I call for judgment and compensation. Your sister Gudrun has been struck and wounded by Brunahild, your queen."

"Surely it is for her husband to make that claim if there has been an injury—" Gundohar looked uneasily at Sigfrid, who was beginning to wear an expression he had seen on beasts trapped in a cage.

Sigfrid had seen Gudrun briefly when she returned, and said that it was shock, more than the scratch, which seemed to be upsetting her. Had the women told him no more, or was he keeping secrets too? *If I cannot trust you, my brother, then we are both lost!*

"Perhaps," answered Grimahild, "and yet there may be reasons why he cannot, or will not, do so. When men ignore the rights of their womenfolk, the women must speak. Therefore, I accuse Brunahild."

"And I will speak for myself in answer!" came a voice, not loud, but quite clear, behind him.

Gundohar jumped. Brunahild was wearing black as well, but she glittered with gold. He caught a heady draught of scent as she brushed past him and stepped down from the dais to confront the old queen.

"You have drawn blood from my daughter and threatened the child whose birth will bring hope to the land. Do you deny it? What compensation will you give for that injury, what apology?"

"I do not deny it," Brunahild said scornfully. "But I think you will find that any compensation due her will be swallowed up in the weregild that is due to me." She took a step closer to the old queen. "I ask you, crone, who know better than any here the arts in which I was trained, do you think I would resort to so clumsy an attack if I truly wished to harm her or her babe?"

"*Why*, then," the words were wrung from Gundohar's lips. "Why did you strike her?" Brunahild turned, and he flinched from the chill of her gaze.

"Because she was wearing the neck ring that was stolen from me. . . ."

"Are you accusing Gudrun of stealing it?" Gundohar began.

"Upon reflection, I realize that if she had done so, even Gudrun would have the sense not to wear it where I could see," Brunahild said with deadly calm. "She said that it was a gift from Sigfrid. How came that ring into Sigfrid's hands?" She stared at Gundohar, and he blinked, trying to hide the fact that he had no idea what neck ring she might mean. Then he glanced at Sigfrid's face and read not confusion, but consternation there.

"Did he steal it from you, my lord? Or from me?" Brunahild's whisper was like the icy touch of a swordpoint just before it is thrust home.

"The ring was mine," Sigfrid said finally, but his voice lacked conviction. "Gundohar gave it to me . . ."

"As a present, perhaps, when you married Gudrun?" Brunahild asked helpfully. Gundohar almost nodded, but the touch of Sigfrid's foot warned him. And of course, if Brunahild thought she recognized the ring, she must have seen it after she came to the Burgund lands.

"He gave it to me later," Sigfrid put in hurriedly.

"After our wedding—" Gundohar echoed him.

"Of course—" She nodded, and began to pace up and down before the dais, holding each man's gaze until he had to look away. They had no more idea what she was getting at than their king, but clearly this was the best entertainment they'd had since the last time they went to war.

"Surely it is more usual for the person being married to receive gifts than to give them . . . but, never mind. Perhaps the gift was given for services rendered. Was that it?" Mute, Gundohar nodded. "And what service, I wonder, might that be? What did Sigfrid do to help you, Gundohar? Did he assist you somehow in your bid to marry me?"

The others were nodding. They had all heard Sigfrid pledge his assistance. But Gundohar felt that icy touch begin to penetrate his heart.

"He taught me his fighting skills," he said weakly.

"Did he?" she asked sweetly. "And how much did you learn?" She shook her head. "I think he did more for you—I think he fought your battles as well and won the combats with me."

Ordwini shook his head. "Lady, we were there and saw it. Your opponent was the king."

"Or someone wearing his garments," she said viciously.

"I am sorry," said Ordwini, "but it seems to me that it must be your word against his, and I for one will believe my king."

"You trust your lord's word so highly?" she asked. "Well, the truth is easily tested. Tell me, Gundohar, of what likeness was the ring you gave to Sigfrid?"

"It was of gold," he began, then stopped, his mind empty, as she laughed.

"Let me help you. It was a lovely thing of ancient workmanship, was it not, of golden cables twisted together, with terminals like dragon's heads."

Gundohar nodded. At least that was something he knew he had seen before, though in his confusion he could not say where.

"A lovely thing . . ." she repeated. "But that, my lord, was the ring you gave to me!" She threw back her veils and they could all see, gleaming on her neck, the massive twisted torque of the Burgund kings. She turned to the others.

"Perhaps you saw me wearing it when he carried me out of the cave? Gundohar had it when he fought me, but if you think back, perhaps you will remember that I was wearing a neck ring of my own when I went to that battle."

"Did she have a ring?" someone whispered, and another man murmured an indistinct answer. *Was she wearing a ring?* Gundohar tried to remember. But the details of her costume were a blur; he could remember only that she had been deadly, and beautiful.

"The man who spent the night with me in that cave took the ring from my neck and replaced it with the one he was wearing. And thus I tell you that Sigfrid must have stolen the ring either from Gundohar, afterward, or that night, from me!" There was a murmur from the men, and even Grimahild was frowning. Brunahild turned to her.

"Do you think Gundohar could forget doing such a thing? You can see that he knows nothing of it. . . . If your daughter knows no more, then I must ask her to forgive me. But if she conspired in this with Sigfrid, then she owes me more than you can know!"

Gundohar waited for his mother to blast her, but the old queen stood leaning on her staff, her eyes hooded so that he could not read them, and said nothing at all.

"No one could blame you if you had asked Sigfrid to act as your champion," Godomar said slowly. "We have seen you fight like a berserker in battle, and we know that you feared to do the maiden harm. . . ."

"It is true then!" Brunahild said in a changed voice. Color flooded her face, then fled, leaving only her eyes glowing in a face that was deathly pale. "I was not crazed . . . my heart did not lie. . . ." She turned her burning gaze upon Sigfrid.

"It was you—" she whispered. "Always, it was you! You are the hero I was waiting for! You won me fairly—by the vows we swore you are my husband!"

They were all staring at Sigfrid now, and Gundohar felt

danger throb in the room. He saw the other man's knuckles whiten as he held his wine cup, and a muscle jump in his jaw.

Say something, he pleaded silently. *Tell them it is not true. Save us all!*

"By the oaths sworn between your kinfolk and the Burgunds, your husband is Gundohar," Sigfrid said finally. Brunahild's eyes blazed.

"Am I a slave to be sold? Am I a mare to be traded at a market fair? I who was Wodan's daughter and one of the Walkyriun?" She drew herself up, and those nearest recoiled from her wrath. "I am no man's wife without my will! But you lay with me in the cave, Sigfrid. Can you deny that you held me in your arms?"

"He did more than that," came a whisper from behind her. "I remember that morning; there was blood on her gown."

Sigfrid lifted his head at last, and meeting his gaze, Gundohar recoiled at the torment he saw there. "My lord," he said in a low voice, "I swear that I have kept faith with you." He looked at them all—all except Brunahild.

"To serve my lord I took his place in the battle, it is true. And that night I guarded his lady. But how could I have lain with her even if I had desired it? She was out of her head from my last blow. The blood on her gown came from my own arm."

Unwillingly, Gundohar remembered his struggle with Brunahild on their wedding night. Truly no man could have lain with her against her will, but while she was unconscious she could not have prevented him. Had Sigfrid taken the gift that Brunahild would not give him? Had he done to her those things that haunted the king's dreams? The thought was unworthy, but it would not go away.

"Can you swear that you have never known my body, Sigfrid Fafnarsbane?" As she mounted the dais Brunahild's draperies flared out behind her like dark wings.

"I swear that since my marriage I have had the love of no woman save Gudrun!" Sigfrid's voice shook as he answered her.

"He lies!" Brunahild said furiously. The whispers in the hall had become a cacophony. Gundohar got to his feet, aware, even through his own anguish, of the need to regain control.

"Silence—" That was Grimahild's voice, pitched with all her old power. "You squabble like children! It is his word against hers, and what proof can there be?"

"Let them take oath upon it!" said Godomar.

"How can they swear?" said Sindold. "The priests have broken the ring of Donar, and we have no holy relics here."

"I will take oath upon Gundohar's spear, the same spear on which we swore brotherhood," said Sigfrid in a strained voice. Godomar rose and lifted down the king-spear from the wall. All eyes followed its dark gleam as it swung around and Sigfrid gripped it fast.

"Hear my oath, you who stand here in this hall, and hear me, all you holy gods. I swear on this spear that the bright blade of his sword guarded the king's honor, for it lay between us all through that night in the cave."

"My oath will uphold yours!" said Godomar stoutly.

"And mine," Gislahar echoed him. Sindold and Deorbehrt came forward after him, and many another, though not all. Gundohar realized then that there were those for whom Sigfrid's prowess was a cause for envy, not honor.

Brunahild waited, her face growing stony, and when they had finished, reached out to grasp the spear. For a moment Gundohar saw their hands mated upon the weapon like the hands of a bridal couple upon the hammer of the smith who hallows them. Then she spoke.

"I will take oath also, that it is Sigfrid who had my maidenhood, and though you shake your heads, you will believe me when his blood stains the blade of this spear!"

"I will swear with you, Brunahild," said Ordwini, though his gaze was troubled, "for you have been a good queen." But though Laidrad and one or two others followed his example, for the most part those who had not already sworn for Sigfrid kept silence.

Gundohar's shoulders sagged. Suspicion would always be with them now.

"Ah, Sigfrid," Brunahild's bitterness made the king wince,

"now you have betrayed me a second time. The first time, I walked in darkness, but now I understand. What was done for love I can forgive, but to deny and betray it—that can never be forgiven. I cursed my god, the father of my heart, when I awakened in that cave. Now I curse you. As you betrayed me, Sigfrid, so those to whom you have given your love will betray you. As Wyrd has snared me, you will be trapped in turn—"

As I am trapped, thought Gundohar. *As we are all snared in this web of my mother's weaving*—He glared at the old woman, who grimaced back at him, thrust out her staff, and knocked the spear away.

"Enough of this—" she said sharply. "Godo, put that thing back on the wall. We have all said far too much this night, and now the matter is for the gods to decide. Gundohar, if you cannot make your wife keep silence, I suggest that you remove her."

At that moment Gundohar would as soon have touched a scorpion, but Brunahild was already wrapping her draperies around her.

"I will be still," she said, "but my words will not be forgotten. Come, *husband*," she said, "obey your mother, escort me from the hall." She offered him her hand with a dreadful smile.

For a moment Gundohar met Sigfrid's gaze, and read there anguish, apology, and disturbingly, shame. As they turned, the edge of Brunahild's mantle swept across the *tabula* board, and the beleagured king and his attackers alike were scattered across the floor.

Gudrun was in bed by the time Sigfrid came in. She sighed with relief. She had been afraid when he did not return, but he stumbled as he moved about in the darkness, and when he lay down beside her she could tell from his breath that he had been drinking.

Godomar and the others must have kept him with them, she thought then, trying to drink the memory of what had happened in the hall away. But it had not served. Sigfrid was lying too tense, too still. She reached out and careful as if she were touching a wild thing, stroked his hand.

"Gudrun—" Even in his whisper she could hear the pain. "You should be asleep."

"My mother came," she said. "She told me what happened. I am sorry. It is my fault, Sigfrid, for letting Brunahild see the ring."

"No! Of us all, the least guilt is yours!"

"I can understand why you felt you had to help my brother win her," she said slowly. "But Brunahild is right to want her ring back. If it will bring peace, I will give it to her."

He shook his head. "She would not take it, not from you."

"She must have something, Sigfrid," Gudrun answered him, "or she will keep brooding and do you some ill."

"The men believed me. There is nothing she can do."

It seemed to Gudrun that Brunahild had done a great deal already, but it was also clear that Sigfrid was not going to listen.

"Why does she hate me so?" he asked, as if he were trying to persuade himself. "I made her a queen."

Gudrun put her arms around him, feeling the supple strength of his body. There were so many things she wanted to know, but she would not ask him. The sweetness of his body next to hers was answer enough, for now.

In the out tide of the night, when even Godo and his cronies had staggered off to bed, Brunahild opened the door that connected the royal bedchamber to Gundohar's workroom. For hours, it seemed, she had lain wakeful, waiting for the moon to sink low enough to shine through their windows, striving to purge the passion from her mind. She was all clarity now, as pure and sharp as the sickle that hung in the sky. It was Sigfrid who had betrayed her. Gundohar was only an instrument, and Gudrun a victim. And tonight Sigfrid had denied her again before them all. There was only one weapon left to her.

She could hear the whisper of the king's breathing as she

entered the room, but if he slept, it was lightly, for at the rustle of her silken bedgown, he stirred.

"Who's there?" Instinctively he was reaching for the dagger on the table beside the couch where he lay.

"It is your wife," she said softly. "Will you call your guards to protect you from me?"

"Why, have you come to murder me?" he asked, but his hand dropped back to his side. "I will not fight you, Brunahild."

She laughed. The moonlight was silvering his rumpled hair. She heard his breath catch as she came closer, for it was shining through her thin gown.

"Brunahild, go back to bed," he said tiredly. "Whatever you would say to me can wait until day."

"Some things can only be said in the darkness," she answered, sitting down on the bed beside him. "I swore once that I would have answers, and I have some of them now. I break no vow to come to you. Your crime was the lesser, Gundohar, and I am minded to make use of you. . . ." She bent over him and her lips brushed his. "Do you love me?"

"You know how I feel about you—" he whispered, "but if you mean to turn me against Sigfrid, leave me now, for I will not betray him."

"No?" Her hand slid across his belly suddenly and she gripped his manhood. He was half-erect already, and as she touched him his member stiffened in her hand. "But you will, Gundohar. You have made me become a woman, and so I must use women's ways. You are the weapon I am forging for his destruction. . . ." She caressed him and he groaned.

When she heard his breathing becoming ragged, she knelt above him. She had not expected to feel passion, and she felt nothing now, but she had oiled herself in preparation, and his phallus slid easily between her thighs as she lowered herself astride. He gasped as she began to move above him, her hands busy upon his nipples and belly in a way that she distantly remembered had brought Sigfrid to a frenzy long ago—so very long ago.

But in moments, it seemed, Gundohar was finished. He gasped and shuddered, whispering her name.

"Yes . . . I am Brunahild. I am your wife and your queen. I am your mistress, Gundohar, and if you wish to have delight from me, you will do my will."

Chapter
Ten ⚶ Wolf-Eyes

Borbetomagus
Hretha's Moon, A.D. 426

On a morning when a wind from the west chased mare's tails of cloud across the sky and the warming air caressed the skin with a promise of spring, a man came running up the road from the river crying that the Huns were on their way. But fast as he ran, Hun ponies were faster, and he had scarcely gasped out his message before Brunahild heard hoofbeats echoing on the stones of the forum, and calls of greeting.

She noted with disquiet how the sound of her own language stirred her emotions. It was a pity that they had not come until now, when she could no longer claim nonconsummation as an excuse to break her marriage. During the long nights of winter, while Gudrun grew bloated as a cow, Brunahild had completed the sexual subjugation of Gundohar.

Riders began to file beneath the arch of the gate into the courtyard and she leaned out the window to see them. It was not an army, only a delegation, but the Hun riders sat their horses with an easy alertness as if they could give battle in a moment, even here. Their bows were on their backs, but they rode unarmored in lapped coats edged with fur and hoods of skin embroidered in bright silk. Gold gleamed here and there from their clothing, but it was on their horses that their wealth had been lavished. Headstalls and harness gleamed with plates of figured gold. She glimpsed a horsetail standard and realized that at least one of the khans must be among them, but before she could see their faces, they passed through the archway that led toward the stables and disappeared.

She turned away from the window. Was it her father? That seemed unlikely, for he served mostly in the eastern lands. Whoever they were, she supposed she must greet them as a queen. She called for her women, who came so swiftly that they must have been waiting, buzzing with speculation, just outside her door.

"Be still—" she said sharply. "They will not eat you. Get out the brocaded tunica, and my jewels."

She was already wearing a gown of fine black wool, banded at neck and wrists with tablet-woven braid worked with gold. Now she exchanged her wrap for a tunica of silk the color of old wine with a brocaded pattern of running horses. Her palla was of crimson wool, as sheer as cotton from India, banded with gold. There were golden threads in her cincture as well, and upon her breast lay a necklet of golden teardrops and embossed discs set with cabochon garnets and pearls, linked by twisted chains.

As she was adding a touch of color to her lips she heard a stirring among the women behind her. She lifted the mirror of polished bronze and saw Gundohar behind her. Calmly she finished her task and then turned to face him, her crimson draperies swirling back from her gold-bound braids like dark flames.

She saw him blink, and with an effort kept her lip from curling. She must greet him now, as always, with unruffled serenity. He had cried, in the throes of one of his fruitless attempts to wake her to an answering passion, that she was like the goddess-statues the Romans had left, as beautiful and as cold. And like one of the images, she had answered him with an enigmatic smile.

He was learning, she thought, that losing himself in her body brought him no closer to what he really wanted from her. In the years when she denied him he had achieved a certain detachment, but now, as the betraying muscle twitched in his cheek at the sight of her, she knew he had no defenses against her anymore.

"You have heard that we have guests, I see." He drew himself up, striving to match her poise. "Will you come with me to the hall to greet them? Your uncle Attila has asked for you."

Brunahild suppressed an impulse to say she was unwell; clearly she was dressed for the meeting; she would not have been believed. And what, after all, had she expected him to say? She had heard that Attila was leading troops for Aetius in Gallia; it should not surprise her to see him here.

But as she walked with Gundohar into the basilica and saw her uncle standing with his commanders, she could not help thinking, *That is the man who sold me into servitude and this is the man who paid the price for me! The only one who is not here is the man who betrayed me.*

They came down the steps of the dais to greet their visitors and Attila held Brunahild by the shoulders for a moment, evaluating her, she thought, as if she were one of his mares. She had forgotten how he was—always looking at things to see what they were good for. But she, in turn, was assessing him, noting the new grey in his beard and how five years had deepened the lines of power graven between nose and jaw.

"Come, drink with me, my kinsman, to celebrate your coming," said Gundohar, gesturing to the servants to bring wine. "This is a noble vintage, they tell me, from the hills near Tolosa."

A young man scarcely out of boyhood, who was standing at Attila's elbow, peered at the seal, then laughed. Gundohar looked at his guest inquiringly.

"It is from vineyards that belong to his father—" said Attila, his lips twitching. "This is Carpileon, Aetius' boy by that daughter of Theoderid he married. We bring him on the campaign. He rides with my son Ellak—" he nodded toward the other young man in the company, "like his father rode with me."

Brunahild looked at Aetius' son with more attention, trying to see in the unformed features beneath the shock of fair hair some reflection of the young Roman whom she had met in

Attila's camp almost ten years before. The boy would not have looked out of place among the Burgunds—Aetius his father was half-Goth, which would make the lad more barbarian than Roman by blood. By conquest or marriage, the tribes were taking over the Empire. She wondered if there would be any true Roman families remaining, at least in the provinces, by the time a century had passed.

But whether their grandfathers had been Roman or Goth, they all spoke Latin. She smoothed the fabric of her tunica, enjoying the feel of the rich fabric that had been woven in the city of Constantine, and thought that perhaps she should be wondering whether in another generation there would be any Germanic families there.

The Walkyriun had feared this, in their endless debates around the fire at Fox Dance. Perhaps they had been right to support the Alamanni against the Burgunds; dimly, in this moment, she could even understand why they had reacted so violently to what they had considered her own treachery. But they might just as well have spared her the pain and themselves the trouble, Brunahild thought bitterly. All their magic was powerless against the lure of silken garments and Gaulish wine.

She turned her gaze to Attila's son and wondered if one day her own people would succumb as well. Like his father, he was dressed in Roman cloth cut in a distinctly nomad style. The Huns seemed to be having no difficulty resisting the temptation to mimic the Empire. They took what they wanted from everyone, Roman or Goth, and tossed the rest away. *All except for me,* she thought then. *I am neither Hun nor Burgund nor Goth. I am an image that Gundohar worships, a memory that Sigfrid fears. I will not be real until he gives my soul back to me!*

The slave held the wine tray out to her and she took a goblet, grateful for the kick beneath the rich bouquet of the wine. In the past few years she had learned to appreciate the blood of the grape—sometimes it could blunt her pain.

"Perhaps Carpileon and Ellak would like to see the city—" said Gundohar. "I will send for my young brother Gislahar to be their guide. They are much of an age." He led his guests toward the benches that had been set around the wrought iron brazier, set in the center of the floor where the long hearth would have been in an old-style hall.

"So, are you travelling to show these young men the world, or is there to be a campaign?"

Attila's lips curled beneath the straggling moustaches and he gave the grunt that was, as she remembered, the closest he came to a laugh.

"It is the Visigoths—this boy's grandfather! Ever since Theoderid and his men deserted the Roman army when they fight the Vandals in Hispania, he thinks he can get away with anything. The word is now that he will march on Arelas, and so Aetius calls to me."

"Why did the Romans let them get away with it?" Gundohar exclaimed. "They had the victory, I am told, and lost it when Theoderid withdrew. They broke their oaths, and still the Romans call them feoderati and pay them the stipend. It is no wonder if they think that now they can do whatever they please!"

Attila shrugged. "The emperor died before they could decide how to punish, then the Romans were too busy fighting each other to trouble about Goths. We were too late to join that war, but this campaign against Theoderid will be good fighting. I think they do not truly wish to win the city, but if they make a good battle, the Romans will pay them more . . ."

Gundohar grinned. The Burgunds themselves had been known to use that tactic at times. It was an ancient game, profitable when both sides understood the rules. The Romans played one set of barbarians against another, and the tribes worked off old hostilities with the emperor's blessing. But the Huns were not feoderati. Unlike the tribes, they did not desire to live in the Empire, only to plunder it. Did Aetius realize, Brunahild wondered, how dangerous an ally Attila could be?

"And Aetius will get a new arm ring from Galla Placidia?" asked Gundohar.

"If he does, he better check it for poison," said one of the other Huns, a big, black-haired fellow who looked like an Alan. "The empress does not like him, no. She wants her favorite, Bonifatius, to be Master of Soldiers for the Empire."

"I thought the new *Magister Utriusque Militiae* was a man named Felix," said Brunahild, pronouncing her newly learned Latin carefully.

Once more Attila smiled. "She does not dare to choose Bonifatius because of Aetius, or Aetius because of Bonifatius. Felix is safe, for a while."

"My father will be the Patrician of Rome one day," Carpileon said loudly. The men looked at each other, even Attila, whom men counted as Aetius' friend, unwilling to echo the boy's unquestioning loyalty.

"He is a great warrior," said Brunahild finally, "and he has done much already. Perhaps he will." And she thought that might even be true. Bonifatius was a good general who had achieved success against the Vandals in the province of Africa, but he had only a Roman army with its unpredictable loyalties. Aetius had the Huns. Attila would be faithful, she thought, to the man who paid him.

Gislahar came in then, and he and Ellak and Carpileon went off together, eyeing each other with wary curiosity like strange dogs. The men's conversation turned to details of the coming warfare, evaluations of Theoderid's fighting strength, and their own problems of supply. Brunahild listened, remembering the lessons she had learned among the Walkyriun. Once, she had dreamed of helping her hero through such battles, but now there was no chance even that some Goth would kill him; though all the rest of her magic had failed, she trusted the spells with which she had warded him to keep him safe against any foe.

It was not until after dinner that Brunahild found an opportunity to speak with Attila alone. Even then, she might not have had the resolve to do so if he had not noticed her watching Sigfrid as he assisted Gudrun, so heavily pregnant by now that she waddled like a cow, from the hall.

"Wolf-eyes . . ." he said reflectively. "Your daughter Asliud has them also. Sigfrid is her father, yes? Does he know?"

"No!" Brunahild said explosively, then, realizing what she had admitted, released tensions she had not known she held in a long sigh. "He does not deserve to know—he betrayed me!"

"Ah, in the fight—"

"You knew that it was Sigfrid who defeated me, and not Gundohar?" It was her turn to stare at him. "Why didn't you stop it?"

"The fight was your condition, not ours," her uncle answered her. "Gundohar's oath sealed the treaty. I thought you saw the substitution, and accepted it to save honor. Is it so bad to be the Burgund queen?"

"To lie beside a man you despise? To never be able to ride free?"

"Go hunting with the men," Attila replied. "Lie with Sigfrid for pleasure. Does Gundohar know that you love his sister's man instead of him?"

"Sigfrid? I hate him! I hate them all!" Hugging her arms, she turned away.

Attila grunted. "Sometimes hate is even better spice than love. I think this makes you want him all the more."

Brunahild remembered the supple line of Sigfrid's back, the controlled grace with which he had assisted Gudrun to rise, and felt a pang in her gut as if she had been stabbed there.

"I cannot bear it . . ." she whispered. "I cannot go on this way. Let me go back to Bertriud and Heimar. I do not know what may happen if I stay!"

"And break the treaty?"

"Break the marriage!" she responded angrily. "What do I care for your alliances?"

"What do I care who you sleep with?" he answered equably. "But the Burgunds would be insulted if you ran away. I do not need angry Burgunds at my back when I am fighting Goths at Arelas."

Slowly she turned back to him, and saw his face still at what he read in her eyes. "You will . . ." she said quietly. "I promise that you will all care, one day."

After the Huns left it began to rain, day after day of steady downpour that found its way through thatching and seeped beneath walls. The Burgunds laughed and wondered if there would be any fighting this year after all—the Goths were not a naval power. But as each day the Rhenus lapped ever higher along its stony banks, speculation became more subdued. Stock had already been driven up from the water meadows; now men began to ask the old Roman families if the waters ever reached the town.

Gudrun stayed with her women in the room where in dryer weather they opened long windows to let in the sun. Now the windows were tightly shuttered, and oil lamps provided an illumination too uncertain for fine work like embroidery. But one could spin in the dark, and spin they did, till Gudrun's fingers were tender and her back ached from sitting too long.

These days, it was true, her back seemed to hurt no matter what she did. Her belly had grown enormous. Sometimes it seemed to her it must be a colt she was carrying, or when the baby was particularly active, a whole litter of wolf cubs. The worst part of it was the way the older women grinned and nodded when she complained. It was spring, and everywhere new life was springing from the ground. Only she, it seemed, was doomed to wallow along forever, burdened by this child.

The equinox passed. Somewhere above the clouds the moon was swelling toward its full. But the meadow where they celebrated the feast of Ostara was a marsh. She did not know where they could go to greet the goddess even if they were sure exactly on which day her festival should fall. The Christian priests were luckier, counting the days to the feast of their god's resurrection according to the emperor's calendar. But the roof of the chapel was leaking and, unless they could fix it, they would have a damp ritual.

That morning Sigfrid and the other men had gone hunting on the other side of the river, defying the weather. They would stay overnight, shivering beneath hide shelters, and come home on the morrow soaked and sneezing, smelling of wet horse and rain. But at least they were outside, doing something. Uncomfortable as they must be, she envied them.

A shutter rattled in the wind and Gudrun heaved herself to her feet to fix it. "Oh no, my lady, sit down—I'll close it," said Ursula, hurrying across the room. Gudrun sighed and set her spindle to twirling once more. On the benches beside the brazier the women were talking; one of the chieftains' daughters was pregnant and would not name the father of her child.

The thread Gudrun was spinning broke and the spindle went rolling across the floor. She swore and started to get up. This time it was Adalfrida who put down her own work, snatched up the spindle, and handed it to her mistress, who looked at it distastefully. Then Gudrun stumped back to her workbasket and stuffed the offending tool inside.

"I'm too restless to sit here spinning," she told the girl. "There must be something else I can do." She saw a broom leaning against the wall and began to sweep up the wisps of wool that had drifted across the floor, ignoring Adalfrida's worried frown.

Her mother looked up from her place closest to the fire, eyed her speculatively, then returned to her work again. Now that she thought about it, Gudrun realized that her mother had been there with the other women more often than not these past days, though generally she kept to her own warm room when the weather was chill.

The old queen was watching her—they were all watching her, Gudrun thought angrily. She swept more vigorously, reaching under the carved chest to get at the dust there. At the end of the room were shelves where they kept supplies for women's work. But with so many using the room these past few days the contents were a jumble.

"Ursula, Gunna, come here—" she said sharply. "These shelves are a disgrace—look, the awls have fallen down among the spindles, and the box of needles has spilled. And the embroidery silks—what a tangle! We must sort them before they grow worse." She carried the basket over to a table and began to separate threads while the others, exchanging amused glances, started on the shelves.

Straightening out the thread gave some relief, but soon enough she was finished. She moved restlessly around the room, examining the others' work until the girls grew nervous, and all the time Grimahild watched her, and never said a word.

The shutter began to bang again, and this time Gudrun strode across the room to fasten it before one of the others could move. She reached out to grasp the handles, her belly pressing hard against the wall, stretched, and got a faceful of rain. The child kicked in protest, and as she pulled the shutter in she felt a sudden gush of wetness between her thighs. For a moment she thought it was the rain, but this water was warm. Had she pissed herself? With the baby sitting on her bladder that had become a problem, but there was no odor. She grabbed the other shutter and slammed it shut, then stood looking down at the spreading puddle of water on the floor.

I should change into a dry gown, she told herself, then sucked in her breath as the familiar ache in the small of her back became a rolling pain that hardened all her muscles. When it let go, Gudrun's mother was by her side.

"I need to return to my chamber—I seem to have wet myself—" she began, but Grimahild shook her head and smiled.

"Your waters have broken, my child. It is the birthing chamber you must go to now."

Gudrun stared at her. *At last!* one part of her mind was crying, glad to have the waiting over, but another part fluttered anxiously. *But I'm not ready—it's too soon, too soon!*

Sigfrid rode in with the others as the last light was fading. They had ranged far up into the forest, but the dozen fat deer they had killed would keep the household in fresh meat for a time. He strode down the corridor to his chambers, looking forward to the spiced ale that Gudrun always kept waiting, but it was little Ursula who met him, her cheeks growing pink as he smiled at her and asked for Gudrun.

"Oh, my lord, you do not know? Since yesterday afternoon she has been in labor. It will ease her to hear you have returned."

"I'll tell her myself as soon as I get dry—" He finished stripping off his muddy tunic. He sat down on a bench and his body servant began to unlace his boots.

"Oh, my lord, the birthing chamber is no place for a man. You will see her when the child is born."

"She has been in labor a whole day?" He frowned, flexed his toes in the bearskin rug, and held out his other foot. "Is not that a long time?" Animal birthings were generally quick and efficient, though herders sometimes had to assist their cows. But he knew very little about how such things went among humankind.

Ursula's gaze slid away as he looked up at her. "Perhaps," she said uncomfortably, "though they say it is always longer with the first child. But we have gone through all the king's house, opening all the doors and searching out every knot and untying it," she went on, "so that nothing will obstruct her. You must make sure that all the ties on the gear you have brought home with you are undone."

"I see—" Sigfrid let the man pull off the other boot and set it aside, laces dangling. He tugged at the cord of his breeches and turned away from her to step out of them, trying to ignore her stare.

"Put on the long robe—" said his man. "It needs no belt and will keep you warm."

He let them dress him, frowning. There was a note of anxiety in Ursula's voice that he did not like, despite her words. But there seemed to be nothing he could do. It was the custom for a man to get drunk with his fellows while his wife was giving birth; perhaps, he thought as he started back to the hall, because it helped him to bear the knowledge that his woman was in danger and there was no way he could help her—that in fact, it was his own deed that had caused her pain.

"Do you think we should send for Father Priscus again?"

Gudrun knew that was Ursula's voice, but it seemed to be coming from a very long way away. For a lifetime, now, she had lain in a dream of pain. In her more lucid intervals, she knew that it was only two days, but though there were moments of surcease, the convulsions that were racking her body never seemed to end.

"What good can he do? Do you think it will help my girl bear this babe to have him gabbling about her sins?" Grimahild replied. The birthing bed was hung about with charms the old woman had placed there. For most of the morning, she had been muttering spells. But they had done no more good than the priest's prayers.

"I meant—" Ursula began, but the old queen would not let her finish.

"I will make an offering to the Mothers," said Grimahild. "They will be more useful by far than a god who tells his worshippers that the joys of the flesh are evil, and that women are a temptation to sin."

But Ursula had meant to call the priest to say the prayers for the dying, and Gudrun knew it. Birthing should not take so long, even for a first child. She felt another useless contraction begin to gather and whimpered. The straw with which they had stuffed the mattress crackled as her body stiffened. Then the pang passed and she lay back again.

She let out her breath in a long groan. And yet this contraction had been weaker than the last one, and the intervals between them were growing longer. That was not how it should be. Perhaps soon they would stop entirely, and she would die with the child still inside her. In this moment of relief, that did not seem so ill a thing, if she could escape from the pain.

"We must do something," Adalfrida's whisper came clear. "The people will take it as an evil omen if she dies, or the child."

"Is that all you can think of?" Ursula replied. "The lady Gudrun has been kind to both of us, I cannot believe that God would punish her by letting her die. She has been so happy with her man."

"I have never understood why you Christians, who sing so loudly about your heaven, speak of death as a punishment!" Adalfrida said tartly. "For Gudrun, death might be a mercy, but I do not want to lose her. Go to the hall and call her husband. Perhaps the sight of him will hearten her."

Gudrun moved her head weakly against the pillow. "Sigfrid

. . . yes, call him—" she whispered. If she could see him it would be better. He was so strong, perhaps he could even take away the pain.

"There now, my lady," Adalfrida bent over her, wiping her brow with a damp cloth. "Rest easy. Surely he will be here soon."

Gudrun shook her head, but another pang was coming. She moaned as it rippled through her, but it was weak, and in a few moments she lay still. Perhaps she slept a little then, for when she opened her eyes again, Sigfrid was bending over her.

She could tell from his expression how the sight of her shocked him, but she was past caring. "I am sorry—" she whispered. "I have tried to fight, but I am losing. I wanted so much to give you a child . . ."

"Live! You must live, Gudrun!" He gripped her hand painfully. "My mother died. You must not leave me as well!"

She clutched at his hand, her fingers twining frantically in his as the terrible clenching of her belly began once more. She clung to the strength in him, but the power that had her in its grip was stronger. Once more she could feel it sweeping through her and this time she cried out. She felt him flinch, but he did not let go.

Things became unclear after that. Perhaps she was fevered, for often she could feel someone bending over her and wiping her brow. Sometimes Sigfrid was with her, at other times it was her mother, her eyes reddened as if she had been weeping. To Gudrun, that seemed of all things the most strange. She tried to ask her to make it stop, as if she were a little girl running to her mother to make the hurt go away, but Grimahild did not seem to hear.

"This is not natural—a young woman, healthy and strong!" A fragment of conversation came to her.

"She strains to deliver, but the babe cannot come," came Ursula's answer.

"It should not be so!" said Adalfrida. "She is young, and wide through the hips. She ought to have given birth easily. There is some other cause here, and if she has been ill-wished the source is not far to look for. Who has the most cause to envy her?"

"Brunahild?" It was only a whisper beneath the babble of other conversations, but Gudrun heard. "The queen?"

"She is barren, and she has the knowledge to do it . . . she was trained by—" abruptly Adalfrida's voice ceased, and in another moment the other women had fallen silent as well. Gudrun forced herself to open her eyes, to turn her head so that she could see the door.

A shape of shadow stood there, wrapped in a dark mantle, her shoulders veiled by a fall of black hair. Gudrun blinked, wondering if Hella herself had come to carry her away. Then the newcomer moved fully into the lamplight, and she saw that it was Brunahild.

"Bird of ill omen, what do you here?" The old queen stepped to bar her way.

"What you, old hedge-witch, cannot do." Brunahild swept past her and stood looking down at Gudrun. "Sister, will you trust me?"

She sounded angry, but Gudrun felt the easy tears well from beneath her eyelids. *I never wanted anything else*—she wanted to say, *it is you who turned from me!* But the words would not come. Mutely she nodded.

"Then I will do what I can . . ."

Brunahild straightened and handed her mantle to the wide-eyed child who came to assist her. She had spoken confidently, but as she looked down at Gudrun her heart sank. She had seen men dead on the battlefield who looked better than the other woman did now. Why indeed had she come?

Yesterday, hearing Gudrun's screams even from the other side of the courtyard, she had found herself hoping that her rival would die. If Gudrun were dead, then Sigfrid would be free again. For a little while she had dreamed of running away with him to live the life they had once planned. And then he had come riding in with Gundohar.

Watching from the window, she had seen his face brighten as he started toward his rooms, and the dream had died. Sigfrid was the one who had betrayed her, not Gudrun. How could she have forgotten how she hated him?

When Gudrun's screaming ceased, she had waited to hear of the birth of the child. Yet the silence from across the courtyard was worse, and at last she had had no choice but to come. But if she could not save Gudrun now, she thought grimly, she might have to flee alone, lest they drown her for the witchcraft of which she had accused Grimahild.

She turned to face her mother-in-law. "Old woman, I do not discount your magic, and perhaps I can do no better. But I was trained by the Walkyriun."

"You were a battle-maid!" said the old queen scornfully. "What would you know of women's mysteries?"

Brunahild shrugged. "It is true that I cared more for the sword than the spindle, but we had to study all the old skills. Wieldrud the midwife made me learn her secrets, whether I expected to need them or no." *And I too*, she thought bitterly, *have borne Sigfrid's child.* "Tell me, how far apart are her pangs, and what herbs have you given her?"

Still frowning, Grimahild began to list the medicines. As Brunahild suspected, they were much the same as the herbs that Huld had taught her to use—infusions of yarrow, birthroot, and motherwort, and oil of pennyroyal. The difficulty was not in stimulating the womb, or at least had not been, until Gudrun grew so tired. But strain as she might, the child would not come.

Brunahild placed her hands upon the laboring woman's rigid belly, trying to feel where the baby lay. Certainly it was low enough—what was the problem? Suddenly she remembered how she had assisted Randgrid when one of the mares belonging to the Walkyriun was having difficulty with her foal. She took a deep breath.

"Pray to the Mothers now, or to your god to help me," she said to the other women. "What I must do is dangerous, but I think that if I do not try she will indeed die!"

She rolled her sleeves up as far as she could above the elbow, then hunkered down in the straw, a bowl of warmed oil beside her. Closing her eyes, she set her hands over Gudrun's womb. It was harder than she had expected to aim her attention. She was out of practice for this; each creak and whisper brought her back to awareness of the others in the room. But she persisted, willing herself to know nothing but the other woman's flesh and the babe imprisoned within.

An image came to her of a river running deep underground. There were words in it, a soft and flowing river voice, like a lullaby sung by the mother she had never known. She had heard that music long ago, when she hung on the rune-tree and listened to the gods. *Mother help me*, she found herself praying, believing in that moment in a power that she had thought denied her forever. *Help her...* she prayed, and the melody became a song. The music was flowing through her. Knowledge came to her, as it had when she warded Sigfrid against all foes. For that moment she became Sigdrifa the Walkyrja once more. Where bitterness had rankled, compassion was welling like the waters of the sacred well.

"*Perthro...*" she sang, drawing the womb rune upended. "*Ingwaz...*" She drew the seed within it. The planted seed will grow. "*Jera...*" In its proper season comes the harvest, all things in harmony. "*Laguz...*" Now the waters are flowing... "*Uruz...*" Strength comes forth to change the world. Change.... She frowned, and then drew the rune of the ice-seed, the hailstone, that striking, transforms. "*Hagalaz!*" she cried suddenly, and felt the babe within the womb kick in answer.

But the kick came from low on the side, not the center as it should by now. What she had feared was the truth, then, and the child was turned in the womb.

"*Hagalaz, hagalaz,* here our need is," she whispered, "let the power of change strike deep within!" She bound together the runes for Hail and Need, drew them on the skin of Gudrun's belly and pressed downward where she could feel the harder curve of the baby's head beneath the taut skin. At the same time she pushed up on the other side where she had felt it kicking, and Gudrun screamed. Another pain began to ridge the belly then and Brunahild waited, but when it had passed, she pushed once more, trying to manipulate the child that struggled within like a badger in a bag.

One of the women exclaimed, and Brunahild saw emerging from between Gudrun's bloody thighs a tiny hand. She swore, dipped up oil and slathered it over her fingers and forearm, then very carefully grasped the baby's arm and eased it back, following it up the birth passage to the opening of the womb, blessing the Mothers that her hands were small. The channel was slick already with the blood that was trickling from the womb, but tight even now. Gudrun moaned as Brunahild thrust two fingers through the opening, pushing on the baby's arm as she maintained pressure on the head from the outside.

Again the great muscles contracted, and she gasped as she felt their strength. Here, surely, was a mighty mystery. The Roman priests who said there was no Goddess surely had never felt this. No warrior, dealing deathblows in battle, ever gripped with such power.

Now that power filled her as well. When the muscles of the birth passage relented once more she pushed again, and this time her fingers touched the hard curve of the infant's skull.

"There, my little one, there—" she murmured, withdrawing her hand. "Now the door is open. Come out into the world!"

The womb clenched again and the watching women cried out as they saw the baby's head show for a moment in the opening to the womb. But Gudrun's body, weakened by her long labor, had not the strength to push it free.

"Push now!" she exclaimed, drawing the strength rune on Gudrun's belly once more, but the other woman only shook her head and moaned.

Brunahild sat back, thinking furiously. Once more she remembered battle. She had seen men in this condition, so weary they could not lift their shields for protection even when a foe came at them with a sword. How had she herself survived it? She was supple with exercise, but narrower through the hips than Gudrun.

Then, with a pain that should not have surprised her, she remembered that when she gave birth she had been wearing the ring. . . .

Brunahild turned to the youngest of Gudrun's maids. "Get

the golden neck ring that your lady wore at the shrine," she said harshly, anguish warring with the exaltation that still filled her. The girl stared at her in amazement. "Put it around her neck!" she exclaimed. "It will save her and the child."

Grimahild had drawn closer. She bent and began to lightly massage her daughter's belly.

"Rest, wait, soon your strength will come to you . . ." she crooned. Then she looked up at Brunahild. "I thought the Walkyriun had taken the knowledge from you. But you still have all their wisdom—why have you hoarded it, woman? There is so much we could learn!"

Brunahild shook her head. She had not known, or perhaps she had not been willing to face the pain of remembering. Only this crisis had brought it back, just as, she thought unwillingly, a dangerous foe brought forth Gundohar's battlecraft. She could feel the power of the Mother-Goddess beginning to ebb within her as others took over helping Gudrun, and trembled as if the Walkyriun were taking it from her again.

Lady, why are you leaving me? her spirit cried. And this time there was an answer: *I am where I always was. It is you who turn away. . . .*

Then the girl brought in the ring and lifted Gudrun so that Grimahild could fit it around her neck.

Brunahild shuddered at the sight of it. "Now the power of the Goddess is in you," she said, her voice cracking. "The Frowe's runes are on that necklet—it is an image of Brisingamen, whose radiance renews the world."

"Hail Froja!" murmured Adalfrida.

"Hail to the Mothers!" said Ursula.

"Hail to holy Earth that givest to all!" Grimahild replied.

And Gudrun took one deep breath and then another, and let them out on a shuddering sigh. To Brunahild it seemed that the other woman's flesh began to glow. And now she could see the contraction beginning, rolling across the mound of the belly.

"Hold your breath, daughter, hold—" cautioned Grimahild,

and then, as the muscle flattened, "now you can push the child—"

The head bulged through the birth canal, then was drawn back again. They waited, and in a few moments Gudrun's body arched once more. This time the baby's head emerged entirely. Grimahild reached between the taut thighs to support it, murmuring encouragement.

Once more, thought Brunahild, *and it will be over.* "You can scream this time," she said aloud, remembering how it had been for her with Asliud. "Shout your battle cry!"

Gudrun tried to smile, then her gaze went inward as her body gathered itself. Her heels dug into the straw and Ursula ran to brace her shoulders. The grunt with which she had pushed before became a moan which grew until it was the shout that Brunahild had asked for. And with that cry, the baby slid out into Grimahild's waiting hands.

For a moment Brunahild wondered if the purplish, wrinkled thing could still be alive. Then its grandmother lifted and smacked it, and the first thin, aggrieved wail became a lusty yell. Color flooded the waxy skin as the baby gulped air. *A new life,* she thought, shivering at the wonder of it. *And every human in the world came into it this way!*

Then the last of her exaltation ebbed abruptly, leaving her drained and dry on the shores of a vanished sea. The baby was clearly a human child now, and, as Brunahild saw with a dull satisfaction, another girl. She hugged her arms, swaying a little with reaction. *Gudrun has given Sigfrid a child, and I helped her!*

The old queen set the infant on her mother's belly, then busied herself with cutting the cord, her movements swift and certain now. Adalfrida brought a cloth and Grimahild swaddled the infant, held it a moment, clucking, then set it in its mother's arms.

"Oh, Brunahild—" whispered Gudrun. "Come and see!"

Brunahild found herself moving to the other woman's side and looked down at her. Gudrun was holding her babe as once she had held Asliud. At this moment that did not seem so very long ago. The tiny features were still folded in upon themselves like the petals of a rose, but upon the forehead lay drying wisps of fair hair. The baby made a little rootling noise, like a small pig, and then, finding nothing, opened her eyes.

A breath of cooler air touched Brunahild's cheek and she looked back over her shoulder. Sigfrid was standing in the doorway. She glanced from the man to the child and back again. From the two faces, so different, the same eyes looked out at her. Asliud's eyes.

But the baby's gaze was wondering and clear, while in the man's face she read shame. Brunahild bared her teeth in a smile as feral as his own.

"She is her father's child for sure," she said softly. "She has wolf eyes." For a moment her gaze lingered on the neck ring, then she turned, snatched her mantle from the chair and wrapped it around her, and swept past Sigfrid to the door.

"Wait—" he said, reaching out to her. "I must thank you. They say that you saved her—"

Brunahild gave a short laugh. "It was not for your sake," she said in a low voice. "And if you keep faith with Gudrun as you did with me, one day she may regret having survived."

Behind her she could hear the babble of women rejoicing. But as Brunahild walked through the passage back to her chamber, her cheeks were wet with tears.

Chapter Eleven The Rune Rod

The Woodcutters' Forest
Blood Moon, A.D. 426

They named Gudrun's child Sunnilda, the battle sow, because she had fought so hard to come into the world. From the beginning the infant grew mightly, though her mother recovered slowly, for she had been much torn by the delivery. But Gudrun delighted in her child. Sigfrid's first terror lest he lose them was replaced by a euphoria which wore off more gradually. This child was like the little sisters whom he had known so briefly. But Sunnilda had wolf eyes like his own. She would never turn from him in fear.

That summer the land was full of rumors of fighting. The Goths continued restive, and Aetius mounted two more campaigns against them. Gundohar led a contingent of warriors to support him, but for the first few months after Sunnilda's birth Sigfrid stayed close to home. It was not until the summer gave way to autumn and mother and child were thriving that he found himself growing restless, not until they came to the moon of slaughter, when the beasts were butchered that could not be fed until spring.

When the weather was fine, the men practiced with their weapons, but the best sport of all was to track down wild boar in the forests and chase after the autumn-fattened deer. For the men the hunt was good training, and the wild game they brought in a necessary addition to the smoked meats in the barns behind the high king's hall.

On a chill evening when the men sat over their ale Godomar announced that he would lead a hunting party out across the river on the morrow, and Sigfrid knew that he could stay cooped up with the women no longer.

He woke in the predawn darkness, for Godo wanted to start early, and rolled carefully out of the bed he shared with Gudrun. He moved around it to the chest where his clothes were laid ready and paused, looking down at her. She lay on her side, with Sunnilda snuggled into the hollow of her shoulder. The light of the oil lamp that they had left burning so that she could see to change the baby's clouts played tenderly across smooth curves of cheek and arm. Gently it burnished the mother's bright hair and struck sparks from that of the child.

Seeing them so, Sigfrid found his chest tightening so that it was hard to breathe. Awareness narrowed to those two sweet, sleeping faces; they justified the world. He wanted to cry out, to hold them tight, to set his great strength against all foes. But he must not wake them, and so he could only stand still, shaken by the force of feelings he could not put into words.

He drew in air in a long gasp and as he let it out, began to regain control. Still trembling, he knelt beside the bed, rested his cheek for a moment against his wife's outflung hand and brushed a kiss across the baby's sweet-scented hair.

Since the birth, though they shared a bed, he and Gudrun had not made love. At first that was because she was healing, and by the time it might have been physically possible, her whole being was focused on the child. In truth this abstinence was not the hardship he might have expected. His desire had always been awakened by women's reactions to him, and these days Gudrun had the milky scent of a mother. The desire that surged in him now was to protect her and her child.

As he rose and began to pull on his clothes he found himself wondering whether he would be able to make love to her even if she wanted him, or if his lust would always be quenched by the memory of how she had looked when she was in labor. He knew now why men were kept out of the birthing chamber. The women had assured him that Gudrun was unlikely to have the same trouble again. But Sigfrid found it hard to believe them. He would give Gudrun no more children. Having seen that agony, what husband would allow his wife to go through it a second time?

The hunters had brought down two deer and were climbing the stony track toward the ridge in search of another when Sigfrid felt Grani lurch beneath him. In another moment the horse had come to a halt, shivering. Sigfrid slid off the animal and began to run his hands down the horse's legs, trying to see where the trouble lay. In a few minutes, Gislahar came back down the path to find out what was wrong.

"I'm out of the hunt, I fear," said Sigfrid, looking up at him. "Grani has sprained something in his off foreleg, and though I could keep up with you on foot, I don't want to leave him."

"You could probably outrun us all," Gislahar laughed. "But can't we send one of the thralls to stay with the horse while you come along?"

"If it were any other horse, perhaps." Sigfrid grinned back at him. "But Grani still has three good legs and I have no mind to pay weregild for someone's injury. There were three men hurt when they brought him back from Hunland, I recall. I will start homeward, resting him, and meet you at the river landing in three days' time."

"Do you need food—" Gislahar began, then shook his head. "I forgot, you have lived in the wilds and know how to forage."

Sigfrid nodded. The autumn woods were a storehouse of food for those who knew their ways. "But I will take that skin of ale you are carrying, if you wish to gift it. Make my apologies to your brother, and wish him good hunting."

Gislahar nodded and untied the hard leather bottle. "We won't kill as many without you there—" he said glumly, but he turned his pony and headed back up the track.

When the hoofbeats had faded, Sigfrid stood for a moment, savoring the quiet. Perhaps this was what he had needed— not simply to get away, but to get away from humankind.

Grani whickered, lifting his foreleg and touching it tentatively to the ground.

"You're right, lad, this is no good place to stop in," Sigfrid said softly. "Let's get back down the hill and find you some grass."

Pausing frequently, they made their way down the slope and back into the thicker forest. As evening approached, the clouds had thickened, descending until the woods were swathed in a pervasive, penetrating mist that made Sigfrid wonder if he had wandered into Nibelheim. What light remained seemed to come from all directions equally, and though Sigfrid understood the lay of the land well enough never to be truly lost, it became clear that he was not going to reach the riverbank before darkness fell.

Presently he chanced upon a pathway that seemed more than a deer trail, and his heart lifted, for the mist had become a drizzle that chilled to the bone. Where there was a path there must be some shelter, and even if it were abandoned, there would be water near, and dry wood for a fire. Even Grani moved out more easily as they wound through the trees. Soon Sigfrid scented woodsmoke, and rounding a stand of birch trees, saw no abandoned hut but a well-built longhouse in the old style, with a gated entrance midway along the side and thatching nearly down to the ground. From behind it a pony whinnied and Grani replied.

He left the stallion in the yard with the reins dangling and knocked on the doorpost. Someone coughed, and in a few moments the door was pulled open. A man peered out at him.

"Who is it? What do you want here?"

"A friend to the house and all within," answered Sigfrid, "who needs a spot to tether a lame horse, and a place to sleep out of the rain." The door opened wider, and firelight fell full upon his face.

"Lord Sigfrid!" the man exclaimed.

To his left he glimpsed stalls and storage. In the entrance to the other half of the house Sigfrid saw a woman leaning on a staff. Forest-trained vision recognized the shape of her before he could make out her features, and he felt an irrational disquiet.

"Lady Grimahild," he saluted her. "I did not know you were here—"

Like everyone else in the king's household, he was aware that the old queen spent much of her time in various houses she had built in the forest, gathering herbs and, so the rumor went, brewing her spells. But he had never thought much about it. Indeed, he tried to avoid her. Ever since she had physicked him when he first came to the Burgunds she had made him uneasy. She looked at him as if they shared some secret.

"Come in—" she said. "There is food and fire. You can even bring your animal inside, if you can tether him so he does not eat my herbs."

Grumbling, her manservant was already shifting bunches of greenery to join the ones that dangled from the other side of the sloping ceiling. As he brought the horse in, Sigfrid could see shelves crammed with leather bags. Rows of baskets were lined up on the floor. She must have enough herbs to dose the entire town of Borbetomagus here!

"A fine animal—" said the queen. "What has gone wrong with him?"

"A sprain in the pastern, I think, from the way he is favoring it . . ."

"Baldur's mount has maimed his foot, has he?" She laughed softly. "If you will, I can do a magic to ease him."

"If he will allow it—" Sigfrid said dubiously as the old woman stumped forward. The horse tossed his head at her approach, but quieted as she blew into his nostrils and murmured some odd, whickering syllables. She ran her hand along the stallion's shoulder and down the leg. Sigfrid saw a tremor run beneath the animal's skin at her touch, but to his amazement, Grani stood still.

"There now . . . there now . . ." She squatted, setting both hands around the foreleg, and began to hum. And then, somehow, there were words in the singing, an odd minor melody that made Sigfrid's neck hair tingle, but seemed to calm the stallion even more.

> *"Fol and Wodan went to the wood*
> *Baldur's mount has maimed its foot.*
> *Then sang Sindgund, Sunna's sister,*
> *then sang Fricca, Folla's sister,*
> *then sang Wodan, as well he could:*
> *Be it bone sprain,*
> *be it blood sprain,*
> *be it limb sprain:*
> *bone to bone, blood to blood,*
> *limb to limb, thus linked they be."*

Grani seemed tranced by the time she had finished. As Grimahild sat back and sighed, the horse remained standing, head hanging, eyes half-closed.

"Ordulf, get me the liniment in the stone bottle by the hearth—" she said to her man. "And you, lad, help me get up again." When the man had brought the bottle, she pressed it into Sigfrid's hand. "Rub this stuff well into his leg. What the spell does not do the herbs will accomplish, and with a day or two of rest, he should be well. While you are doing that, my man can bring in some fodder and I will give a last stir to the stew."

The old queen proved to be as good a cook as she was a horse healer. By the time Sigfrid left Grani munching happily, the smell of the food was making his belly growl. As he ate, his apprehensions were forgotten.

"Is it good?" Grimahild asked. She herself had eaten very little.

"It is wonderful," he answered. "Have you taught Gudrun to cook this?"

"There is very little that my daughter has consented to learn from me," the queen said dryly.

And thank all the gods for that, thought Sigfrid, applying himself to his food.

"Even though I helped her to the husband she wanted," the old woman laughed softly. "Ah, lad, I thought it was Baldur himself who had come to us when I saw you at the door."

Sigfrid flushed, wondering if he should be watching out for mistletoe.

"The blind god hit his mark, and the fragile twig speared its target, and the just god fell to treachery . . ." Grimahild chanted. "The laws of the world were turned upside down that the law of Wyrd might be fulfilled. The one god who will survive Midgard's doom dwells now in the land of the dead. Is that not a wonder?" She fixed Sigfrid with her clouded gaze, and he wondered whether she was seeing him at all.

"I have wept for Baldur, in my day," she continued softly. "But no longer. For in that ritual we do not mourn for him who feasts now in Hella's hall, but for our world. And I am growing old enough so that what comes after my time is no longer of much concern to me."

"Not even the fate of the Burgunds?" he dared to ask.

Her look grew fiercer. "For the Niflungar, I have done more than they know. But will my wisdom be enough for them? I learned the old earth-magic, and gave Gundohar a brother who can use it, but he fights for the Huns. When will he come home?"

Sigfrid blinked. Word came to them from time to time that Hagano had been making a great name for himself in Attila's service, but he, for one, had not missed him. He had heard the rumors that Hagano was not the old king's child. Had the queen slept with one of Ragan's kind?

"I married Gundohar to a Walkyrja, but will she protect him?" the queen continued. "And then there is you—"

He stared back at her, his head reeling. "What about me?" He summoned up the strength to reply.

"A hero out of legend . . ." She nodded, smiling craftily. "Wodan's wolf-child. You are heir to even stranger powers. Why have you not used the treasures you won?"

"Your daughter is wearing one of them," he said angrily,

straightening. "As for the others, I do not desire that kind of power, and neither do the Burgunds. In the world that is coming the only might they will care for is that of Rome."

"You are strong . . ." she said softly. "You resist me. Drink, Sigfrid." She poured ale into a horn and held it out to him. "Once you tasted a potion of my brewing and grew drunk on the beauty of my daughter . . ."

Sigfrid stared at her, and after a few moments had the small victory of seeing her look away. He remembered vividly how exquisite Gudrun had seemed to him when he wakened after the old woman had dosed him. Was that the only reason he had wanted her? Then he thought of how she had looked that morning when he left her sleeping with their child. He still loved her, but now it was in a different way. After six years, he knew every inch of her body, with all its imperfections, as he knew his own. He realized that he could no longer say if she was beautiful. She was simply Gudrun.

"And who will I desire if I drink this?" he said harshly. "You?"

She looked up, startled, then began to laugh, and as shadow sculpted away sagging flesh and the lines graven by the years he saw her resemblence to Gudrun, or rather to what Gudrun might someday be.

"I could make you want me—" she cackled maliciously. "And make you forget it after. To look at your sinewy arms and your strong thighs stirs memories of old lovers. Be grateful that I have lived so long that the old fires have died."

He lifted the horn in salutation, drank, then looked back at her, frowning as a new thought surfaced like a silver pike in a dark stream.

"Is that what you did to me when I came to Borbetomagus? Did your spells make me forget Brunahild?"

Slowly her smile faded. "Sigdrifa—" she said sharply. "It was Sigdrifa you had been searching for."

The ale grew sour on his tongue. "You think yourself so wise! Old woman, did you not know? Do you not know even now what you have done? Sigdrifa was her war-name among the Walkyriun, the only name she gave me. Sigdrifa *was* Brunahild!"

This time he had the bitter satisfaction of seeing Grimahild pale. "She has said nothing—"

"Nor have I! What good would it do? This wyrd has been long in the weaving. All we can do is to follow it to the end."

Grimahild pulled her shawl around her, rocking back and forth on her stool. "He did not tell me," she whispered. "Why did he deceive me?"

"It seems to me that we have all betrayed each other," said Sigfrid, wondering whom she meant. "But I have kept faith where I can. The oath I swore when Brunahild accused me was not a lie. But I ask you now, old woman, who gave you the right to play Norn with our lives?"

"It was not I," she whispered, still rocking. "You will have to seek your answers from my master. Run with the wolves tomorrow, Sigfrid Sigmundson, and perhaps you will find him."

"Who?" he leaned toward her, but Grimahild shook her head and pulled away.

"I am an old woman," she said harshly. "I need rest. Wolf-kin must seek answers from the lord of wolves."

Gudrun rolled over in the big bed, reaching for Sigfrid, and grasped a handful of the sleeping furs. Half-awake, she remembered that he was away and hugged the furs to her, running her fingers through their rich softness. The first winter of their marriage Sigfrid had hunted often, and brought in enough foxskins to cover the bed. On her other side Sunnilda lay sleeping, snug in her own nest of blankets. Gudrun sighed, surprised to find how much she missed her husband. She had grown used to having him always near in the nine months since the child had been born.

She closed her eyes, but sleep would not come to her. She imagined Sigfrid curled in his cloak on the cold ground with the others—a harder bed than this one, but she had no doubt that he was sleeping. She felt a momentary flare of resentment that he should be out and doing while she was tied to her child, replaced almost immediately by surprise. For almost a year Sunnilda had been the world to her. She had refused to let another woman nurse her, but the child would be walking soon. Already she was growing interested in other people, and as she became a separate person the bond between them was bound to thin.

Perhaps as others took over more of Sunnilda's care, Gudrun could pay more attention to Sigfrid. She realized suddenly that although he had been with her constantly, she had been treating him as a support and a protection, part of the magic circle that included herself and the child, but until he went away from her she had not looked at him for his own sake at all. *No wonder,* she thought ruefully, *he has not tried to make love to me!*

Longing to have him in her arms hit her suddenly, and she blinked back tears. This would never do. She rolled out of the bed and crossed the room to the carved chest, lifted the heavy lid, and rummaged through the folded garments kept there. In the bottom, as she had remembered, was the stained linen bag in which Sigfrid kept his wolfskin. For a moment she wondered if he would mind her touching it, but after five years of marriage what secrets could there be between them? She drew the skin from its covering and held it in her arms.

It still retained a hint of the wild smell and the rankness of the original tanning, but mostly it smelled of Sigfrid, a healthy male musk that made her take an instinctive quick breath as she felt responses that for a year had been quiescent begin to stir.

For a moment Gudrun wondered if this was a good idea. But she was lonely, and the fur was warm. She took it back to the bed with her and crawled beneath the covers, holding it in her arms. Perhaps if she could pretend that Sigfrid was with her, she would be able to sleep.

She stroked the soft fur, imagining it was Sigfrid's hair. And then it seemed to her that it was a living wolf she was touching. Even as she wondered when sleep would come to her, Gudrun slid into dream.

She was walking in the forest with the great wolf by her

side, as she had once before. But this time it was dark; the treetops stirred restlessly beneath the stroking of the wind with a sound like the whispering of a voice just too soft for her to understand the words. But she could tell that the wolf heard. His ears pricked; she could feel tension in the muscles beneath the soft fur. And then the wind gusted, and the whispering thinned and grew until it was a howl. For a moment the wolf stilled, rigid, listening. Then he was away. She called out, but his stride did not even falter. She tried to follow, stumbling on the rough ground. But he was gone, shadow to shadow. Gudrun wandered, weeping, until she found herself awake, wound in the bedclothes, crying into the soft fur.

If Sigfrid had been there, he would have cuddled and caressed her, stroking her back and buttocks, fondling her breasts and probing all her secret places until another kind of tension replaced it, which he knew better than anyone how to ease. Sighing, she cupped her breasts, squeezing them gently, tweaking the nipples as Sigfrid liked to do until they grew hard beneath her hand. She ran her own hands down her sides, and then, holding her breath, touched herself where he had given her so much pleasure.

But though her flesh throbbed with need, there was no release. It was nearly dawn before exhaustion claimed her and she slept at last.

When Sigfrid woke the next morning he waited a moment before opening his eyes, listening. His night had been troubled, full of dreams in which he had run through the forest as a wolf, and then, still in wolf-shape, made love to Gudrun. He had half expected to wake up in the forest with Grani beside him, but he could hear the crackle of a fire and smell porridge cooking. When he did lift his head, he saw the houseposts and benches in the light that came in through the open door. So it had not all been a dream.

Ordulf, laconic and unfriendly as ever, ladled him out some porridge. The old woman was nowhere to be seen. That was a relief to Sigfrid. It seemed to him they had said too much to each other the night before.

He went into the other half of the building to look at Grani, who appeared glad to see him, but quite content to stay where he was. When he had given the horse more hay and water, he felt along the foreleg. The swelling had gone down, but from the way the animal moved, the limb must still be tender. Grimahild's spells had clearly done something for him, but he was not yet ready to travel—the best evidence for that was the fact that he had not yet tried to kick the wall down.

Sigfrid went outside again, breathing deeply of the damp morning air. It had stopped drizzling, but the cloud still clung to the forest, veiling it in mystery. In broad daylight these trees had seemed tame to him, but swathed in mist, they had become strange, like one of those woods through which heroes pass on their way to the Underworld. The wildness within him rose up in answer. Grimahild had called him wolf-kin, and since he came to the Burgund lands there had never been a day when the calling to release the wolf inside him had been stronger. And here, it seemed to him, it would be safe at last to let it run free.

Perhaps that part of the old woman's advice had been good, anyway. Sigfrid laughed aloud, the sound swallowed up by the damp air, then went back inside to tell Ordulf how to tend Grani while he was away.

He had not brought the wolf-pelt along, but he knew that he did not really need it to change. It was enough to strip off his human clothes and with them, his human identity. Clad only in the "wolf-pelt" of hair that grew across his shoulders and down to a point along his spine, he emerged from the shed where he had left his clothing and with a single step disappeared into the mist between the trees.

For a moment he stood still, breathing deeply. Scents carried easily in the damp air. From behind him he could smell woodsmoke and the warmer scents of cooked food and horse and man, but the rich odors of decaying leaves and wet earth and the smell of water-soaked bark were stronger. From farther off he could smell crushed mint and more faintly, the stink of fox. With each breath, human awareness faded. With scent, his hearing grew sharper. It seemed to him that he could feel his snout lengthening, his posture altered into a half crouch.

The disturbing memories of the night before grew dim; what had the passions of men to do with the being he was now? He lifted his head, throat muscles quivering, and released all his pain in a long howl. From wolf-height he saw an opening in the bushes before him. All animal now, he passed through it, moving more freely as muscles loosened, leaving scarcely a scuffed leaf or bent branch to show where he had gone.

Sigfrid ran through the forest, exulting in the free play of muscle beneath his skin. He followed the trails the deer used, and branches that would have caught in human clothing brushed easily past bare hide. He was not yet hungry. It was movement he needed, an escape from all the restraints that had cut him off from his true self. He moved faster than a horse could go in this terrain, and far more swiftly than any ordinary man.

Around noon he came over the ridge and caught the scent of Godomar's hunting party as he crossed the trail. A sense of humor more lupine than human set him to stalking them. He pulled the tail of Godo's horse and faded back into the trees before they ever saw him. A few, sharper-sighted than the rest, glimpsed a pale shape among the shadows, but none of them guessed it was a man. He retreated a little farther, and yipped mockingly. As the horses began to rear and the men to swear, he shook with something between a growl and human laughter.

The hunters were too busy trying to control their mounts to come after him, but the man-wolf had not reckoned on the dogs, with noses as good as his own and no preconceptions. The dogboy slipped their leashes and they came boiling into the woods, yammering with an excitement that turned to frenzy when one of them picked up his trail.

Sigfrid growled menacingly and the leaders hung back, but the pack instinct was too strong for that to stop them for long. The barking redoubled in fury—*our teeth are sharp, our jaws are strong*, cried the dogs, *and we are many to your one. Run, wolf, and we will chase you! Turn at bay, and we will bring you down!*

The man-wolf snarled defiance and leaped away, moving faster than he had ever gone before. After that, he saved his breath for running. Behind him the dogs chorused their blood-lust in many-throated harmonies. The horns of the hunters belled with ominous sweetness, but this wolf combined a man's wit with the animal's cunning. Soon the hounds were strung out in a wavering line behind him. He splashed through a brook, waded downstream, and then cut back through the woods the way he had come. He surprised several stragglers, breaking the necks of two and leaving them dead on the trail, and paused, panting. Up ahead the leaders were whining in confusion, then one of them found where he had doubled back and gave tongue. Behind him he could hear men shouting as they drew near.

He growled deep in his throat. Suddenly the game had ceased to be amusing. Sigfrid stared about him, trying to think like a man. The land sloped steeply here, with many outcrops of stone, less apt to hold a scent than the damp soil. He leaped up, grasped an overhanging branch and swung forward to land lightly on a knob of granite, leaped from there to another and sprang away down the hill.

A sheer cleft in the hillside opened almost beneath his feet, more than a man's length across, faced with tangled greenery and tumbled stone. For a moment he wavered, but the mad-dened hounds had found his trail once more. *Run wolf, run! We are many, many, many*, they cried, *and you are only one!* He gulped air, made a swift circle to find the best approach, and sped toward the brink.

As the first of the dogs burst through the bushes he leaped. They howled furiously behind him as he hurtled through the air. Then his foot touched the far side, slipped, he flung him-self forward, scrabbling with all four limbs, rolled into a deep patch of bracken, and lay still. The garnet-colored fronds had scarcely ceased to quiver when the riders emerged from the trees.

He did not dare to move, but he could hear them, swearing

colorfully above the frustrated yelping of the dogs. A spear came hurtling across the chasm and gouged a track through the bracken, coming to rest a handspan from his thigh. It took a long time for the dogboy to whistle the hounds into order and get them leashed once more.

"Whatever it was, we've lost it—" Ordwini's voice rose above the general babble at last. "And it's growing dark. We had best find the path and our baggage while we can."

"I don't like to leave a hot trail—" said Godomar sullenly. "Besides, the wolf owes me for two of my dogs!"

"And me, for my spear," said someone who sounded like Laidrad.

"Do you really want to try climbing down into that chasm as the shadows fall?" asked Ordwini. "Or bumble around in the darkness to find a way around?"

"Leave it be, my lord," said the dogboy. "Let it go. No mortal animal could have made that leap without wings. This was no wolf, but some creature of trolldom we were following—"

"He speaks true—I saw it!" said one of the others. "Pale as a ghost and as big as a man!"

Sigfrid listened, stifling laughter and wishing he dared part the bracken to see. An awakening owl hooted above him; he looked up and saw a blur of pale feathers as it lifted into the air and soared out over the chasm.

"Look there, he's turned himself into an owl!" came the cry.

"He's coming for us, my lord, please, let's away!"

Sigfrid heard more oaths and a great crashing in the undergrowth as men and dogs and horses blundered back the way they had come. They were not quite out of earshot when he lost control entirely, turned over on his back in the bracken, and began to laugh, great peals of laughter that rang through the darkening forest as if he were some creature of the Otherworld indeed.

By the time Sigfrid crawled out from his hiding place, the sun had set, but in the lingering half-light he could see well enough to recognize landmarks. His flight had brought him

a long way from Grimahild's house in the forest, and though
he supposed he could burrow into a drift of fallen leaves, he
would need water. The spring of the linden trees lay below
the cleft in which he had hidden Fafnar's hoard, and from the
lay of the land, he judged that it was near.

Brushing off bits of bracken and wincing at the sting of cuts
and scrapes he had not noticed before, he picked up the spear
and swung into a steady wolf-trot, moving so lightly, even in
the half-dark, that he scarcely stirred the leaves. A startled
hare burst out beneath his feet, and in another stride it was
spitted on his spear. Tonight he would have food, anyhow,
even if he must wolf it down raw.

Presently, as he continued on his way, he became aware
that something was keeping pace with him, moving invisibly
through the undergrowth to either side. Sigfrid stilled, all his
senses questing outward, and in a moment was rewarded by
the gleam of two pairs of yellow eyes; wolf eyes. He ventured
a yip of greeting, and as they answered, shapes appeared beneath them as if his notice had summoned them. He watched
with a prickle of wonder as two mist grey wolves flowed onto
the path before him and trotted on ahead, pausing from time
to time to see if he were following. If indeed they were not
some figment of his longing, he had not seen them since he
ranged the woods around Ragan's forge when he was a child.

Thus, he was not altogether surprised when he glimpsed
the flicker of a campfire by the springs where he had hidden
Fafnar's gold. The mist wolves trotted ahead of him into the
clearing, fawning on the man who sat by the fire, but Sigfrid
stopped short at the edge of the light, staring.

The fellow was dressed like one of the charcoal burners
who plied their trade in this forest, with a hide apron over
his tunic and leggings of blackened leather. The cape that
covered his shoulders was patched together from worn furs,
its hood drawn forward so that all Sigfrid could see of his face
was the grizzled beard. But no wood burner would have hailed
without fear a naked man who appeared at his fire, or played
so familiarly with wolves. The hair that grew along Sigfrid's

spine lifted as that chill that was not quite fear rippled through him again.

"Hail to you, Sigfrid. I see you have brought us some dinner—" The old man spoke softly, sitting as still as if Sigfrid were some wild creature he was trying to entice to his fire.

"One hare . . . is not much—" Sigfrid struggled to remember the human words.

"I have bread and wine," said the stranger. Sigfrid came slowly forward and laid his spear down beside the fire, peering at the face beneath the hood. One eye was lost in shadow, but the other transfixed him as his own wolf-gaze could hold other men, until he had to look away.

"You know my name," he said then. "What do I call you? Helmbari, or perhaps Farmamann?" Those were names this wanderer had borne when he met him before.

The other laughed and held out his hand for the hare. "Or Grim," he said, gutting it with a single strong stroke of his knife, and throwing the offal to the wolves. *Or Wodan*, thought Sigfrid uneasily. Living in Christian lands he had forgotten how to talk to gods.

He cleared his throat. "So, Hidden One, what do you want with me now?"

"Such suspicion!" The old man shook his head. "But at least you do not recoil, waving crosses and splashing holy water about like rain. People used to fear me, with some reason, but they also sought the gifts I bring. These days, they call me a devil. Soon the demon is all they will be able to see, not knowing that in every thought, and every memory, I am there."

"They called *me* a demon this afternoon," Sigfrid said bitterly. "But I will call you Father of Wolves."

The old man looked up from skinning the hare. "That is well, for I have loved the men of your line." Firelight burned in the silver of his beard, glittered on the surface of the waters welling from the rocks beyond him, and picked out the cleft where Sigfrid had hidden Fafnar's hoard.

"Should that comfort me?" He held out his hands to the flames. "My father bled out his life on the battlefield. Did you love him? I know a woman whom you once called daughter. How has your love served her?"

"Sigmund . . . lived well and died well and dwells now in my hall with the heroes—" Grim's voice rang as swords ring when they meet in the fray. "Brunahild—" He sighed, and when he spoke again his voice had gone flat as a cracked blade. "Brunahild has cut herself off from me. . . ."

"Because you betrayed her!"

"*You* betrayed her!" The old man straightened, seeming suddenly larger, and Sigfrid recoiled. "You chose to stay with the Burgunds. You chose to marry Gudrun."

"Did I?" muttered Sigfrid, remembering his conversation with Grimahild. "Brunahild was certain you meant me to be her hero. Why did you allow me to abandon her?"

"*Allow you?*" Grim looked at him in amazement. "Do I look like one of the Norns? And even they only spin the strands of character and inheritance into threads for Wyrd's weaving. Perhaps the Christian god predestines the fall of a sparrow, but you must not confuse him with me."

Nonetheless, thought Sigfrid, *you allowed Brunahild to believe that I was her destiny.* But he did not say so aloud.

"Everything that lives is always choosing, and those choices, constraining each other, are woven into the web. Some things are already in the weaving, and cannot now be changed. Their consequences are the wyrd that binds you. In Hunland, you made the choice to substitute yourself for Gundohar."

"He or Brunahild might have been killed, otherwise—" Sigfrid protested, but Grim was shaking his head.

"Is dying the worst fate you know?" He pointed to the hare that was roasting now over the fire. "All things die to the world that others may dwell there. Wolf, you live by killing. Why does it matter less for a hare to die than a man?"

Sigfrid's stomach growled at the scent of the meat. "It matters to the man," he said, shaken by sudden laughter. "Did this beast choose to die at my hand?"

"The wise, be they man or beast, know when it is time to make an ending," Grim said gently.

He lifted the spit from the fire, laid the roasted hare on a flat stone, and carved off a haunch, which he handed to Sigfrid. The second haunch he cut into pieces, and began to feed them to his wolves. Sigfrid bit into his, wincing as the hot juices burned his tongue, remembering how Fafnar's blood had burned him. The flesh was tough, but sweet. He swallowed, and as the meat went down he remembered the triumph in Ragan's eyes as he gave himself to Sigfrid's sword.

"Do you know, old one, when that time will come for me?"

"If I knew that," came the answer, very softly, "do you think I would have allowed Baldur to die? That he must dwell in Hella's realm at the end of the Age of Gods and be lost to me, I knew, but I would have delayed it if I could have foreseen the cycle's ending. I am certain only of my own fate, and by whom I will fall. And even Ragnarok I will put off, if through the choices of humankind I can preserve the world."

"How can I believe you?" Sigfrid leaped to his feet, knowing now what master Grimahild had served. "To how many kings have you promised victory, and then allowed them to die? Brunahild told me that you had promised I would stay with her."

"Even now, you do not understand!" exclaimed the god. "I know what wyrd is coming into being. You choose how to see that reality! Your choices become my knowledge of what will be!"

Sigfrid shook his head. The world spun around him, shadow and substance forming and re-forming in endless complexity.

"Why are you telling me this?" he cried desperately. "What do you want from me?" In the silence left by his words all sounds seemed louder—the hiss of the flames, the crack of bones as the wolves gnawed them, the trickling of the spring.

"It is long since you have looked on your treasure . . ." The words were so soft it might have been Sigfrid's own heart speaking. "You came here to see it. Bring out the hoard, and let it shine in the light of the fire."

The other's outlines wavered, as if a larger, brighter figure were sitting there. Then Sigfrid pulled himself together, blinking, and saw only an old man. But Sigfrid still could not meet his gaze.

"Why, do you desire it? Men offer treasure to the gods, but I have never understood what the shining ones want with gold!"

"Bring out the chest, Sigfrid," Grim repeated, "and I will answer you."

Sigfrid tossed the bone on which he had been chewing to one of the wolves and stepped over the rivulet where the waters of the spring ran away into darkness. The rocks with which he had blocked the opening of the cleft were still secure, moss and grasses growing among them as if they had fallen there naturally. Carefully he worked them free and pulled the chest from the gap into which he had wedged it. There was mold growing on the wood, and the hasps were corroded, but not too badly. He scraped off the worst of it and haggled the latch free.

Inside, the oiled leather sack was still whole, and though the bronze pieces had corroded and the silver darkened, the gold shone with undiminished luster. One by one he drew the pieces out and laid them on the ground. There lay the arm rings and the torques of twisted gold. There was the flagon of Greek design with a pair of drinking cups all scrolled over with acanthus leaves. Beside it lay a leaf-shaped dagger, its bronze turned a leprous green, but the hilt was bound with gold wire, and the guard and pommel were gold. Bowls of bronze and silver overflowed with coins bearing the blurred faces of forgotten kings.

"There it lies," said Sigfrid, "and little good has it brought me. Shall I choose another neck ring from the hoard to repay Brunahild for the one I took away?"

"She would not thank you. There is no other like that one," said Grim, "as there is nothing like the rod that lies there at your feet, wrapped in a piece of skin."

Sigfrid knelt to pick it up, and the tattered leather fell away. The rod was about the length of his forearm and as thick as his thumb, with the rough figure of a bird, perhaps an eagle, at one end. At some point after its making it had been graven all over with runes, like the ones scratched into the neck ring. He held the rod in the firelight, trying to remember Brunahild's attempt to teach him what they were, and felt a tingling where he held the heavy gold.

"They are all there, Sigfrid—" said Grim softly, "all the mysteries of Might and Meaning. These are the runes I gave to humankind. He who understands them rules his own fate, because he understands the wyrd of the world. Take up the rod. Take it back to the city of the Burgunds and wield it there."

"Wield it?" asked Sigfrid. "How? I could carve the runes on an oak bough—why should this gold be different? And what would I do with it? I am a warrior. I carve out my own fate with the point of my sword."

"Indeed," said his companion dryly, "as you did when Fafnar and Ragan died at your hand?" Sigfrid flinched. That was an old grief, but not forgotten. "Would it not be better if wisdom showed you how to use your sword?"

"Do you want me to challenge Gundohar's kingship?" Sigfrid glared at him. "I will not do it—there is a bond of blood between us!" He flung the rod down, clashing musically, upon the hoard.

"How do you know what you will do," Grim said quietly, "who so quickly forgot the oaths you swore to Brunahild?"

Sigfrid turned away, staring into the darkness, but he could not still his trembling. First one wolf, then the other, came to his side and leaned against him. Instinctively he began to caress them, a little comforted by the feel of the soft fur beneath his hands.

"The world is changing," said the voice behind him. "You must change with it, and so must I. Carry the runes into the world that is to be."

"I am not the one to do it—" Sigfrid answered in a shaking voice. "I do not understand them, or you. I am a wolf. I will serve my leader and protect my family. Find another son to work for you among men!"

"I will . . . I must . . ." The reply was almost too soft for his hearing. "Yet this much I foresee, that you will serve me in the end. . . ."

There was a sound like a long sigh, and then silence. The wolves poked their cold noses into his palms and slipped away.

When Sigfrid mastered his shivering enough to look again, he saw the old man slumped in a heap, his hood fallen back so that his face was fully visible in the glow of the coals. Sigfrid bent over him, feeling for a pulse. The man's eyes were closed, but they both appeared to be normal. He was breathing with the stertorous regularity of a drunkard, and Sigfrid noticed now the wineskin that lay by his side.

It was almost half-full. Sigfrid unstoppered it and set it to his lips, not ceasing to drink until the wine was gone. He needed it, and an empty wineskin would make it easier for the fellow to account for a lost evening. After a few moments the new fire in Sigfrid's belly began to burn some of the chill away. In the fading light of the coals the treasure glittered balefully. Frowning, Sigfrid began to pack it away again, putting the rune rod in last, wrapped in the raw skin of the hare. When he had gotten the chest wedged back into the cliff, he replaced the rocks so that the moss appeared to have grown undisturbed.

When he was finished he saw that one golden coin still lay winking on the ground. Grinning mirthlessly, he laid it on the chest of the sleeping charcoal burner to pay him for the wine. When the fellow woke he would think he had been dreaming. Sigfrid found himself wondering the same thing, but he did not think he could have imagined the things that the god had said to him, and he had certainly not cracked all those bones.

When the poor fellow did regain consciousness, Sigfrid himself must be far from here. At least the food and rest had given him a second wind, and a late-rising moon would give him a little light. He should be able to reach Grimahild's steading and retrieve his clothes before dawn. If he were lucky, Grani would be well enough to walk, and he could take the horse and be off to the river landing without meeting Grimahild. He did not think she had the power to read in his face what had happened to him, but he dared not take the chance.

He had resisted her, and he had stood against the will of the god, and he did not know if he had been right to do either. All he was sure of was that even if he betrayed all else, he could not deny the wolf within.

Sigfrid covered the coals with ashes to give the man a little comfort in the morning. Then, silent as one of Wodan's wolves, he faded into the forest.

Chapter
Twelve Reunion

Borbetomagus
Eggtide Moon, A.D. 427

T hat winter, the second since the boy Valentinian had assumed the purple and the sixteenth of Gundohar's kingship, was a hard one. Snow fell heavily in the mountains, and a swift thaw in the spring sent melting waters through the land like an invading army, drowning cattle and sweeping homes away. What word got through said that the weather had been even worse elsewhere. In Rome the Tiber had overflowed its banks, killing many, and the marshes around Ravenna made the city into an island.

Gundohar stared at the watery sunshine. It had been raining on and off all week, even though the feast of Ostara was past, and he wondered how the boy-emperor was facing his problems. Had they even told the child that anything was wrong? He had some sympathy for Valentinian, having himself been thrust into kingship before he was grown.

But that was half his life ago. It seemed a very long time to him since his father had died, but Gundohar could remember how it had felt to be king in name while surrounded by people who were all older, more powerful, and certain they knew better than he did what he should do. Valentinian had Galla Placidia, his mother, to govern for him, born to the Imperial power and forced by her gender to exercise it through others. Gundohar had had Grimahild.

He wondered if he would have her much longer. The old

queen had been ailing all winter. Thinking back, he realized that it was after her last expedition to gather herbs in the autumn, that time Godomar had taken the men hunting and they had all come back yammering about were-wolves, that she had begun to fail.

When Gundohar was younger he had resented her interference, but he thought now that her knowledge of the strengths and weaknesses of the great families that dominated the clans was probably what had kept him in his kingship. He suspected that where threat or persuasion would not answer, she had used other means. Certainly there had been some unexpected, and highly convenient, deaths during the early years of his reign. But he had never dared to ask if she had arranged them by magic or poison. He supposed that of all her children, only Hagano was likely to know.

And he had to admit that after the battle of the Longstone field, and especially after his marriage to Brunahild, his mother had seemed content to advise without meddling. But even now, she still seemed to know more about what was going on among the people than anyone else around.

He sighed and lifted the roll of parchment that had just arrived, all crusted over with Imperial seals. But the device they bore was that of the prefecture of Gallia, not Rome. Carefully, he slit the seals and pulled open the parchment.

"Ad Gundicharium, Rex Burgundiorum, ex Flavio Aetio, Comes Domesticorum, Magister Militum intra Gallias, salve—"

Holding the roll so that it caught the light, he scanned the neatly scripted lines. Their essence was clear—Aetius had been in Rome and was taking the route northward through Rhaetia as soon as the passes cleared. He planned to continue along the Rhenus before following the Mosella westward to Treveri, the same route, thought Gundohar with a small smile, that the Burgunds had followed four years before when they collected the "taxes."

"I expect to reach Borbetomagus by the ides of Maia," the letter continued. "I look forward to seeing how you have dealt with the feoderate lands. I wish to confer with you regarding their defense, and review the forces at your command."

He's going to fight Theoderid again this summer, thought Gundohar, *and he thinks he may need us. Hiring Huns is expensive. . . .* Once more he smiled. The Burgunds could be expensive too. Since settling along the Rhenus their numbers had grown, and the country around Divodurum was rich. Ordwini, whose holdings lay nearest, was already beginning to extend his influence westward from Argentoratum. If Aetius wanted his help, the price would be those lands.

What other concessions, he wondered, could he wring from the Romani in exchange for cooperation? It occurred to him that to frame a suitable reply he needed a head more devious than his own. This was the kind of situation that Grimahild would understand. Perhaps the challenge would amuse her. Rolling up the parchment, he set off to find her.

"Is the queen here?" Gundohar's question came clearly as the gate to the garden was opened, and Gudrun looked up in surprise. "I was told she was taking the sun."

Gudrun glanced over at her mother, who appeared to be dozing while little Sunnilda sat on the ground beside her, turning over the pebbles in the path.

"Not in the mouth, darling—hold the pretty rock in your hand—" she said automatically, and then, raising her voice, "We are in the grape arbor, brother, on the outside path." In a few moments she saw him coming past the rosemary bush, which had survived drought and flood and once more seemed likely to take over the garden if not restrained.

"I suppose there is a little sunshine—" he said dubiously, squinting up at the sky.

"More than there has been for some time," Gudrun agreed. "I wanted to take advantage of it. It is hard for a child to stay cooped up, and I thought that our mother might benefit from the fresh air."

He looked at Grimahild, who sat with her eyes closed, swathed in shawls. "Is she asleep?"

"My eyes may be failing, but there is nothing wrong with my ears," came a voice from within the shawls. The old queen straightened with a sigh. "What is it, my son?"

Once, she would have known he was coming before he got here, thought Gudrun. *After all her struggles to hold on to the power, now even the thought of it is a burden she does not want to bear.* The quick color came and went in Gundohar's face, and she thought that he was aware of it as well.

"I have a letter from Aetius," he said brightly. "He is coming to visit, and I think he will ask our help in the summer's campaign. I wanted your advice on how we can turn this to our advantage. What should I ask of him?"

For a moment the old woman's gaze focused fully on her son, then it went inward. "Hagano—" she said finally. "You will ask the Romani for more land when the general comes, but I do not think he will want to give it to you. In your reply, ask him, as a favor, to request his friends the Huns to let Hagano come home. We are linked already by marriage— there should be no need for hostages between us. Tell him that Hagano's mother is old and sick and would like to see her missing son."

"Mother—" Gundohar exclaimed, coming closer. "What—"

She cut him off with a wave of her hand. "I am old, and at my age one is never entirely well. But you may say I am at death's door if that will serve. It is time for your brother to come home."

Hagano . . . thought Gudrun, feeling suddenly cold; Hagano the changeling child, who when they were growing up had been ever devious and sometimes cruel. But of them all, only he had inherited their mother's peculiar brand of wisdom. Did Grimahild suspect that her time was short? Did she want Hagano back to advise Gundohar when she was gone?

Sunnilda, tiring of examining stones, grabbed her grand-mother's skirts with both chubby hands and pulled herself upright. Gudrun made a grab for her, but Grimahild waved her back.

"Let her be. It is natural for the young to stand upon the old. I do not mind. She is the brightest thing in this garden. See how her hair shines in the sun. . . ." She touched the bright curls, and Sunnilda tipped back her head to stare up at her. "Sigfrid's child . . ."

For a moment longer the child held her grandmother's gaze. Then, with the swiftness of the very young, she lost interest and, letting go of Grimahild's skirt, held out her arms to Gudrun.

"Come to me then, my darling," crooned her mother. "There's a good girl, you know you can."

Sunnilda's face brightened and she gurgled with laughter, then suddenly she was walking, small legs barely keeping up with her forward motion, but never quite falling until she reached her mother's arms. Gudrun's arms closed around her, exulting in the solid, firm flesh and the sweet smell of her hair. As she lifted her head she saw that Gundohar was watching them, and looked quickly away from the naked longing she read in his eyes.

He wants a child . . . she thought in wonder. *Not just to have an heir, but to love. I think he would be a good father. Is Brunahild barren, or is she refusing to give him what he so badly needs?*

Her mother was watching Gundohar too, but in the old woman's eyes, instead of the look of impatient exasperation which had been her usual response to her son, Gudrun saw sorrow. Then the king straightened, and his face resumed its usual shuttered calm.

"Then I will write the letter, and let us hope that soon your son will be home."

Warriors were gathering in the long meadow by the river when Hagano rode up the road that led from the landing toward the town. It seemed very strange to be riding past the neatly tilled fields of the coloni after living in wild lands that had never known Roman law; it had been strange, even, to make his offering as he crossed the river to Father Rhenus instead of to Mother Danu. He had been almost a moon on the road since the summons came, wondering with every step whether his mother was really ill. But Attila had believed it, or pretended to, and one did not argue with the khan.

Could he be content with the gentle hills of Germania

Prima after the wild crags of Pannonia, and confine himself
within geometric enclosures after seven years of living with a
people who still preferred to dwell in felt *gers* which could be
packed up at a moment's notice and moved? But the sight of
armed men gathering on a field was more than familiar. The
surge of excitement that pebbled his skin receded a little as
he drew closer and saw that their swords were wrapped with
leather for practice. Then he saw the Roman standards beside
the platform from which they used to watch the games and
began to understand.

One of the Burgunds caught sight of him, and in moments
he was surrounded by a grinning, chattering mob of men. He
was relieved when his brother Godomar pushed through the
throng and clapped him on the shoulder.

"Holy gods, I'd hoped for this!" he exclaimed. "Mother said
you would be back when Aetius got here. I should have
known better than to doubt her word!"

"Is all this display for him, then?" Hagano asked.

"It's for the Visigoths," said Godomar, "though they don't
yet know it. If we impress the Roman, he'll let us have a good
crack at them, and we've a better chance of doing it with you
on our side!"

"I should go see our mother—" Hagano began, feeling
rather as if he had encountered a young whirlwind.

"She's waited this long, she'll keep till sunset," his brother
said cheerfully. "Your arms are in your pack, aren't they? Well,
get them on! Brother, we need you here."

The water meadow had been green that morning. Now,
what could be seen of it from the roofed platform where the
king sat with his guests was brown, churned to mud by the
feet of the men whose bright tunics and gleaming metal ornaments and armor seemed to have sprouted like strange flowers from the field. But these blooms were in motion, though
there was no wind. The day, in fact, had dawned bright, still,
and clear, as if the weather itself wished to help the Burgunds
impress the visitors from Rome.

Gundohar supposed they would have to find somewhere

else to pasture the cattle—that field would not recover this year—but it was worth the loss of good grazing. He thought he had never seen his warriors show to better advantage, and as he watched them sparring he felt a surge of pride as powerful as if he had been watching the exploits of his own child. It was not just because four of those fighting there were his own kinfolk—Godo and Gislahar, and Sigfrid, and Hagano, who had just arrived. The simile went farther, for in a sense they were all his children, the whole tribe. Certainly he worried about their welfare as much as any father could do.

At one end of the field targets had been set up for spear-throwing. At the other men were running, fully armed, as if to charge upon a foe. In the middle, groups of a half a dozen men stood back to back with their shields locked while as many more attacked them, their swords wrapped in leather to avoid lethal blows, while others clashed in individual duels. But the cries he heard were of challenge or triumph, not pain. It was like watching a battle without the stink of blood or fear. The men moved like stallions, glorying in their strength. How, he wondered, could a pageant dedicated to the arts of death seem such a celebration of life?

The men clearly felt no contradiction. They were applying themselves to the demonstration with real enthusiasm, displaying their prowess to impress the Roman general who could lead them to loot and glory. The king looked over at Aetius, who was observing with a critical eye. *He sees neither the pathos nor the splendor, only how he can use them in his war. And that is as it should be,* Gundohar told himself. *I think too much for my own good or theirs.*

"They show well—" The Roman, as if feeling his gaze, turned to him.

"They want to fight for you."

"Do *you*?" Aetius asked, measuring him. Startled, Gundohar met the other man's eyes, forcing his own features to calm.

"If it is for the good of my people, yes, of course I do. The younger warriors need the experience, the older ones an outlet for their energy, and the Burgunds need gold to replace the cattle we lost in the spring rains."

"But you do not enjoy battle, do you—" said Aetius equably. "I do not criticize—sometimes such men make the best generals, because they fight from necessity. I see that your brother has lost no time in reestablishing himself in your warband."

He pointed to the field, and a breath Gundohar had not realized he was holding eased out of him in a long sigh. He had hardly had time to embrace Hagano when he arrived, but he looked brown and fit, and the training the Huns had given him showed in every move.

"What about your other warriors—" asked Aetius. "Who is that man with the wolf crest on his helm?"

"That is Sigfrid, son of Sigmund the Wolsung. He is my brother-in-law," said Gundohar, and smiled.

"That is Sigfrid . . ." Gundohar's words pierced the babble of conversation behind Brunahild. Like the spear that was thrown above a foe to dedicate him to Wodan, Sigfrid dominated the fighting. The less skilled avoided him, but the good ones, the young men with the greatest need to test their skill and win glory, attacked one after another, as stags in the fall wait to challenge the master of the herd. And one by one Sigfrid defeated them, and laughed.

At moments like this, when everyone's attention was on their own talk or the spectacle, it was safe for her to acknowledge Sigfrid's beauty. The king's brother Godomar might be physically stronger; even in practice he felled men as if he were hewing trees. Hagano, bringing down his opponents with swift, efficient blows, might have as much battlecraft. But no one else moved with the grace of a wild thing, combining all talents in such a triumph of mated strength and skill. Brunahild could allow herself to watch him so long as she did not remember how it felt to hold that splendid body in her arms, but only how he had betrayed her.

Then Sigfrid knocked his latest opponent flat and turned toward the platform with lifted sword, grinning triumphantly. The sight of him was like a stab beneath her breastbone, and Brunahild knew that she had passed the limits of safety. For a moment she closed her eyes, then turned resolutely to Father Priscus, who had been invited in deference to the orthodoxy of the Roman visitors, and seated by her side.

"So, good Father, are you enjoying the spectacle?" she asked brightly.

Priscus, looking even more sour than usual, shook his head. "They are preparing for fighting, and it is an offense to God when Christians go to war. But as Bishop Augustine has told us, the world is topsy-turvy. How could it be otherwise when a Roman army which is still half-pagan goes to war against a barbarian who is a Catholic king?"

"Oh, surely not half—" said the queen, smiling.

"Flavius Aetius retains that man Litorius, who is still an unbeliever, as his second in command. How can he expect God to give him the victory?"

"Would it be different if the Visigoths were Arians like their Eastern kindred?" asked Brunahild.

"Of course—" said the churchman, looking at her in surprise. Then he appeared to remember that she was herself still half a barbarian, and schooled his features to an expression of condescending patience which Brunahild had always found particularly annoying. "There is one God in heaven, and one Church below—eternal, holy, and Catholic."

"But there are two emperors, and I was taught that God is three persons in one essence . . . like Wodan—" she added mischeviously. She was rewarded by the sight of his face changing from its normal ruddy color to a rather alarming shade of purple before he could get the breath to answer her.

"Wodan is a devil, who betrays his worshippers—" he began, but Brunahild shook her head.

"That is true," she said with bitter certainty, "but all gods are treacherous. Did not even the Christos say he came not to bring peace but a sword? And it must be so, for the tribes do not seem to fight any the less now that they are becoming Christians."

"It takes time—time—" said Father Priscus, still sputtering. "The sword will be sheathed when there are no more ungodly men in the world!"

After Ragnarok, then, or the Apocalypse that John of Patmos had described so vividly, thought Brunahild, for surely men would not cease from fighting each other until the ending of the age.

"Ah there—look—Hagano has taken out his man!" Gundohar's exclamation brought her attention back to the field. "My thanks to you, Aetius, for persuading the Huns to let him return to us. I can see that he has learned a thing or two from Attila, and we have missed him."

"Everyone learns from Attila," said Aetius dryly. "It is because I learned from him when to be bold and when to seek safety that I am Master of Gallia today."

Brunahild turned to look at him, comparing the man he was now with the young officer she had met at Attila's camp ten years before. His light hair was greying now, but he was still tall and well muscled, in body more a Goth than a Roman, though his face had something of the eagle look she had seen in pictures of old emperors, and his eyes were as dark as her own.

"You seem to be handling the empress well enough at any rate," said Gundohar, laughing.

Aetius grimaced. "The woman is a fool. She hates me because she thinks I threaten her power, and favors Bonifatius because she thinks he can contain me. Bonifatius!" He shook his head. "The man who gave North Africa to the Vandals. They make a fiction of loyalty, but the province will never be Roman again."

"And yet you gave the lands along the Rhenus to the Burgunds—" said Brunahild, becoming curious. "What is the difference?"

"The difference, khatun," said Aetius, giving her the Hunnish title as he addressed her directly for the first time, "is that I am sitting here with you. The Burgunds are becoming Roman, while the North Africans will soon be barbarians. And yet the kind of Roman you are becoming is a new thing, and despite having been married to Athaulf, this is what Galla Placidia does not understand. She looks at the Goths, and thinks only of forces she can call upon."

"And when you look at us, what do you see?" said Gundohar softly.

"A new world that needs no Second Coming," said Aetius, smiling a little as he met Father Priscus' glare, "supported by the vigor of the tribes, harnessed by Roman values, Roman law. Good father, you need not frown at me, for I think that your Church will be at the center of it. The tribes will become nations, all part of one Empire, but these nations will themselves be mixed peoples—Gauls and Romans and Germani of all tribes together.

"It is happening already—" He turned to Gundohar. "You may remember your cousin Gundrada, who was married to a great-grandson of that Athanaric who preserved the Goths from annihilation by Rome a century ago. She has borne, just recently, a son called Gundiok, who bears the blood of both the Gothic Balthi line and that of the Niflungar."

Brunahild heard him with an internal shiver. *A new thing* . . . she thought, gazing out across the struggling men to the silver gleam of the river. Beyond it the eastern hills rose in folds of blue-hazed green, gateway to the land from which all these new peoples had come. *It is true, and I am here to bear witness. But when the world is made anew, how much that was good in the old one will be lost?*

Gundohar was looking thoughtful. He was no longer the half-fledged youth who had faced her on the Longstone field, or even the eager young man she had fought beside the Danu. He had grown into his face at last, his forehead getting higher as the fair hair began to thin, and new lines accenting the set of his eyes and the strong muscles of his jaw. It came to her then that they could have made a powerful team if she had loved him. She wondered if he would be strong enough to lead his people through all the changes that were coming, but though she had lived among the Burgunds for almost six years, she found it hard to care.

Someone murmured in the king's ear and pointed toward the field.

All the other contenders had apparently been defeated, even Godomar, and Hagano and Sigfrid were fighting each other. All their other combats had used up the first flush of vigor for both of them; this bout would be won by pure skill. Brunahild sat forward, recognizing the marks of Attila's training in Hagano's balanced stance and the darting movements of his sword. He knew when to strike and when to hoard his power. Every motion revealed the brain behind the blade. But though Sigfrid's fighting lacked its earlier exuberance, attack and defense were a single flowing sequence, one move unfolding from another with a beauty that could not be anticipated, yet had the satisfaction of total rightness when it came.

Brunahild found that she was holding her breath; they were all holding their breath, watching these two fighters who were so different in style and spirit, yet nearly matched in power. Everyone else in Gundohar's following had long ago given up trying to take Sigfrid in combat. But Hagano had been sparring with the best of Attila's men, the warriors with whose help Aetius had preserved the Empire. He might be the only fighter who could come even close to matching Sigfrid, but as Brunahild watched, she realized that even his battlecraft was not going to be sufficient to counter the protections that she herself had set upon Sigfrid and the talents given him by the gods.

But at least Hagano could give him a fight. Both men had slowed now. Perhaps that was why Brunahild could see the finish coming; Hagano saw it too, but he could not force tiring muscles to respond as Sigfrid's sword caught him in the side of the head and took him down. In another instant Sigfrid was standing over him, the tip of his sword above Hagano's throat. Brunahild only realized that she had been holding her breath when at last the fallen man lifted one hand to acknowledge Sigfrid's victory.

Sigfrid stepped back then, grinning hugely, saluting Gundohar, and then his fallen foe. He bent then to help Hagano to his feet, but on the face of the king's brother there was no emotion at all.

"Da!" Sunnilda's cry brought Gudrun to her feet as Sigfrid pushed open the door. His face was still glowing with the day's exercise, his hair darkened to the color of oak bark from the dip in the river that had followed. Gudrun looked at him and felt a sudden warmth. Watching the fighting this afternoon she had glowed with pride. Being close to him now, she felt a different kind of fire. Sigfrid saw the child, swooped like a striking hawk, and scooped her up, tossing her into the air. Her gurgles became a shriek of delight as he caught her again and nuzzled his face against her tummy, growling.

Gudrun reached out protectively as he started to throw her into the air again, then drew back as Sigfrid looked at her in surprise.

"I won't drop her, and she is not really frightened, are you, my cubling?"

Sunnilda waved her arms in the air as her father shifted her in his arms; two pairs of golden eyes looked back at Gudrun with identical glee. No, thought Gudrun, Sunnilda was a Wolsung. She would not give way easily to fear.

"She's getting to be a big cub now—" she answered, "but it is almost time for a big girl to be in bed."

It was hard to believe that the child was a whole year old. But the changes in her own body confirmed it. She had begun to want Sigfrid again last fall, but when he returned from his hunting trip he had been distant, and she had feared rejection. During the winter all desires faded, waiting like banked coals for the spring, and of course there had still been the inhibiting presence of the child. But for the past moon, Sunnilda had slept with the slavewoman instead of her mother. After a few nights of tears, she had seemed to accept the change. Once more Gudrun and Sigfrid had the bedchamber to themselves. Spring had come, and her body was responding to the new life that was pulsing through the world. It had hurt to watch him this afternoon. He was too beautiful.

Sigfrid gave the child another toss and hugged her, then surrendered her, protesting, to the nurse who came to take her away.

"Sit down," she told him, "and let me finish drying your hair."

"It's not cold—" he began, but she laughed at him.

"It will dry in tangles. Do you want to go to the feast looking like a haystack?" She pushed him down on a bench and reached for the comb. His hair had grown long over the winter. Carefully she combed out the silky strands. As it dried it seemed to grow thicker and more springy, with a wave that made it cling to her fingers. She felt a quiver run through her flesh at the touch of it—but it should be his hands, not his hair, that were caressing her now.

She let her own hands slide through the loose locks and stroke down his neck, kneading the hard muscles that ran down into the shoulder, relearning the shape of them. She traced the shape of his shoulder and the lovely joining of muscle where the bicep swelled the upper arm, over the curve of the shoulder to the flat slab of his pectoral, fingers slipping delicately over the light furring of hair to the hard nub of his nipple and pausing there. His breath caught, and she pressed her breasts against his back, kissing the nape of his neck.

"Sigfrid," she whispered, "it has been so long!" She felt the tremors that were shaking him and brought her other hand around to caress him. For a few moments he held himself still, then he turned, rising and lifting her almost in the same motion, carrying her to the great bed and laying her down. As his robe fell away she could see that he was half-aroused already and smiled, feeling the sweetness of desire begin to throb between her thighs.

"Listen, Gudrun." He eased down beside her, capturing the hand that tried to stray downward. "I love you, but you almost died bearing Sunnilda. My mother died from trying to give Alb a son. I can't risk that, dear one. I can't let you bear another child. . . ."

She shook her head, whimpering, torn between despair and desire. "I am healed, Sigfrid, truly! And I want you—you cannot stop now!"

"I know . . ." He drew a shaky breath. "Do you think I do not know?" He stroked her face, and his hand slipped along her neck to find her breast beneath the loose neck of her gown. "And I will not deny you what you need."

Gudrun clutched at his arm as he handled her, gasped as

he pushed up her skirts and stroked the aching flesh between her thighs. She felt herself arching to meet his probing fingers, and clung to him. But it was with the hands that had dealt such hard blows on the battlefield, grown no less skillful but far more tender as he touched her now, with which he entered her. And though she tried to pull him to her, his skill had mastered her body, and before she could try to break his will with her own caresses, he brought her to a convulsive climax, calling his name.

When she could think again, he was gone. The need that had tormented her was gone as well, but even more than that very specific pleasure, she had wanted Sigfrid's weight upon her body, wanted to feel him finding his own release in her arms. She rolled over, pressing herself against the faint warmth that remained where he had lain, and cried.

Gundohar sighed as the door to the feasting hall closed behind him, cutting off the sound of male laughter and voices raised in song. Inside, Sigfrid and Godomar still sat with Aetius' officers, working their way through another amphora of wine. They were welcome to drink themselves into a stupor— it would not be the first time some of the feasters had finished the evening on the floor of the hall. But the Magister Militum had the sense to seek his bed when the hour grew late, and once Aetius had left the table, Gundohar was free to seek his own.

Brunahild had very sensibly retired as soon as the men settled down to serious drinking. He wondered if she would still be awake, and his step quickened. Gods, but she had looked magnificent, clad all in crimson silk with amber and pearls and all of her ornaments of gold. The color would have overwhelmed any other woman, but it set off her dark beauty. At dinner she had laughed and flirted with Aetius, glowing like a coal in a sea of flame. Afterward, the general had commented upon her beauty, and he had seen the women of Rome.

And she was his. Gundohar felt a flicker of pride in that fact even as he wondered what welcome he would receive.

He had never, after that first night, pushed her to violence, but he was still unable to tell which signals meant she would allow him in her bed and which were the prelude to a furious rejection. The uncertainty wore on him, as perhaps it had been meant to. If he had moved to a separate suite of rooms, or better still, divorced her, he could have spared himself a great deal of pain. After so many years without children, it might not even cause too much comment. But there was always a chance that this might be the night when she would turn to him, and even the scornful amusement with which she accepted his advances was better than nothing at all.

As he approached their rooms he heard voices from within. The queen was still up, then, talking to her women. The conversation halted a moment as he entered, then flowed on. The maids took their tone from their mistress, and they knew that these chambers were Brunahild's domain, where even the Burgund king might come only by sufferance of his queen.

Brunahild wore only her undergown, of thin silk dyed so deep a purple that her eyes, catching the color, seemed almost black. One of the maids was brushing out her long black hair. It was nearly as long, now, as it had been the first time he saw her, thick and glossy as a horse's tail. Each strand caught the lamplight as the woman drew the brush through it, then fell away in a trail of shadow as she lifted the next.

"I am glad to find you still awake," he said carefully. "I feared Aetius would sit over his wine till dawn."

"Did the Roman finally tell you what he is doing here?" she asked.

Gundohar nodded, his gaze following the rhythmic strokes of the brush on Brunahild's hair. "It was more or less as we suspected. There's trouble in Dacia, and half of the Huns will be busy there this season. If Theodorid tries his usual summer exercise, Aetius wants us to make up the numbers."

"And he'll pay?"

"Enough to replace the beasts we lost in the flooding, and grain to see us through till next year." Gundohar loosened the massive brooch of gem-set gold that held his mantle and tossed it across a chair, undid his belt so that his tunic fell free. He crossed to the table before the window and poured wine from the flagon that was kept waiting there.

"What, more wine?" Brunahild asked mockingly. "Did the Romans guzzle all you had in the hall?"

"They will by morning." Gundohar grimaced. It had been his most expensive vintage. "I left Godo and Sigfrid trying to drink Aetius' two tribunes under the table. I'd wager that Godo, at least, won't give up until the last of it is gone." He lifted the cup and let the wine, a pale, fragrant stuff made from the grapes that grew between the Rhenus and the hills, slide down his throat.

"The flower of the Burgunds against the pride of Rome . . . no doubt it will be a battle for the bards to sing."

"Not me," he muttered, turning back to her. "I would rather sing of your beauty. You were splendid, tonight, in that gown. Every man on Aetius' staff envied me." She smiled, slowly, with a promise in her eyes that made his blood pulse, and waved to her women to go.

"And what about me?" she said then. "Would their wives envy me the love of a man who sat like a slug on the platform while his warriors took their knocks on the field?"

Gundohar flushed crimson, but he had learned to deal with this kind of thing after so many years. "Perhaps," he said evenly. "If he were dealing on even terms with the master of half the western world! This time I will not rise to your teasing. Pull in your claws, Brunahild."

Something dangerous flickered in her gaze. "Oh, why? Anywhere else I must obey my lord and master, but I am the ruler here. . . ." She rose, shaking her hair back over her shoulders with a sinuous motion that displayed the lovely line of her throat, and ran her hands down her body, drawing the thin silk tight over the curve of her breasts and the swell of her thighs.

Gundohar felt an answering tightening in his groin, hating himself as much as he wanted her, knowing that this was why he did not leave her. Even now, with a single gesture, a flicker of the eyelids, a word, she could turn his blood to flame. She watched him, reading his response as easily as if he had spoken, and laughed.

Gundohar closed his eyes. *I am a king*, he told himself. *Why do I allow this woman to torment me?* He tensed as he heard the rustle of her gown. Then he could feel her near him. His head swam as he breathed in the spicy scent she wore. Her fingers stroked down his neck, then pinched suddenly, hard.

"Am I your mistress, Gundohar?" she asked softly. Her fingers brushed his chest, and he groaned. "Bow down to me, mighty king. . . ." He shook his head, trembling. "Then open your eyes—" she snapped suddenly, and startled, he obeyed. She had pulled off her gown and stood now clad only in a golden necklace that dangled between her breasts, cloaked in her raven hair.

"Froja, I only wanted to love you," he whispered. "Why do you do this to me?"

"Because it is all I *can* do—" she answered bitterly. She turned away, poured wine and drank, then turned with the goblet in one hand. With her other, she cupped one breast, offering it. Her nipple was hard. He looked at it and felt his own flesh stiffening with sweet pain. "Here is the wine you desire. If you would taste, you have only to kneel to me."

He swayed, feeling desire loosen his limbs, fighting the old battle once more. Among the tribes, only a man who had chosen to live as a woman, or a boy who was learning from an older warrior, or a thrall, allowed himself to be used as a female. It was a mortal insult to accuse another man of submitting, as he, feeling his need for this woman overwhelm his senses, was doing now. Groaning, Gundohar went down first on one knee, then the other. Brunahild reached out and pressed down on his head until he bowed down to the floor itself and kissed her white feet.

She laughed then, long and bitterly. Dimly, his forehead resting on the cool tiles, Gundohar understood that she was mocking herself as well as him.

"Very well then, slave, you may serve me—" Brunahild went to the bed and lay down upon it, spreading her thighs. And

Gundohar, cursing his own weakness, pulled off his tunic and came to her.

While Gundohar was spending himself in Brunahild's bed, Sigfrid downed another beaker of Roman wine, Aetius dreamed of conquest, and Gudrun, her cheeks still tear-stained, lay alone. But Hagano, who had drunk only a little wine at the feast and had never lost sleep over any female, went to say good-night to his mother in her rooms above the garden. He had arrived just in time to join in the fighting. This was the first moment he had been free to go to the old queen. Now that he was here, he wished he had never come.

In seven years among the Huns he had faced battle with no more than an anxiety lest he shame his kindred and his name, and later, a commander's concern for his men. The sight of a thousand Goths drawn up and arrayed for battle inspired only calculation. But his mother's face, gaunted by illness and so wrinkled that the skin lay pleated on the bones, filled him with fear. When he left, Grimahild had been slowed by age, but still the unyielding, uncomfortable rock on which he had built his life. Now she was a husk that any wind might blow away. Now she was old.

"You need your rest," he said, rising. "I should go."

"Sit!" There was enough of the old snap in her voice to bring him to attention. "If you live long enough to grow old, you will learn that sleep is as likely to come by day as by night when it comes at all. I will not sleep again until it is nearly morning. You may as well keep me company!"

He stopped halfway to the door, and slowly turned. Appearances could be deceptive. Perhaps Grimahild had not changed after all.

"Sit down—" she repeated. "It hurts my neck to look up at you. Tell me, my son, were you happy with the Huns?"

Hagano frowned, wondering if he could find the words to explain how it had been to live with folk whose own blood-lines were so mixed that no one cared about his, with a leader who could tell the worth of a man at a glance and give him what reward he had earned. How could he tell her that even though he had been a hostage, among the Huns he had felt free?

"I can see that living with them has been good for you . . ." she continued when he finally sat down. "You are thin, but harder, and strong, whereas I—no—say nothing! I do not need you to tell me!" Her cackle of laughter became a fit of coughing, and he brought her water. "You are afraid to look at me!"

He stared into the fire. "Attila told me I must go see my dying mother, and I was sure it must be some trick of yours to get me home," he said finally. "But now I see that it was true."

She lay back with a sigh. "I was wrong about your courage. Or perhaps it is just that having been away so long, you can see. At least none of my other children has had the guts to say that to me. I wonder why it is so hard? You would go into battle singing."

"In battle you can kill your enemy." He managed a grin and turned back to her.

"Even the greatest of warriors eventually falls to this foe," she reminded him. "Donar himself could do no more than hold his own against old age. It is how you fight that matters—you know that as well as I."

"Are you fighting this?" He caught her gaze, and this time it was she who looked away.

"I am still here . . ." she answered at last. "But I sent for you . . . because I think it will not be for long, and there are things that you must know."

Hagano found himself on his feet as if to meet a challenge, looking down at her. "I came because I was ordered to, but even pity for you cannot make me stay—"

She looked at him curiously. "Do you expect me to beg for your love? I have Gundohar to mouth pious sympathy, and Gudrun, though I suspect they are saying what they think I expect to hear, not what they feel. But I have never demanded love from my children, only obedience, and loyalty."

"I am no longer your little boy," said Hagano.

"That is good," she answered, "for what the Burgunds will

need in the days that are coming is a man, and one who thinks with his head, not his balls, or his sword."

"What about Gundohar?" He realized that he was still on his feet and sat down again. "These days he seems to be the pattern of a feoderati king. And there's Sigfrid, with everyone fawning on him as if he were Baldur returned. Why do you need me?"

"Gundohar thinks with his heart," said Grimahild. "And Sigfrid thinks like a wolf among dogs. But Sigfrid is the problem, my son. Sigfrid is the reason I wanted you to return. You are the only one I can tell how my wisdom has failed, for you are the only one who knows what I have done."

"I don't understand," he said flatly. "I thought that Sigfrid and Gudrun were a model couple, and I saw Gundohar displaying Brunahild like a prize heifer at a market fair."

"Do you know why Brunahild required to be won by combat?" asked the old queen. "She was waiting for Sigfrid."

"But Sigfrid was actually the one—" Hagano stopped. "Waiting? What do you mean?"

"Sigfrid was the only one who could defeat her because he had been her lover. Brunahild was the Hun girl he had been looking for."

Hagano swallowed. "Does she know?"

"She knows that Sigfrid replaced Gundohar in the combat. She knows that he betrayed her, but not how, or why. She hates Sigfrid, Hagano, and though Gundohar still dotes on her, she takes it out on him, I know."

"And Sigfrid?"

"He is still tender to Gudrun, but he knows that I tricked him somehow into marrying her. I am afraid, Hagano, not of death, but of what may happen here. And there is nothing more that I can do. The task will be yours, my son. Somehow you must find a way to save Gundohar."

Grimahild fought for breath and then began to cough. He lifted her, holding the cup to her lips, and saw the skull beneath the skin. He had seen that look before on wounded men, and knew its meaning.

"Promise . . ." she whispered, fighting for breath. "Promise me!" Even now, her eyes compelled him.

"I swear," he said at last, "to do what must be done."

She relaxed then, and for a moment he thought that he had lost her. But now she was breathing more easily. He held her, his nostrils filled with the scent of mortality, and thought, *We are all bound now. . . .*

Chapter
Thirteen Waldhari

Provincie Belgica Prima
Litha Moon, A.D. 427

After the Spring Festival, when the cattle that had survived the winter had been driven from the soggy lower meadows to the high pastures, and the grain was beginning to wave in the muddy fields, Gundohar started gathering his men. It was a measure of how well the Burgunds had adapted to their new land that he could not hope to summon them until the labors of the summer were well under way. The martial display he had put on for Aetius had been limited to the warriors of his own war-band and those of some of his major chieftains. To muster the full strength of the Burgund war-host took careful planning, and time.

Nonetheless, by the beginning of Litha Moon, the first half of Gundohar's forces were marching westward, led by Sigfrid and Godomar. With them went most of the comitatus, while the king and Hagano, attended only by Gundohar's own house-guard, gathered the rest. They were sitting in Gundohar's work chamber, discussing the effects of the floods on the food supply in Gallia, when the courier from Attila arrived.

He was one of the khan's own men, a wiry, grinning fellow called Tuldik, who could ride anything with hooves. He bowed to the king, beginning his message in halting Gothic, and then, seeing Hagano, broke into a torrent of speech in the language of the Huns.

"What is it? What is he saying?" Gundohar demanded, look-

249

ing from Tuldik to Hagano. There was excitement in the little man's voice, and anger, and appeal. Hagano was frowning. Did Attila want him back again?

"He says that Waldhari has run away with Hildigund and the khan's war-chest—" Hagano began, and Tuldik cut in with another burst of gabbling. Hagano said something in Hunnish and turned to Gundohar.

"If you are to understand this, I will have to give you some history. Waldhari is the son of Theoderid's sister and Albharius, a major chieftain among the Tervingi Goths. He was sent to the Huns at about the same time I was, along with a girl called Hildigund, the daughter of Hairarik, a king of the riverbank Franks. There was some talk that their fathers had meant to betroth them, but of course that was all put aside when they became hostages. Hildigund went into the household of Queen Ereka, Attila's principal wife, and Waldhari was with the rest of us in the war-band of the khan."

"So you know him—" said Gundohar, beginning to understand his brother's reaction.

"I ate and slept and fought beside him for seven years. . . ."

Gundohar nodded. Men who served together in a war-band could become very close. Hagano had grown grimmer and darker in the past seven years, the heavy bones of his face thrusting against the skin. He might well feel more of a bond with this Gothic hero than he did with his own brothers, after so long.

"And now he has stolen something from the khan? It is a pity that you weren't there to talk him out of it—" said the king, watching him.

"A pity indeed—" For a moment his brother's face showed some emotion, as quickly denied. "For it seems that to reach home, Waldhari and Hildigund must pass through our lands, and Attila is asking us to find him and recover the gold."

"How did Waldhari get it in the first place?" Gundohar put in, playing for time while he tried to understand what was going on here.

"The khan travels so much that his chief wife keeps charge

of his treasury. Waldhari was left to guard the household, and Hildigund showed him how to get at the gold."

He liked the man, thought the king. *He doesn't want to fight him. Can we talk our way out of this somehow?*

He looked at Hagano and laughed. "Surely the khan has more men than I do, and better trackers, too. You and I have an army to get together—if this man had come a day later he would not have found us here. I sympathize, but surely this is not our affair. Attila may send his Huns to hunt Waldhari across the Burgund land with my good leave."

Tuldik said something else and held out a message case with a Roman seal. Hagano raised one eyebrow as Gundohar unrolled it and began to read. After a moment the king looked up again.

"It would seem," he said carefully, "that catching Waldhari may become our business after all." He turned to the precise Roman lettering once more. "The letter is from Aetius. Attila is with him in the west—apparently the queen sent a courier to him in Gallia as soon as it happened, and he sent the man here. Waldhari must be travelling much more slowly, burdened by the treasure and the girl. The treasure consists of most of the payment made by the Romans to Attila for last year's campaign, a tidy sum for the Goths to play with. Aetius says—" He looked down at the parchment.

> *"The gold would be worth more to Theoderid than an army. It must not reach him. You are therefore required to use all your resources to find and seize Waldhari. A proportion of the treasure will be your payment, equivalent to what you would have received for participation in the western campaign. In the name of the emperor, I charge you, let this be done."*

Hagano blinked and turned to the messenger. "Aetius proposes to pay the Burgunds with Attila's gold?"

"Yes! Yes! Then pay us more. You catch Waldhari, you do not have to wait for Rome to pay!"

"And if we don't catch him, we can wait for it till Baldur

returns," Hagano said bitterly. "You don't have to tell me, brother, how badly we need to replenish our own treasury. But it won't be easy. Waldhari may be one man against an army, but he is crafty as well as strong."

"He is good, then?" asked Gundohar. "Better than you?"

Hagano grimaced. "The best fighter in Attila's war-band."

"Better than Sigfrid?"

"Sigfrid is not here!" Hagano snapped suddenly. "I am afraid that you and I, brother, will have to do!"

"So you and Hagano are going off to be heroes!" Brunahild set down her spinning as Gundohar came into the room. He looked at her in surprise. "Do you think I would not make it my business to find out what a messenger from my uncle had to say?"

"Then I need not explain," he said pleasantly after a moment's pause. "We will be taking my house-guards, but you will have to see to the rest of the warriors as they come in. I will leave Sindald and Ecgward to assist you. If you keep the men well fed and well exercised, you should have no difficulty."

"And what about you?" she asked sweetly. "Will you and your war-band have any difficulty, going after one man?"

"I would rather not be going after Waldhari at all. He is a sword-brother of Hagano, and he has never done any harm to me. He and his woman could pass with my blessing—"

"If it were not for my uncle's gold," she finished for him.

"Burgund gold," he corrected her. "Or did you not hear that part of it? The Huns will be paid, whatever we do, but Aetius has left me little choice. If I want my people to eat next winter, we will need that money to buy grain."

Brunahild looked at him, wondering why she felt so irritated. Perhaps it was because Waldhari and Hildigund were living the life she had dreamed of when she was Sigfrid's companion, defying kings with only love and courage to defend them. She would lose that dream a second time when Gundohar and his warriors hunted them down.

"Go, then," she said coldly, "and win your gold, but do not

expect me to wish you victory. You should be able to manage that without any prayers from me!"

The day after Attila's messenger arrived, Gundohar had sent out word to all the Burgund settlements to watch for Waldhari and Hildigund. But Hagano had read his old friend fairly—the fugitives knew they would be followed, and were going carefully. Whether it was Waldhari's woodcraft, or discreet distributions of Attila's gold, no one reported their presence until they had passed through the eastern Burgund lands.

The king had expected to catch them when they tried to cross the river, but they found a boatman to take them over below the regular ferry crossing. Still, at this point they had to come out into the open, and so, on the fourth day after the alert, a farmer's son came ambling in on his father's plow-pony to tell the king that a man and a woman had landed below his father's vineyard and were moving westward through Ordwini's lands, heading for Belgica.

Gundohar sent his fastest riders after them, while the rest of the house-guard followed more slowly. As they neared Argentoratum, a messenger came back to tell them that the fugitives, hoping to lose their pursuers in wilder country, had turned south into the forest of Vosegus. The king swore, knowing his numbers would be little use to him in such terrain.

But there was no help for it. They followed the markers that had been left for them, just over a dozen men and their servants, winding in single file up into the rocky fastnesses beneath the tangled trees. Gundohar's scouts showed him the tracks they were following—a pack mule, heavily laden, and a lighter pony, which must be carrying the girl. But it was the footprints made by the man that interested him, big prints, with a long, easy stride that reminded him of Sigfrid's.

He gazed up the canyon they were following, where pale stone caught the sunlight as the crags lifted above the trees. The trail had grown narrower, and from time to time they encountered fresh landslides or newly felled tree trunks that lay across the path and had to be laboriously cut up before the riders could get through. Somewhere up there, Waldhari was waiting. He wondered if they might not come to wish they had Sigfrid with them after all.

Five days after the Burgunds left Borbetomagus a scout came scurrying down the trail to tell him that the canyon dead-ended in a fissure in the mountain, the source of the little stream. In a few minutes Gundohar could see it for himself. The stream trickled beneath two great masses of rock that leaned together like wrestling trolls caught by the sun. The space between them was barely big enough to get a pony through, but hoofprints in the sand showed clearly that they had done so, and not returned.

In another light Gundohar might have thought they had gone straight into the mountain, but the slanting afternoon sunlight shadowed a deeper darkness behind the stones. The shaggy-haired men who lived in these hills assured him that there was space enough there, barely, for the fugitives. But except from the front there was no way to come at it. Cliffs overhung the cleft, so that even if the king could get some men up there, it would do little good to shoot arrows or roll stones. But if the Burgunds could not get in, neither could Waldhari escape them.

They had brought the bear to bay—now they had only to draw him out of his den.

That night they made camp in a straggling line along the stream. As Hagano rolled himself in his blankets, listening to the grunts and rustlings as other men settled themselves to sleep around him, it seemed to him that this could be any of a hundred nights he and Waldhari had slept on hard ground out hunting, or on campaign. The only difference was that this time, Waldhari was the prey.

He stared upward, where a few stars winked mockingly through the branches of the trees. It was mostly oak and beechwood here, though the heights were crowned with evergreens. A wind from the west sighed softly in the branches. The past few days had been clear and fine, but it seemed to him that weather was coming in on that wind.

Or perhaps it was the approaching conflict of men, not the elements, that he was sensing. The king would have left him to muster the rest of the war-host if he had asked it, but the only thing worse than being here would have been to stay in Borbetomagus, explaining to their mother why he had let Gundohar go after Waldhari alone.

Among the Huns, the hostages who served in Attila's house-guard had all been strangers. When all were equally foreign to the people among whom they were serving, no one expected to feel at home, and they became each others' kindred. Now, even though Hagano was back with the people among whom he had been born, he felt closer to the man they had come to kill than to anyone here, except perhaps for Gundohar. He sighed and closed his eyes. There was no help for it now, and morning would come soon.

But whether it was anxiety, or because even a few moons sleeping in beds had softened him, Hagano did not sleep well. He dreamed he was back with the Huns, trading blows with Waldhari in the practice yard. His opponent, a huge man with a red beard, was laughing as he always did in battle. Hagano grinned, fighting with all the might that was in him, and even as he fought found new battlecraft called forth by his opponent's skill.

He had never been happier. And in that moment, it seemed to him that above the sound of blows he heard someone calling. *"Hagano, Hagano, is this all you want to be?"*

Then the scene darkened, and suddenly it was a bear that he was fighting, a giant red beast that raked the air with huge, taloned paws. He shouted, and Gundohar came running up to help him. They attacked together, but the bear was a match for both of them. Roaring, he slashed Gundohar's thigh. Hagano glimpsed his brother rolling away, spouting blood, and hewed with all the strength that was in him. He felt the blade connect with one of the mighty paws, but the other was blurring toward him.

He felt first the impact as it struck his head, then blinding pain. He reeled back, one hand clapped to his face, and felt the hot blood pouring from what was left of his eye. It seemed to him that he fell through endless darkness. A voice followed him, whispering—

"Some see with one eye more truly than others with two. Let this be your warning. If you choose this path, you choose Me. . . ."

"No—" he muttered. "No!" And then suddenly someone was shaking him. He struggled, then got his eyes open—both eyes—and looked up into his brother's worried face.

It was morning, and men were stirring sleepily all around him. Morning, and he was whole. The fight with the bear had been a dream.

"Are you all right?" Awkwardly, Gundohar patted his shoulder.

Hagano stared at his brother, still shaken. Only a dream—and yet it had the sharp clarity of prophecy. To fight Waldhari would bring disaster, but how could he convince Gundohar?

"My lord," called Gamalo, "I can see smoke rising from the cleft. They're still in there. Shall I tell the men to eat now?"

"Yes, of course—" the king said over his shoulder.

"Listen, brother, I have a stave for you—" said Hagano. With a flicker of humor he saw Gundohar's eyes widen at the idea of his dour brother playing with poetry.

> *"Red bear raging, ringed by hunters,*
> *Strikes with wound-swords, slaying many,*
> *Leader's leg with talons slashes,*
> *Brother's eye's bashed by the bear."*

Gundohar blinked, the agile mind intrigued despite the stress of the moment. "This was your dream? Waldhari is the bear?"

Hagano nodded. "Brother, we will be the ones to suffer if we attack him. I have never had so clear a warning. Let us turn back—leave him and his woman alone."

Gundohar sat back with a sigh. "I cannot. The men will call me coward, and I cannot afford that. Even less can I afford to lose that gold."

"You have proved yourself in battle and so have I!" snapped

Hagano. "And as for the treasure—the Burgunds survived bad seasons before they had Roman gold to fall back on. We can do it again!"

"Before, we were not living on Roman land! What have seven years among the Huns made of you, Hagano? A man may be maimed in any battle, so what is different now? Do you love this Visigoth more than your own blood-kin?"

Hagano stared at him, knowing that, indeed, that was part of it. But the thing that had him sweating was not so much the fear of being wounded, but of what that maiming might mean.

"Do what you must, Burgund king," he said heavily. "But I tell you now that no good will come of it. As for me, when the god himself has warned me of disaster, I will not fight a man who was my friend."

The morning sun was just topping the rim of the canyon when Gundohar led his house-guard up the slope toward Waldhari's lair. There were twelve of them, all picked fighters sworn to die to protect him. Feisty as fighting cocks, touchy and quarrelsome in peacetime, only in battle could they earn the arm rings he had given them and the mead they drank in his hall. They had grumbled when the rest of the war-host marched off to win glory in Gallia, and this expedition, however one-sided, was the best chance they had to earn some of their own. And there were certain romantic aspects to the situation. Perhaps the poets would find something in it to interest them, and immortalize those who fought this day.

Their steps crunched loudly on the stones below the cleft, but the thin trail of smoke that twined lazily above it was the only thing that moved.

"Waldhari son of Albharius," cried Gamalo, "you trespass on Burgund land. Gundohar our lord awaits you. Come out, Waldhari, and pay your respects to the king."

A raven called from a pine tree that clung to the cliff face above them, but there was no other sound.

"They must be in there," said young Betavrid presently. He was one of the newest of the band, chosen to replace a man who had fallen in last summer's campaign, and fond of practical joking. "Unless they have grown wings!"

"Are you sure there's no way out but this one?" Helmnot replied.

"I'll wager you my new arm ring they are in there!" said Betavrid. "They've gone to ground."

"Why don't you go knock on the door then," asked Gerwit. "See if anybody's home?"

"Very well!" The boy looked to Gundohar for confirmation, then began to climb the last few feet, whistling tonelessly. He reached the gap, and banged the shaft of his spear against the stone. "Ho, Waldhari, can't you hear me knocking? At least you could come to the door!"

Betavrid bent forward to peer inside, something moved, and he lurched back again, dropping his spear.

"Well, is he there?" Gamalo asked at last.

"I . . . don't know." Slowly the boy turned. He was clutching at his solar plexus, and blood seeped between his fingers. He looked from one to another, and managed a ghastly grin. "But his spear . . . is. . . ."

He took a step forward and became even more ashen; then his face contorted and he crumpled suddenly, rolling down the hill. He came to rest at Gundohar's feet, arms outflung, blood flowering in a red stain beneath his heart. For the space of one pulse and then another the blossom grew. Then it ceased, and with a last shudder, Betavrid was still.

Gundohar heard a soft growling from the men and felt the hair on his neck lift. Before, this had been a game to them; now they were angry. He wavered between sorrow and satisfaction, knowing that they would not rest until Waldhari had paid the price for Betavrid's loss.

"A brave deed, Waldhari, to strike from hiding—" cried Gerwit.

"Almost as brave as to send twelve men against one . . ." The reply came from within the cleft, lazy, almost amused, its deep tones amplified by the rock walls.

"We will face you one by one if you will come out to us,"

Randalf replied. His voice shook, and Gundohar remembered that he had been close to Betavrid.

Shadow moved in the entrance, then the sun struck red sparks from the hair and beard of one of the biggest men Gundohar had ever seen. He held the spear that had killed Betavrid with an arm like a young tree trunk, though the rest of the body was covered with a long shield on which had been painted a red bear. *Hagano was right*, thought Gundohar, *in his dream.*

"His size must slow him," said Gamalo softly, but the king wondered. He was beginning to wish very much that Sigfrid was here. Waldhari looked at them one by one, and grinned.

"Well—here I am."

Randalf spat out an oath and charged uphill toward him. Gundohar groaned, for though Waldhari was outnumbered, he had the advantage in both reach and ground. He hardly seemed to move as his opponent charged him, but before Randalf could close, that deadly spear flickered once more. Randalf yelled and swayed, but he had not even hit the ground when Gerwit sprang up the slope after him.

The attacker's spear rattled against a shield that was suddenly between it and the target; Waldhari shoved, and as Gerwit spun away, his opponent's spear followed, thrusting him through the side. Two more men followed and received the same treatment. One was killed immediately by a spear through the throat; the other was holed in the groin, and took a little longer to die.

"That's five of you gone," said Waldhari pleasantly. He did not, damn him, even appear to be sweating. "The odds are a little better now. Who's next? You need not wait for an invitation—I am always at home."

But Gundohar's men had learned caution and were retreating to a safe distance down the slope, carrying their dead.

"Combat on equal terms, hah!" Tanastus spat into the dust. "The man is a troll!"

"He's twice the size of any ordinary man!" exclaimed Helmnot.

"And twice as fast, too," added one of the others.

Eleuthir, the only one of the band who was older than Gundohar, grunted, tugged off his metal cap, used it to dip water from the stream and passed it around among the men.

"It seems to me that all of us against him barely evens the odds," Eleuthir said then. "I think we will have to rush him all together and pull him down." They all looked at Gundohar.

"But is that honorable?" asked the king. Eleuthir frowned.

"With all respect, my lord, honor requires that Waldhari pay the price for our comrades slain!"

"Rush him!" said Helmnot. "Let his blood feed the ground!"

"Aye—all together—" the others were echoing.

Gundohar recognized the note, like the belling of hounds. It might work. With enough dogs, a hunter could bring down a bear. And in any case, he did not think he could stop them now. "Very well," he said at last.

Together they moved back up the slope. "On my signal," said Eleuthir. Men nodded, began to spread out to either side.

"So you are back—" Waldhari began. "Who will be next to feel my welcome?"

"Now!" shouted Eleuthir.

Baying, the warriors rushed their foe. Steel flared in the sunlight as spears stabbed inward, drumming on Waldhari's shield. The roar with which he answered was like a blow; Gundohar saw the flicker of his spear. Someone's blood sprayed the stones; a man reeled backward; another was screaming. He stabbed with his own spear, felt it catch on the shield, and wrenched it free.

A flicker of motion from above caught Gundohar's eye. He looked up just in time to dodge as a small boulder came hurtling toward him. A woman's face showed over the top of the mass of stone; he could not tell if she was beautiful, for she wore a mask of fury now. *Hildigund . . .* thought the king, *helping her man.* He felt a stab of regret, knowing that Brunahild would never have fought so for him. She reappeared with another rock; it crashed down among the struggling men, and Helmnot, stunned, dropped his guard and fell prey to Waldhari's spear.

Gundohar stood it a little longer, but it was clear that his men could not succeed, they were only getting in each other's way.

"Back!" he cried. "Down the hill, men, now!"

This time, when they withdrew, there were four bodies to carry, Eleuthir and Trogus as well as Helmnot, and scarcely a man among them was without a wound. *Nine men dead!* Gundohar groaned silently. From their camp among the trees the scouts must be watching. He wondered what tale they would tell of this day. If he had had the luxury of thinking like a bard, he could at least have gotten a lament from the tragedy, but now he had to think like a king. Hagano was down there too, sitting on his shield. Gundohar suppressed a spurt of anger. His brother should have been by his side, helping him to comfort his dying men.

"Burgund king!" Like an echo of his thoughts, he heard Waldhari's call. "This carnage is senseless. Will you talk with me?"

Gundohar started back up the hill.

"No, my lord," said Gamalo, "he'll strike you down!"

"I don't think so," said Gundohar. It was he who could not afford to be honorable now.

Waldhari was waiting for him, leaning on his spear. The king took a sour satisfaction in noting that the bear on the linden-wood shield had been hacked almost beyond recognition. They had broken his spear for him too—the one he was holding now was one of their own. However, he did not appear to have been wounded.

He came to a halt just over a spear's length away.

"So you are Hagano's brother," said Waldhari. "He used to talk about you. You are not quite what I expected, Burgund king. . . ."

Gundohar kept his features still, promising himself that when this was over he would have a word with Hagano. "Did you think I came here to write poetry?" he answered. "I wish I had—for you, unfortunately, are living up to my brother's description of you far too well."

"Hildigund counseled me to seek a safe-conduct from you when I entered your lands," said Waldhari. "But I thought that

Hagano would stop you from coming after me."

"I would have been happy to give it—" Gundohar began.

"Then why—"

"—If your request had arrived before Aetius' letter came," the king continued, and watched understanding follow regret in the face of his foe. "My people suffered badly this winter. That gold you are carrying will buy grain to get us through next year."

Waldhari nodded. "What if we split it between us?" he asked. "Or if I gave it to you as a ransom to let me and Hildigund go?"

Gundohar frowned, thinking, then shook his head unhappily. "If you had made that offer when we got here, I might have chanced it, but you are of royal kin, and you must understand that reputation can be as necessary as gold to a king. You have killed too many of my men. If I let you go now, they will call it cowardice, and no one will follow me."

"Will it help you if I kill the rest of them—if I kill you?"

"Then men will say that we died with honor," Gundohar answered steadily. And in truth, at this moment, that did not seem so ill an ending. Death would free him from the burden of kingship and the pain of loving Brunahild.

"Then I must fight you," said Waldhari. "I salute you, Gundohar, as a worthy foe!"

The king nodded, but as he turned away, he wondered how long the other man would think so. As the afternoon wore on, a little breeze was beginning to blow up the canyon, and an idea had come to him which was not honorable at all.

They rested until it was nearly sunset. Waldhari had gone back into the cleft, and the dead had been buried. The place looked deceptively peaceful. But Gundohar had set the scouts to felling brushwood, and as the shadows lengthened, men moved back up the slope carrying wood in their arms.

It was clear that so long as Waldhari had the rock at his back they could do nothing against him. They had to get him out in the open, away from his refuge, where they could wear him down. With every moment the wind grew stronger, rising from the warm lowlands to swirl up the canyons. Gundohar gave quiet orders and men piled their sticks against the rocks and before it, leaving only a narrow passageway. It was a variation on a technique still common in the northlands. Usually men preferred to come out fighting rather than be burned alive in their halls.

Inevitably they made some sound. Soon a head poked above the stone rampart, and they heard voices within. Gundohar gestured to the scout who was holding the torches.

"Light the wood—" he said harshly.

Only three of the king's guard were left now, but they began to grin as they spread out beyond the piled wood, ready to cut Waldhari down. It had been set alight at the far edges, but already smoke was beginning to curl inward through the passageway. One of the horses whinnied in alarm. The flames would not reach inside, but the cleft would act like a chimney. When the fire was well started, nothing inside would be able to breathe.

"Send out the woman, Waldhari, and we will see her to safety," called Gundohar.

"As for you," Gamalo added, "come out fighting or choke inside—we don't care!"

Wind gusted and the flames roared hungrily. Black smoke billowed inward and they heard someone coughing. The girl had better come out quickly, thought Gundohar, or she would not make it. Had she decided to stay there and die with her man? He tensed. Beyond the screen of smoke something was moving—

"Wait, it might be the woman!" Gundohar began, and as they hesitated, Waldhari, sword flaring, seemed to materialize from the flames.

The sword fell and a man screamed. Gundohar drove in, felt the jar all the way up his arm as he struck the shield, and wrenched with all his might, grinning as he felt the weakened wood give way. Waldhari flung the useless mass aside, pulling the king's spear with it, and Gundohar drew his own sword.

Slowly, the three Burgunds closed in. The king glimpsed Gamalo's face beyond their foe's shoulder.

"Get him!" he screamed, saw Gamalo's sword rise, Waldhari's blade flaming to meet it. He swung, sliced through metal plates and hardened leather and knew it was not a killing blow. As Gundohar pulled his sword free he sensed someone else charging in beside him.

Waldhari's return blow arched toward him, but the other man stepped into its path. Hot blood sprayed across his face as Tanastus took the blow that had been meant for his lord. Then something struck the king across the side of the head; flame and darkness swirled around him and he knew no more.

"Hagano! Hagano!"

The call boomed down the slope, and Hagano, crouched with his head in his hands as if the reality of what was happening would be changed if he did not hear or see, came to his feet, staring. The voice was so roughened by smoke he could not tell who was calling, but the tall figure silhouetted against the dying flames was unmistakable. As he recognized Waldhari, Hagano felt as if a swordblade had twisted in his own gut, and a rush of rage that made him understand at last where his true loyalty must lie.

"Come up here and get your wounded if you care for them—your brother still lives . . ."

Swaying, Waldhari ducked back into his refuge as Hagano scrambled up the slope toward him. He could see that two of the men were beyond helping. Gamalo lay clutching his guts and moaning, but though the king was covered in blood and had lost his helm, he was only unconscious. If Gundohar was still alive, then Waldhari must have liked him, Hagano thought grimly.

That night was a very long one. Around midnight Gamalo, not much helped by Hagano's rough bandaging, ceased at last to moan. But Hagano's main care was for his brother, who lay shivering and muttering despite all the cloaks he could wrap him in and the warmth of their fire. A little before dawn his breathing eased and he seemed to pass into a normal sleep. Hagano lay down beside him, and despite his determination to stay on guard, presently sleep took him as well, and this time he had no dreams at all.

When he awakened, his brother's eyes were open, and he was staring around him as if he had never seen a tree before.

"Gundohar!" The vague grey gaze turned to him. "How many fingers do you see—" Hagano held up his hand.

"Five . . ." The king blinked. "And can you please speak more softly? I feel as if a herd of horses had trampled my brain."

Hagano sighed, surprised once more by the depth of his relief. "No," he said quietly, "it was only one bear."

But now that he thought about it, he should have been hearing horses, a dozen hungry horses who had run out of grass to graze. He gave a quick look around him—there were none to be seen, and the spears that had marked the graves of Gundohar's men were gone as well. But the soft ground beyond the stream was churned to mud, as if a number of beasts had passed that way.

"Waldhari!" Gundohar sat up suddenly, winced, and touched the side of his head gingerly.

"Gone—" said Hagano. "He has taken the horses. The scouts ran off long ago. And your men are dead."

Gundohar groaned, with more than physical pain. "For me . . ." he whispered. "They died for me!"

"That is what their oaths to you required of them," said Hagano grimly. "They died well, and no doubt by now they are feasting in Wodan's hall."

Gundohar took a deep breath, reached out to the nearest branch, and levered himself upright. For a moment he swayed, then his sight seemed to clear. "But Waldhari lives. We must go after him—"

"Brother, has that blow addled you? You are in no state to travel, and Waldhari has taken all the horses anyway. He will be hours ahead by now."

"He is tired . . . too," said the king, "and so many horses will slow him. I have . . . to try." He took a wavering step toward the stream, half fell to his knees, and scooped chill water over his head, gasping as it trickled down his neck. Then he drank.

When he sat up again, he was still pale, but his eyes were clear.

"Thank you, brother, for taking care of me. I will understand if you do not feel you can go with me—Waldhari is a noble man." He looked down the trail.

"So are you . . ." muttered Hagano. He heaved himself to his feet with a sigh. "You will never catch him that way," he said more loudly. "But I talked with the scouts while you were up there playing bait-the-bear. There's another trail over the mountain, no good for horses, but a shorter route to the Divodurum road. That's the way the scouts ran. If you're strong enough to climb it, we might get to the other side in time to cut him off."

"I will get there—" said Gundohar, and his brother blinked, for the first time seeing in his face a resemblance to the old king, Gipicho.

Yes, he thought, *I begin to think you will.* He gathered up their weapons, rolled cloaks into packs to hold their food, and stamped out the remnants of their fire. As they started up the hill, a raven fluttered from a branch and winged ahead of them. Hagano felt cold sweat breaking out on his skin, but Gundohar was digging his spear shaft into the ground and pulling himself upward, and Hagano had to follow him.

It was late afternoon by the time they reached the road, but to Hagano's amazement, Gundohar's condition had improved with exercise. The road showed no evidence of recent passage by horses. Always assuming the fugitives had decided to come this way, the brothers were in time. Hagano did not know whether to be glad or sorry.

"There, where the trail goes through the copse of hazel trees, we will confront them," said Gundohar. "I do not think they will run away."

If you had any sense it is you who would be running, thought Hagano. The raven he had seen before, or perhaps another, was watching them from the trees. But his brother had acquired a strange serenity. Hagano realized that, for the first time, Gundohar had become truly dangerous, because he had become completely focused on coming to grips with his foe, and that mattered more to him than whether he lived or died.

And so they took up their positions, and a little before sunset they heard horses coming up the road.

The fugitives had roped them together in a long string, half of them led by Waldhari, and the other half by Hildigund, and as expected, they were going slowly. Gundohar let the girl and her string go by. Then he stepped into the road ahead of the man.

"Waldhari, son of Albharius," said the king, "there are deaths between us. You may not pass."

There was a stunned silence, then Hildigund reined her mount around and the horses she led began to plunge. She was a sturdy girl with gold-brown braids, no great beauty in ordinary terms, though she was splendid now, with the light glowing in her eyes like fire.

"He's mad—" she shouted over the squeals of the horses. "Ride him down!"

"You won't do that—" said Gundohar, and Waldhari sighed.

"No. It is time we made an end." He looked over at Hagano. "And have you also turned against me? We swore oaths of brotherhood once, as I recall."

"I remember," said Hagano harshly, "but blood binds better than words, and he is my brother as well as my king."

Waldhari nodded. "Hildigund, you must take charge of the horses, and promise not to interfere."

"But they are two to one—" she protested.

"Do you think those odds are too great for me?" As Hildigund, swearing, began to round up the horses, his smile became a grin.

"She will go free," said Gundohar, "no matter what happens here."

"I believe you." Waldhari slid down from his saddle and handed the rein to the girl. He nodded toward the grass beside the road. "That meadow will do nicely."

Gundohar's fair head flamed in the red light as he moved out to face his foe. He could not have borne to wear a helm, and Waldhari had lost his. Hagano, who was the only one with everything undamaged, sighed and set his own war-cap down. They had gone beyond self-preservation or battlecraft. Who won or lost would depend on courage now and the will of the gods. But they were all tired. He did not think it would take long.

Waldhari struck first, so swiftly he nearly ended it then, but Gundohar managed to wrench himself out of his path, whipping his own blade around with more strength than grace, grazing Waldhari's side.

The king gulped breath and came upright in fighting stance as his foe's sword arced around. Blades clanged as he met the blow; for a moment they strained together, swords held two-handed, but Waldhari was the stronger. Slowly Gundohar's blade was being borne down. *Give way!* thought Hagano, and as if he had heard him, his brother released the pressure suddenly, stepping aside and out from under, slicing upward with a quick twist that parted the ties that held Waldhari's metal-plated breastplate and tore through the tunic beneath, leaving a long red gouge on the fair skin.

Waldhari leaped back and shrugged out of the hanging pieces. Amazingly, he was laughing. "My thanks, little king. It has been a long day, and that leather was growing heavy. I will move more easily now."

Gundohar smiled back at him, swaying a little, and Hagano felt his heart sink, realizing that the unnatural energy that had sustained his brother must be failing now. He moved slowly toward him.

For a long moment Gundohar and Waldhari faced each other, swords poised. The big man's eyes were shining, but in his brother's eyes Hagano saw only that strange serenity.

He expects to die. As that knowledge came to him he saw Waldhari begin to move. But Hagano was moving too. The Goth's blade hissed down, and Gundohar tried to parry, but slowly, too slowly. Then Hagano was there, knocking his brother aside, and the stroke that would have split him only kissed his chest and belly, and at fullest extension tore through the muscles just below the joining of abdomen and thigh.

Blood welling, Gundohar fell. But Hagano had no time to see to him. That bitter blade was seeking his own life now. Steel rasped as his weapon met it, then whirled away. His sword and Waldhari's danced together as they had so often in the practice yard while the Huns made wagers and cheered them on.

Waldhari had been the best of them, but at times Hagano had nearly matched him. And now, unwounded and less wearied, he must be his master. Gods, how well he knew this man, his every trick and parry—as well as Waldhari knew Hagano's own. He found himself fighting as never before, matching blow for blow in a deadly harmony; and for a few moments then, he was a god.

Then the rhythm faltered—Waldhari had brought his blade up just a fraction too slowly. And in that moment Hagano knew that this time he would win. But even then, old habit kept him from killing. The blow that might have ripped the other man's chest continued onward as Hagano sought to disarm him. But Waldhari was turning too quickly. The blow glanced from the swordhilt and ripped through the muscle and tendon and bone of his right hand.

Waldhari yelled, his blade flying free as hot blood spurted from a suddenly nerveless hand. And Hagano stood, staring as if spellstruck as the sword wheeled toward him through the air. He felt first the impact, then the blinding pain as its tip struck the bone beneath his eyebrow and then flicked across his left eye.

A long time later, as it seemed to him, Hagano became aware that someone was tending him. He felt pressure over the throbbing agony that had been his eye and realized it had been bandaged. An arm went behind his head, lifting it, and he felt something touch his lips.

"Drink," said a woman's voice. "It will help with the pain."

He opened his lips, gulped as strong wine went down his throat, and began to cough. "My brother—" he whispered when he could speak once more.

"He's all right," came Waldhari's voice, roughened by pain.

"Though it will be awhile before he's walking."

"Or before you swing a sword," said Gundohar weakly.

Hagano managed to get his good eye open, and saw his brother lying on the other side of a little fire. Waldhari, his arm in a sling, sat nearby, and Hildigund was offering the wine to him, her lips twisted in a grim smile.

"Between the three of us, we could just about make up a figure to frighten crows from the corn," said Waldhari. But Hagano thought of a tale he had heard once among the Gaulish farmers, of the Master of the Animals, who had one eye, one leg, and one arm.

"We'll be going on in the morning," said Hildigund. "We'll leave your horses, and tell the folk at the next village to fetch you. The treasure we are carrying will be my dowry. I am sorry I cannot give you any of the gold."

"You are very gracious," said Gundohar, and it was clear from his tone that he meant it. All the fury seemed to have drained from him with the blood he had shed. No one could doubt that he had done all he could, and perhaps that was enough, even though he had not won.

But Hagano, letting his head fall back and gazing with his good eye at the firelit branches above him, thought he saw a dark shape that might have been a raven waiting there. Gundohar might heal, and Waldhari could learn, like Tiw, to fight with his left hand. But Hagano knew that he had dreamed true. From now on he would see as Wodan saw, one eye on the world without, the other on the darkness within.

Chapter
Fourteen Homecoming

At the beginning of harvest, when the barley was beginning to hang its head and the emmer wheat was turning gold in the fields, the Burgund war-host came home. The men were bronzed from a summer's campaigning, decked out with the spoils of war and eager to boast of their battles. At the head of the procession rode Sigfrid and Godomar, grinning hugely and wreathed in summer flowers.

The warriors had done well, thought Gundohar, watching them from the porch of his feasting hall. It was no fault of theirs that the pickings of the battlefield were all they would get for this summer's campaigning. The harvest was proving better than he had hoped, but cattle took longer to replace. What was left in his war-chest would have to buy more beasts come the spring. The spirits of his forefathers were probably laughing at him—in the old days, some lean seasons were only to be expected, and folk tightened their belts or starved till Earth relented and grew generous with her bounty once more. But the Burgunds had become used to a regular food supply. If it failed them, they would not blame the goddess Erda, but the king.

At least he had a week or two of grace before the harvest feast at which they would celebrate their victories. Sigfrid had brought home the first contingent, but they must wait for Ordwini and his men. He grudged the expense, but a show of abundance now might stave off gossip later on.

"Sigfrid's sword was swift to slay, out by Arelas—" from the street came singing. *"Godo drove the Goths away, back to Tolosa!"*

Gundohar forced his lips to smile and wave back as the warriors marched by. They sang of Burgund victories in Aquitanica, praising the men who had led them there. If anyone ever made a song about how he and Hagano had fought Waldhari, it would have a very different theme. It had been two moons since he and Hagano had come home from their campaign, not on their war-horses proudly leading their men, but stretched out in a farmer's wagon like thralls. At the thought, his leg began to ache and he shifted position on the hard bench. There had been times then, and even now, when he wished Hagano had not saved him from Waldhari's sword.

With the help of a stick, he could get around, and Grimahild said that by next summer he might be able to sit a horse again, but he would never again walk without limping. And for a time the wound and everything around it had been fevered; it might be that he would never be able to beget a child.

> *"By Burgund men the battle's won,*
> *out by Arelas,*
> *Theoderid's day now is done,*
> *back at Tolosa!"*

The warriors sang and the people cheered as they marched by. Gundohar smiled, and waved, and wondered how soon he could take some more of the poppy syrup his mother had brewed to stop the pain.

"Wasn't the procession splendid?" Marcia folded Brunahild's mantle carefully and laid it in the chest by the window. The girl was not usually so talkative, but apparently the afternoon's show had excited her. "The men looked so fine, marching in through the gates with their swords all shining in the sun!"

"Very fine," said the queen, sitting down so that Marcia could brush out her hair. The whole town was excited. Even from here she could hear sounds of celebration. They were not waiting for the official feast of victory; every tavern had thrown wide its doors tonight, and they would be drinking and boasting until dawn.

The evening was warm. In the draft from the open windows, the flame of the lamp flared. *Like a swordblade flashing,* thought Brunahild. *Like Sigfrid's sword—* His image seemed to grow suddenly from the light before her until she saw him as she had that afternoon, riding at the head of the army. The summer's work had hardened him and given him a new authority. They used to call the gods the Shining Ones. Today, Sigfrid had been a god.

She shut her eyes, shaken by longing so sharp it went beyond desire. What she felt was *need,* not so much for his body as for the spirit that filled him, or perhaps for the part of herself that she had given away. Once she had been Sigdrifa, Bringer of Victory; this summer Sigdrifa had been Sigfrid's Walkyrja, invisibly protecting him. It occurred to her then to wonder if her spirit would have flown free and been with Sigfrid always if she had died bearing his child.

This woman they called Brunahild was only her lesser, human self, the part that endured this body and played the role of Gundohar's queen.

The flame flickered in the other direction, she heard the tap of a stick upon the tiles and knew that Gundohar had come in. Her woman gave a last stroke to her hair and began to bustle about, putting things away. Then she left them alone.

"So, the war-host is home . . ." she said conversationally. Gundohar glanced up at her, then continued pouring wine. "Marcia thinks they made a fine show. All the city is praising the victors of Arelas." The king grunted and took a long swallow. From the flush in his face, she suspected that this was not his first drink of the evening, but that was nothing new. "What a pity it is," she added viciously, "that you weren't leading them."

"Brunahild—" There was warning in his tone, but she only laughed.

"And didn't Sigfrid look splendid at the head of your army?"

She rose and began to pace back and forth, feeling the loose silk gown that was all she was wearing caress her body like a lover as she moved. "So strong . . . so healthy . . . so *virile!*" There was a loud click as the wine cup was set down.

"Why Brunahild, are you *asking* me to sleep with you?" Gundohar leaned against the windowsill, watching her.

"You haven't approached me since your encounter with Waldhari," she said sweetly. "I was wondering if you still can. . . ."

A faint voice deep within her observed that this was hardly fair, when the man had been recovering from such wounds, but as she saw the color fade from his face and then come flooding back again, she suppressed it. There was nothing she could do to Sigfrid, but Gundohar was a willing victim, and tormenting him helped, a little, to ease her own pain.

"Not that you have ever been much use to me. Perhaps I should go out into the streets and find some healthy young man who can serve me. Or perhaps I should seduce Sigfrid," she added, turning the knife in her own wound, "and see if he can give me a child."

"Woman, I have borne much from you," Gundohar took a halting step toward her, "but you will keep silent now!"

"Why should I? If one man insults another, they draw swords and fight, but you have taken that choice away from me. Words are the only weapon I have!"

"Then use them with honor," her husband said harshly. "And remember that you are a queen!"

"And you are a king—" She swept the hair back over her shoulders and laughed. "Poor little king, who needs other men to fight his battles, and other men to—"

"No!" With an agility she had not expected, he crossed the room and gripped her arm. "You are my wife, Brunahild!"

She turned her face away. "Whatever gave you the idea that was an honor I desired?"

She heard the rasp of his breath and smelled wine. Then, with his other hand, Gundohar gripped her face and turned it. His eyes were blazing, and she remembered how he had looked when he fought at the Longstone field. This was the face he wore in battle. She realized with an obscure satisfaction that she had awakened the animal that lived deep inside him at last.

"Do you want my hatred, Brunahild?" he hissed. "Was my mistake trying to win you with love?"

His grip was painful, but it tightened when she tried to get free. He pulled her against him, lips drawn back in a snarling grin. "My leg hurts, badly," he said, "but sometimes agony like this can sweep all other pains away. I am still a man, Brunahild, whatever you may say!"

"Let me go," she muttered. "You're hurting me."

"Good! I meant to," he answered her. "And I will do it again, since that is what you seem to want from me!"

"If you leave marks, everyone will know, and what will they say?"

"They will say that I have been beating you, bitch, and wonder why I didn't do it before!" He began to laugh, and a chill of danger thrilled along her nerves.

I am a Walkyrja, she thought, remembering how she had wrestled him into submission before. And now he was weakened by his wound. *He cannot treat me this way.*

Brunahild jerked suddenly and broke away, but Gundohar still had her arm; as she reached to loosen his grip he struck her on the side of the head with his other hand. Dizzied, she rocked back, and gasped as he hit her in the shoulder. Her arm went numb. If she could pull free, she could outrun him, but his grip was like a vise. If she kicked him in the groin, he would faint, but as she started her move he punched her in the belly and she doubled over. His fist followed, battering head and shoulders as she went down.

This is not happening . . . this cannot happen to me. . . .

He fell heavily on top of her, wrenching her arm. She bucked beneath him, flailing with her free arm, but his other hand was on her throat now, the long fingers contracting until her vision blurred and she could hardly feel her limbs. She had been trained to fight off an attacker, but it had been a long time since she had practiced, and even training was no guarantee against a man possessed by berserk rage.

She heard cloth rip, and bucked again as Gundohar forced himself between her thighs. He let go of her throat then, and sense and vision began to come back in waves of blood and darkness as he battered against her, convulsing after a few moments with a cry not of triumph but of agony.

Then he collapsed across her body, breathing in harsh gasps. After a few moments Brunahild pushed him off and he rolled onto his back on the cold tiles. She sat up, beginning to ache now where he had hit her. In fact, she hurt everywhere, and most deeply of all in her soul. Long ago, the Walkyriun had doomed her to be taken by the first man who found her, but until tonight, she had never lain with a man against her will. She hated the one who had done it. But it was Sigfrid who had first seduced her and then, when he no longer wanted her, tricked her into marriage with Gundohar.

Slowly Brunahild got to her feet, and without looking at her husband, made her way over to the pitcher and basin and poured water with a shaking hand.

I will make him suffer for this, she thought, *but first I will kill Sigfrid, who made me into a woman who could be treated so.* Then she began to scrub her body, but she knew that not all the waters of the Rhenus would wash the memory of this night away.

"Woofy, Da, woofy!"

Sigfrid grunted as a warm weight attached itself to his leg and looked down at his daughter, who was holding on to him as if he were a tree. Her nurse came scurrying down the path after her, but seeing the child with her father, drew back again.

"What does she want?" asked Gislahar, with whom he had been crossing the garden, discussing the possibility of going hunting the next day.

Sigfrid felt himself flushing. "I used to play . . . 'wolf' . . . with her, before we went on campaign. I'm surprised she remembers."

"Wolfie . . ." Gislahar began to grin. "I should have known! Godo would love this—what will you give me not to tell?"

Sigfrid glared at him, then laughed. "My new Frankish cloak pin?"

Gislahar whistled. "You really *don't* want them to know!"

"Da—*now!*" Sunnilda clutched at his breeches, looking up at him.

"Mustn't keep a lady waiting," said Gislahar, stifling more laughter. "I'll leave you two alone!"

When he had gone, Sigfrid sighed in relief and knelt in the path. Suddenly shy now that she had his attention, Sunnilda looked away.

"Well, and have you been a good wolf cub?" he asked softly. "You've grown, little one—" He felt a pang, seeing how much she was getting to resemble the little sisters with whom he had played this very game long ago.

"Let's see how much you remember . . ." Sigfrid got down on his knees and forearms, whining inquiringly, and her eyes came back to his, as amber as his own. After a moment she imitated the sound, more accurately than she could yet manage human language, and he smiled.

"I'm the daddy wolf, and you're my cub—" He barked suddenly, and startled, she sat down in the path. "That's right, that means to sit still!"

"*Bite* Da!" Sunnilda said, glaring.

"Well, you can try!" He grinned at her, cocking his head to one side. Her eyes lit up and she launched herself toward him, squealing. He let her knock him over and rolled over onto his back, his attempts to growl mingling with laughter as she bounced on his chest.

He blinked as a shadow fell across them, dimming the child's fair hair.

"Oh, my lord, you'll not want her sitting on you, getting your fine tunic all dirty in the path," said a woman. But that voice came from behind him.

Sigfrid sat up abruptly, clasping the child. For a moment she struggled, then nestled against his chest, peeking up at her nurse, who had spoken, and at Brunahild, who stood between them and the sun, her dark cloak trailing behind her like a broken wing.

Her face was in shadow, but he could see the tension in her body. Still holding Sunnilda, he came to his feet. "You've been a good cub, but it's time to go with your nurse now."

"Don't *want*—" she began, but he silenced her with a warning growl.

"The queen wants to talk to me. I'll play with you another time." He handed her to the woman, who carried her, still protesting, away.

"*Do* you want to talk to me?" Sigfrid asked when they were alone. She turned away and as the sunlight struck her face he saw the purpling bruise on her jaw. "Blessed gods, Brunahild, you look as if you have been in a fight. Has Gundohar taken to beating you?" He began to laugh, then stopped abruptly as the fury in her face told him it was true. "I'm sorry—" he began.

"Sorry! Are you sorry you bound me to a spineless fool?" she said in a shaking voice.

Not quite spineless, thought Sigfrid, remembering the bruise, but it was true that Gundohar's courage did not become apparent until his back was to the wall.

"At least he can give you honor and a home—" he said quietly.

"Is that what you thought I wanted?" She turned to him, eyes blazing, and her sallow skin and narrow features were transformed. He remembered then that her beauty had always been in motion, and realized how rarely he had seen it since she became Gundohar's queen.

"Is that what you want—truly—Sigfrid Fafnarsbane? Then do not teach Gudrun's daughter the wolfing ways, or she will never be happy here. Nor will you, no matter what you may think now. A wolf among dogs is either their master or their slave!"

"I *am* happy here . . ." he said then, but he spoke with a little too much emphasis, even to his own ears. Brunahild heard it (how could he have forgotten how well she knew him?) and began to laugh.

"Today, when they are praising you, perhaps you are. But what will you do when the nights grow long and men tremble when they hear the wolves howling outside their doors? Sigfrid, Sigfrid—" She laid her hand on his arm, and looking into her eyes, he realized that she was still beautiful. "I could have made you king of the world!"

He took a deep breath, willing his pulse to still. "Brunahild, it is no use speaking of what might have been, or the choices we might have made. I am bound to Gudrun now, and to our child."

"Your child—" she repeated in a strange voice. "Would it surprise you to know that there is another girl-child with wolf eyes living in my sister's hall? Her hair is redder and of course she is taller, being five years older, but they are very much alike, I am told. Her name is Asliud."

He stared at her as if she had spoken in a dialect he did not understand.

"Oh!" said Brunahild. "You are as great a fool as Gundohar!"

"Our daughter?" His voice cracked, and suddenly he was remembering how they had hunted and played together in the snow through the short days of the winter he had spent with her, and how they had lain together through the long nights. "Why did you never tell me?"

"I was waiting to show her to you," she said in a low voice. "But you never came. The next time I saw you—to know you—I was married to Gundohar and Gudrun was hanging on your arm."

"We'll send for her—" Sigfrid knew he was stammering, but he could not seem to get his voice under control. "There is plenty of room for her here!"

Brunahild stared at him, and for a moment her fury was replaced by simple amazement. "Indeed? And what would the Burgund lords say when they learned that their king's sworn brother had sired a child on his queen? Do you suppose Gudrun would welcome your child by me? No, Asliud is safer where she is. But you will never see her, Sigfrid."

He reached out to her, but she struck his arm away.

"You will never hold your firstborn child in your arms!" she hissed. "And you will never again lie with me!"

* * *

The weather of harvest month held fair and clear. From the banks of the Rhenus to the hills, the grainfields were aswarm with harvesters, the men moving from field to field as each plot ripened, with their womenfolk binding behind them; one week cutting barley, another, oats or rye or the precious wheat that made the king's bread.

A few mornings after the return of the war-host, Hagano rode out among the fields. The town was too full of warriors, and he had no mind to sit listening to them tally slain enemies whose numbers grew greater with each telling, or worse, to hear them fall sympathetically silent when he came near. It was an honorable wound, but men hit in the eye often took a fever to the brain and died. Hagano was fortunate that only the tip of Waldhari's sword had touched him, but as he had foreseen, it was sufficient. In the two moons since the fight, it had become clear that he would never see out of that eye again.

He had told himself—too often—that he ought to feel lucky. As he grew accustomed to the limitation he was learning to compensate, to turn his head more to see around him, and use other cues to judge distance. A one-eyed man could still fight. Wodan himself— he thrust that thought away.

He had dreamed of the god for three nights running. He would find himself walking along a lonely lane and come to a crossroads. Sometimes there was a gibbet set up there where the body of some criminal had been hanged as a warning, sometimes only the crossing itself, and the three roads unwinding into shadow. His feet would begin to drag as he neared the center and he would stop when he stood there, listening to the wind. That was when the voice would speak to him, as if the wind were whispering—

"Where are you going, Grimahild's son? Which way will you choose?" And when he could neither move nor answer, he would hear laughter, and then, *"When you see as I see, you will know what to do . . ."*

So far he had resisted, but even in the king's house, folk were not so Christian that they did not recoil with a sign of warding when they met him unexpectedly. In the next moment, of course, they would apologize, but Hagano knew whom they had thought him to be. At least when he rode out he could pull a broad-brimmed hat down over his brow, and those he met would think no more than that he wanted protection from the sun.

Old One, I never sought to be your priest, he thought grimly, *and I do not want that honor now. I may carry your mark, but I will not serve you!*

Reapers pausing at the end of a row looked up and saluted him, recognizing one of their lords in any horseman, and a son of the royal house as soon as he drew near. Hagano drew rein cautiously, for sometimes the harvesters would surround the farmer who approached his field, or any stranger, and make him pay a ransom before they let him go.

"Does the work go well?" he called.

One of the men wiped sweat from his brow and squinted up at him, shading his eyes with his hand. "Very well, sir. We'll finish this field by eventide, and this is the last of the king's corn. But this sun is hot as Muspel's fires."

Hagano nodded. A townsman would have said Satan's fires, but the veneer of Christianity grew thinner the farther one went into the countryside. He could feel sweat damp on his thighs where they touched the saddle and trickling down his back. Beyond the field, though, a winding line of trees showed where some watercourse came down from the hills. The reaper was already turning back to his work. Hagano nodded and reined his horse through the stubble in the direction of the stream.

It was blessedly cool in the shade by the water. He dismounted and knelt to splash his face and neck, tossing his hat aside, while the pony plunged its nose gratefully into the stream. When he had drunk his fill, Hagano sat back with a sigh. There did not seem to be any reason to move on. Hidden here, no one would trouble him. He felt his eyes growing heavy and lay back on the grass, the rein still in his hand. In the sweet music of water flowing over stones he heard the singing of the spirit of the stream. In this place of peace, perhaps he would not dream.

If dreams did come, they were not dire enough to wake him. It was shouting from the field that brought Hagano back to awareness. He washed the sleep from his good eye, bathed away the discharge that had run from his blind one, and peered through the screen of greenery.

The sun was sinking toward the western hills, its long rays falling at just the angle that makes everything it touches seem to glow from within. In the field, the harvesters were beginning to bind up the last sheaf they called the Old Man with braidings whose patterns had been old when the Gauls came into this land. The cut ends of the stubble glinted, and the sheaf shone with living gold.

So did the rider who was coming down the path from the hills. The coat of his pale stallion rippled with light, gold glinted from hair sun-bleached to the color of wheat by a summer in the open, gave the faded tunic he was wearing its own color, and flamed from the tip of his hunting spear. He rode wrapped in isolation like a haze of light, letting the horse choose its way. It was that, as much as the harmony of horse and rider, that sent the prickle of awe along Hagano's spine.

He was not the only one to feel it. "Ho!" called one of the men. "See how Fol comes riding through the corn! A blessing, lord, upon the harvest!"

"A ransom, rather," cried a woman as the stranger roused and turned to look at them. "He shall bear the Old Man away!"

"What is it?" asked the rider. "Do you need help?" The women looked at each other and began to laugh.

"Indeed we do, my lord," said the one who had called out. "And you are just the lad to give it, if you will get down off that tall horse and come into the field."

"Of course, if you need me," said the rider, laughing. "For every beast in the forest has gone to ground to escape the heat, and my hunting brought me nothing today."

Hagano stiffened and parted the bushes further, turning his head to see, for surely that voice belonged to Sigfrid! He watched, knowing what was coming, as Sigfrid slid down from Grani's back and one of the men led the stallion away.

"Do you know who that is?" said one of the men at Hagano's end of the field.

"The Lady's husband, who was with her on the Donarberg ... the Leaf King!" said his companion. "He gives himself to us—a good omen for the end of the harvesting!"

Several of the women had begun to pick up straw ropes that had not been used in the binding while the others gathered around him, waiting until the horse was safely tied.

"What do you want—" Sigfrid began, and at that the women threw themselves upon him, squealing with laughter, grabbing him by the arms and body, and dragging him toward the last sheaf. He struggled, but not too roughly, and in another moment they all went down together in a tangle of bare legs and straw. From what Hagano could see, Sigfrid did not appear to mind all the woman-flesh that was being pressed against him, but when they released him and he discovered that his arms and legs had been bound to the sheaf and a straw rope was tightening around his neck, he began to frown.

> *"The men are ready, the scythes are bent,*
> *the corn is great and small,*
> *the victim to the field is sent,*
> *the barley-king must fall!"*

With a rhythmic rasping the harvesters whetted their blades. Sigfrid began to test his bonds. "You've had your fun," he said, "now let me go!" But the women shook their heads as the men continued their song.

> *"The barley-king now we will beard,*
> *All with a naked sword,*
> *Meadows many we have sheared,*
> *and many a prince and lord,"*

The prisoner was beginning to struggle harder, and Hagano eased out of his hiding place, realizing that Sigfrid did not understand the local custom, and afraid someone would get hurt soon.

> *"But if he'll bring out ale and beer,*
> *to hearten thirsty men,*
> *we'll end the joke; if not, I fear*
> *the sword will strike him down!"*

Sigfrid had gotten to his knees, the fury of a bound beast beginning to blaze in his eyes. But one of the women had a good grip on the noose, and it was a toss-up whether he would break free before she strangled him. It was time, thought Hagano, to make an end.

"Let him go—" his deep voice rang across the field. "I will pay the ransom. This man belongs to me!"

He strode across the stubble, turning his face to the red glow of the setting sun so that they could see who he was. The woman who was holding the noose dropped it as if it had stung her and the others began to back away.

"The Old Man . . ." came the whisper. "The Old One himself has come for him!"

Hagano had time for a muffled curse as he realized who they thought he was, but for once the superstition might be useful. He drew his dagger and bent over Sigfrid to cut the ropes, and several of the harvesters, making warding signs over their shoulders, turned and ran.

"My thanks to you," said Sigfrid, standing up and brushing straw out of his hair. "I rode out from the town today because it stifled me, and to be trapped like that"—he shuddered—"for a moment, I felt the berserk fit coming on!"

"I know," said Hagano dryly. "That is why I intervened."

The man who had spoken to Hagano before brought his pony up from the stream and the horse began to nibble at the grain scattered on the ground.

"I will see that ale from the king's cellars is sent out to you," said Hagano, pulling himself into the saddle. The man's gaze went from him to Sigfrid, who was already mounted on Grani.

"We will drink your health, lord, and his. . . ." The man

bowed deeply and backed away. Hagano shook his head and reined his pony toward the road. When he looked back, he saw that the reapers had come back into the field and were carefully gathering up the scattered stalks of grain.

"The gods know what kind of a tale the country-folk will make of this," said Hagano as they turned onto the main road that led back to the town.

"Well, it is true, you do look a bit like old One-Eye," Sigfrid answered him. Hagano stared, and Sigfrid flushed a little. "Does that sound crazy? Several times I have seen him, or so I believe, when he took over a man's body for a time."

Crazy? thought Hagano. Perhaps, but he remembered a shadowed figure on a woodland path who had traded riddles with his mother and realized that it was probably true.

"But now that I think about it, I see more of a resemblance to someone else I knew," Sigfrid went on. "Except for your coloring, you have a great look of Ragan the mastersmith of the earthfolk who raised me. . . ."

Hagano's pony snorted at his sudden jerk on the rein. *Earthfolk . . . bilwisse . . . wild man . . . bastard. . . .* When he was a child, he had learned to dread those names. A challenge rasped from deep within him. "What do you mean?"

At the tone, Sigfrid pulled in as well, his eyes widening. "He was a hard man, but a good master—" he floundered, beginning to realize that no words would be the right ones. "He was good to me. . . ."

Hagano glared at him, the emotion that would have been powerful in two eyes focused into one terrible gaze. "*Wolf,* I am Gipicho's son! Never suggest that I am anything else again!" He wrenched the pony's head around and rammed his heels into its sides, and as they bucketed forward, snarled over his shoulder, "I should have let them cut you down with the grain!"

For the harvest feast they had garlanded the king's feasting hall with summer flowers, and tied sheafs of grain to the pillars. The effect was one of abundance, and as the noise level grew, it seemed to Gudrun that most of the warriors drinking at the long tables would see no difference between this feast and the celebration of any other year. Only those who came from the farms surrounding the city would know in how many fields, whether because of witchcraft or soggy ground, the grain had been blighted before harvest time. There was grain in the king's storehouses, but would it be enough to get them through the coming year?

"Look at them! They guzzle like swine," said Hagano, beside her.

"Be thankful they are here to do so!" she said tartly. "And not lying cold in the hills like Gundohar's guard!"

He turned to the left so that he could look at her, and she held herself from flinching. The milky gaze of his blind eye was bad enough, but it was almost worse to face the bitterness in the one that could still see.

"We would have fewer mouths to feed," he said deliberately, "if Sigfrid had lost more men."

"My husband's success this summer was the only bright spot in an otherwise disastrous year!" Gudrun flared, and then flushed, realizing that once more she had risen to his teasing. She waited for his sneer of triumph, but he was looking at Sigfrid, and slowly her anger gave way to an odd chill of fear.

He meant it—she thought then, her gaze following his. Sigfrid and Godomar had been given the place of honor at the center of the king's table. Gundohar sat beyond them, with Brunahild by his side. Godo, flushed and expansive as always by this point in the evening, was downing more than his share of the wine. But it seemed to her that Sigfrid had been drinking more than usual as well.

Did he have some worry? For two days she had scarcely seen him, and when she did he greeted her with an impenetrable cheerfulness, as if he still had his armor on. Sunnilda's nurse said he had been talking in the garden with Brunahild, who sat tonight with her head and throat swathed in a silk veil to hide the bruises she said she had gotten falling down the stairs.

Gudrun's women had spent the past few days debating whether to believe her. Gudrun herself had said nothing, but her brother looked like a lost soul, and it was clear to her that things were worse between the two of them than they had ever been before.

There was more amiss here than the harvest. Gudrun could feel it, like the hidden currents that ruffled the smooth surface of the Rhenus, but no one would tell her what was wrong.

One of the thralls leaned over to clear the fragments of bread away and Godo clapped his big hand over his own scraps, laughing.

"Don' take it away. Gods know when we'll get more!" He appeared to think this was funny, but the silence that spread around him was icy. Slowly he realized that perhaps he had said the wrong thing and lifted his palm.

Sigfrid looked at him, blinking, and then back at Gundohar.

"Is it money you need? Because of Waldhari? Why didn't you ask me? I have a treasure, you know, and no use for it. I can buy grain for you with gold from Fafnar's hoard. . . ." The silence deepened, as Gundohar flushed dangerously and then went pale.

"How very generous . . ." Hagano said finally. "But you have already led our armies to victory. I think we can manage to feed our people ourselves." He smiled sweetly, but there was venom in his words.

"I only meant—as a brother—" Sigfrid's reply faltered. Gudrun looked from him to the others, but their closed faces gave her no answers. Like Sigfrid, she knew what he had said was unfortunate, but no more than he, did she understand why.

The scent of cooked meat reached them as the great doors at the other end of the hall were flung open, and Gudrun found her mouth watering despite her tension. Staggering beneath the weight, two thralls brought in a board on which rested one of the oxen that had been roasting outside and set it down on the trestles that had been placed in the middle of the hall.

"Here's a noble feast for heroes!" cried one of the men. "Who shall carve it?"

"Not you, Drogo!" exclaimed one of his benchmates. "If I hadn't pulled you out from under a pile of Goths, you wouldn't be here!" Laughing, they began to call out other names.

But that was only in play, and soon enough the names that emerged from the chanting were those of Sigfrid and Godomar, who stood up, warming themselves at the adulation as if it were a fire.

"So," said Gundohar when the tumult had stilled a little, "which of you shall it be?"

Sigfrid hesitated, but Godo clapped him on the back. "You cut it this time," he said, grinning. "You killed more than me!"

Sigfrid laughed then, sprang up onto his bench and vaulted over the table. His crimson tunic glowed in the torchlight, and all his gold jewelry blazed. In that moment he seemed to Gudrun as splendid as any god.

The men thought so too. "Sigfrid!" they chanted as he strode down the aisle, drawing his sword. "Sigfrid Hundredkiller! Sigfrid Fafnarsbane!" Steel flashed as he brought it down, and a hot wave of blood-scent filled the air.

Gudrun would not have heard the little hiss of indrawn breath if Hagano had not been sitting beside her. She turned, though everyone else was looking at Sigfrid now. But Ordwini and some of the other lords were frowning. In Hagano's face was a bitterness that made her flinch, Gundohar's eyes were dark with shame, and in Brunahild's face she saw a mingling of exultation and hatred that was the most disturbing of all.

Chapter Fifteen

Challenges

Borbetomagus
Yule Month, A.D. 427

For almost two moons, since the beginning of the winter season, Brunahild, like the sun, had alternated between intervals of brilliance and long periods of gloom. When she did rouse, it was in bursts of furious activity which could take any form from a plan to whitewash all the rooms in the palace to setting all the woodcutters to bring her feathers and carcasses of dead ravens or rousing everyone before dawn to go herb hunting. Her times of seclusion were at first a relief to Gundohar, who feared any reminder of his madness, and even more that she would drive him to it again, but after a time, as those periods grew longer, his anxiety grew. Brunahild's women took meals to her, but reported that she ate little. Meeting her only at intervals, the king could see that she was growing thin.

In desperation, he sought counsel from his mother, who sat huddled before the hearth in her rooms. A storm had rolled in that afternoon. As the early winter darkness deepened, the wind moaned beneath the eaves in melancholy accompaniment to the crackling of Grimahild's fire.

"I am afraid my wisdom failed when I advised you to wed Brunahild," said the old queen. "She has brought no good to you or to the Burgunds."

Gundohar shook his head, remembering how his lady's lips could curve in amusement, her winged brows lift in scorn. "I would have taken her anyway," he said sadly. "I still love her, and now she hates me. But I meant only good, and if I did not fear to start a war, I would send her back to her people and set her free."

"It is not you she hates, my son," said Grimahild, "but herself. She is gnawing at herself like a trapped beast."

"You may be right—I have feared she will do herself some injury. But how can I stop her, Mother? The last person to whom she would look for comfort is me!"

"She does not want comfort. She wants revenge. It would be better to let her die, but I see that you will not accept that solution. Send Sigfrid to speak with her—perhaps hatred will rouse her. But I warn you, if she does, you may wish you had left well enough alone."

Hail rattled suddenly against the walls. It had been like that all afternoon—never quite warm enough for rain or cold enough for snow. Unsettling, dismal weather; just to think about it deepened his gloom.

"Anything would be better than this death in life," said Gundohar, but his mother only shook her head.

"I am an old woman. Once I thought I could control fate, but I know better now, and things that once seemed to me to matter greatly do not seem so important any more. You have wound your wyrd, and the Norns are busy at the loom. I thank the gods that I will not live to see that weaving done."

"Well, I am young," answered Gundohar with a spurt of bitter laughter, "and I will not sit idle if there is anything I can think of to do."

He rose and stood looking down at her. *Why are we all so enmeshed in hatred,* he wondered, *when all I wanted was love?*

Grimahild had sunk back into her shawls and seemed to be dozing. He blinked; for a moment he saw a mass of stone instead of a human figure, as if she had already become one with the earth. Then a log popped on the hearth and she stirred. He bent and kissed her on the brow and went out to find Sigfrid.

*   *   *

Brunahild lay alone in the great bed, listening to the storm. Since darkness fell the rain had settled to a steady pattering, monotonous and hypnotic. It was so easy simply to lie there and listen, letting the sound carry her like a river—the River Gjoll, perhaps, that roared past the gates of Hella's realm. A part of her understood her danger, but she found it hard to care.

There was a sound outside her door, perhaps the changing of the man on watch there, but she willed herself not to hear. To hear nothing, see nothing, and feel—especially to feel— nothing was death in life, but it gave her the illusion of peace.

Then the door swung open and golden light flared into the room. She stirred, ready to send whichever of her servants had dared to disturb her out faster than she had come, and was a little surprised at how hard it was to move. Then awareness shocked through her and she jerked upright, for the flicker of lamplight showed her broad shoulders and sinewy arms and flames dancing in a pair of amber eyes that held her own.

"What—" She coughed and tried again. "What are *you* doing here?"

"They tell me that you do not rise and work with your women; you do not play at board games, or drink wine or mead in hall," said Sigfrid. "You do no embroidery with thread of silk and gold, and give no one your counsel."

He shut the door behind him and began to move around the room, lighting lamps from the one he carried, until all the chamber was filled by their golden glow.

"I cannot make the sun shine, but at least I can bring you light," he answered, but his voice wavered a little as he looked fully into her face for the first time. "Holy gods, Brunahild, you looked better when first I found you, except that now you have more hair!"

"How *dare* you remind me of those days!" she hissed, shifting to her knees so that she could face him. Already it was easier—her strength was coming back to her—she realized abruptly that it was because the part of her that she had given him was so close to her, because *he* was here.

He stood still, looking at her. "Because I think that it is from those days that all your troubles come . . ."

"*My* troubles!" For a moment she was speechless. "You speak as if you had no part in them! I do not love Gundohar, but it was you who did me the greatest wrong!"

"Brunahild—" he said in a low voice. "Cannot you believe that I never meant to do you harm? If I deceived you, it was to save your life."

"You took my maidenhood and gave me a morning gift to seal the bond. I swore to wed only the man who could best me in battle, and you conquered me. You, Sigfrid—not King Gundohar! You have stolen my honor—what good is my life to me?"

He struck the table with his fist and she heard wood crack. "What do you *want*, Brunahild?"

"All the things for which Gudrun did not even have to ask," she answered bitterly. "I wanted to keep your fire and bear your children and warm your back with my breasts; I wanted to be your Walkyrja, your shield, your soul!"

"You said once that you would never try to trick me into something I did not want," Sigfrid said then. "But from the first moment I saw you, you began to force me into your concept of a hero—you turned me into your reason for existence because you had lost your own!"

"Do you think so?" she said bitterly. "It seemed to me that you were glad enough to have someone show you a road, and glad to lie in my arms! Was that so great a crime? Did it justify so great a treachery?"

"I gave you to a man who could give you wealth and power—and a home, as I could never do! It was for your own good, Brunahild!"

"*For my own good*—" she repeated, staring at him in amazement. "How kind of you! How very thoughtful. . . . Do you really believe that, Sigfrid, or are you only trying to make me think you are a fool?" Her voice rose. "Did it never occur to you to ask me if that was what *I* wanted? Didn't you realize that I would rather have slept under a hedge with you than in silken sheets with any other man?"

She drew a shaking breath. "No . . . of course not. It was more convenient for you to have me out of the way, and therefore you concluded it must be better for me! Perhaps I should not be surprised—every other man—my father, my uncle—thinks the same way. But I was a Walkyrja, Sigfrid. It was my right to choose, and you took that right away from me!" She was poised on the edge of the bed as if she would spring at his throat, and he backed away.

"If I chose for you, at least I chose well! I have made you queen of a great people and wife to a noble man. Is that not sufficient compensation?" He turned away and stood looking at the hunting scene frescoed on the wall, and Brunahild, seeing the beautiful balance of his back and shoulders, felt as if she had been stabbed. Outside the wind was rising. A gust of rain slammed against the shutters as it wailed away.

"Does Gundohar know that he got your leavings? I thought not! Sigfrid, the only compensation I desire is to see a keen sword reddened with your blood!" she exclaimed. "For almost ten years part of my soul has belonged to you, and from you I have had nothing. That bond is an open wound through which my life is draining away. If you were dead, I would be free!"

"It may come to that," he said heavily, turning back to her. "But do you really think that you will survive me, if things are as you say?"

She stared at him, and for once it was the golden wolf-eyes that shifted away. "Do you think that I care?"

"Oh, Brunahild, Brunahild—live! Love King Gundohar and me—I'll give all I have if only you'll not die."

"Love you!" she exclaimed. Suddenly she could stay still no longer. She slid from the bed and stood up, swaying. He reached out to her and she struck his hand away. "Have I ever ceased to do so? Or perhaps it is hate I feel—I can no longer tell the difference between them!"

On a table by the window a dagger was lying. A swift step brought it to her hand and she turned, holding it ready, and firelight flickered along the blade. At the movement, Sigfrid's body flowed instinctively into a defensive crouch; then she saw him straighten again, hands open at his sides.

"You cannot know what it has been like for me," she whispered. "When I enter a room I can tell, even before I see you, if you are there. And then you touch Gudrun, or speak to her as once you spoke to me, and I remember that of all women I am the most hateful to you now!"

"No . . ." Sigfrid whispered, moving towards her. "You are wrong. I loved you more than myself. I, too, was deceived, but I did the best I could, and if I could not lie beside you, then at least we were all together, and I could see that you were well."

"It is late to be saying so. What relief can there be for me now?" She took a deep breath, feeling more power flow into her the nearer he drew.

"If my heart's blood will ease you, slay me!" he cried.

Even if Brunahild's eyes had been closed, she would have known he was near her. She felt him like an approaching flame. She stood with dagger poised, trembling, until he was so close that the sharp point caught in the rough weave of the tunic he had on.

Their eyes met, and slowly he began to lean into the blade. She gasped as a pricking in her own breast became a point of pain that shot throughout her body, jerked back, and flung the weapon away.

I cannot kill him! she thought wildly. *If he is to die, someone else will have to strike the blow.*

"Sigdrifa—" Sigfrid said hoarsely. His hands closed on her shoulders and he drew her to him. Heat pulsed through her body; she heard his heartbeat speed as if he had been running. Without willing it, she found herself reaching up, relearning the shape of his body with her hands.

"You are fire in the blood!" His hands ran down her back, molding her body against his, and she felt the strength of his desire. "To death and beyond it I am bound to you. . . ."

The oaths they had sworn to each other in the forest echoed in memory, and once more she felt around her neck the weight of the golden ring. But the ring belonged to Gudrun now, and there were other vows that bound her to Gundohar.

With a groan Sigfrid bent, searching for her lips like a thirsty man. He found her mouth and as they clung, Brunahild felt the life leap in her like a flame. Wind howled around the eaves of the palace, or was it only her own pain? Once she had thought that all would be well if she could only hold him in her arms; but she had forgotten how it was when they came together. This was not comfort, but a fire that could consume the world.

And then, suddenly it was not Sigfrid but Gundohar's hands that clutched at her, his passion that burned. She wrenched herself away.

He reached for her. "Lie with me, Brunahild!"

"No. In death or beyond it, you may claim me, but not here. Better I should die than to have two husbands in one hall!"

He looked at her. His breath came hard as if he had been running, as if with another such breath he should burst the seams of the tunic he wore.

"Then I will leave Gudrun and we will run away!"

She looked at him, and all her wrongs rose up in her and the fire that had flamed in her blood turned to ash. Too much had happened; the simple passion with which she had responded to him long ago was corrupted now.

Desire me! she thought bitterly. *Burn for me!*

"What good would that be? A wolf becomes a dog if he is chained! I do not want you," she said coldly, and in that moment it was true, for she had wanted a hero, and if he fled with her, he would be dishonored.

"I do not want any man."

He stared at her, the wild breaths that had shaken him subsiding until outwardly he appeared calm once more. But she could see the conflicts that had torn at him burning in his eyes. *Good,* she thought grimly, *now you will suffer as I suffer. Now you understand.*

Sigfrid turned then and left her. Brunahild sank down upon a bench, feeling as if a great storm had passed over, leaving her stranded on a barren shore. Yet this was not the apathy that had imprisoned her before, but a narrow islet in the midst of a flooding river, or thin ice above a deep pool. This storm had passed, but she sensed she had found no more than a temporary serenity.

Through the opened door she could hear someone speak and Sigfrid's brief answer, then Gundohar came limping into the room.

"Sigfrid said that you were talking again," the king said hesitantly. "Will you tell me what has been troubling you?"

Brunahild looked at him and began to laugh. In this cold place where she was now, everything seemed appallingly clear.

"I don't want to live. Sigfrid has betrayed me, and when you forced him to win me, he betrayed you! Death must pay for it—yours, or mine—or his. His would be the simplest," she added in a conversational tone, "for if he lives, you will lose everything anyway; wealth, and power, and me. . . ."

Hagano sat by the fire in the smaller building that had been built in the Burgund style adjoining the old Roman basilica that was now the king's feasting hall. Here, benches were set up beside a long hearth for the folk of the king's household to take their meals. Sigfrid and Gudrun ate in their own chambers, and Godomar, newly married, lived now on an estate of his own, but it had been a long time since Gundohar had dined privately with his queen, and Hagano, who had no wife to comfort or torment him, had taken to eating in the hall as well so that neither of them would be alone.

Most of the warriors sitting on the benches were new to the king's service, men recruited after the war-host returned from Gallia to replace those killed by Waldhari. Once, Gundohar had asked Hagano to captain his house-guard and he had refused, arguing that he was too grim and strange for them to trust him, saying that the king needed a hero for the job. And they had found their hero. But Sigfrid, he thought frowning, was even stranger than he himself, especially these days.

And these men who saw Hagano every day, eating and drinking and belching like any other man, had grown used to him. In a way it was an advantage to be starting out with a new group. They had no one with whom to compare him as a captain. Perhaps they would never feel wholly at ease with him, but the years in Attila's war-band had taught Hagano how to handle men. He could lead them now.

There was a little stir and the warriors got to their feet as Gundohar came in, moving carefully as if his leg were hurting him. He greeted them with a brittle cheerfulness that Hagano found more disturbing than overt gloom. When they were children Gundohar had been as transparent as a running brook. He had learned to hide his feelings better since becoming king.

But those same years had taught Hagano patience. He waited, apparently content with small talk, until the men finished eating and went away, and then, when his brother would have followed their example, took his arm.

"Something is troubling you, and you need to tell me. Is it Brunahild?"

For a moment Gundohar seemed to be looking through him, then he capitulated suddenly.

"She says Sigfrid betrayed both her and me. She wants him dead or she says she herself will die. I do not know what to do."

Hagano closed his eyes. Their mother had warned him about Brunahild's hatred of Sigfrid, when first he returned to the Burgund lands. It had been clear even then that the situation was dangerous. And now it had come to this.

"She is my wife and he is my sworn brother!" the king exclaimed. "He swore he did not lie with her in the cave and I believed him. Gods—she was unconscious, in no condition to tempt any decent man. Whom should I believe? How can I choose between them?"

Should Hagano tell the king that Brunahild had never really been his? Knowing that both Sigfrid and Brunahild were telling the truth did nothing to solve their dilemma, and he had no wish to reveal the role their mother had played in the treachery.

"Do you want me to give you the counsels of reason?" he asked. "Your queen is a contentious woman, and she has given you no heir, but by keeping her you keep Attila's goodwill. Sigfrid is a valuable warleader and rich, and he has done you no harm, but if he becomes too great a hero, he could challenge your authority. And he would be very hard to kill."

Gundohar stared at him. "You are actually considering it . . ."

Hagano shrugged. "Is that not what you need from me?" Gundohar had improved since they were children, but he was still too soft. Someone had to make the hard choices for him. Once it had been their mother. Now the role was falling to him.

"I cannot do it!" said Gundohar. "He is Gudrun's husband, and I love him as if he had been my brother born!"

"You love your wife, too," observed Hagano. "In the end, it is not whom you love, but what the Burgunds need that must decide which of them you choose."

And whom would I choose? he wondered then. *Gundohar loves them both, but Brunahild has always been an arrogant bitch, and Sigfrid . . .*

Scowling, he remembered how Sigfrid had beaten him in the games, and how blithely he had blundered onto the one area in which Hagano was still vulnerable, his birth. For that, he hated him. But Hagano realized now that he would not be able to trust his own judgment until he knew whether Sigfrid's suggestion that Ragan the Smith might have fathered him was true.

"Sigfrid . . . There is something I must say to you. This is Sunnilda's second winter. I am not even nursing her anymore, and I healed from the birthing long ago." Gudrun's voice was low, but Sigfrid had been made acutely sensitive to the overtones of women's voices by his interview with Brunahild a few days before, and he stilled, hearing the uncertainty there, and the pain. "She should have a brother. It seems a long time since we lay together. All the old wives tell me I should have no trouble next time. Will you give me another child?"

He sat very still, wondering what to say. Gradually, the memory of how Gudrun had suffered bearing Sunnilda had faded, and in truth, he had been thinking the same thing. But not now, not tonight, when his flesh still ached with wanting to take Brunahild's slender body once more in his arms.

I can make neither her nor Gudrun happy, he thought despairingly. *How could I have chosen so disastrously? I only wanted someone to love.*

"Sigfrid—" She moved toward him, sliding her fingers gently through his hair and over his shoulders. He could scent her desire. "I need you to love me. . . ."

Not me, you do not need me— He groaned and laid his cheek against her hand. *I will only bring you pain.*

She sighed and leaned closer, and panic rose in him as if her soft hands were fetters. In the next moment he found that he had slipped through her arms and was standing, facing her from several feet away.

"Something is wrong!" Gudrun reached out, then, as she saw him flinch, let her hand fall. "You must tell me, my love. I will understand!"

Sigfrid shook his head. It seemed to him that these days every time he spoke he only made matters worse. He would do better to keep silence now.

"Is it some misunderstanding with my brothers? Or something about Brunahild?"

He looked at her in alarm. In a moment she would have the story out of him, and then where would they be? How could she understand when in truth he himself did not really know? Anything he could tell her could only give her pain.

"I have been cooped up too long indoors," he said swiftly. "I need to go running." And that was the truth. He needed to get away from women and their demands, and the confusions of the world of men. He was a wolf among dogs, and he still did not understand them. Perhaps he should have studied some other kind of animal when he was growing up—something more solitary, like a bear.

She stood aside as he rummaged in the big chest, her blue eyes dark with concern. "Be careful," she said as he drew out the wolfskin. "There will be evil rumors if you are seen." Her voice shook as if there were things that she too dared not say.

"No one will know . . ." he answered with as much confidence as he could muster, remembering how once he had said the same thing to Gundohar. But in truth, he thought as he tucked the rolled-up hide beneath his arm, just now he did not really care, so long as for this one night he could run free.

The day had been sunny, but as Hagano walked across the courtyard to his mother's rooms a fine drizzle was beginning to fall. A new storm was moving in, driven by a restless wind.

"*Hagano—*"

He turned, for a moment certain that someone had summoned him, but there was no one closer than the two men on guard at the gate, and they did not appear even to know he was there.

"*Hagano, stand still and listen to me. . . .*"

Hagano shook his head. Whether it was the wind or something stranger, he would not listen. For weeks now that voice had been haunting him, as deceptive as the things he saw sometimes with the eye that was no longer there. Usually he could stop the illusions by eating or drinking, or talking to men. He quickened his pace across the stone cobbling toward the guards.

"No, I didn't see it," one of the men said as he approached them, "but Drogo did, and he wasn't drunk, not on guard! He told me in sober truth that he had seen someone come out of the palace in the shape of a man, and then it dropped down to all fours and drew a mist around it and loped away."

There was a snort of disbelief from the other man. "Then the fumes of the wine he had been drinking were still clouding his brain. No doubt he saw a beggar looking for a warm place out of the wind, and then a dog came by and he got confused. The priests have taught us that men do not turn into wolves!"

"The priests do not know everything," the first guard replied. "But it is only a few days until Yule. This is the season when the trolls come out of their holes, and hags ride the wind. Why not wargs as well?"

He recoiled as Hagano came into the circle of torchlight, fingers flickering in a sign of warding, and the other man crossed himself.

"My lord!" the Christian guard exclaimed as Hagano pushed back his hood and gave the password. "Forgive me—you looked like some spirit, looming up out of the mist so suddenly." He stepped aside, but Hagano noted that the other man's fingers were still flexed and his gaze averted as he went by.

He drew his cloak around him, suddenly chilled, though it was not nearly cold enough for snow. That too was disturbing, for by now the hills should have been white.

"A green Yule makes for a high gravemound," said his mother when he commented on it. "In freezing weather the hags who shoot disease into men do not ride. Is that what you came to tell me?"

For a moment Hagano considered asking her about the voice he had heard, but he thought he knew what she would say. Then he forced a laugh, and turned back to her.

"No. It is about Gundohar—" When he had finished recounting his conversation with the king, Grimahild sighed.

"Do not say that you told me so—I know it," said her son. "What can we do?"

"It might be for the best if Brunahild died, but Gundohar is still bewitched by her, and she has powerful kin. Yet unless he is forced to it, he will never consent to harming Sigfrid."

Grimahild lay back against her cushions, her deep-set eyes hooded by lids like old parchment. With her veined hands crossed in her lap, she seemed to him incredibly old. And yet despite all the times she had assured him she was dying, her spirit was still strong enough to make him afraid.

Hagano frowned. "And we need Sigfrid's strength—I seem to remember that was the argument for bringing him here. He bears a charmed life anyway. They say he has never taken a wound in any of his wars."

"Sigfrid is charmed—yes—by Brunahild. It is she whose spells protect him, and she is the only one who would know how to counter them. *You* swore no oath of brotherhood; if you knew them, you could kill him, and then, when Gudrun inherited his treasure, you could take the magic things from the hoard. That neck ring that caused all the trouble was one of them. Sigfrid told her about others, a royal wand all covered over with runes that confers mastery, for instance. If you had that, you would be Wodan's son indeed . . ."

Grimahild still looked old and fragile, but her voice trembled with excitement as she spoke of the hoard. Hagano's ruined eye began to ache and he covered it with his hand.

"Once, long ago, you said that he was not my father—" he said harshly.

"That was before he claimed you . . ."

"I am not Wodan's priest, and I am not his son!" Hagano exclaimed, uncovering his eye. "This was an accident, nothing more. I want nothing to do with the gods. But I think the time has come for me to know who *did* father me! Tell me, old woman, or I will leave this place and let you all sort things out on your own!"

"Hagano . . . Hagano . . ." She shook her head. "Why does it matter to you? You are who you are."

"It matters," he said carefully, "because Sigfrid said I have a look of Ragan the Smith, who fostered him. That Sigfrid should know more than I do about my parentage is not to be borne. Am I one of the earthfolk, mother? You must tell me now!" His single gaze held hers until at last it was she who looked away.

"I was living in the forest, gathering herbs and preparing medicines, and spells . . ." she said at last. "Gipicho was off fighting someone—I think it was the Huns that year. A man came to the cottage and asked hospitality." She paused, remembering. "He was a smith of the earthfolk who had served many kings, but he knew more about the wildlands than anyone I ever met—the names and spirits of each plant, and how the power ran beneath the ground. The hospitality of my bed was his price for teaching me."

"And he was my father?"

"At first I was not sure, for you were born fair-haired, while he was dark as a fox's pelt in the rain. But as you grew like him in feature—yes—then I knew."

And I knew as well, thought Hagano, surprised at how painful it was to have it put into words.

"And there was no love between you? It was only a transaction, the price you paid for power?"

Her eyes unhooded suddenly and he realized that she was laughing.

"Listen, my son—that is all that any man's love has ever meant to me. It was no different with Gipicho. What passion there was in my heart was for the god who taught me his mysteries. I tell you this now because it does not matter anymore," she said softly. "Soon I will know if he deluded me. And as for you, though you may deny it, Wodan has put his mark on you, and he will have you in the end."

The Yule feast that year was less lavish than usual, but there was plenty of wine and ale. Sigfrid drank deeply, and by the time they led the boar around the hall, the sense of unease that had disturbed him when they sat down to feast had been dulled by a golden haze. He did not understand it. At the autumn feast all men had praised him. But this winter nothing had been going right for him.

At least Brunahild was not there—she no longer kept to her bed, but she refused to serve in any royal role. Gudrun had done duty for the queen by bearing one horn of mead around the hall and then gone away. That was a relief too— her hurt silence had been almost as hard to bear as Brunahild's hostility, but he could not explain why he could not make love to her.

The pig was bigger and more docile than a wild boar, his shoulder the height of a man's thigh and covered with bristly red hair. This one had been garlanded with greenery, and given a bowl of the same ale the men were drinking to mellow him. He followed his keeper into the hall with only a little hesitation, seeming to enjoy the attention. It was a good sign, ran the whispers along the long tables. The sacrifice came consenting, and would bear the oaths men swore upon his ridged back to the god.

In the old days a priest would have led the boar among the long tables, and they would have praised Fro explicitly as they prayed for peace and good seasons. Now the song spoke only of the Lord, and left men free to decide which god they were praying to.

"In our next battle I will slay a hundred of our enemies!" Ecgward stroked his hand along the coarse hair that covered the boar's spine and the animal grunted in pleasure. The men around him laughed.

"You will have to strike harder than that, lad, if you mean to fulfill your vow!" Godomar grinned and the young man flushed. He still resented having been left behind when everyone else was off gathering glory.

Sigfrid held out his horn as the servant went by with the wine flask. As the boar moved up the hall the boasts were getting bolder. Some men wanted women, others treasure. *What do I want?* thought Sigfrid muzzily. *More wine!* He set the horn to his lips and swallowed, feeling the stuff burn all the way down. Most men seemed to find comradeship in drinking. Perhaps if he drank enough, they would accept him at last.

"I will make my clan great and wealthy!" said Laidrad as the boar came to him. At least he was honest about it. There were some here, thought Sigfrid, who veiled their ambitions in flattery.

Did Gundohar see through them? They had placed Sigfrid next to Godo. The king sat next to him, in the center, with Hagano just beyond him and then Gislahar. Sigfrid could just see his profile. He looked troubled, his gaze abstracted, as if he were still brooding over his defeat by Waldhari. If he did not wake up and take notice, the men would lose faith in him. What would it take to make him see?

Now they were bringing the boar to the high table. Gislahar, who had suddenly reached the age when women meant something to him, turned red and murmured a prayer for success with the girl he was courting. Hagano muttered something that no one could hear. They brought the boar around to Godomar, leaving the king for last.

"By this time next year I will be the father of a son!" Godo stroked the boar as if he could absorb some of its fertility while the men made lewd suggestions about what part of the beast he should eat when it had been killed and the cooking was done.

Then the pig was poking at Sigfrid's knee. He looked down at it and saw something wild begin to glow in its eyes, as if it recognized the wolf within him, just as he could see the wild boar beneath this tame beast's skin. Godo had drawn back and he could see Gundohar's uncertainty and the distrust in Hagano's bleak gaze.

Perhaps it was the wine, but suddenly they seemed ridiculous, and he laughed. The boar tried to back away as he reached down, but he was faster and gripped it by the long hairs of its crest.

"This is my oath, that I shall be the greatest of heroes! They will still be singing my name when a thousand years have passed!"

The boar squealed angrily as he let it go and straightened, staring at Gundohar. *Top that, my brother! Tell them that you will be the greatest king the world has known!*

If they had been wolves, the pack-king would have glowered until the challenger had to look away. And for a long moment Gundohar held his gaze, so long that the men around them began to murmur uneasily. But in the end, it was the king who could not sustain that silent struggle. His gaze shifted, and Sigfrid sighed. *Oh, Gundohar, was I wrong when I promised to follow you?*

The pigboy tugged at the leash and pulled the boar over to the king.

"I swear," said Gundohar carefully, "that I will do whatever is necessary so that my people can survive!"

That was better, thought Sigfrid, drinking again. But the king still would not meet his gaze.

Then the boar was taken off to be butchered and the men settled to their drinking again. Winter was the traditional time for telling tales, and the Yule feast the best of all. At this season, when the nights grew long and even in the daytime clouds hid the sun, things walked the world that had little love for men. A story of horrors outside made men appreciate the warmth and fellowship indoors all the more.

One man told of the mere-wives, monstrous hags who lived in the marshes of the northern coast or at the bottoms of deep pools. Sometimes, it was said, they mated with creatures even worse than themselves, and gave birth to beings that walked the world, feeding on humankind.

"I have a tale," said Laidrad when that story was done, "of a king who married a woman who had ten brothers, and at the wedding feast he killed them, and her father, all but one who escaped to the forest and lived there as a wolf's head, shunning humankind."

"Where's the strangeness in that, Laidrad?" said his companions. "That happens all the time!"

"Not like this. The woman knew her obligation to get vengeance for her kinfolk, you see, and when she bore sons she sent them out to their uncle in the forest, and when they could not pass the tests he set them he killed them. And the queen knew then that she would never have a child strong enough to do what must be done if her husband fathered him, and so she changed shape with a witch-woman and went out to her brother and lay with him, and bore a strong son."

"Ah," said his hearers, letting the slaves refill their horns. "That's more like it." Sex and death were what they wanted, thought Sigfrid, but he was frowning, for it seemed to him that he had heard something of this story before.

"She sent this son out to live with his uncle-father in the forest, and one day they found two wolfskins hanging on a tree, and when they put them on they were wolves. . . ."

"*Wargs . . .*" came the echo, and men crooked fingers protectively.

Sigfrid felt a chill run through him. Even through the haze of wine he could remember his mother's voice telling him this, and the softness of the wolf fur beneath his hands. He knew, better than anyone, who the two wargs were, and the powers of the hide that lay hidden in his rooms.

"And did they kill the king who had murdered their kinfolk?" asked Gislahar, interested only in the story.

"Oh yes, they set fire to his hall, and having assured her vengeance, the woman walked back inside and burned with her lord." Laidrad got to his feet and stood looking up at the high table. "After that the brother became a king, and in time the wife he took poisoned his nephew-son. But the sons she bore him were killed in turn. Indeed, that was a family that luck did not follow. But the king lived to be old, and in his old age he begot another son."

Sigfrid stared at him, struck speechless by the man's gall in telling that tale. Then the wine haze grew red around him, and in his breast he felt the berserk heat beginning to burn. *Not here!* he told himself, *not now! You cannot break the king's peace in the king's hall!*

But Laidrad was looking at him now. "So, Sigfrid Sigmundson!" he sneered. "Do you still have your father's wolfskin? Was that you whom my men saw running across the fields when last the moon was full?"

"Oh come now," said Godo into the silence. "Moonlight plays tricks on the eyes, especially when a man is full of wine!"

"Are you accusing my men of lying?" sneered Laidrad.

"He is saying they were mistaken," Gislahar said angrily. "What they say they saw is an impossible thing."

Sigfrid looked at the boy and managed a smile, but he was acutely aware that neither Gundohar nor Hagano had defended him. There was a silence, and now everyone was looking at him, and the longer it went on the more suspicion grew in their eyes. Danger shocked through his system, and suddenly he was sober once more.

"Laidrad—" he growled. "Are you challenging me? I will take oath that I have done no harm to anyone here; in my own shape, or any other that a fevered imagination may contrive. And that oath I will uphold body to body against you or any other man!"

He stared Laidrad down, but he could not stop the muttering that whispered through the hall. Sigfrid felt very cold, for the illusion of fellowship had misted away with the fumes of the wine. His accuser dared not fight him, nor would anyone else, for warg or not, they believed him invincible. But they would remember that he had not denied Laidrad's words.

How could he? He could not deny his eyes, or the way the hair grew on his back, or the wolf on his helm. He could not deny the wolf within.

Chapter
Sixteen

 Fever

Borbetomagus
The Outmonths, A.D. 428

The first three moons of the year that men call the Outmonths fulfilled the threat of Yuletide, being chill and wet with neither the freezing cold of snow to preserve the land nor the fury of heavy rain to wash it clean. Those moons were always hard ones, when the last supplies stored for the winter ran low. This year, all things were out of balance. Even such food as remained molded in the storerooms, and the Burgunds, hungry, wet, and chilled, were easy prey for the hag-spirits that ride the storm winds, shooting their arrows to bring disease to humankind. Soon they began to die.

It was not the plague, but some sickness just as deadly, that began with a headache and fever that rose until the patient was burning. Then red spots appeared on the body, with sweating and chills. Again and again the cycle would repeat, until there was nothing more on which the fever could feed. Sometimes a victim was strong enough to endure until it burned itself out, but mostly they died.

Old people and young ones died; infants and strong warriors. Godomar's pretty young wife died with her child unborn, and near the beginning of Hretha's Moon, the old queen, Grimahild, breathed her last and they heaped her gravemound high.

Hagano had expected to feel grief, but there was only emptiness. He told himself that it was the way of the earth for the old to die and the young to take their places, but all his life her spirit had driven him, and now there was nothing. He moved into her rooms and sorted through the bags of herbs and the pots of potions and the rolled parchments full of spells. But she was not there. Only sometimes, when he sat out on her mound, it seemed to him that he heard her whispering to him, and was a little comforted.

The days lengthened and the weather warmed as the season turned toward Ostara. The cows calved and came into their milk as the grass thickened, so there were butter and cheese for those whose bellies could accept them, and some spring greens, but not much food of other kinds.

The land was full of rumors: an evil conjunction of planets ruled the heavens, a two-headed calf had been born, wild men had come into a village and carried off a child, and some creature that was far too cunning for any natural wolf had been savaging sheep and leaving them dead in the fields. The priests preached loudly against the old gods and adjured men to repent their sins before the Last Judgment, which surely must come soon, but at night around their fires, folk told tales of other cycles of disaster and the darker remedies that men had used to stave off Ragnarok in elder days.

On a morning a week or so before the feast of Ostara, the king rode out to visit Ordwini. Whenever the weather was damp, which was most of the winter, his leg still pained him, but he knew that he would have to start exercising if he expected to lead an army that summer. And whatever happened, he was determined to do so. He wanted to fight, and if the world was ending, so much the better. He needed battle to wipe the memory of this whole past year away.

Gundohar had thought it would be good to get away from Borbetomagus, where Brunahild's despair seemed to have shrouded the entire palace in gloom. But though he had known how terrible the fever had been in the town, he had not realized how it had ravaged the countryside. When he rode through fields where the young grain should have been poking its first green shoots through the soil and saw them still unplowed, or hamlets where from half the houses no smoke showed, he began to understand just how bad it had been. Only the graveyards had been fully tilled that dreadful spring.

Three days into their journey, Gundohar sent a rider ahead to tell the folk of the next hamlet that they would be stopping there that night, and would expect such hospitality as the place might afford. Here were none of the rich estates on which he had established his warriors, and the chieftain who held these lands lived too far off the main road to be worth visiting. It would have to be the village, and he did not want to descend on them without warning.

Ordwini's hall was only a half-day's journey farther, but Gundohar's leg was beginning to hurt badly, and he thought he could be quite content with bread and water if only the hamlet had a bed. The place consisted of no more than half a dozen houses, but it seemed unusually quiet as they rode in, with no shouting children, and only a few barking dogs. Before the largest of the buildings a few men were waiting for him.

"My lord king—" The eldest inclined his head a little as Gundohar reined in. Hagano raised an eyebrow at the tepid welcome.

"Did my messenger tell you that I was coming?" asked the king. "I am sorry to descend on you without warning, but I have an old wound that will not allow me to ride farther today. We have brought our own provisions, so we will require no more than shelter from you—" He paused, waiting.

"That is well," said the elder, "for we have no food to spare. And I should warn you that we have had sickness here."

"There has been sickness everywhere!" said Gislahar impatiently, and the king gave him a warning frown.

Gundohar slid off of his horse, wincing as the injured muscles took his weight, but at least it was a different kind of pain. The villagers did not seem hostile so much as dispirited. It would not be a jolly evening, but the thatching looked sound, so at least they would keep dry.

The evening meal was finished and the king was beginning

to wonder how soon he could go to bed when Ecgward, who was on guard, came to tell him that the elder who had greeted him was waiting with some other men outside.

"For God's sake, it's his own house—of course they can come in." Stretching out his leg to ease it, Gundohar turned on the bench so that he was facing the door. The men came in, as dour as before, and stood shuffling their feet and looking at their leader.

"Well, what do you want with us?" asked Hagano finally. "Out with it! We've had a long day on the road and the king is tired."

The elder nodded and coughed. His beard was shot with grey, but Gundohar realized that what he had taken for age were the marks of poor feeding and illness; the man was not really much older than he.

"Have you come to ask for money? I know that times have been hard, and you will not find us ungenerous," he began, but one of the men was shaking his head angrily.

"What good is gold to me? My sons—" he cried, and the warriors around Gundohar stiffened. Then the elder hushed him.

"You must forgive him. His children all died when the sickness came."

"I understand," said the king. "There has been loss in my household also. But if it is not about payment, then what have you come to say to me?"

The elder looked at him strangely. "Payment . . . well, perhaps in a way it is. When the season is as bad as this, one begins to search about for a reason. We are only poor men here, of no great ancestry, and yet we have served in your wars, lord. We have our honor, and we remember the old ways. Since the new faith came in the old gods have not received their offerings, and it seems to us that they must resent that. But even in the old times, when it was time for a cycle's ending, the blood of cows and horses was not always enough to bring the new age in."

"What is he talking about?" One of the warriors, Apius, a

man of Roman blood, crossed himself. "Does he want the king to murder someone to appease his demons?"

But Hagano, his face darkening, had eased forward until he stood between his brother and the villagers, and one or two of the other warriors, remembering what they had heard of the old ways, began to finger their swords. Gundohar looked from one to another, and felt the first thin chill of fear brush down his spine.

The elder saw too, and his features contorted in a sour grin. "Are you afraid of us? Look, we do not even have swords! And yet"—and now he turned back to the king—"your men are right to fear. We come only to tell you, but others will do more than that, if you do not listen to us now."

"What is he talking about?" Gislahar said loudly. He was in the first flush of his young manhood now, his fair hair shining in the light of the fire. Gundohar looked at him and his heart wrenched, for he was beginning to understand only too well. *What if they should choose him?*

"Your fathers knew, my young Niflung. It was Gipicho's brother they sacrificed when the last plague came, and the gods were appeased by that, and it was not necessary to offer the king."

It had been said, now. Some of the men were muttering in outrage; but others looked afraid. Apius drew his sword.

"My lord, let this fool pay the price for speaking such madness!"

"Go ahead—" Now the elder was laughing at him. "You may kill me if you please. My daughter and her babe were my only remaining kin, and I buried them yesterday. But spilling *my* blood will change nothing. I am no threat—" His gaze locked with Gundohar's. "It is your people who cry out to you! Perhaps it is because of the new god, or because we are new in the land. But royal blood must feed the earth. Someone will do it. Far better if it were offered willingly . . ."

"Out!" cried Apius. "If my lord will not let me kill you, at least I can remove you from his sight! The Christos died for all of us, and his judgment will fall heavy on those who try to delay his second coming by killing men!" He grabbed the man by his worn sheepskin vest and hustled him toward the door. The elder did not try to resist him, and the others, losing what little courage they had had, scuttled after.

"I want the rest of you outside as well—" said Hagano crisply to the king's guard. "Make a perimeter around this house. Better to lose a night's sleep than to be burned in our beds. We'll leave at first dawn."

His face hidden in his hands, Gundohar listened to the clink of metal and the scuffle of feet as the men filed out. He had been aware of the old custom as he was aware of the deeds of Airmanareik, as a grim memory of elder days. It was a shock to find that his people remembered as well, not as a piece of ancient lore, but the same way they knew the spells they chanted over their cattle and the herbs they used for medicines. If they remembered it in one hamlet, they would know of it in others, and he could not go guarded every moment. If enough of the folk feared sufficiently, one of them would find a way to spill his blood on the ground.

Presently he became aware that Hagano had come back from disposing the guards and was sitting near him, his grim presence curiously comforting. There had been a new bond between them ever since they both lay bleeding beside Waldhari's fire.

"It is not fear for myself that is making me shiver . . ." he muttered, "or not entirely. It was their anguish that chills me like a wind off of ice, that feeling of sick despair. What if he is right, Hagano? Is this the price I must pay for being king? It would almost be easier to let them take me than to live in fear, always wondering when the blow will fall."

"A man of the royal house they must have, or one who has been like a king . . ." Hagano said in a strange voice, and Gundohar roused, staring at him. His brother was frowning into the fire.

"What do you mean?"

"Our mother told me once that the balance of life was maintained by making the offerings. But the seasons of the world turn in cycles. The greatest of these will be the time that the Christians call the Second Coming and our people call Ragnarok, when all that we know comes to an end. The gods themselves will die, and their passing will be the final offering so that a new world can begin. But there are lesser cycles, and to win new life for the land the death of a godlike man is often required."

"A king . . ." said Gundohar, understanding at last.

"It is not the man, but the office, that is important for the ritual. It must be a man who has received royal honors—who has stood before the people as a god. Sigfrid did that for you when he married Gudrun, and during the drought, I am told, when they danced for rain. Last fall, the harvesters caught him in the fields and his ransom was never paid. He is already marked for sacrifice. If he died, the requirement would be fulfilled, and Gudrun would inherit his gold."

"No!" Gundohar sat up angrily. "He is not a Niflung! He does not owe the Burgunds a life, and we have no right to take it, for he has done nothing wrong!" Hagano turned to face him and he flinched from his brother's lightless gaze.

"Our mother charged me to guard the Niflungar," Hagano said finally. "To keep that trust, I will do whatever is required. You may be willing to take the risk that they will kill you, but can you truly forbid me to protect you by finding a substitute, knowing that if I do not, it may be Godo's blood that flows, or Gislahar's?"

Gundohar turned back to the fire. The logs had burned down to coals, glowing golden as the fabled treasure of Fafnar's hoard. "But Sigfrid is invulnerable," he said finally, meaning it as an objection. "He would be very hard to kill. . . ."

The words hung between them, and as the coals faded, Gundohar realized that he had given his brother permission to do it, if he could find a way.

"Mistress, there are some women who ask to see you. They say they have feathers . . ." Marcia's voice was carefully neutral. These past few moons Brunahild's women had learned that was the best way to approach their queen.

Brunahild recognized the tone and felt a moment's sorrow.

But there was no mending it now. She nodded, and pulled her shawl up to cover her tangled hair.

There had been a number of such visitors since she had put the word about that she was buying ravens. The cloak to which she was sewing the feathers was two-thirds covered now. Some thought it was her way of dispensing charity, to pay for carcasses whose only other use was to frighten crows from the fields. Some said that when her feather cloak was finished she would turn into a raven and fly away. They thought it would be good riddance, and perhaps they were right. In truth, she herself did not fully understand why she felt compelled to recreate the regalia the Walkyriun had taken away from her.

Brunahild pulled the folds of the shawl closer as the women entered, country people by the look of them, in wraps of coarsely woven cloth the natural brown of the wool over unbleached linen gowns. But there was something in the way the first one moved—She straightened from her bow and Brunahild recognized the open, long-boned face and the thick fair hair, though eight years had darkened its gold. The last time she had seen her that face had been averted in rejection, and she had worn a cloak of midnight blue.

"Raganleob—" she said softly, "it has been a long time. Have the Walkyriun sunk so low they must beg door-to-door?"

Her younger companion flushed, then turned her face away, but Raganleob only sighed. Brunahild felt a flicker of shame. The other woman had been a few years ahead of her in training, and had always treated her fairly.

"I am sorry—I did not mean to speak so sharply—may I offer you some tea?" She gestured toward the bench on the other side of the brazier. The days were warming, but it was still chilly inside these stone walls, or perhaps it was only she who was always cold now.

As the minty fragrance of the tea that Marcia was pouring spread through the room they surveyed each other in the way of women who have not seen each other for a while. Brunahild was under no illusions regarding her own appearance; she had grown thin and haggard and the first threads of silver were beginning to show in her dark hair. But life did not seem to have been much kinder to Raganleob.

"How fair the alfs, how fare the Aesir . . . and how fare the Walkyriun?" Brunahild adapted the old greeting and laughed.

"Badly—" Raganleob's smile twisted. "Since they cast you out, nothing has gone well. I thought at the time it was unjust and that no good would come of it, but I was the least in their councils. There was nothing I could do."

It was a lame excuse for destroying her life, thought Brunahild, but she did not say so. In the past years she had learned something about compromise.

Raganleob continued, "After Fox Dance burned, the wise-women scattered to what is left of the tribes. The Huns are on the move again, seeking more territory, and no one's lands are secure. It seems that all things are coming to an end. We have met all together only three times since, and then it was only to argue. Your curses bit well."

Brunahild shrugged. Once that would have given her satisfaction, but it seemed to her that her whole life had become a curse now.

"We heard that you were gathering feathers," Raganleob said diffidently, "and wondered if you were practicing your old crafts once more. . . ."

Brunahild gazed at her in astonishment. "You took that power away from me—or tried to. What do you want from me? Patronage or protection? I can give you some gold, but here the priests of the White Christ rule."

"I know that," Raganleob straightened. "I was going to ask something quite different. Hlutgard and Hadugera and many of the other older ones are dead and their knowledge lost, but the Broken Mountain is farther from the reach of Rome and there some of our sisterhood still dwell. They would welcome us, and you especially, for you were the best of our generation. Come with us, Sigdrifa! You have no child to hold you and they say you are not happy here. Our troubles began when we condemned you. Perhaps if you returned we could all begin to heal . . ."

Brunahild stared at her, torn by a confusion of emotions she thought she had forgotten. Outrage and a malicious satisfaction were among them, but they were swiftly overwhelmed by the sense of loss.

"You are too late . . ." she whispered. "Sigdrifa died eight years ago . . ." *Sigfrid killed her . . . This is only her shell that you see here . . .*

"We have brought this for you—" said Raganleob, unwrapping her bundle. Brunahild drew a quick breath. On the linen lay the plumage of a raven, beautifully tanned with the skull still inside as only the Walkyriun knew how, already sewn to a linen headpiece. The black wing feathers glistened softly in the lamplight. Jet beads had been set into the skull for eyes. It seemed to Brunahild that they were watching her.

"I can give you nothing, nothing!" Brunahild felt sudden tears burn in her eyes.

"Then receive this in compensation for what we took from you!" Raganleob held it out and Brunahild received the linen folds into her arms. How light it was to bear so great a weight of power!

It will serve for my burial. But I cannot die yet. Sigfrid must be punished too. . . .

Raganleob and her apprentice got to their feet. "We are dwelling near the Mothers' shrine—" She named a chieftain whom Brunahild had long suspected of holding to the old ways. "Send word if you have need, and we will come to you."

Brunahild was still weeping when they left, her tears giving their own bitter baptism to the ravenskin. The plumage would have to be blessed, she thought numbly, old memories stirring as she tried to remember which herbs must be used. She did not have them all, but she recalled now that the old queen had kept a great store of such things in her rooms.

After supper, Hagano found his steps turning toward his mother's old rooms. They were cold now, and beginning to get dusty, but he had refused to let her things be moved. Some of the slaves refused to go into that wing, whispering that the old woman's spirit walked there still. Hagano had not been there since returning from the visit to Ordwini, but to-day, while they were out hunting, an arrow had narrowly missed Godomar. When they checked the trees, no one was there, but the message was clear. If they did not offer up one of the royal house voluntarily, the people would make their own choice.

Hagano did not fear for himself. The common people knew he was not the old king's son, whatever polite fictions their lords might use. And even if it were not so, he did not think that since he had lost his eye any man who honored the old ways would touch him.

But for that very reason he thought they would accept Sig-frid as a royal sacrifice, especially if he died at Hagano's hands.

Yet Gundohar was still wavering, and when Hagano re-membered how angered he had been when Sigfrid called him a son of the earthfolk he doubted his own motives in offering to be the executioner. And in any case, as Gundohar had pointed out, unless Sigfrid himself consented, the man would be hard to kill. Perhaps in those rooms where his mother's shadow still lay, some inspiration would come to him.

As he opened the door, he saw something moving. Hagano backed away, fingers flexing to ward off evil, and the lamp went out, leaving only an impression of a figure swathed in dark draperies. For one wild moment he wondered if the slaves had been right. But if this were his mother's ghost, surely he had nothing to fear from her.

"Who's there?" He took a torch from its sconce in the cor-ridor and peered into the room.

Standing in its center, wrapped in a dark cloak that revealed only her pale face and staring eyes, he saw Brunahild.

"What are you doing here?" he snapped, harshly, because he had been afraid.

"I am the queen . . ." she said in a low voice. "I could have claimed these rooms for my own. But I want only a few herbs. Will you slay me for a handful of wormwood leaves?"

Hagano considered her. He had sometimes wondered if during the years he was away the old witch had taken the young one under her wing, but if she had, Brunahild would have known her way around these rooms. "You are looking on the wrong shelves," he said aloud. "I will find it for you."

Why are you here when my mother lies in her mound? He wanted to get her out of here as quickly as possible, without even asking why she was seeking the herbs. Memories of all the times he and his mother had talked here shook him; he took a quick breath; he had thought he was past that part of his grieving.

What was it the old queen had said about Brunahild? *"It is she whose spells protect him . . ."*

Slowly, the bag of herbs still clutched in his hands, Hagano turned.

Brunahild also had recovered her self-possession. As if she had read his mind, she said, "You do not love Sigfrid." She was watching him with a heavy-lidded gaze that made his pulse quicken. For the first time he began to understand how she had fascinated Gundohar.

"That is so," he said gravely, wondering where this would lead.

"Sigfrid betrayed me," she hissed. "When I become a raven, I will carry his soul away. But someone must kill him for me."

Hagano dropped the bag of wormwood onto a table and pulled a bench toward the lamp. "Sit down, my queen, and tell me just why you want Sigfrid to die. . . ."

Slowly, she complied, and he leaned against the chest, deliberately positioning himself so that the shadows cast by the lamp would hide his ruined eye. Brunahild looked up at him.

"Are you doing the god's errands, now that he has turned against Sigfrid and me?" Seeing his face change, she laughed. "Or do you still think that you are free? Don't trust Wodan, Hagano. He makes you choose, and when you choose wrongly, he abandons you."

"And is your guidance better? What would you have me choose, Brunahild? If you want Sigfrid dead, then kill him yourself." Hagano crossed his arms casually, but his heart was pounding.

"I have tried, but I cannot do it," she whispered hoarsely. "He is protected. I gave him part of my soul."

"And how did you do that?" Hagano's words slid like oil across hers. "Tell me. . . ."

"I inscribed every part of his body with runes of power . . ." Brunahild's voice sank so low he could hardly hear her.

"Which ones?" he asked, fascinated and appalled as she bent forward, drawing the runes on a body that only she could see. "And was that all?" he asked when she was done.

"I protected his skin with a holy oil compounded of sacred herbs. That is why no weapon will wound him. All except his back—" she said then, as if she had just remembered it. "I ran out of oil before I could cover it, and I did not think it mattered. Sigfrid would never run from an enemy."

But he would turn his back on one he thought a friend, thought Hagano, feeling suddenly weary. *If Sigfrid is to die, I must take him from behind, by treachery.*

"And if I kill him for you, Brunahild, will that make you happy?" he said aloud.

"No," she said starkly, "but perhaps it will bring me peace. Do it, Hagano—I will pay whatever price you ask."

"Any price?" he laughed, remembering how girls who once had suffered his attentions now avoided him. "Will you lie with me?"

Brunahild stared at him, her expression unreadable. "If you desire it."

For a moment longer he held her eyes, then turned away. "No thank you. My brother's bed is already dishonored, but I will not take Sigfrid's leavings!"

He heard the gasp of indrawn breath and knew that he had hurt her, but he refused to feel pity, remembering that she had just told him how to kill a man whom she once had loved.

All day the wind had been fitful; stormclouds were building to the west, and the setting sun stained them with crimson. Gudrun watched the light fade from that wounded sky and shivered, not entirely because of the wind.

"Mama—" Sunnilda reached up to tug at her hand, and she picked her up, not so easily as she would have even a few months ago. For a child of three winters she was well grown. She pointed at the sky.

"See how pretty the colors are—"

"Red. Like eggs," the child answered. "Is Ostara when? Tomorrow?"

"Not tomorrow, but it will be soon." Gudrun sighed.

Sunnilda's nurse must have been telling her about the old celebrations. Some of the women had hinted that Gudrun should organize something, now that her mother was gone. It was almost the time for their celebrations in the old reckoning, although as usual, the way the Christians calculated their feast put it a few days after. Still, though Gudrun was not much of a Christian, she had never learned all the details of the pagan ceremony. Better, she thought, to let it go by than to put on some patched up travesty, especially since she doubted that anyone felt like giving thanks this spring. But perhaps they could color some eggs for the child.

The clouds deepened from a velvety crimson to a purple like an emperor's cloak. Then there was only a featureless darkness that obliterated even the evening star. A chill wind was rising and she shivered suddenly.

"Come, little one," she said softly. "Night is falling and there is nothing left for us here."

When she returned to their rooms, she was surprised to find Sigfrid there. The chieftains had begun to gather for the Spring Assembly, and she had expected him to eat with the men in the hall.

"We are going hunting in the morning," he answered, "and these days, even Godo knows better than to drink too deeply the night before. I thought that rather than struggling against temptation I would spend the evening here with you."

Gudrun eyed him doubtfully, for it had been some time since he had seemed that eager for her company.

"Is there food?" he asked with a sudden grin that made her heart ache. "Or do I have to go out tonight as well and bring home an Ostara hare?"

"I will ask my maids to fetch enough from the kitchens to serve you as well," she said tartly. "I was just surprised." She turned quickly away, afraid he would think she was reproaching him.

Then it came to her that she should have expected this. Gudrun had heard some of the wolf talk, and seen how men were beginning to look at him. Despite his humor, he might have good reasons not to eat in the hall.

"Sigfrid," she said carefully. "Is anything wrong between you and my brothers?" She could sense how he looked at her, but she kept her gaze on the tablecloth she was laying down.

"Of course not. Why should there be? I told you—we are hunting together tomorrow, and they particularly requested me to come along."

"Don't go!" It slipped out before she thought. She stood perfectly still, staring as first one tear, then another, fell into the pattern of the cloth. She heard a shutter rattle. The storm must be coming in.

"Gudrun—" he said very softly. Then he gripped her shoulder and she felt his breath stir her hair. "Gudrun, my little one, don't cry."

Oh gods! she thought. *Why doesn't he tell me there is nothing to fear?*

He pulled her closer and she gave way suddenly, knowing it was probably a mistake, but unable to stop. He was so solid and warm, so *alive*, surely nothing could ever happen to someone that strong!

"I'm sorry—I'm just being foolish," she said at last. "Gundohar wouldn't break his blood oath, and besides, they need you in the battle line!"

"Gudrun," he began, "I do love you. I only wish—" He stopped as the maids came in with the food, and she bit off a curse at their timing. Sunnilda and her nursemaid followed, and as the child ran to her Gudrun put her mind to preserving an appearance of cheer.

Throughout that meal they spoke mostly to Sunnilda, like new lovers afraid to look at one another for fear of what their glances will reveal. The child blossomed under their combined attention, prattling and laughing till her nurse shook her head, wondering how she would ever get her to sleep when dinner was done.

Sigfrid held his daughter for a long moment when at last the woman prepared to take her away. "Good-night, my cubling. Go with your nurse now or I will eat you!" Softly, he growled. But the girl's yellow eyes stared fearlessly into her father's, and she laughed. "Laugh, then," said Sigfrid, grinning back at her, "that is as good a way to say good-night as any. Sleep well!

"The child is big for her age—" he said to Gudrun when they had gone.

"Yes . . ." she answered. She was trembling like a maiden. Curse the man that he should be able to do this to her after so long! But she would curse him even more roundly if after all those sweet words he went out again, or simply curled up on the other side of the great bed with his face to the wall.

But when he had made sure the door to their chambers was closed, Sigfrid came back to her. Above the sound of the wind outside she heard the whisper of her name, and turned to meet his kiss. As his arms closed hard around her she forgot all the reproaches she had planned to heap upon him if ever he turned to her again. There was no longer any meaning in the rules she had intended to lay down to salve her pride.

I won't ask if he is sorry he's neglected me, her heart was babbling, *or why he is being so tender to me tonight. Whatever this means, I will not cry. I don't want to know. There is only now.* And then she gave herself up to his embrace.

It seemed to go on for a very long time. She sensed a simplicity in the way he kissed her, a clarity that had been in him when they were first married and then had gone away. She had thought that it just went with growing older, and accustomed to one another's ways. But suddenly it was as if they had never kissed before.

One by one, he unpinned the fibulae that held her wrap at her shoulders. Indoors, in the warmer weather, she was wearing no tunic beneath it, and her bare breasts seemed to press themselves into his hands. She rubbed her hands across the taut fabric of his tunic, yearning for the skin beneath, and arched herself against him until his own breath began to come faster. He unclasped his belt then and dragged the tunic over his head, and as his hands went beneath the cloth of the wrap to untie her woven girdle, she loosed the cord that held his breeches and reached for the living flesh that rose to her touch so eagerly.

He laughed then, deep in his throat, and lifting her as easily as if she had been the child, carried her into the next room.

"Let us make a little brother for Sunnilda—" he said as he sank down beside her. "Avoiding risk will not make life longer. I was wrong to refuse you before."

But Gudrun could not have answered him if she had wanted to. Even before his hands ceased caressing her belly and moved lower, she was aching with need. She cried out when he entered her; she had grown as tight as a virgin, it had been so long, but as the sweet pressure filled her every nerve ending seemed to burst into flame.

And then he began to move within her, and all other awareness crisped away.

That night Sigfrid loved her as if to make up for all the times he had stayed away. The storm that released its showers of rain outside was matched by the tumult within; their first desperate joining gave way to long, slow explorations that gradually built, again and again, to ecstasy until at last Gudrun slept exhausted in his arms.

But despite the sweet lassitude that weighted his limbs, Sigfrid lay wakeful afterward, listening to the sighing of the wind and the gentle breathing of the woman at his side. The moisture of their coupling still linked them; they lay twined so closely it was hard to say where his flesh ended and hers began. He knew without question that he had given her joy. In the midst of all the death that had surrounded them they had celebrated life, and surely that was a good thing. So why could he not sink into satisfied sleep as well?

The wind was growing louder, and it seemed to Sigfrid that he could hear voices. Carefully he detached himself from Gudrun and opened the shutter of the window in the other room. Beyond the walls of the courtyard he could see the dark shapes of trees like women dancing, swaying and shaking their boughs at the troubled sky. They looked like dark disir, spirit-women, dancing out a spell . . .

By the feel of the air he judged it was the out tide, the hours between midnight and rising. The king's house slept, except for one light that burned across the courtyard in the queen's rooms. Brunahild was waking too. He wondered how often she had stood at her window and looked across at his. For so long he had not allowed himself to think about her, but since their last meeting he could not forget her. Even now, when his body was spent from making love to Gudrun, his spirit yearned toward the woman whose hatred for him burned like a dark flame. Gudrun was his mate in the world of men, and called forth all his tenderness . . . but Brunahild was the shadow self he had so long denied—his soul.

I love both, and I have wronged both, he thought sadly, *but Brunahild most of all . . .*

A gust of wind tugged at the shutter in his hand like a messenger that warns of the approach of an army. There was no rest in the heavens. From afar he could hear a tumult, as if an enemy were indeed coming upon them, but by the prickling of his neck hairs Sigfrid knew that tonight it was no mortal host that roamed the skies.

As if in anticipation of the king's hunting tomorrow, he heard from the sky a bitter calling, like horncalls, or like the belling of hounds. *It is wild geese crying as they wing northward,* he told himself. That was a music he had heard often enough as a child. But he had never heard the geese cry with such painful urgency.

The wind gusted and he blinked, for though the stars were hidden, across the sky lights came flinging like a shower of burning coals or sparks from the hooves of running horses. Sigfrid stood shivering, knowing that any sane man would bar the shutters now and hide beneath the bedclothes. But he had never yet run from a thing he feared, and now it seemed to him that he could almost see the horses. Dark shapes rushed across the heavens with more legs than any horse should have and streaming manes and tails. He saw spears waving, and the pale glimmer of faces. Battle hags screamed across the sky, guiding slain warriors: Goths that he had faced in battle, the sons of Hunding, and lastly Fafnar the shapeshifter and Ragan his fosterer, whom he had loved, and slain.

Sigfrid clung to the windowsill. But after that tumult came a great silence, and two wolves made of mist that trod the empty air. He straightened, already knowing the hunter that followed them on his eight-legged steed. He held his breath, heart pounding. It had been easier when the god spoke to him through the flesh of men.

"*Sigfrid—*" He heard the call, but could not tell if it was with his heart or his ears. "*Sigfrid, ride with me—*"

The skull-face of the horse swung toward him. The god's eye blazed, and in it Sigfrid saw madness, and all the wildness that had sent him running as a wolf through the fields surged up in answer. He had dreamed of this, with Sigdrifa at his side.

"*Here is an escape for you—*" came the call. "*Ride with me!*"

But the woman on the bed stirred and cried out as if she were dreaming. Sigfrid fought down the frenzy, and as he did so the face of the god also grew still.

"No. I am a killer, but I am also something more—" Sigfrid whispered, looking up at him. "I cannot run away—"

"*The choice is yours,*" said Wodan, "*and yet you will come to me . . .*" He lifted his spear in salute, and Sigfrid stared in amazement, for on the god's cheek shone a tear. Then the wind rose once more and the god's cloak swirled around him. The great horse leaped into motion, and in a rush and a roaring and breaking of branches the Wild Hunt swept on.

Shivering, Sigfrid slammed closed the shutters and drew the bar. As he went back to the bedchamber, Gudrun started up, crying his name.

"It's all right—" He put his arm around her. "The wind had loosed the shutter and I closed it again." Gudrun clutched at him, shuddering, and he pulled her down against him, murmuring her name.

"Sigfrid, it was my dream, my dream!" she whispered when

she could speak again. "I had a stag that walked with me in the forest and I loved it dearly, but a raven came flying down, screaming, and the other beasts attacked the stag and tore it to pieces!" She shook her head in frustration. "It seems silly, to hear it, but I can still feel the grief that filled me when I saw its blood on the ground. Sigfrid, don't go hunting tomorrow. I am afraid!"

"Hush, love, hush. I am a wolf, remember. If I go hunting, it is the deer that will die!" Sigfrid stroked her hair until she ceased from sobbing, and then he set himself, very deliberately, to love her back to sleep again.

Afterward, he held her in his arms, knowing that he would not sleep now. Despite his reassurances, his own vision and Gudrun's dreaming were omens, and he could not ignore them. He could think of no reason for the Niflungar to turn against him, but ever since Gundohar returned from visiting Ordwini there had been an odd constraint in the king's manner, and Sigfrid had never trusted Hagano. They could well mean some harm to him tomorrow, but surely he was a match for them.

Gudrun whimpered in her sleep and nestled against him, and he kissed her soft hair. If his death was fated, she would be left alone, but he could not ask them for her sake to spare him. He had done so many evils, not knowing what he did or what it would bring. If this once he had been given warning, all he could do was resolve to meet the challenge well.

In all his life, the one thing he had never betrayed was courage. Brunahild had reason to hate him. But even if the men he had loved as brothers had somehow become his enemies, he would not run away.

Chapter Seventeen

The Offering

Charcoal Burners' Forest
Ostara, A.D. 428

Dawn broke red and rainy, the color fading from the clouds gradually, as if the last drops were washing it from the sky. As Hagano walked across the courtyard, he saw it littered with branches and broken roof tiles brought down by the wind. His good eye felt sore and grainy with sleeplessness and the other one was aching, but from the chatter around him, he was not the only man who had been kept awake, nor was he the only one to hear horncalls in the heavens or see the spectral hunters who rode that storm.

"It was the Wild Hunt," said one of the trackers, "with old Wodan himself at the head of them. An evil omen for someone, no doubt of that."

"For all of us, maybe," said one of the younger men. "God knows it would be no surprise, the way things have gone this year! Perhaps this time the world really is going to end."

"May God preserve us!" One of the hunters crossed himself.

"Or the gods—" His companion looked at Hagano and made the old warding sign.

I am not Wodan, Hagano said silently, turning away. *Wodan is riding the stormwind, and whispering in the new leaves.* It was only a whisper this morning, but last night that voice had drawn him from his bed to the window. He could still hear it in memory. . . .

"Hagano, my son, listen to me!"

329

"Leave me alone, old man—" he had told that whisper. *"I do not belong to you."*

"Then what will you serve?"

That question was still unanswered. Hagano rubbed at his forehead, wincing at the sweet clamor of barking dogs as they brought up the hounds.

"Brother, are you all right?" Gundohar's voice brought him around. "If you are unwell, you don't have to come out with us. I don't see Sigfrid here, and he wasn't in the hall for dinner," he said brightly. "Perhaps he is not coming. Indeed, after such a night, I'm wondering if any of us should hunt today."

Hagano pulled himself together. "I am well enough to do what must be done. I know now how he can be killed, Gundohar."

The king blinked, and Hagano knew that he had been hoping they would not find a way. Perhaps he had hoped so as well, before he talked to Brunahild. For three days he had carried the knowledge of what she had told him, like a spear in the gut. Then Godo had proposed that they all go hunting, and Sigfrid had consented, and Hagano had seen how it must be done.

There was an outburst of laughter as Godomar, who had spent the night drinking after all, came into the yard. He looked bleary and hung over, but he grinned at the teasing.

"Watch out for stray arrows, Godo!" said someone. The men laughed, but the king grew pale.

"That is why, brother," Hagano said quietly. "An offering must be made, and if it is to be Sigfrid, it must be done before the Assembly. Remember how the warriors cheered him at the autumn feasting. He could split the kingdom if he felt himself in danger—there are too many men in our war-host who remember how he led them to victory."

I am trying to convince myself, thought Hagano as he waited for the king to reply. Then he saw Gundohar tense and turned.

Sigfrid had come out from the far wing of the king's house, moving with the swinging grace that belonged to no other man. He was dressed all in green for the hunting, with his spear, a bow on his back, and the silver-mounted aurochs horn by his side. The young sun glinted on the oak brown of his hair. Some of the hunters drew back as he passed, whispering, but even those who nodded in greeting did not approach him. There was a stillness about him this morning that prevented familiarity.

"The Leaf King," whispered Gundohar, and Hagano nodded. Sigfrid was coming toward them, smiling.

Hagano cleared his throat. "Lord, I would bring your king-spear on this hunting. May I take it from the hall?"

"The oath-spear?" Gundohar's voice cracked, but he managed an answering smile as Sigfrid neared. "If you must—" he said, and Hagano edged backward.

"Is your brother not coming?" he heard Sigfrid ask as he moved away from them.

"He will join us later," Gundohar replied.

Hagano could hear the strain in his brother's voice, and knew how hard he was finding this. *But it is harder for me,* he thought grimly, thinking of the runes he must draw on the blade to counter Sigfrid's protections. *I'm the one who will have to use the spear.*

Brunahild stood at her window, her dark cloak wrapped around her, watching the hunting party form up in the courtyard below. She leaned against the frame, for her bones ached with weariness. It had been days since she had slept properly, and she had certainly had no rest the night before. She knew that Sigfrid had been wakeful too, for she had felt first the joy he shared with Gudrun and then his tension as he listened to the storm.

But though she too had seen the Wild Hunt, she did not know how he had responded, for she had heard only the belling of the spectral hounds, louder than the yapping of the dogs below, and the calling of the One who led them. She could hear it still—"*Sigdrifa, my daughter, where are you? Come to me. . . .*"

But she had cowered beneath the covers, whimpering in

grief and terror, until the wind died away and she knew that they were gone.

The voices of the men below seemed flat and tuneless after that calling. Some of the warriors were teasing each other about the women they had left snug in soft beds. From Sigfrid's smile, Brunahild guessed that Gudrun was among them, sleeping in exhausted satiation after the loving he had given her the night before. *Sleep on, my sister*, she thought, *and smile, for you will be weeping soon. . . .*

Brunahild watched dry eyed as a slave brought Grani up and Sigfrid leaped to the horse's back with that easy grace that always brought an ache to her throat, but not, this time, the release of tears. Would she ever weep again?

The chief huntsman blew his horn and the horsemen began to form into some kind of order, taking up their own horns to sound an answer. Her breath caught as Sigfrid lifted the aurochs horn to his lips, and the deep sweet tone belled out across the yard, louder than all the others, pulsing in the chill air. The line of his arm and the cording in his strong throat made their own music, achingly beautiful. *Now I will weep*, she thought, watching him, but her eyes remained dry.

And then, as they began to move out, Sigfrid looked up, and she saw that his eyes were clear and full of peace that brightened, as his eyes met hers, into love.

That was when the sudden tears betrayed her, blurring her vision so that she could see no more. She was still weeping when, a little later, Hagano rode out after them, carrying the king's spear.

The way the hunters had taken was clear, but Hagano did not immediately follow them. He went instead to his mother's cottage in the forest to use the magic Brunahild had taught him to dedicate the spear. The house was cold and damp. Even before the old queen's death it had been long since she had visited there. Water had come in where the thatch was ragged and mice had made their homes in the bedding. But he did not have to sleep there, only to work a spell.

He built a fire in the pit in the center of the room and

hung a cauldron of water above it, then began to search the shelves for the herbs he would need. As Brunahild had warded Sigfrid with herbs, so with herbs Hagano meant to break that protection and any other spell that bound him, even the witchcraft his own mother had used to make Sigfrid forget Brunahild. Before he died, all his sins must be remembered.

Toadflax and holy thistle, elf-bane, elecampane, venom-loather, he chose—herbs of purification and unbinding. One by one he cast them into the cauldron. When the mixture was steaming he added fennel, boar-throat, spear-leek and finally, mistletoe. He stirred the dark liquid as it began to bubble, nostrils wrinkling at the acrid odor, binding the herbs to his will with his own spell.

> *Nine herbs I cast, nine herbs I conjure,*
> *Nine glory-twigs by the high god shattered:*
> *Against nine spells these herbs have power,*
> *Against nine spirits they shall battle:*
> *'Gainst spell of elf, 'gainst spell of worm,*
> *'Gainst spell of witch, 'gainst spell of Walkyrja,*
> *'Gainst spell of cunning folk, of kin and kind,*
> *Against all bindings and all protections,*
> *My power seeks them, my power breaks them,*
> *By wit and word and will I bind them*
> *To empower what they wash against all spells.*

When the brew had steeped enough to bring out the power, but before it grew so hot it would spoil the weapon's temper, he plunged the spearhead into the cauldron.

For another space he held it there, chanting the spell, feeling the power of the brew transferring from the water into the steel.

Then, when he could feel the change in it, he pulled it out and with the sharp point scratched a red line across his left arm. Three times he spat on the wound, and with the mixture of blood and spittle drew runes across the graceful silver knotwork that twined through the dark metal of the blade.

Tiwaz, that justice should be done; *Naudhiz*, for the fulfilling of fate; *Hagalaz*, for a violent transformation, and *Ansuz*, to dedicate the victim to the god.

So now my blood is also on this spear, he thought grimly. *But my oaths are different.*

"By the blood I have spilled and the spells I have sung, this oath I offer." He held up the spear. "With this blade I shall let Sigfrid's life out. May the gods receive his blood as a royal sacrifice, and Brunahild be avenged . . ."

He upended the cauldron, dousing the fire, and then, wrapping the spearhead carefully, went out to join the king's hunting.

In such a lean season the prospect of fresh meat gave an edge to the hunters' enthusiasm. As they moved into the forest, Sigfrid found his memories of the night and its visions fading, and with them, his sadness. The air was sweet, swept clean by last night's wind. With every breath new scents came to him from the moist ground. Grani danced beneath him, and he laughed suddenly, his senses extending through the forest until he felt the life within it as an expansion of his own.

Why had he been afraid? If he chose to disappear among the trees, no man here could follow him. In the royal hall he might fear treachery, but not here. In the woods he was king, and no creature of the wild would harm him. Gundohar, who as the morning progressed had begun to display a manic gaiety of his own, had offered a prize to the man who took the noblest game. Sigfrid grinned at that, for he had already seen beasts that no one else was noticing.

"My thanks to you, brother," he told the king. "Is this your subtle way of making a gift to me?" He saw Gundohar wince as if Sigfrid had caught him out, and laughed.

A winged black shadow flickered through the trees above them and he saluted the raven. *Lead me to the game, brother, and you will have your offering!*

Then the dogs began to clamor as they caught the scent of the stag whose tracks Sigfrid had already seen on the path and he gave Grani his head as the hunters surged after them.

By noon, a dozen beasts had been slain and sent back to the camp to be butchered and transported to the town. Half of them had fallen to Sigfrid's spear or bow. But the sport had been good enough so that everyone was in a cheerful humor, and ready for some rest and a meal.

Sigfrid's final contribution was to surprise a half-grown bear and bring it bound and snarling into the clearing where they were dismounting, but after the men had scattered and the horses began to plunge hysterically, he took it away again and let it go.

He was still laughing when the servants with the packhorses brought up the food.

Hagano stood with folded arms, leaning against an oak tree. Some of the men had spread their cloaks on the ground, others sprawled on the soft grass where the sun came through the trees. The air rang with their boasting as the men who had killed that morning repeated their victories in words and those who had not described how in the afternoon's sport they would surpass them.

There was some debate as to whether Sigfrid's bear should count, since he had not actually killed it. To Hagano's ear, the chaffering did not seem entirely friendly. The men had been frightened, and they did not like it.

"Forget the bear then," said Sigfrid, tossing the bone on which he had been gnawing to the dogs. "I'll bring down a nobler beast this afternoon."

No, I will—thought Hagano, watching him.

When at last he had caught up with the hunters, he had kept to the rear and kept the cloth bound around his weapon so that no one should ask why he had come hunting with the king's war-spear. He could feel the moment to use it drawing nearer. His gut clenched with awareness and each time Sigfrid laughed it surprised him.

"There's food here, but what are we to drink?" Sigfrid asked. Most of the men had been drinking from the leather water bottles they carried, but he had none.

"I don't know," said Gundohar, who had presided over this

meal with a brittle gaiety that should have given the game away. He looked around him as if expecting wine to spring from the ground and his gaze met Hagano's. "It's my brother's fault—" he laughed shrilly. "He was supposed to arrange for the provisions."

"Well, Hagano," said Sigfrid, "are you determined to keep us all thirsty?"

My spear is thirsty . . . he thought, but he managed to smile. "I am sorry," he said aloud. "The servants did not expect us to roam so far. No doubt they are still back on the trail somewhere with the rest of the ale. But there is a spring with good water just past those linden trees. Listen and you can hear it—"

As he gestured, the men stopped talking. In the silence the musical chuckling of the little stream came clearly, mingling with the whisper of wind in the trees. He thought there were words in it, but he could not yet understand them.

"We stopped there the first time you ever came hunting with us, do you remember? Before you married Gudrun."

Memory flickered in Sigfrid's eyes and Hagano nodded. He had felt the same sense of recognition when he realized that the chase had brought them to the spring where he had given Sigfrid the drink that delivered him to the old queen's witcheries. They had come full circle, and perhaps Sigfrid was beginning to understand it now.

"Let's drink then," said Laidrad, shaking his flask. "This was only a drop to get me started." He clambered to his feet and started down the path.

Sigfrid rose too, though he had lost his open smile, and he and Gundohar, with most of the others, followed him. Only the men most loyal to the king had been invited to the hunt today. Hagano came last, carrying the spear.

The place did not seem to have changed. Bright green moss carpeted the rocks that lay jumbled above the fissure from which the water was welling, and it still trickled in a steady stream into the little pool. Laidrad was already drinking, slurping up the water in his hands, and the others waited behind him. But Sigfrid was hanging back, behind Gundohar.

"Ho, Laidrad, isn't this the place where they found your spear?" Hagano said when the man had finished. He had heard the story just after he returned to the Burgunds, and thought it might be useful.

"What spear?" asked some of the newer warriors.

"The one that the were-wolf stole from me!" said Laidrad, frowning. "Two winters ago the dogs got on his scent when we were hunting up on the ridge. We thought it was a wolf we were chasing, until we came to a chasm that no wolf could have jumped and he leaped over it. One of the men said he saw it change in midleap into a naked man who disappeared into the bracken. We didn't know what to believe, but I cast my spear after it. The next day, when we sent men around to get it, the spear was gone."

"And they found it here?" The men had drawn closer, beginning to bristle already as folk did when they confronted the uncanny.

"A charcoal burner found it. He said the warg had come upon him and cast him into a charmed sleep. When he woke, the spear was beside him and in the dust around him were the prints of a wolf mingled with those of a naked man. And one other thing—the creature had left him a golden coin."

"A generous were-wolf," said someone, laughing nervously, but men looked around them as if the forest had grown darker suddenly.

"It was an old Roman coin, wasn't it," said Ordwini slowly, "like the ones Sigfrid gave us from his hoard. . . ."

There was a sudden quiet as men turned to look at Sigfrid, who had gone first red, and then pale. They were remembering the accusations that had been made at the Yule feast, and Laidrad's story was acquiring a new significance. Only the wind in the trees seemed to have grown louder. Hagano felt a tightness in the back of his head and along his shoulders. "*Soon . . .*" the wind seemed to whisper, or perhaps it was in his head that the voice was speaking. "*Soon . . .*"

"You never told us where your hoard was hidden, Sigfrid," Hagano spoke into the silence. "Is it here, perhaps? Under a tree or behind some stones?"

Sigfrid took a step backward, toward the spring, and Laidrad turned on him.

"*You* are the warg! You came out to hunt with us and then turned back, but never said where you spent the two days until we returned. You're the one who goes loping across the fields when the moon is full!"

"And kills the sheep in the fields!" said one man in a low voice.

"And brings the sickness that kills men," another echoed him.

"This is foolishness—" said Godomar, but his voice held no conviction. Gislahar looked as if he were about to protest more strongly, and Hagano held out a warning hand.

"No, little brother. This has been brewing for a long time. You must let them have their say—"

"Surely the Wolf Age is coming when the people die and troll kin walk the world!" whispered Ecgward. "Only a bloodprice will end the cycle so that life can begin anew."

"When a man gives himself to do the Devil's work he becomes a demon and must be slain," said Apius, crossing himself. From the others came a low muttering.

Hagano reached behind him, and as he touched the spear, it seemed to him that another hand closed over his own.

"*Why, War Father?*" shocked, his spirit cried. "*He is your son! Why are you helping me?*" and then he trembled, because for the first time an answer came clearly.

"*When my children die, my hand is always on the spear. . . .*"

Sigfrid listened to that muttering and the disbelief that had paralyzed him lifted, for he recognized the sound. He had heard the same growl of menace when a wolf pack turned on a stranger. He felt the pelt of hair across his shoulders bristle and his eyes narrowed as he looked from one to another, grinning as they flinched from his gaze. He had left his weapons back with the horses, but there were stones in the streambed. It was a pity that there was not time enough to get at the weapons that lay hidden in the rocks with the rest of Fafnar's hoard. But he still had the strength of his arms and the power of his will; it would not be so easy to bring him down.

"Do I look like a demon?" he said softly, holding out his hands. "This is flesh like yours—"

"Is it?" asked Ordwini. "Then why does no weapon wound you? We have all seen you come unscathed from battle time and time again." The murmuring from the men grew louder.

Sigfrid straightened. "And in those battles, how many of you have I defended? You have no case against me. I have done no harm to any here!"

"And what of your sins against the king's honor?" asked Hagano, very softly. "What of your sins against the queen?"

Sigfrid felt a cold fist clench beneath his heart, and all the premonitions of the night before returned to him. *This is no squall that has blown up unexpectedly. It was planned to happen this way.* His gaze went from Gundohar, who was staring at the ground, to Hagano, waiting beneath the linden tree.

In the shadow, his wild hair seemed dark, and the socket of his missing eye darker still. There was a power in the way he stood there that made Sigfrid remember how men looked when they were being ridden by the god. *"Old man,"* he thought, *"have you betrayed me too?"*

Then Hagano stalked forward. Sigfrid saw that he was holding Gundohar's spear, and started like a wolf that feels the trap begin to spring. All the green forest was still waiting behind him. In a moment he could leap the stream and be gone from here. The teeth of the trap that was closing were inside him.

"Upon that spear our blood was mingled. Earth's womb received it." He looked at Godo and Gundohar. "You swore me brotherhood. Will you betray that bond?"

It was Hagano who answered him. "Have you forgotten that you swore another oath upon this spear?"

"I remember—" Godo found his voice. "He said he had not lain with Brunahild in the cave."

"But can you swear that you never lay with her?" asked Hagano, and Gundohar looked up, his face flaming. "Who had her maidenhead, Sigfrid? When was it that she brewed the spells that have protected you?"

There was a long silence. "It is Brunahild who has woven this web to trap me . . ." Sigfrid said softly at last.

"No, it is Wyrd," came Hagano's implacable reply.

For a moment Sigfrid's gaze met his, then moved to the shifting leaves of the linden tree. Where were the birds who should be perching there, he wondered, telling him what to do? He saw only one bird, a black one, and it was not singing, and then, as the wind stirred the branches, he realized that there were two.

Run! said a frantic voice within him. *Even with their dogs these foolish men could never catch you. Become the wolf again, and you will be free!* But that was the way out that the leader of the Wild Hunt had offered him, and he had refused. He could run away, but luck would never follow him after. He would become what these men had called him. He would be a wolf's head in truth, and every man's hand would be against him.

The god had told him once that a man's wyrd is twined by his own choices. Had his own deeds truly brought him to this day? If the Burgunds must judge him, Sigfrid thought then, let it be for the truth of what he had done, and not for lies!

"After I killed Fafnar," he said, still looking at the linden tree, "I heard that the Walkyriun had bound a maiden on a fire-swept mountain. I found her and nursed her back to health, and through the winter that followed we taught each other the ways of love. I called her Sigdrifa . . . Bringer of Victory. I did not know she had another name." He turned his gaze to Gundohar, and saw awareness and anguish warring in the king's eyes.

"We swore vows to one another," he went on, "and then we parted, I to get arms in the land of the Franks and she to her kin in Hunland to wait for me." He heard a gasp of indrawn breath and knew that they were all beginning to understand now. "But I came here, and some spell made me forget those vows and remember only the brightness of Gudrun's eyes. I did not see Brunahild again until I had already sworn to win her for another man."

Which one would I have chosen, he wondered, *if I had not been spelled?* It came to him then that it was because he had not known his own nature truly that the old queen had been able to confuse him so.

"In Froja's name, I loved them both, but there was no way I could keep faith with one without betraying the other."

"Then Brunahild swore truly when she said you had her maidenhood—" said Godomar.

"In the land of the Huns there is a little girl with eyes like mine, whom I have never seen. . . ." Sigfrid swallowed, wondering if he would ever see her now. Sunlight, striking through the leaves, blazed suddenly on the water, as bright as the neck ring he had given in turn to both of the women he had loved.

I have betrayed them both, he thought painfully, *but what else could I do? And now the snare that I myself have woven tightens around me and I see no way to evade it. Does a man know his path only at its ending? Fight or flee, there is nothing that I can do that will change what I have done!*

Was this what he had sensed last night, without consciously knowing? Was this why he had tried so hard to plant new life in Gudrun's womb?

"For myself I will say only this—" His glance swept the circle, and even now, men's eyes flinched away. "In all that I have done, I never meant ill to any man."

In the silence that followed the only voice that spoke was that of the stream. Sigfrid, listening to that musical murmuring, thought it sweeter than the speech of men and remembered that he had come to the spring to drink, it seemed a very long time ago. No one was moving. Perhaps they did not dare. Or perhaps they understood that now it was between him and the gods. He licked dry lips and turned to Gundohar.

"We came here because we were thirsty, but I will not go before you—drink, my lord." He gestured toward the stream. Gundohar blinked, and Sigfrid realized that though his words were humble, he had spoken as if he were giving orders to his sworn man. *I always thought he was the king-wolf,* he realized suddenly, *but it is I.*

And understanding that, he knew, finally, why the man he called king feared him. Gundohar was already obeying, bending to scoop up water from the stream. Sigfrid watched him, aware of the radiance of the sunlight, the scents of moist earth and greenery and the soft touch of the wind on his cheek as he had never been before.

Then Gundohar finished drinking. Awkwardly, because of his bad leg, he got himself upright again. For a moment his eyes met Sigfrid's. "Leaf King, forgive me—" he whispered. Then he turned and limped away.

Sigfrid looked after him. *Is that who I am?*

None of the men who circled him had moved. *They do not dare,* thought Sigfrid. He turned away from them and bent down to the water, newly aware, after watching Gundohar, of how smoothly his own muscles moved. The stream flowed clear and bright, its ripples reflecting leaf and sky and his own face in an ever-changing pattern that had its own unity. Its clean touch sent a tingle through his skin.

"Water of life, flowing from Earth's womb—" Sigfrid whispered, lifting it to his lips, "hallow me. . . ."

The water slid down his throat, coolness spreading through his body like a blessing. It was then that he heard the thrumming in the air behind him. Even then he might have ducked or rolled, wrenched his body out of its way. But the spear was part of the moment's unity.

"The wise know when it is time to make an ending . . ." said the raven called Memory. And Sigfrid had never yet run from an enemy.

And then he felt a blow that drove the breath from his lungs and knocked him forward into the stream.

For a moment there was only confusion. When he was able to open his eyes, he lifted himself on his forearms, wondering why it was so hard to breathe. Presently, looking down, Sigfrid saw the blade of the spear jutting out through his chest, blood crimsoning its silver inlay and falling in slow drops into the stream. *My blood,* he thought numbly, *my blood is the offering.*

He felt movement behind him and heaved himself onto his side, gasping as the spear shaft bumped against the ground. Hagano was coming toward him, but it was Ragan that Sigfrid saw.

"Ragan's son . . ." he whispered as the other man knelt beside him, "takes vengeance with Ragan's spear . . ." Any single thread of fate he might have broken, but there were too many strands to this weaving.

Hagano's face contorted, and Sigfrid realized that he had struck back after all. "You never meant harm, yet harm was done," said the other man harshly, "and now the price is paid."

Sigfrid drew breath and coughed, feeling the blood beginning to fill his lungs. There was no pain yet, only pressure, but he had seen too many deer die not to know it would come soon. *Brunahild, I forgive you . . . be free. . . .* He shook his head, knowing something had gone from him, but he was growing too tired to think any more.

One of the ravens launched itself from the linden tree in a long swoop that brought it to rest above the hoard. It was cool and dark behind those stones. It seemed to Sigfrid that perhaps he could find comfort there, safe in Earth's womb with the other offerings. Grunting, he started to crawl toward it.

The men, even Hagano, stood away from him, their faces stamped alike with pity and horror. But they no longer mattered. Sigfrid tried to shift one of the stones, but his strength was leaving him. It seemed to him that he could hear wolves howling, but perhaps it was only the ringing in his ears. He fought for breath, coughing, and tasted blood.

"*Wolf, your brothers are calling—*" said the second raven, circling. Sigfrid nodded. He must take the wolf-shape. That was how to escape them. He set himself to remember the transformation, sinking toward the earth as his strength ebbed away.

The spearpoint touched the ground and he felt the first jolt of pain. But he reached out with arms that no longer seemed to belong to him to embrace the earth, and as the spear tore back through his chest, agony blossomed through every nerve like a flower of fire and set him free.

It was the ravens who told them it was over. It seemed to Gundohar there was accusation in their cries. Three times they circled Sigfrid's body, then winged away westward. In the forest a wolf howled, and then another, setting off a hysterical yammering from the dogs.

In the end Sigfrid had died so easily, with scarcely a quiver. Later the king heard talk that some of the men had seen a wolf made of mist arise from the body and trot away, but he had seen only that gradual collapse, like a child falling asleep. It did not seem possible that someone whose presence had been like a flame could lie as still and as cold as the stones.

And I allowed it to happen, Gundohar thought numbly. *How could I do that? I loved him.*

Then Hagano walked over to the body, set his foot on Sigfrid's back, and jerked out the spear. "Well, brother, will you give me the prize for this day's hunting? Surely no man ever brought down a nobler prey!" He looked down at the blood that had followed the spear from the wound. "Thus do we deal with all who threaten the Niflungar!

"Fafnar's hoard is hid here somewhere," he added in the same hard tone. "It belongs to our sister now. We must dig it out and take it back to her as compensation for her loss." He turned, and Gundohar saw madness in his gaze.

"Nothing will console Gudrun for this, ever," whispered Gislahar. Tears were glistening on his cheeks already. "This was an evil thing, and I think that in time to come we will all curse this day."

One of the men made the sign of the horns and backed away from them. The others had gone silent, as if all their hatred had washed away with the blood that had flowed down the stream.

"Get the horses," said Godo, "and the rest of you, gather branches to make a litter so that we can bring him home."

He is home, thought Gundohar. *We should leave him here where he belongs.* But he said nothing. The circlet of royalty still bound his brow, but in dying Sigfrid had taken with him all that was wild and wonderful. He would have only the powers of humankind to rule with now. *Mourn, oh ye warriors, for the king of the forest died this day!*

Hagano stepped past the sprawled body and slid the spearpoint between two of the stones that filled the fissure above the spring. For a few moments nothing seemed to happen. Hagano's muscles bulged and the spear shaft bent like a bow. Then there was a crack, and he fell backward. The spear flew from his hand, its blade broken, and stones began to tumble downward, narrowly missing Sigfrid's outstretched fingers. Suddenly Gundohar could see a dark cleft beyond them. The last rocks bounced and rattled away as Hagano struggled to his knees and reached in, grunting as he dragged the moss-grown chest into the light of day.

"Is that why you did it?" asked Gislahar. "Because of greed?"

"No," the king found his voice at last, "because of need. But I don't understand what Hagano is after now."

His brother had got the lid to the chest open and was pawing through its contents. Gold gleamed in the sun. Gundohar saw him pick up something wrapped in drying hide and drop it with an oath.

"Close the chest, Hagano," he said sharply. "Whatever is in there belongs to Gudrun. Let her count over the gold."

His brother looked up, shaking his head uncertainly. "There are things of power here—our mother told me—but I cannot see them, I cannot feel them. It is all dark now, and He has gone away . . ."

"Sigfrid is gone indeed!" Godomar snorted. "You yourself made sure of that. Why are you surprised? Close the chest as the king ordered and let us treat his corpse with such honor as remains to us. You have done enough for one day!"

Hagano moved away from the body, stumbling as if his vision were wavering, and clung to the oak tree.

Grunting, for Sigfrid had been a big man and his corpse was heavy, they got it onto the litter the men had bound together from boughs. The whole front of his chest was bloody and there was a little red froth on his lips, but his eyes were already closed, his expression serene. Gundohar pulled off his cloak and laid it across the body.

Diana L. Paxson

"Wear this, my brother," he said softly, "for you died like a king."

They brought up two horses and tied the stretcher between them, and then, slowly, because the ways were narrow and treacherous, began the journey back to the river and the world.

Chapter
Eighteen   The Fire

Borbetomagus
Ostara, A.D. 428

$\mathbf{A}$ll that day Brunahild lay open-eyed upon her bed. Her women looked in on her from time to time and then retreated again, murmuring uneasily. She did not seem to be in pain of mind or body. She was only—still. But in that state, which was like a waking dream, Brunahild's spirit ranged on the wings of Muninn far through the fields of memory.

She remembered how she had lain prisoned on the white rocks of the Taunus after the Walkyriun had destroyed her identity among them, and cried out to the god for a hero so that she could be a Walkyrja once more. And Sigfrid had come with the morning, young and strong and concealing his own soul's half-healed wounds. She had been so certain, then, that he had been sent to fulfill her dreams.

She thought of the tenderness with which he had nursed her back to health, careful not to hurt her by handling her too roughly, body or soul. *Would I have told him more if he had used less courtesy?* she wondered then. That had been her first error, to hide the truth of who she really was from herself and from him. *Is the purpose of our lives to find out who we really are?*

She had taken his forbearance for granted, and taken the space she needed for her own healing, until, in her pride, she determined to prove that she was still a Walkyrja by warding him against all ills. *And that was my second error,* she told herself, *to be so desperate to prove myself that I forgot my own need for detach-*

ment, and so I gave a part of my soul away . . . Is the purpose of our
lives to become whole?

And all that had happened before Sigfrid bound himself to
her by any vow. Her third mistake, she supposed, had been
to bind herself to marry the man who defeated her in battle,
supposing her own cleverness would protect her, putting her
own interpretation on every omen until she was caught completely. *Did I really trap myself? Is this what you meant, All-Father,
when you said that I must choose?*

As she was now, she could choose nothing. And so she lay
as the slow hours drew on toward their nooning, listening to
the dying wind.

And it came to her, finally, how Sigfrid had looked at her
when the hunters rode out that morning. It was the look of a
man at peace with himself and his wyrd. *He has forgiven me his
death,* she thought, *not even knowing I condemned him. Cannot I
forgive him my life?*

It was then, as the sun passed its zenith and began to de-
cline, that she felt the change—an expansion of awareness, as
if some sense long lost were reawakening. Brunahild's
breathing quickened, and as she drew in the soft air, she felt
life tingling through her veins. She stirred and sat up, opening
her eyes as once she had opened them to greet Sigfrid and
the dawn.

"Hail to thee, Day . . ." she whispered. And then her face
changed, for she understood what had happened. Sigfrid was
dead, and her soul had come back to her.

Gudrun spent the day working in her garden. Though there
was still a pleasant soreness between her thighs from their
lovemaking, after such a night as Sigfrid had given her, she
could not bear to stay indoors. It seemed to her that every
part of her body must be glowing, and she blushed like a
bride on the morning after her wedding when people looked
at her, sure that they must be able to see. At this moment
even Sunnilda's presence was an intrusion, and so she told the
child's nurse to take her to look for wildflowers by the riverside.

It was certainly true that the garden needed her attention. The walls had protected it somewhat from the force of the wind, but the ground was littered with bits of straw and roof tile and broken branches dropped by the storm. And when she had cleared the debris, Gudrun found that the effort had been well worth her trouble, for despite the weather, the blue violets were peeking from beneath their heart-shaped leaves, and on the side of the garden where the sun shone first and longest, golden daffodils trumpeted back their joy to the day.

By sunset the garden was combed and tended, almost purring with content in the deepening light. Gudrun stood up, stretching, and began to think about a bath. The hunters might well take advantage of the fine weather to get in a second day of sport—but if Sigfrid should return that evening . . . She smiled reminiscently, resolving that he should find her clean and scented and ready to welcome him.

She blinked and looked up as a shadow brushed the path before her. Two ravens flapped heavily overhead and settled on the rooftree of the feasting hall, calling harshly. And like an echo, from the direction of the river came the sound of horns.

Gudrun's pulse raced as she listened, but though the mournful music grew louder as they neared, she did not hear the deep note of Sigfrid's horn. Of course that meant nothing—sound did strange things over a distance—but she was frowning as she made her way through the gateway to the porch in front of the feasting hall.

When she came out into the daylight she saw that Brunahild was already there, standing at the top of the steps where she could look down the street that led to the river road.

Gudrun eyed her doubtfully, surprised to see her there. These past moons the queen had been so strange, it was probably pointless to wonder what she was doing, but there was a difference in her today that Gudrun could not quite identify. Brunahild was wearing a white gown, but that was not what had changed. She stood serenely self-possessed, with her dark hair lifting a little in the light wind, and to Gudrun she looked almost like the girl who had been her friend so long ago.

"The hunters are returning," Gudrun said brightly.

"Yes, and we must be ready to greet them," answered Brunahild gently, "for they have brought home a noble prey."

Others had heard the horns and were gathering as well. Gudrun rubbed her hands on the skirts of her gown, wondering how much of the garden she had gotten on her face when she wiped sweat away, and wishing she had found time for that bath.

She heard the hounds then, barking ecstatically as they caught the scent of home, and the echo of hoofbeats following. But why were they coming so slowly? Usually successful hunters returned at a gallop, hallooing their victory and letting the slaves bring up the slain beasts after. The ravens were still perched on the rooftree. Gudrun looked back at the road, suppressing the first flicker of fear.

Gundohar came first, reining down his big bay, with Godo beside him. That eased one anxiety, but the horse she was looking for was grey. Then the next group came around the corner of the chapel—two riderless horses with something tied between them. Her breath caught, and Ursula, who had come onto the porch behind her, reached out and took her hand.

"Someone has been hurt," said a voice behind her. "Killed, more likely," came the reply, "or why would they bring him here?"

The little procession moved across the square. She could see now that the horses were carrying a litter with the king's cloak spread across it. What lay beneath was hidden, but a thrall was leading Grani behind them, and his saddle was empty.

Gudrun could not believe what she was seeing. Sigfrid's scent was still on her skin, his seed still liquid between her thighs. It could not be he whom they were bringing home this way.

They came to a halt before the hall and the princes dismounted. They brought up the led ponies, untied the litter, and laid it on the first broad stair. It was Brunahild who moved first to meet them, coming down the steps with an eerie grace and drawing down the cloak to reveal the face of the man who lay there. She bent and kissed his lips. Through the silence that held them all her whisper came clear.

"Ah, the taste of your blood is the same, but your lips are cold. Once my kiss drew your spirit back to your body, but this time it has gone where it will be harder to follow. . . ." She sat back, looking down at him.

"Sigfrid . . ." the muttering began behind her. "Sigfrid is dead."

"How?" whispered Gudrun. She took first one tottering step and then another. Only Ursula's grip kept her from falling as she moved down the stairs. "How could he die?"

Godomar shook his head, flushing with shame and anger. "A wild boar gored him, sister," he mumbled, turning his face away.

"I do not believe you," she cried. "He belonged to the forest—no beast could slay him!" She fell on her knees beside the bier and pulled the cloak away. All the front of Sigfrid's green tunic was dark and stinking with blood, but it was clear that whatever had pierced his heart had broken through from behind and burst the fabric outward. She rocked back with a groan.

"No wild beast did this, it was some creature more vicious than any in the forest. I am a king's daughter, and I can recognize the wounds made by the steel tusks and iron claws of men!" She shook her head, gasping. "And this was done by treachery—a wild boar does not spring from behind! Which of you is the beast who killed him? Come here, and let these wounds weep when their maker draws nigh!"

Her gaze fixed one brother after another. Godo looked angry and young Gislahar was weeping. In Gundohar's face she saw guilt. Then the men who were standing behind him moved apart and Hagano came forward, carrying the fragments of the king's spear.

"I am the boar who has killed this royal stag," his voice grated. "And in the back, because it was the only way. I take the guilt of it upon myself, and the shame."

"But why?" she whispered, staring up at him. "He was the strength of the kingdom—"

"To save the kingdom," he answered her, "he had to die."

Another whisper went through the crowd. Some were frowning, but others nodded, as if they understood only too well. She heard a woman's voice begin the ritualized, mournful ululations with which they used to celebrate the death of Baldur when they still lived on the other side of the river, when she was a child.

Hagano turned away abruptly, and Gudrun's strength left her. She sank down upon the body, drawing her hands down Sigfrid's arms and feeling for the shape of the long muscles she knew so well. But there was no resilience to the flesh she was caressing, and he was so cold. The body had stiffened; touching it was like embracing a piece of wood carved into the shape of the man she loved. It was not Sigfrid at all. She jerked back, whimpering, and felt the soft hands of her women pulling her away.

"Shall we take him to the church?" asked one of the warriors.

Brunahild got to her feet and shook her head. "They would not accept him; Sigfrid was not a christened man. Besides, they have one sacrificed god there already, they do not need another one."

"Where, then?" asked one of the women.

"Bring him to my chambers," said the queen, "and we will bathe his body and anoint it. Fetch his feasting clothes and his ornaments and his arms. Let him lie in the great hall thereafter so that all the chieftains may do him honor. Tomorrow let men build a royal pyre in the water meadow where you hold the games, and on the day that follows we will give him to the fire."

As Gudrun's women led her away, she heard the sounds of mourning spreading through the town. *When he was alive they called him "warg" and feared him, but now that he is cold they remember that he was a hero . . .*

"Weep for him—" her women said, patting her hand, but

her eyes were burning, and she saw nothing but that parody of the man that she had loved.

Brunahild looked at the bier on which they had placed Sigfrid's body with a critical eye, adjusted a fold of the drapery that covered it, and moved his arm a little so that his hands were clasped more becomingly. Most of the night had passed before he was cleansed to her satisfaction, his great wound bound up and his skin anointed with sweet herbs. Then they had dressed him in his byrny of grey leather with gilded rivets and his wolf-crested spangenhelm. But the mantle that lapped him was of royal crimson—a piece of silk from the city of the emperors—that belonged to Gundohar.

Ah yes . . . she thought with a bitter self-mockery, *they butchered him like a stag, but they will bury him like a king.* She had already sent for Raganleob to come to her—together they would bless the pyre.

The women who assisted her to prepare the body had been glad to leave her alone with him. If they thought her actions strange, there was nothing new in that. They could not know that she had become a stranger to herself as well. The emotions she ought to be feeling now were too great even to be summarized as sorrow. She was whole at last, but there was nothing left in the world that could stir her, not even Sigfrid's empty shell lying before her. There was only this dispassionate awareness of what must be done.

Where are you, my love? she thought, looking down at him. *Where does the wolf run now?* Better than any, she understood that he was no longer in this body, for she had known the touch of his spirit better than her own. But did he wander at the threshold between this world and the other, or had he found his way to Wodan's hall?

Gold glittered from the tags of his lacings and his swordbelt and the shield that leaned against the bier, but it was not enough. Frowning, she dragged open the great chest that they had set beside him and began to select arm rings and platters, the flower of Fafnar's hoard, to lay around him. Let the chieftains envy the wealth with which Sigfrid might have bought himself a kingdom, and which now would win him a place of honor in the Hall of the Slain.

As Brunahild reached for a golden goblet, her fingers brushed something softer—a piece of fur in better condition than any of the other wrappings in the hoard. She felt a tingle, and curious, lifted the thing into the light. The rabbit fur had stuck in places, but when she got it free she saw that she was holding a wand of gold whose head had the shape of a bird. Its surface was graven all over with runes.

She frowned. She had been curious when Sigfrid described it among the treasures of the hoard long ago, but he had not been able to tell her what it was for, because he did not know the runes. Brunahild held it to the light, tracing the shapes with her finger, murmuring their names.

They were all there—the twenty-four signs of power that had been graven into her own consciousness when she hung on the tree of testing to become a Walkyrja. Around the top and bottom of the wand ran an inscription in smaller characters—*"He who holds this hallowed rod, with mind and might the world will master!"*

She held it to her breast, feeling the power in it. Perhaps she should place it in Sigfrid's hands, but he had never wanted to master the world of men—he had another kingdom. And it occurred to her then that when Hagano dug out the hoard he had been looking for something. If Wodan had wanted him to have the wand, he would have put it into his hands.

"Father"—she closed her eyes—*"Can you still hear me? Can I hear you?"* She stilled, and it seemed to her that she heard, as if from a great way off, the sound of wind. She swayed as a pulse of warmth surged from the rune-wand to her breast, just where Wodan's spear had pierced her in her first vision, long ago, and sat down suddenly on the step below the bier.

At the top and back of her head the tingling intensified; she trembled and felt strong hands steadying her and a Presence that seemed to flow inward, pressing her spirit deeper into her body. Tears started to her eyes and she sucked in breath, understanding only now how lonely she had been.

"*High One, why have you been so far from me?*" her spirit cried, and closer than her own thoughts, the answer came, "*I am where I have been always, in every thought, in every memory, in every pain . . . I told you once that my children must share my suffering, but I bear theirs as well. It is you who cut yourself off from me. . . .*"

For a moment it was all she could do to breathe, then she thought of the man on the bier.

"*You said once that I would be the instrument of my hero's destiny— but all I brought Sigfrid was destruction. Was this your will?*"

"*Sometimes one must betray the thing that one loves best, for the sake of the world. You have given him lasting fame . . .*"

"*Is that enough to justify all the pain?*" she cried.

"*He did not desire the gift I would have given him. An undying name is more than most men win in one lifetime, and it will serve my purpose to have men tell his story. That will have to do.*"

Brunahild struggled to breathe, for she was feeling his sorrow now, and it went far deeper than her own. "*I love you . . .*"

"*It changes nothing—*"

Brunahild shook her head tenderly, feeling their roles oddly reversed, as if she were a mother explaining some difficult concept to her child. "*It does for me.*"

After that there was a time when no thought was possible, only a wordless awareness that this was what he had needed from her. At length, when the intensity receded, another thought came to her, "*Why is it only now that I understand?*"

"*Ah, my daughter, don't you know?*"

And presently it came to Brunahild that she did know, had indeed known from the moment when she realized Sigfrid's death, and she smiled.

Gundohar and Hagano walked slowly along the corridor to the chambers the king once had shared with Brunahild.

"She is mad, or fey," the servant had told him. "She has summoned all the daughters of chieftains who served her and is giving away her ornaments and clothes."

In truth, he was not sorry to leave the hall where Sigfrid's corpse presided like a king over the chieftains who had gathered to drink his funeral ale. But it was Brunahild who had betrayed him, and he himself had consented to the deed. What in the world could they say to each other now? Hagano strode like a grim shadow behind him. He could not even guess what demons warred behind his brother's single eye.

From the queen's chambers he heard an uneasy murmur of women's voices. As they neared, the door opened and Ordwini's sister came out smoothing a mantle of fine dark green wool around her shoulders, her cheeks flushed, and her eyes cast down.

"My lord!" The blush deepened as she saw him, she ducked her head in greeting and almost scurried away.

The long windows of the queen's chamber were open, and the room glowed with color. Gundohar blinked, then realized that it came from the lengths of fabric that were draped everywhere. Light glanced and glittered from ornaments spilling out of caskets set open on tables and stands. Half the women in the royal household seemed to have crowded into the room, moving from one heap to another, fingering the fabric, then looking at the queen with troubled eyes. The king shook his head. He had not realized that Brunahild had accumulated so many treasures over the years.

In all that jeweled display, the one thing without color was the queen herself, who sat on a bench in the middle of the room in her white gown.

Gundohar cleared his throat. "My lady, how is it with you?"

Brunahild raised one eyebrow, but did not answer. It was her woman, Marcia, who turned to him.

"Sir, since morning she has been at this, telling us to bring out all her goods and giving them away. Do you wish to forbid it?"

"The things are hers . . ." the king said, frowning, and then, "has she said why?"

"Oh, my lord," said Gunna, "we fear she means to do something desperate, and is distributing her possessions so that folk will mourn. But those who still follow the old ways believe that she wishes them to die with her, and are afraid."

"Ah," Hagano observed softly, "I'll warrant little Ordlieb means to do neither. No wonder she looked so ashamed."

Gundohar felt fear congealing in his belly. He looked at his wife and thought that never, unless it were on the day when she had spared his life on the battlefield, had she been so beautiful.

"Brunahild—" He went towards her and the other women backed away. "It is not true, is it? I cannot lose you too!"

She was not weeping; she did not appear ravaged by sorrow. Indeed, though she had sought Sigfrid's death, he had yet to see her show any sign either of sorrow or of joy. But there was something daunting in her serenity.

"Tomorrow a great hero goes home—" she said quietly. "My women must be richly dressed to bid him farewell."

"Is that all? How I want to believe you!" he said desperately. "Live, Brunahild, and I will make it all up to you—"

"Oh, do not hinder, if her face is set toward Hella's kingdom!" Hagano cut in behind him. "She has never brought luck to any. And if she must be reborn, let it be far from here!"

"How sweetly you persuade, good brother," said Brunahild. "But you have made your own luck now, and far will it follow you. It is not I you should fear, but kindred who are nearer. Gudrun will not soon forget that you struck her husband down."

"Do not curse me, witch—" Hagano began, and Gundohar laid a hand on his arm. But Brunahild was smiling.

"Hagano," she said, "I do not need to." She sighed and then looked up at Gundohar. "Do not grieve for me, husband."

Gundohar shook his head and knelt awkwardly before her. "Brunahild—I never meant to wrong you. I love you . . ." She frowned a little, and he wondered if she were seeing him at all.

"Perhaps too much," she said then, and he flinched from her still gaze. "You made it too easy for me to wrong you. But I will stand by my choices. If you can do the same, you will fare well. Forgive me, and I will pardon you." She smiled a little, but her focus had gone inward once more.

She was as beautiful as a Walkyrja, thought the king, and as far beyond his reach, wife though she had been. *I have lost everything now*, thought Gundohar, *the woman I loved and the man who was my dearest friend*. Suddenly desolate, he struggled to his feet and allowed Hagano to lead him away.

"I have buried seven sons and a husband, all killed in battle," said the old woman, the wife of one of Gipicho's chieftains. "I wept for them, and eased my sorrow. You should let your tears flow, Gudrun. They will give you ease—"

Gudrun shook her head and turned her face back to the wall. The old women had been coming to her all morning, telling her tales of woe that would make a stone weep. But she was young, and Sigfrid's scent was still on the pillow. Though her heart ached as if it would crack in two, she could not cry.

They had brought her child to her, begging her to live for her sake, but when Gudrun looked into Sunnilda's amber eyes she could think only of those other eyes, so like, that would never smile on her anymore. She supposed that her nurse had taken the girl away after that, but she found it hard to care.

"I saw my husband slain and was carried off as a captive into Hunland," said another. "Seven years I served as a bond-maid. By night my master used me in his bed, and by day I combed the hair of my mistress and tied the thongs of her slippers. You still have a home and honor, Gudrun. Weep for your man, but be grateful that you still have kinfolk to care for you."

How can I be grateful, she thought numbly, *when it is my own brothers who killed him?* Or two of them, anyway. Young Gislahar had come to her early that morning and told her the full tale of Sigfrid's slaying. She ground her face against the pillow, trying to ignore the futile attempts at consolation. It was only when the talking stopped entirely that she roused.

She saw her women retreating through the far doorway. Brunahild was standing beside her, with her hair unbound and a dark blue mantle over her white gown.

"Do not reproach me, Gudrun," the queen said softly. "For all that I have harmed you, you and your kinfolk sinned against me as well."

Gudrun nodded, remembering Gislahar's words. "Did Sigfrid ever love me?" she whispered. "Was he ever really mine, or was it all a delusion born of my mother's spells?"

"Is that the worm that gnaws you?" asked the queen. "He loved you. All these years my spirit was open to his like a raw wound to the wind. He delighted in you as a flower rejoices in the sunshine. Believe me."

"But you loved him . . ." Gudrun said, staring into the other woman's changeable eyes. A tremor ran through Brunahild's body, half shrug, half shiver, and Gudrun recoiled, as if she had glimpsed depths beyond her understanding beneath the still surface of a pool. Then the moment passed, and the queen held out a long bundle.

"Listen—this is part of his legacy. Your brothers may try to take the rest of the hoard from you, but this rod, and the neck ring Sigfrid gave you, Hagano must not have. They are the keys to a magic beyond his understanding, though even he may come to wisdom someday."

"I cannot take it. Without Sigfrid, how can I live?" whispered Gudrun.

"You have a daughter who needs you," said Brunahild sharply. "Live for her. The only thing you can do for Sigfrid now is to guard your inheritance. If Sigfrid had been willing to take the rod as well as the ring our wyrd might have been different. Do you understand?"

"No! All I understand is that I have lived a lie!"

"So have we all, Gudrun," Brunahild said somberly. "But I think that perhaps most men spend their lives trying to understand what they truly are. Our deceptions were greater than most, that is all. Take the rod, and keep it safe with the ring. Perhaps you will be the one who learns to wield them."

Gudrun stared at her. What Brunahild was saying made no sense to her, but she took the package the other woman pressed into her hands. Then the queen smiled, and in her thin face Gudrun saw a sudden glimmer of the laughing girl she had met at Halle.

"Keep them safe, Gudrun, and you may yet be blessed. Remember the promise of the Lady you saw in the sacred well, and do not think too hardly of me . . ." She turned, dark hair and dark mantle seeming to fade into the shadows as she moved toward the door.

It was then, finally, that Gudrun felt the grief that had been frozen inside her crack, and she gave way to her tears.

Shortly after noon of the third day, the procession set forth from the town to carry Sigfrid to the pyre. Their way led through orchards where the road was strewn with flowers brought down untimely by the wind, across the meadow where Sigfrid had so often been victorious, past the cairn where the women made the Ostara offerings. The wagon was attended by all the Burgund chieftains and their house-guards; they had all drunk deeply of his funeral ale, and had nothing but good to say of him now.

To Hagano, riding just in front of the funeral wagon with Gundohar, their mourning seemed a mockery. *Now that the wolf is safely dead you may praise him, whom alive you were ready to drive out with stones.* He doubted if any man there felt the bitterness of Sigfrid's death as keenly as he did, except, perhaps, for Gundohar. *We were the ones he most endangered, and yet we are the ones who suffer most for his loss.*

They came at last to the green grass by the river where they had built the pyre. It was well made, of good seasoned logs drenched in oil, with kindling under them. It ought to burn well. Hagano watched grimly as they lifted the bier to the top of the pyre and settled it there. Sunlight glittered on the wealth of gold laid around the body. But he had made sure that the bulk of Fafnar's hoard was still secure in its chest back in the palace. Gudrun's it might be, but he suspected that the Burgunds would need it in time to come.

A silence fell, and Gundohar stepped forward to give the oration. He looked pale and strained, and Hagano saw people whispering. Everyone knew that it was the king's brother who had done the killing, and since Hagano was standing free and unharmed beside him, it was clear enough that the king must have willed it. No wonder they were all agog to hear what Gundohar would say.

Gundohar went up to the pyre, and for a moment seemed to speak to the silent figure that lay there.

Did you love him, brother? Do you think he will listen to your apologies? You would do better to take heed to the living. But though Hagano's thoughts were bitter, he knew that his own choices had bound him to Gundohar for good or ill.

Then the king turned to face them. His cheeks were wet, but his voice rang out strongly, and one remembered that he was also a bard.

> *"Holy the hero whom now we hallow,*
> *The pyre awaits, the people praise him.*
> *By his blood the Burgunds' bane is banished,*
> *His offering all ill o'ersetting.*
> *Now comes the nightfall, never will we see*
> *Again his likeness, last of legends;*
> *This fire the fiercest, as he the fairest;*
> *The elder age with him is ended."*

Is that what we are mourning? thought Hagano. *The death of a legend?* There was a little murmur of appreciation, and Hagano wondered if the people had understood any better than he.

As Gundohar started to walk away from the pyre, Gudrun stepped out from among her women, her face blotched with weeping and her golden hair streaming unbound. She was wearing the neck ring that had caused so much trouble, and there was something else, that he could not quite see, in her hand. "Sweet words, my brother," she said softly, "and said in a fair voice. My own is cracked from weeping. But though my words are not so fine, you will have to hear them." She straightened, drawing breath so that everyone could hear. "The man who lies here was the noblest of warriors and the kindest of husbands, who never fled from an enemy. The bonds that brought him down were those of love and loyalty. And so the greatest of hunters became the hunted, and the most faithful of friends was betrayed by those he thought his brothers. I accuse you, Burgund king, of willing the deed.

There is no compensation you can make me for the loss of such a husband! And since I have no battlecraft to exact a vengeance, let my curse compel you—"

"Be silent, woman!" Hagano strode forward. "Keep your curse from the king—mine was the arm that struck the blow. The blame, and the shame, belong to me. But it was needful. The people and the land were dying, and blood was required. Sigfrid had been honored as a king; at the end he understood, and consented to make the offering."

"Did he? Well, I did not, but never fear, you have not been forgotten." The hair rose on the back of Hagano's neck at her laugh. "The wyrd that I have called down upon Gundohar on you will bite doubly, but for you, the knowledge that your deed was the cause will bring the greatest pain."

"Let be, Gudrun, let it be—" said a new voice. "If there is blood-guilt to be shared out, some of it belongs to me. But I will provide my own compensation. The flame has been made ready that will carry the hero to freedom. Let us not keep him waiting . . ."

It was Brunahild's voice, but as Hagano turned, he saw not the Burgund queen, but a Walkyrja, robed in white as the priestesses had been robed in ancient days, and cloaked in a dark mantle sewn with the feathers of ravens. Her face was framed by a full plumage, mounted as a headdress. The sharp-beaked head rested on her brow, its stone eyes glittering balefully, and the shining wings flared down to either side, their dark feathers mingling with the shadowed waves of her hair. Two other women stood behind her, Walkyiun by their garb, though he had never seen them before.

Gundohar made a little helpless gesture, and Brunahild smiled. "Do you deny my right to conduct this ritual? Or my knowledge, or my power?"

"Priestess, you have the right," he said brokenly. "Let fate be fulfilled."

Did his brother truly understand what was happening? It was clear to Hagano, but he would be the last to stop her now.

She turned then to Gudrun. "In life you called this man

husband. Will you allow me to serve him now?"

Gudrun looked up. "Forgive me—" she whispered, and Brunahild stepped closer and took her face between her two hands, whispering. For a moment Hagano saw them, fair and dark, as two halves of something greater; the one all earth, the other already moving beyond it, and yet somehow the same.

"Sister . . ." said the queen more loudly, "do you begin to understand?"

"Our ways part here. Send him home, Brunahild," Gudrun whispered, "and I will guard his memory." For a moment longer they embraced, then the queen stepped back.

"Bring his horse," said Brunahild.

Two grooms brought up Grani in his golden harness, tossing his head at the scent of death and plunging. A lashing hoof took one man in the thigh. Then Brunahild reached out for the bridle and spoke to him, and the stallion stilled. Godomar came forward, a bronze axe in his hands. The horse stood quietly as the queen whispered, appearing not to sense the bright axe lifting behind his head. She stepped back as the blade flashed down. The great body reared, hooves flailing, as the head fell, and bright blood spurted across the logs. Then the rest of the body understood its death as well, and crashed into the pyre.

"Is it time?" asked Godomar. Someone had handed him a torch, and he lifted it.

"It is almost time," said Brunahild, and very sweetly, she smiled. "But he must have a sword to take with him to Wodan's hall."

Light flashed from steel, and Hagano saw that from beneath her cloak she had drawn Sigfrid's sword. He eyed it hungrily, for he had heard many tales about that blade. If it had been placed with the body earlier, perhaps he would have found some way to substitute another weapon. Had she guessed that, he wondered, and was that why she had hidden it until now?

For a moment Brunahild stood looking around her. Hagano followed her gaze and saw that two ravens were waiting in the young ash trees by the shore. He felt a chill, and his ruined eye began to ache, but Brunahild nodded, moved lightly past him, her feather cloak rustling, and stepped up the stacked logs to the bier.

The other two Walkyriun had moved to either end of the pyre and stood with arms lifted, waiting.

"Here is your sword, my beloved," Brunahild's clear voice carried. "I will give you a worthy sheath for it—" She bent over the bier, and the folds of the raven cloak fell forward. "—and a bride to serve you in Wodan's hall!" He could not see what she did, but he saw the jerk of her body, and even before she straightened he knew what she had done.

Wodan! he thought. *Is this your work as well?* and knew, with the certainty of prophecy, that one day a blade would bite his heart too.

"For me the sword—" she gasped, "as for you the spear." She turned, and they could all see the blade half-buried in her breast and the bright blood staining her white robe. "Now you may light the fire!"

Brunahild heard the first crackle as the fire took hold of the lower logs, but the agony in her breast was a greater flame. She had not expected there to be so much pain. Through the sound of the flames she could hear Raganleob and the girl chanting the spells that would speed her on her way.

She was crouched with the hilt of the sword braced against Sigfrid's side, gripping his shoulders, with most of her weight upon her hands. But since she could still breathe, she judged that the blade had not yet pierced her heart. Poised between life and death, her thought spanned worlds between two heartbeats. Oddly, she remembered the last moments of childbirth, when she had been sure that one more push would tear her in two.

Wodan's wisdom is like that of a woman, she thought then, *who is willing to sacrifice all for the sake of life, knowing that life and death are two parts of a single whole.* Sigfrid was the offering for Gundohar. "Allfather—" her thought lifted suddenly. *"Was Baldur the offering for you?"*

"Be easy—" the answer came to her, and she felt once more

the sense of strong hands holding her, *"your work is almost done. Embrace your beloved, my raven. Seek for the wolf that runs through the land of shadow as your teachers told you, and bring him home."*

Brunahild looked down at Sigfrid's still face and thought, *Yes, it is time.* She released her breath in a long sigh, giving it back to the god. And she did not know if it was because her own arms could no longer uphold her or because those others were lowering her, ever so gently, that she sank down along the swordblade until she lay at last outstretched on Sigfrid's breast.

Gudrun watched as the flames rose higher; a wall of fire that warded the last embrace of the two who lay atop the pyre from any who might try to hinder them. She knew that Godo and Gislahar were beside her, ready to catch her if she should fall, but she stood in isolation, like the other two brothers whose shapes wavered through the flames.

As she watched, Gundohar gasped and turned his face away, and Hagano reached out to grasp his arm.

"Do you mourn?" she cried. "By your own deed you are betrayed! It is not over, *brothers*—" Her voice cracked on the word. "Do you think they are silenced?" She gestured toward the pyre with the rune rod, and Hagano's eyes widened. "Receive now Sigfrid's legacy!"

She sucked in breath, and with it an exaltation beyond grief. The rune rod was tingling in her hand. "A time will come when your enemies surround you, and then you will miss the strength of Sigfrid's strong arm. A time will come when those you trust betray you, and then you will miss Sigfrid's loyalty. A time will come when death is near you, and Sigfrid will not be there to delay your doom! You may weep then for his loss. But I will be there, my brothers, and I will laugh!"

As abruptly as it had come, the prophetic power left her, and she sank to the ground, digging her fingers into the moist soil.

Once, a lifetime ago, she had come here with her eyes full of dreams and watched a hare bleed out its life upon the stones. Now the life that Sigfrid had given her was ending, consumed by those flames. Was vengeance all the world held for her now? For a moment it seemed to her that a voice answered from the roaring flames of the pyre, but she could not understand the words. But the earth was cool. She rested her forehead against it, taking comfort from the deep throbbing of the nearby river that was the lifeblood of the land.

As sunset cast its own glow across the meadow the fire began at last to die. Where the pyre had been there was now only a tangle of glowing logs. But a wind that had sprung up with the coming of nightfall picked up bits of mixed ash, or perhaps they were feathers, and carried them to the Rhenus.

Gudrun watched them drifting downward to the water, watched them until the light faded and the two ravens that had been observing from the ash trees rose heavily into the air and flapped away.

Background & Sources

 Those readers who are familiar with Wagner's *Ring* operas will have noted that this book covers essentially the same material as *Götterdämmerung*, with the difference, of course, that neither Wodan nor the world are destroyed at the end! Writing the book was rather like assisting at the divorce of two close friends, who phoned up to cry on my shoulder in alternate scenes. To understand the forces that drove them into conflict was the challenge.

For the more historically minded, the following notes may explain some of my choices. In including Hengest in my list of heroes in the first chapter, I am following Alan Bliss in suggesting that Hengest was originally of a royal Anglian family that had formerly ruled the Jutes, who served as a retainer to Hnaef Half-Dane and appears in the Anglo-Saxon Finnesburgh fragment. He is also, of course, the Hengest who led the Jutes to Britain. I diverge, however, on his chronology, preferring to follow Morris, who places Hengest's arrival in Britain around 428 and gives 441 as the date for the first Saxon revolt.

Burgundian history is lost in the mists of the north. The bard's account here is based as far as possible on what they believed (or might have liked to believe) of themselves, drawn from material presented in Perrin's *Les Burgonds*. From the evidence available, they seem to have originated on the Baltic Sea, in Posnania, the north coasts being considered a part of Scandinavia. According to Jordanes, the Gepids wiped out the Burgundians, but it is more likely they simply mauled them badly while they were passing through on their way to Transylvania. The battered Burgunds then seem to have moved south, and encountering the emperor Probus on the Danube, given up the idea of entering the Empire in Illyria and turned westward.

Only a few words from the Burgund dialect have survived, including *hendinos* and *sinista*. The exact interpretation of these terms is disputed by the scholars, but hendinos seems to have meant something like high king, and sinista, related to "elder," originally a figure whose function was somewhere between the advisory role of the chief Druid in early Ireland, and that of an independent judex or the lawspeaker elected by the chieftains of Iceland.

The difficulty in analyzing ancient German political structures, of course, is the fact that they were constantly changing. The trick is to guess correctly for any given period how far the evolution might have gone. In the third century, the sinista seems to have played a central role. Based on the structures of the Anglo-Saxons at a similar stage of monarchic development, I am assuming that by the fifth, the Burgund sinista would have become an advisory figure something like the thyle or thul.

In the period covered by this book Gundohar is in the midst of the transition from tribal chieftain or leader of a military democracy to feudal king. During this period all of the feoderate tribes were engaged in an uneasy process of accommodating themselves to life in the Empire. This including coping with both a changed lifestyle and economy. The gap was often bridged by warfare, as much an economic activity for the tribes as it was for the Vikings later on. Whether fighting for the government or against it, the object was to make enough of an impression to win an increase in the payments. All-out war was to the interest of neither party, since the enemy of this summer might be next year's ally, and vice versa.

Grimm and Fraser record a rich folk tradition in the Germanic countries, including elaborate rituals for spring. Eostara, or Ostara, is an ancient goddess associated with spring, the east, and the dawn who gave her name to the month in which the Christians celebrated Christ's death and resurrection. The oldest painted Easter egg found in Europe is from a Roman grave near Worms.

It is Grimm who identifies Phol (Fol) with Baldur. Phol's Day is May 2, which would make the festival of Baldur coincide with the Celtic Beltaine. Walburga, who gave her name to Walpurgisnacht, was according to legend the daughter of the English King Richard I who founded a nunnery, but her name probably came from an older fertility deity, whose worship would have been celebrated with wild dancing around the bonfire on mountains such as the Brocken. The Latin song quoted is a medieval spring carol, "In vernale tempore," originally sung to the tune now used for "Good King Wenceslas."

The wild man tradition has survived all over Europe, and may represent a folk memory of a native primate related to Bigfoot and the Yeti. In some places, the kinds of customs associated with Beltaine in Celtic countries were relocated to Whitsunday. The Maypole, however, is a major image of spring in southern Germany, where every town has its blue-and-white-striped pole permanently set up in the central square.

The practices featured in the rain-making ceremony, including the prayer to Donar, are based on Germanic and Baltic materials, but they bear a remarkable resemblance to the kind of sympathetic magic employed for this purpose all over the world. The same goes for the harvest ceremonies, and whether they came to Britain with the Anglo-Saxons or were learned by both Celts and Germans from the pre–Indo-European farming culture, the cutting of the last sheaves is celebrated in essentially the same way.

For those with interest in such things, the Latin quotes from the baptismal service are from the Gothic Missal, one of the oldest liturgical collections surviving, reprinted in a collection titled *The Ancient Liturgies of the Gallican Church*, edited by J.M. Neale in 1855 and now published by the AMS press. The oddities in the Latin are those of the period, not my own. The words of Brunahild's abjuration are adapted slightly from

an actual Saxon text quoted by Grimm in Volume 1 of his
Teutonic Mythology—

"*Forsachistu diabolei?*"

"*Ec forsacho diabole end allum diobolgelde end allem dioboles wercu-
mend worum. Thunor ende Woden end Saxnote ende allen them unholdum
the hiro genotas sint.*"

The language is close enough to English to hardly need
translation, and is in fact much more inclusive than the equiv-
alent question in the Latin text.

It was, however, an official practice of the Roman Church
to co-opt pagan shrines, festivals, and even deities whenever
possible. The pagan Romans had already begun this process
by identifying local divinities with their own, and setting up
shrines in the Roman style with latinized names. The *matronae*
are the Latin version of the goddesses of birth and family.
Their shrines were found all over, usually near a sacred spring,
and they were often Christianized as the Three Marys. The
springs of Bad Durkheim, near the old Celtic ringfort below
the Donarberg, are still a noted spa. The song is adapted from
a nursery rhyme from Switzerland. Sometimes Christianiza-
tion was long in coming—the citizens of Trier were still being
criticized as late as the fifth century for maintaining a shrine
to Artemis.

Students of early medieval literature will recognize in
"Waldhari" the ninth century Latin poem "Waltharius." Although in this version Gunther has unaccountably become a
Frank and Hildigund a Burgundian, the names and setting
make it clear that this story, which can be correlated with
some references in the *Nibelungenlied*, belongs to the same cycle
of legends. The poem presents a sprightly summary of the
events, culminating in the lines,

> "*King Gunther's foot was lying there,*
> *and Walter's hand was lying there,*
> *and also Hagen's twitching eye,*
> *Thus, thus the men have shared the treasure of the Avars!*"
>
> (ll. 1402–4)

I retained the tradition of Hagen's lost eye, but made Gunther's wound somewhat less drastic, since he is going to need both feet in Book III.

In choreographing the final episodes of the story I am once again mixing traditions from the *Volsungasaga* and the *Nibelungenlied*. All the sources are agreed that Sigfrid's death was agreed on by the king and Hagen, and that he was taken from behind and unawares.

Although this is the point at which Wagner concluded his operas, all of the medieval versions of the story treat the death of Sigfrid as only the first half of the story, the second part being the means by which justice is brought to his murderers. Whether or not one believes that Gundohar and Hagano had reason for their action, it is undeniable that the death of Sigfrid becomes the central event against which their later lives are measured.

What happens then will provide the material for the third book of this trilogy.

Some sources of particular interest include:

Phil Barker, *The Armies and Enemies of Imperial Rome*, Wargames Research Group, 1981.

Walter Goffart, *Barbarians and Romans, A.D. 418–584, The Techniques of Accommodation*, Princeton University Press, 1980.

Jacob Grimm, *Teutonic Mythology*, Dover, 1966.

A.H.M. Jones, *The Later Roman Empire, 284–602*, Johns Hopkins University Press, 1990.

Charlotte G. Otten, *A Lycanthropy Reader: Werewolves in Western Culture*, Syracuse University Press, 1986.

Jennifer M. Russ, *German Festivals and Customs*, London: Oswald Wolff, 1983.

G. Storms, *Anglo-Saxon Magic*, Folcroft Library, 1975.

J.R.R. Tolkien, *Finn and Hengest*, ed. by Alan Bliss, Boston: Houghton-Mifflin Co. 1983.

Waltharius and Ruodlieb, ed. and trans. by Dennis Kratz, Garland Publishing, 1984.